SEVERAL DECEPTIONS

Jane Stevenson was born in London in 1959, and brought up in London, Beijing, and Bonn. She learned to read at the age of three, since when she has done little else. She now teaches in the Centre for British and Comparative Cultural Studies at the University of Warwick, and divides her time between living in a village in Warwickshire and travelling in Europe. Though she has published on a variety of academic subjects, this is her first collection of fiction. Her first novel, *London Bridges*, is published by Jonathan Cape in 2000.

Jane Stevenson

SEVERAL DECEPTIONS

Published by Vintage 2000

2 4 6 8 10 9 7 5 3 1

First published in Great Britain in 1999 by
Jonathan Cape

Vintage
Random House, 20 Vauxhall Bridge Road,
London SW1V 2SA

Random House Australia (Pty) Limited
20 Alfred Street, Milsons Point, Sydney
New South Wales 2061, Australia

Random House New Zealand Limited
18 Poland Road, Glenfield,
Auckland 10, New Zealand

Random House (Pty) Limited
Endulini, 5A Jubilee Road, Parktown 2193,
South Africa

The Random House Group Limited Reg. No. 954009
www.randomhouse.co.uk

A CIP catalogue record for this book
is available from the British Library

ISBN 0 09 927374 8

Papers used by Random House are natural, recyclable products made from wood grown in sustainable forests. The manufacturing processes conform to the environmental regulations of the country of origin

Printed and bound in Denmark by
Nørhaven A/S, Viborg

To Maureen Freely and David Morley
optimi amici

Thanks are also due, and gratefully offered, to Peter Davidson, Bob Hendrie, Elisabeth Knottenbelt, Jill Macdonald, Loredana Polezzi, Sander Schimmelpenninck, Frank Thackray, Adriaan van der Weel, and the Ven. Yeshe Zangmo.

Contents

The Island of the Day Before Yesterday

I always found when I was young that the most obscure period of time was that which was too old to be news and too young to be history – the day before yesterday, as it were.

Rupert Hart-Davis to George Lyttelton, 8 April 1956

In retrospect, I am strongly inclined to blame the whole thing on Umberto Eco. If that fat plutocrat in Bologna had not brought a temporary glamour to the otherwise forgettable concept of 'an Italian semiotician', the *Sunday Times* would never have thought of asking me for my story. Sofia would not have left me. I would not now be the laughing-stock of Macerata, where I have lived for thirty-odd years. And Dora – Dora would still be Dora, damn her to hell.

Some of it was true, of course. Mamà was, indeed, a society beauty, a contessa, and an incompetent, if occasionally charming, film actress in the Palaeozoic era of Italian cinema. Daddy's DSO was perfectly real, and he really did write *Night Winds in Algeria* and *No Watch upon the Rhine*, all by himself, unlike the action-men of today – I have seen the notebooks he did it in, filled from cover to cover with his small, firm, backward-sloping script – he did know T. E. Lawrence, and go around with Peter Fleming and Paddy Leigh-Fermor, which is to say that he was genuinely part of that strange and very British little clique of men-of-action with a tiny gift for prose about whom the world has heard so unnecessarily much. That ghastly little bint from the *Sunday Times* had it all at her fingertips, who'd done what, and with what, and to whom, as the limerick puts it. But they would have been the most minor of minor figures on the stage of the glitterati, practically third spearcarriers from the left, if it wasn't for that bloody photograph. Don't tell me you haven't seen it. You probably owned a copy when you were a student, since it's been Athena's sixth best seller overall for the last decade (I asked them), somewhere up there with Marilyn on her grating and James Dean standing by the car which killed him. Spring in the Bois du Boulogne, the chestnut trees just sifting down their petals, though the trees still blaze with white candles of blossom. It's dawn, and they've clearly been dancing all night, but they don't look jaded or sordid. They are holding hands. He is in uniform, devastatingly handsome, his youthful face vulnerable and tender as he looks down at his girl, who is radiant with love. A pale, bias-cut satin dress outlines her perfect figure, shows off her lovely, unbrassièred breasts. Her feet are bare: he is carrying her tiny satin slippers in his free hand. I'm not going to deconstruct the damned thing. What's more, I'm not going to tell you that it was a set-up, or that she was coked to the gills, or he'd just been shagging the Algerian waiter in the Club Morocco. They were young: it was taken two years before I was born. For all I know, it's 'true', they *were* that glamorous, they *were* that much in love. In any case, it is of absolutely no significance. Athena gives the name of the photographer, not the names of the couple. The millions who buy the poster every year aren't buying Emilia Corsi, last seen in public playing a frightful Roman hag in *La Dolce Vita*, and Nigel Strachey, racing-driver, war hero, and master of tight-lipped, manly prose. They're buying a sentimental icon of a generation retrospectively perceived as glamorous and doomed: 'and then the war came.'

If those who buy the thing ever wonder about the couple at all, they presumably imagine that the boy in uniform was killed. He wasn't, as it happens. Despite his best efforts (you can read his flying stories for yourself: rather to my surprise, Cape reprint them about every five years), he survived the Battle of Britain and other epic encounters with the Luftwaffe, and unlike many a returning warrior, came back to a perfectly satisfactory social and financial position, sufficient to employ a nanny, and send me to Eton and Caius, and to a life comfortably lived between a flat near Fitzroy Square and the *piano nobile* of a very acceptable palazzo in the Via Giulia.

That is, I hope, sufficient about my parents. The only thing to add, perhaps, is that while I have inherited some measure of their looks, they were not as fashionable in my day as they had been in theirs. My heyday was the Sixties, and a matinée-idol profile counted for little in that epoch of flashing eyes and floating hair: I could only have put it to use if I had decided on a humble but meritorious career modelling for knitwear manufacturers. As it happened, I had also inherited a more bankable gift, a modest ability to write. I went into journalism, edited the *Contemporary Review* for a time, and in a moment of unusual energy, wrote a book on the spaghetti Western as a sociocultural phenomenon. I had become bored with London society, which, *pace* Dr Johnson, is perfectly possible. On the strength of the book, and Mamà's contacts (though you would not have thought it to listen to her, she was the daughter of a notably intellectual family), I was offered a professorship in the University of Macerata, an agreeable small town at the top of a very steep hill in the Marche, and settled down to the life of an Italian professor, which is one of blameless, if cultivated, inactivity. I should add that the university, while small and obscure, is not recent. The Law Faculty traces its origins back to 1252, while the institution as a whole dates back to a bull of Paul III issued in 1543. In due course, I married a daughter of the local noble family, my charming Sofia, and periodically, I extruded another book on some subject roughly within the field of semiotics. Not an adventurous life, perhaps, but adventures are not to everyone's taste. I have no doubts of my legitimacy, but all the same, I preferred collecting majolica to wrestling headhunters in Borneo or attempting to break the land speed record. I had plenty to write about without putting myself at personal risk, or even inconvenience. I had never consumed heroin, gone to India, or slept with a man, unlike most of my English friends, but I did not feel that these omissions had left gaps in my life – I had reverted, in fact, to the tastes and inclinations of the generations of Corsi *professori* which had so uncharacteristically produced Mamà. Though occasionally bored, I was perfectly happy: I look back on that boredom now as the land of lost content. It is a peculiarly excruciating sensation for a man of above average intelligence to know that he is responsible for his own downfall. But as I said at the beginning, I am also inclined to blame Umberto Eco, and above all, the *Sunday Times*.

What happened to precipitate disaster was the death of my father. He lost Mamà in the early Seventies, to cancer of the breast. After a period of adjustment, during which Sofia and I worried about him a good deal, he settled down contentedly to widowerhood. He sold the Rome flat – which had always been very much Mamà's domain, and which I suspect reminded him unbearably of her – gave her jewellery to Sofia and the best of her movables to me, and settled immovably in London, lunching daily at one or other of his clubs (the Travellers' or the Oxford and Cambridge), writing letters to publishers correcting small points of factual detail in works of fiction and non-fiction alike, becoming greyer and apparently smaller, gradually permitting his world to contract. I visited London perhaps once a year, and he invariably took me to lunch at one of the clubs. Fortunately for the maintenance of his routines, Sofia was not in the habit of accompanying me on such jaunts: she is one of four sisters, who have maintained an extraordinary (to me at least, an only child) closeness: at any opportunity, they desert their respective families and go to a spa or a beauty-farm of some kind in a close-formation middle-aged gaggle. Like the husbands of my sisters-in-law, I have come to accept this fatalistically, as part of the necessary structure of life.

One morning near the end of the summer term, I received a phone call from London. Daddy had been found peacefully dead in his bed by Mrs Pettigree, the charwoman who came to his flat three times a week. There was no indication that he had suffered in any way: the immediate diagnosis was of a fatal thrombosis, though this would have to be confirmed by post-mortem since he had managed to achieve his end without medical assistance. We were upset, of course, but not heartbroken: the element of personal distress was, I have to say, mitigated by the prospect of his not inconsiderable estate. Tactful to the last, he had also contrived to release me from one of the most unpleasant duties of the year – the University had promptly and sympathetically agreed to release me from my duties, and I had therefore escaped the annual Hell of examining.

Sofia immediately took the *rapido* to Florence, from whence she returned with a variety of becoming and fashionable black garments. We flew to London, and ensconced ourselves in a dismal but efficient hotel in Holland Park (why are the English so extraordinarily bad at running hotels? Never mind: *revenons à nos moutons*: that question will keep for another of my tiresome little books). The funeral was a successful occasion, as these things go. Daddy was sent down into the dismal earth of Kensal Green amid an ocean of floral tributes (including one in the shape of an aeroplane – in the stress of the occasion, I never discovered who this was from), bewailed by an extraordinary array of elderly gnomes, goblins and grokes, most of whom had not set eyes on him in decades. They were (I thought to myself, as Sofia wept becomingly by my side) a poor advertisement for *la dolce vita* in its more advanced phases. Pot bellies, watery, alcoholic eyes, deep, bronchial coughs, broken veins and puffy, sodden complexions abounded. After the funeral itself, Sofia declared that she had started a migraine, and went back to the hotel in a taxi. The *leitmotiv* of the subsequent reception was provided by the words 'my God, you look well', uttered in tones of disbelief and envy by various acquaintances from my days in the *jeunesse dorée* who had, without exception, worn a great deal less well than had I.

Once the funeral was over, it was time to take stock. The obituaries were numerous, and flattering. *The Times* printed one of Daddy's 'war hero' photographs, but the *Guardian* dug out one of the Cecil Beaton studies of my parents together, together with a frankly illiterate piece of prose evidently written by a film fanatic who would have much preferred obituarising Mamà. It also mentioned 'Dawn in the Bois' – now I think about it, this must have been where the trouble really started. One of these days, I will lay hands on the hack responsible, and roast him over a slow fire. Sofia, firmly and without regret, left me. She had a date of long standing with Maria, Laura and Giulietta: I would have been foolish to expect her to break it, especially since (as she pointed out with perfect good sense) she had no relevant knowledge or skills. Daddy's flat, which I had not actually entered for some time, had proved to be full almost to the ceiling with books and papers of one sort or another.

'You need a secretary, *caro*, not a wife,' she observed. 'Ring up an agency, and they will send you someone suitable. Someone who will make it a little job, not a private thing.' Sofia was quite right. It needed the professional touch – not only because there was so much of it, but also because the element of professional detachment would be a valuable addition. My relations with Daddy, as I hope I have indicated, were affectionate without being intimate, but I defy any person of sensibility to spend a couple of months thus immersed in the life of a parent without becoming a prey to melancholy reflection. Sofia then thought of something else. 'Not a secretary bird, *tesoro mio*. An ugly secretary.' There too, you may be surprised to hear, I agreed with her entirely. What's that rhyme which so delighted my simpler contemporaries at Cambridge? 'Higgamus, hoggamus, woman's monogamous, hoggamus, higgamus, man is polygamous.' Perhaps true in the majority of cases, but not universally so. I had not the slightest desire to be unfaithful to Sofia; but I was aware, through observation of various contemporaries at moments of crisis, that the irrationalities of even very civilised bereavement might suddenly impel me in uncharacteristic directions. I did not wish to find myself lusting wildly after a pinheaded floozy of twenty. How little I knew.

So, with the best possible intentions, I saw Sofia off at Heathrow, with a number of drawings by Picasso, Cocteau and Derain which I did not intend the Inland Revenue ever to know about secreted at the bottom of her case, returned to the hotel, and consulted the Yellow Pages. I then rang an upmarket employment agency, and asked them to find me an experienced secretary/PA with some experience of handling literary manuscripts. The second lady I interviewed appeared to be ideal. She had worked for a while in a publisher's office and as a librarian, had a variety of other relevant experience, and seemed marginally literate. Equally to the point, she was also a lumpy spinster of approximately my own age, the epitome of dullness, unbecomingly clad in an outfit which included upswept, blue-rimmed spectacles, a white crochet cardigan of distressingly handmade appearance, and blue plastic beads. I was so delighted by her that I sent Sofia a telegram at the spa, for the amusement of her sisters: *carissima mia*, I have left you for the ugliest woman in London. Yours unfaithfully, Simone.

She of the upswept spectacles, etc. was called Dora. Miss Dora Prentiss, a name which I would consider a guarantee of chastity in itself to any man of sensibility. But she was not without talent with respect to the job in hand, which was just as well. When I put the key in the door of the flat that first day, with Miss Prentiss one pace behind exuding a powdery odour of cheap talcum and instant coffee, I realised that I had, if anything, underestimated the scale of the problem. I was also heartily grateful both to Sofia and to Miss Prentiss, since it almost immediately became obvious that the archaeology of my father's life was also the archaeology of my own, to an extent which made the continuous involvement of a disinterested outsider something of a psychological, as well as a practical, necessity.

How can I describe the scene before us? I think I can best start by accounting for it. As Daddy's capacity for physical derring-do declined, perhaps unsurprisingly, literature, or at least writing, came to play a larger and larger part in his life. I personally had found as I got older that parties tired me and gave me indigestion: since Daddy, unlike myself, had started with the physique of a hero, it took him far longer to erode his constitution than it had taken me. I do not know, of course, whether he would have continued frisking so indefatigably into his sixties had it not been for Mamà, but that spoilt darling's taste for glittering social occasions had been inexhaustible, and Daddy would, I know, have inconvenienced himself a great deal further than indigestion to give her a moment's pleasure. Mamà's enjoyment of parties was, I rather think, due to the fact that she contrived to maintain a surprising amount of her early beauty into her middle years. It was only once cancer began its secret work that she finally turned away from the bright world she had loved with such admirable consistency and energy. In consequence, the pair of them were still prominent members of London, as well as Roman, society throughout the fifties and sixties. As early as my sixth-form days, Mamà (who had come to enjoy the universal cries of 'your son! he *can't* be') bought me some evening clothes, appointed me Cavalier Servente in chief, and started taking me to parties. I am happy to say that she suffered from no pretty maternal illusions about adolescent male sexuality: under her observant, sardonic, but far from unsympathetic tutelage, I met a number of 'attractive older women', and became the object of insane envy among my lusty but pudibond peers, condemned as they were to work out their frustrations among themselves or in furtive encounters arising indirectly from tennis clubs and dramatic societies. As a lifelong loather of all forms of organised sport, it gave me immense satisfaction to possess a reputation which caused even the mighty heroes of the cricket pitch and the first boat discreetly to seek my advice. I still remember the sheer pleasure of having my housemaster tell me, publicly and in no uncertain terms, after I had returned for the Michaelmas half with a string of empurpled love-bites rising out of my collar and disappearing up behind my right ear, that I was lowering the tone of the House. It was an age, and a time, when such a remark was an accolade beyond any that could be conferred by a silver tassel on one's cricket cap: it allowed me to maintain a revolting degree of diligence and conformity in my studies, secure that the words 'filthy little swot' would never come my way.

I digress. The point I was trying to make, before I was distracted by *schadenfreude*, is that my parents and I had, to a truly remarkable extent, an overlapping group of friends and associates. I began to write in my late teens; and my father was in a position to introduce me to journalists and publishers, who kindly agreed to read my amateur effusions. Since Daddy had also contrived, in his reticent way, to teach me a number of tricks of the trade, I suspect that even my tyro efforts were somewhat better than average. My parents were also admirably unworried by me. At eighteen, I was to be seen in public costumed as, roughly, the young Baudelaire: my mother, in a severe Balenciaga shift-dress, her still lovely eyes black-ringed as Nefertiti's, merely laughed like a drain. My father, who was perfectly well aware of my adventures among the grass- or rather glass-widows of Fitzrovia, saw no reason to mention either Oscar Wilde or army barbers. All that I recall in the way of criticism from either of them was Daddy pointing out that the style of the times did not really suit me: a judgement so abstract, so neutrally expressed, and so obviously true, that it caused no offence. Anyway, to cut a long story short, leaving the war years out of it, Daddy moved in circles frequented by writers and artists and reported by gossip columnists, between approximately 1945 and 1975: my own London period, which went rather further into the world of photographers, rock-stars and poets, thus overlapped with the last ten or so years of his. I, of course, had gone on to an entirely different sort of life. But Daddy, as he aged, had become increasingly absorbed in his own place in what he saw as contemporary history. Looking around the flat, with Dora Thing padding at my heels, it became ever more obvious that he had bought every diary, volume of letters, biography, autobiography, collection of anecdotes, and critical work that he could lay his hands on relating to anyone he had personally known – an extensive, and formidable, list. He had kept all correspondence relating to those remotely in the public eye. There was an archive of photographs, there were diaries, and there were bits and scraps of memoir and autobiography, beginning from different points, in a number of different notebooks, started and put down on a variety of occasions. God knows what else there was: what there was not, I observed, was a television. He had spent his long, lonely hours as a chronicler of his own time, or perhaps even as *laudator temporis acti*: fond though I was of the old darling, I am well aware that my brains come from the Corsi side of the family.

A dip into the collection of biographies, etcetera, confirmed the overall picture yet further. Each one was briefly reviewed on the flyleaf, with military tidy-mindedness: 'Pure fantasy', 'Basically factual', 'Tendentious'. They were meticulously annotated in the margins, in ink. This is a typical sample. 'Actually on the Weds. Cf. Connolly *Journal*, 158.' In effect, the old man had lived his life twice over. It was perfectly clear that he had had no end of fun from it the first time: I could only hope that he had also enjoyed it the second time around. I took a deep breath, filling my lungs with the smell of my father's life (books, furniture polish, tobacco, and Yardley's English Lavender), and turned to my new secretary.

'Well, you see the problem, Miss Prentiss.'

'Where do you want me to start, Professor Strachey?'

I sighed. 'It's an extraordinary archive. I must say, I had no real idea of the scale of it. I'm beginning to think that we might persuade an American university library to take the whole thing off our hands. He'd have liked that, I rather think. So obviously, the first step towards this happy conclusion is to inventory the lot. Start with the letters; they're likely to be the most important. I'll go out in a minute, and buy an extremely large quantity of cardboard files and index cards. Go through the correspondence boxes, and start sorting them by name of sender: if you can read the writing, give them a quick flick through and see if any of them are intrinsically interesting – is anyone describing anything important, or noteworthy, or amusing? If you find anything which strikes you as remarkable, I don't know, an account of visiting a brothel with John F. Kennedy or something, make a note, or mention it to me directly: I'm going to be doing exactly the same at the other end of the dining table, with a different box. If there's any correspondence that isn't in English, of course, just pass it straight over. I gather you do have some idea of who these people might be? If someone mentions Dylan, who might they be talking about?'

'Dylan Thomas?'

'Excellent. Kenneth? Cyril? Tom?'

'Er . . . Kenneth Tynan? Cyril Connolly? Oh, dear. I don't think I know the last one. Tom Jones?'

'Right with the first two, Miss Prentiss. Mr Jones, I think, moved in rather different circles. It was dear old Tom Driberg that I had in mind. Never mind, it sounds as though you're likely to get the hang of things in no time. We'll take *Who's Who* through, and a handful of the more obvious biographies: if you're stuck on a name, try looking through the indexes. You can ask me, of course, but I won't necessarily be here all the time, and it might be as well to get into the way of finding things out for yourself. Now, do you think you can cope?'

'Oh, yes. I think it will be interesting.' Behind the spectacles, her pebbly little eyes gleamed with something like enthusiasm. I suppose, if one stops to think about it, temporary secretarial jobs are, by and large, tedious. This one promised tedium enough, from my point of view, but I began faintly to surmise that from hers, it might seem positively exciting. I was also surprised and gratified to find how well informed she was: evidently, by pure luck, I had come across someone with a genuine interest in the period and its writers.

Excellent, I thought, poor fool that I was. If the earnest Dora contrives to bring an element of engagement to this project, she will be happy to work on her own, unsupervised (I am not a professor because I adore the role of instructor. Quite the opposite), and moreover, driven by enthusiasm, she may become, in a reasonably short space of time, passably efficient. She and I began to move boxes and books into the dining-room, boxes to the table, reference books to the sideboard, and set up two work-stations, one at either end. I discreetly bagged Mamà's chair for myself, since the thought of seeing Dreary Dora in it depressed me so much, leaving her to take Daddy's. The woman seemed to have something on her mind: she was glancing at me, and biting her lip.

'What is it, Miss Prentiss?'

'Professor Strachey, do you think I could borrow some of the books? To read, I mean, in my own time? I'll be very careful with them. I've always liked biographies.'

'Of course', I said, astonished. 'Read what you like. I'm only glad you find it that interesting.'

Which said, I left her to look round, and trotted out, regardless of my doom, to purchase essential supplies: files, file-cards, coffee, milk, and so forth. I remember that the only thing on my mind was that I was rejoicing that I would not need to buy dust masks.

Thanks to Daddy's fastidious habits, and the regular interventions of the excellent Mrs Pettigree (who had, I was touched to observe, sent a bunch of flowers for the funeral), the piles of data, though formidable in themselves, were at least more or less clean to handle.

The next fortnight or so passed without incident. Dora, with what struck me even at the time was almost excessive zeal, chewed her way through Daddy's library evening by evening with the industry of a locust. During working hours, the work of filing proceeded apace. A goodly proportion of the letters did, I was happy to discover, emanate from a number of satisfactorily famous luminaries of the mid-twentieth-century literary landscape, and contained a number of interesting anecdotes and even pieces of analysis which (as Dora was increasingly able to assure me) had apparently not yet appeared in print. I thought, with increasing complacency, of the Modern Literature Archive in the Harry Ransom Humanities Research Center at the University of Texas.

Increasingly, I was finding, it was the thought of the scholars of Austin – i.e., of a substantial cheque written in dollars – that sustained me from day to day. While it was clear that Dreary Dora was ever more fascinated by the material we uncovered, I was not. To me, the whole thing went to confirm my original decision to leave London and become an Italian *professore*: I was bored to tears. But Dora's reaction to Daddy's faintly pathetic archive reassured me. I came gradually to consider her as a species of literary miner's canary. The thoughtworld of *Daily Mail* readers and public library users was something wholly beyond my experience, and it seemed to me that if she continued to be fascinated by these trivial episodes from the private lives of individuals of no real or permanent historical significance, then perhaps it was my own reaction which was out of the ordinary. And where there is interest, there is money.

Then, as I was drinking a somehow subtly unsatisfactory cup of coffee at the hotel one morning, I was handed a much-franked letter, which had started from London, addressed to me at the University of Macerata, and had then been forwarded back to London by a secretary. It contained an approach from a journalist in the pay of the *Sunday Times*, a certain Ms Janice Chapman. She assured me of the profound interest and significance of Mamà, Daddy, and even myself, and angled hopefully for an interview and a photo-biography. This communication reminded me instantly why I had been so glad to get out of journalism, and irritated me profoundly. For one thing, it was written in the sort of breathless, suburban-schoolgirl style which, while it is marginally an improvement on the arch mimsiness of the *New Yorker* and its imitators, makes English journalistic prose so fundamentally sickening to any educated person. A good many adjectives of superlative tendency were sprinkled about in it, used with the slap-happy imprecision of a punt-gun. Its content was equally annoying, since the degree of enthusiasm expressed seemed to me distinctly disproportionate to its cause. I would not have said myself that the fact that in my eighteenth year, I had once been discovered during the course of a Faber launch-party shagging the late Mrs— up against the wall in a coat-cupboard, and that a notoriously foul-mouthed old sodomite had proceeded to be funny at her expense, qualified me for a place in literary history. The mere fact that this and a number of similarly trivial incidents were reported in the endless flood of memoirs and biographies, only went, to my mind, to confirm the ineffable stupidity and decadence of the British reading public at the latter end of the millennium. They had no inflationary effect on my ego, which has better things to do with itself.

I would not like you, gentle reader, to imagine that that last remark implies that I attach any exaggerated importance to the half-dozen or so books with my name on the spine. They are ephemera which, in this new Saturnian age of lead-type, I feel constrained to produce. It is merely that in the course of the last thirty years, the lesson I have learned from the most civilised nation in the world is that the talented but not superlative should be content to exist, to enjoy themselves, and to be modestly rewarded during their lifetime. I have learned a great deal from the simple fact that my wife has never had, or sought to have, a job: she toils not, neither does she spin. The literary fame which arises from mutual *frottage* among self-publicising nonentities is something which, viewed from the loggia at Macerata, no sane person would value or aspire to. I do not consider that mere ability, which I possess, gives one any claim on the interest of future generations whatsoever. Ms Chapman, it was clear, thought very differently, and it had not occurred to her for one moment that I might disagree with her.

It was while I was sitting there, letting my distasteful coffee get cold, that my annoyance with the whole dreary business suddenly embodied itself in an idea. I must try and reconstruct the movement of my thought: this is important. As you will remember, I am a semiotician by trade. This world of adultery, alcoholism, dope, and intermittent beta-plus literary production which so fascinated Dora, Ms Chapman, and apparently, thousands of otherwise sane members of the book-buying public, had by now become, without question, a system of signs. In particular, I had been very struck by the rhetoric of *verismo* which motivated so many of these dreary accounts, the fascination (shared, of course, by Daddy, bless him) with 'what really happened'. It was clear from a brief but intensive study of my father's collection that much of the stock-in-trade of the modern literary biographer could be described in the following formula: 'this is a story which has often been told, but what *really* happened is . . .' Whereupon some additional fact, or factor, is invoked, to change the causality of the event in question, and the whole conspiracy of writer, publisher and reader apparently feel satisfied that an act of history has taken place. The notion which flashed across my mind was to insert an alternative reality, a sort of *gedankenexperiment* on this basic structure of obsessive reconstruction, which would both illumine it as a cultural artefact, and call it into question. I would persuade Dora, who by now knew a remarkable amount about my erstwhile world *as it was reflected in narrative* (which is of course, all that matters: that was what Ms Chapman knew too) to collude with me in inserting her into history. I was getting quite attached to her, since she was so clearly giving me approximately double my money's worth, and it was quite clear that the poor creature would have liked nothing better. I could not, of course, gratify this desire in reality, but it occurred to me that, like Chesterton's donkey, she might find that an afternoon's glory, 'one far fierce hour and sweet,' gave her something to look back on when she found herself, in future years, clerking for Gabbitas & Thring. As she uncomplainingly did the donkey-work to which her limited education and intelligence condemned her, she would be able to console herself with the thought that once, 'there was a shout about my head and palms beneath my feet.' Thus, I would by a purely gratuitous action, bring a moment of sunshine into a dull life. The worst that could happen was that Ms Chapman would accuse me of pulling her leg, flounce out in a huff, and the article would not be written. Since the only purpose of the article, as far as I was concerned, was to strengthen my hand with Austin, Texas, and I thought the material was quite strong enough on its own, this was not a prospect which appalled me. If I pulled it off, on the other hand, Sofia would laugh, and at my leisure, I would write an entertaining but philosophically serious work on the fictionality of historicism. And for once in my life, I would have thought of something before bloody Eco, whose effortless ubiquity in every corner of my profession was beginning to cause me serious annoyance. I am, as you will have gathered, not unduly solemn about the value of my contribution to the literature of ideas, but the thought of producing something which might cause Uncle Umberto a nasty moment of professional envy gave me, I have to admit, a definite *frisson* of satisfaction.

Having worked this thought through to its conclusion, I folded up the letter, went up to my room, pulled out a gun, and shot myself dead. No I didn't: this self-exculpatory nonsense is not being written from beyond the grave. I merely wished you to pause for a moment, to register the stark horror of the fact that I ruined my own life as a consequence of five minutes' worth of bright idea, a tiny buzz of collegiate rivalry, and an uncharacteristic moment of altruism. I folded up the letter, left the hotel, and went off cheerfully to try the whole thing on Dora. Her initial reaction, perhaps unsurprisingly, was suspicion, alarm, and disbelief.

'What do you mean, you want me to have been there?' she cried, looking wildly around. On all sides, there rose mountains of minutely detailed evidence for the pastness of the past, in the form of day-by-day lives of the moderately famous. Or so it must have seemed to Dora, Miss Average Reader that she was.

'It's not as difficult as it sounds,' I said, reasonably patiently. 'I know it looks as though the books have got the whole thing down; but you'll find there are plenty of gaps if you look for them.' I went back to the study, and started riffling through Daddy's photograph collection. It did not take me very long to find a *caracteristico e tipico* David Bailey, of me in the early Stones Age, disporting myself at some moderately decadent party. The focus is strongly on my face, bright-eyed with booze: I have a reefer in one hand, and with the other, I am supporting an indeterminate and extremely stoned female (the actual identity of whom I have long since forgotten), whose features are obscured by her long dark hair. Did we really believe that it was an age of freedom and liberty? My inability to remember even the names of most of my female contemporaries suggested that they had been, in effect, interchangeable accessories whom my Sofia would heartily have despised. Never mind that; it strengthened my present case. 'Look at that,' I said to Dora, slapping the thing down in front of her. 'I haven't a clue who the girl is, but there's nothing stopping us saying that it was you.' Seeing is believing, to a simple mind. Dora stared at the photograph like a medium; soaking herself in it. Gradually, the expression on her face changed from pinch-featured panicky dumb resistance to something more like holy awe. 'I've no idea what you looked like in your twenties,' I lied – I knew exactly. She'd been one of those girls with chubby knees rashly accentuated by white stockings who prowled up and down outside Biba's in twos and threes, too frightened to go in, clutching their plastic handbags. 'The only thing that matters now is that you are approximately five feet five inches tall, and so is she.'

'But I can't,' she said feebly. 'It's not true.'

'My dear Dora,' I said. 'You have read an almost obscene quantity of London-based literary reminiscence in the last couple of weeks. Their overall message, you must surely realise, one which was once pithily summed up by Saint Jerome: *tot codices, quot versiones*. That is to say, for any event, there are as many different versions as there are commentators. They contradict each other all over the place. Most of them were too drunk or too stoned at the time to remember whether it was Friday or Christmas. If we add *our* version, all that will happen is that people who do not in fact remember you, will assume that you inhabit one of the numerous gaps in their actual memories, and will act accordingly. Earnest young biographers will assume that where I went, you went also, and will therefore write you into their own narratives. If you can just contrive to keep your head for a couple of hours, it is virtually certain that if people are still writing this kind of' – I was going to say 'rubbish', but thought I had better spare her feelings – 'stuff in 2007, you will find your own name in the indexes, sure as fate. Won't that give you some satisfaction? Wouldn't you like to be famous?'

'But it's not fair.'

'Dora, my dear girl. The world is not fair. It is not fair, for example, that you, who would clearly have enjoyed the whole thing so much more than I did, were not born to my social advantages. Think of it as class revenge. A member of the reading public gets her own back.' She continued to look terrified, and mulish. 'After all,' I added, 'what on earth have you got to lose?' This, after some little while, appeared to bring her to a decision.

'All right, Professor Strachey. I'll do it.'

'Good girl.' I went and got a bit of my father's writing paper, and wrote a note to Ms Chapman: 'Dear Ms Chapman, Dora and I will be happy to receive you at my late father's flat at any suitable time: do get in touch, yours, &c.' I folded, addressed and stamped it, then called a taxi. 'Put your coat on, Dora. I am going to buy you a dress.' She made a sort of inarticulate noise, which can only be rendered as '!!!', but I paid it no heed: I was trying to think.

In my darling Sofia's opinion, London couture is only fit for some pigs (I quote), but needs must. The taxi arrived, I put Dora into it with a firm, but not unkindly hand, and climbed in after her. 'Harvey Nichols,' I told the driver. When we arrived at that crass monument to the English upper-class aesthetic, I tucked Dora's damp and tremulous hand under my arm, and took her up to ladies' fashions. There, I stopped a passing floorwalker, and asked her to find me a senior saleswoman. Some short while later, a grey-haired woman with a shrewd, assessing countenance and a string of very good cultured pearls appeared, and asked how she could help. I looked her straight in the eye.

'Madame is a gentlewoman, of mildly bohemian inclinations. She requires a suitable and becoming afternoon dress, with appropriate shoes and so forth. She also needs the attentions of a hairdresser, and some guidance on *maquillage*. Please explain the situation to the functionaries responsible; she does not wish either to look like a retired prostitute, or like a middle-aged clone of the ex-Princess of Wales. I propose to sit here on this convenient little gilt chair where someone can keep an eye on me, and I will stay here for as long as this takes. When you have done all you can, I will sign the cheques without a murmur.'

The saleswoman looked me over for a long moment, a world of cynical experience in her face.

'Certainly, Sir,' she replied, and led the gibbering Dora away to some inner fastness. I pulled out a pocket copy of *Il Principe* (underestimated, in my view, as a work of comic fiction), and made myself as comfortable as possible: I was expecting to be there for some time.

In the event, the whole thing took about three hours. Kindly hands brought me coffee from time to time; and I was permitted to visit the lavatory. When Dora was returned to me, I must say, I was agreeably impressed. The awful glasses, I had become aware, were mainly needed for reading. She could manage without them; and I was therefore unsurprised to find that the stylist had suppressed them with a firm hand. Their absence gave her gaze a swimming, unfocused character, by no means inappropriate to one who had allegedly spent her youth drinking and smoking dope: the eyes themselves were marginally better than they had appeared through smeary and poorly proportioned lenses. Looking her over, I was well satisfied. It occurred to me that it is one of the minor ironies of life that the wages of sin are not necessarily distinguishable from the wages of frustration and ignorance. The stylist had cleverly not attempted to plaster over the enlarged pores, the bags beneath her eyes, and so forth. With considerable subtlety, he or she had merely suggested that the collapse of Miss Prentiss's youthful charms, if indeed there had been any, came into the same bracket as the ruin of Miss Birkin's looks, or Miss Faithfull's: damage as testimony to a life lived in the fast lane. The frock, similarly, cast the most flattering gloss over poor Dora's collection of spare tyres that I could possibly have hoped for. She did not, in my view, look appetising, but at least it was possible to believe that if she were thirty years younger, and about twenty kilos lighter, Mick Jagger might have thought her worth undoing his zip for. I signed the bills without demur: Harvey Nichols had done well by us.

The next morning, Ms Chapman rang me up on her mobile. It sounded a bit as if she were phoning from Beijing, but she assured me that she was merely in a traffic jam on the M25. Shouting at one another above the hiss and crackle, we arranged that she would come on Friday afternoon. Dora immediately panicked, of course, but I pointed out to her that an interview is not an interrogation, or an oral examination. 'Given the past which we are implying for you,' I said, 'no one will be expecting you to remember *anything* accurately. The phrase "I honestly don't remember" will stand you in good stead, provided that you refrain from accompanying it with an apologetic little laugh. If you get flustered, refer her to me. This will lead her to believe that you are a sweet, old-fashioned girl, but you don't mind that, do you?'

She flushed, unbecomingly. Perhaps she had picked up a note of sarcasm? It is hard to understand the perceptions of the extremely stupid: irony, I knew, passed straight over her head. She continued to look annoyed.

'I'll do my best,' she said, sulkily.

'Dora, my dear,' I said gently, 'no one could ask for more. The stakes are not that high. Absolutely nothing can happen to you. No one will sue you for libel. They don't even know your address. If we make idiots of ourselves, then the *Sunday Times* will pull the interview.'

'But I don't want them to,' she blurted, 'I really don't.' There were actually tears in her eyes. I will never understand that woman.

The hours and days marched by ineluctably. Then it was Friday, our appointment with doom. I dressed with some care, in a casual suit from Ermenegildo Zegna, and surveyed myself with justifiable satisfaction, congratulating myself on the fact that the only visible reminder of my youthful self which I retained was my waist measurement. Dora reported for duty in a high state of nervousness, having achieved a respectable simulacrum of the stylist's work on her face: he must have given her a diagram. After lunch, I opened a bottle of Brunello, and insisted that she drink some.

'Better tight than tense,' I observed. 'It all helps the mood.'

'I don't have much of a head,' she muttered. I laughed:

'For God's sake don't say that to Ms Chapman! Or if you do, add the magic words, "these days".'

Dora took a swig from her glass, and looked at it in mild surprise. 'It's actually quite nice,' she observed.

The words '*Dio mio*' escaped me before I could repress them. 'I'm so glad you like it,' I said, as sweetly as I could. She was half-way down the glass by the time the doorbell rang, and beginning to look more relaxed. 'Just stay there,' I said hastily. 'Good luck,' and went and answered it myself.

Opening the door, I found myself confronting a skinny female dressed out of Gap or some such dismal emporium, wearing large, round, brightly coloured glasses which gave her the appearance of a minor Walt Disney character. Her hair appeared to have been eaten by rats, though she may have imagined that she had undergone a layer cut of some kind. She peered up at me, apparently in some surprise.

'Professor Strachey? I'm Janice Chapman.'

'Of course. Do come in. Dora is in the sitting-room.' She followed me in; I made introductions, poured her a glass of wine, and settled her down on the sofa beside Dora. The latter, now the whole business had actually begun, was surprisingly calm; perhaps with the calm of the tumbril, though in retrospect, I am not so sure. I smiled professorially at Ms Chapman, and took charge of the conversation.

'Where would you like to start?' I invited.

'Oh, with the photograph. You know, "Spring in the Bois"? It was only when I saw your father's obituary that I realised it had been anyone at all well known. It's such a famous image in itself, I thought our readers would enjoy knowing how it fits into contemporary history.'

I was surprised: I had at that point almost forgotten about 'Spring in the Bois'. Having lived outside England for so long, its popularity as an image had not impinged on me. Also, I had forgotten the crass workings of the English journalistic mentality.

'Of course,' I said, marking time while I hauled the relevant facts from the dark backward and abysm of time, 'Though as you'll probably realise, it was taken some time before I was born.'

'But do you know what the immediate story is behind it, Professor Strachey – can I call you Simone? When did they meet? Why were they in Paris?'

That, at least, I could answer. The bits and scraps of paternal autobiographising had focused strongly on his early manhood, and the circumstances of his meeting with my mother were well covered (though I have to admit, some of the stories Mamà told me about her own family's reaction to his proposal, funny though they were in themselves, had been discreetly suppressed: I saw no reason to revive them in this context). I launched into a rhetorically appropriate, and largely factual, *récit*: both ladies appeared to find it moving.

'I can let you use a fragment of autobiography which my father must, I think, have written shortly after my mother's death,' I concluded. 'It might perhaps help you with tone and atmosphere?'

'He clearly saw this as one of the key moments in his life?' prompted Ms Chapman. *Dio mio*, I should bloody well think so. I thought it best to change the subject.

'I did realise that you would be interested in photographs,' I said. 'I assume you will want to use several? I sorted out some of the most interesting.' Opening the folder on the coffee-table, I handed them one by one to Ms Chapman, who took them reverently, then passed them to Dora, who returned them in sequence to the folder. I had included an early publicity photo of Mamà, looking almost edible in her youthful beauty, and one of Daddy in uniform, with the sort of glazed, Monarch-of-the-Glen nobility then in vogue. Ms Chapman received these politely, but her enthusiasm visibly rose once we reached the 'name' photographers of my parents' high and palmy days. Fortunately, there were enough of these to make the whole thing very much worth her while, including a very good and unpublished Beaton of Mamà taken some time in the late thirties, and an excellent Norman Parkinson from her flourishing middle years. As we went through, we came, of course, to the Bailey photograph I have already described. 'It's not a very good picture of Dora,' I said apologetically, as I handed it over. 'We were all such chauvinists then, were we not?' As I had hoped it might, from her generally Libberish appearance, this triggered a Pavlovian reaction. Her attention was entirely and successfully diverted to the photograph as a cultural artefact. Using it as the text of a feminist sermon, she waved it about, and gave us a dull five minutes on Steinem, Solanas, Sontag, and the rise of the Women's Movement in its social context, alluding at intervals to its informational iniquities (or inequities) while Dora stared, transfixed with terror. Not for a second did she think to question the identity of the woman thus imperfectly represented. I began to feel remarkably cheerful, and poured us all another glass of Brunello. A second 'Dora' photograph, a Tony Armstrong-Jones of a girl almost completely obscured by floppy hair, floppy hat and white lipstick, photographed in a crowded coffee-bar, passed almost without comment. Miss Chapman set her glass down absent-mindedly, and turned to look at Dora, who was carefully tying the strings on the photograph portfolio.

'Simone mentioned that you'd be here when we set up the interview,' she began, 'but I have to say, I hadn't remembered that you'd been part of the scene. Tell me, what was it actually like?' This was it. I crossed my fingers furtively in my jacket pocket, and sent up a brief but fervent prayer to St Mercurius, patron of fraudsters. An expression of complete panic flitted across Dora's bunlike features, but she gained a moment by reaching for, and sipping from, her glass of wine, and when she spoke, her voice, to my considerable relief, was fairly even in tone.

'It's all a long time ago,' she temporised. 'You know, you can end up sort of feeling that in your twenties you were really someone else?' Oho, dangerous ground, my little Dora. But Ms Chapman was nodding and smiling, oozing empathy from every pore.

'God, yes! I look at my own old photographs sometimes, and say, was that really me? You must get that so strongly, with this stuff.'

'Actually, I was really struck with what you were saying, Janice.' Dora was clearly gaining confidence. I wondered if the ladies quite realised how often the words 'really' and 'actually' were surfacing in their discourse: I was just waiting for 'honestly', a sure symptom of someone lying through his teeth. But Dora was doing well. While her speech pattern still breathed the stagnancy of the Thames valley, she had picked up one or two helpful tricks, presumably from the Harvey Nichols total immersion experience. Her vocables were still semi-literate, but they were indisputably posher: she said, for instance, 'atchly' rather than 'ackcherley'.

'It was all much more Establishment than it looked at the time. There was an awful lot of the Old Boys' network – you know, Humphrey Lyttelton was at school with Simone?'

'Though quite a lot older,' I put in hastily. I have my pride. But Dora was well away, perhaps thanks to the second glass.

'Even people like Heathcote Williams and Nicky Haslam turned out to be Old Etonians when you got to know them. Half the men you met had been at Eton or Cambridge. Basically, there were two sorts of men in the Sixties, tough boys from the East End with nothing to lose, like Bailey and Sassoon, and public schoolboys, who didn't know what losing meant. Women didn't really fit in at all.'

'What about Mary Quant?' asked Ms Chapman. 'Now, she really was a Sixties woman who wasn't just a pretty face.'

'Well, yes, okay. She achieved something for herself, of course, but she married a public schoolboy. It took his confidence as well as her talent to get her as far as she got. You just had to scratch the surface, you know, and you found the same old game, played by the same old rules. It was all men talking to each other. Working-class boys those days expected their girls to keep their traps shut, and the other lot weren't used to talking to women at all, so of course, they didn't.' I felt a pang of compunction, as she spoke, for my parents and their relationship, which had borne not the slightest relationship to the grotesque caricature which Dora was perpetrating. She was beginning to irritate me: I was longing to interrupt, but dared not put her off her stride.

'And how did you feel about it?'

'Well, honestly, at the time, I thought it was wonderful. None of us knew any better, you know? I may have been following Simone around like Mary's little lamb, but I was still having so much more fun and freedom than I'd been brought up to expect. We really did *think* we were liberated, you know. It's only looking back on it that you start to wonder why we ever put up with it. They talked about a Brave New World. But in reality, men like Simone edited journals, and women like me made the coffee.'

I could bear this no longer. 'Extremely badly, as I recall,' I put in. Both women gave me, simultaneously, the same condescending stare.

'This is really fascinating,' said Ms Chapman.

'But my dear Dora,' I objected, 'is it absolutely necessary to explain the fact that I edited the *Contemporary Review* and you did not by recourse to the concept of a vast international conspiracy? I'm sorry to be unchivalrous, but do you not think that in this context, the fact that I and my fellow editors had been to university, while you and your fellow coffee-makers had not, was of some direct relevance?'

'Did you ever meet Iris Murdoch?' asked Ms Chapman. I considered her tone impertinent.

'I did indeed. Since Dora thinks it important, you might care to know that she is another female luminary of the Sixties who was married to an Old Etonian. I remember her as a bright-eyed little academic bag-lady of a wholly recognisable kind. I believe her to be wholly sound on Sartre, and her book on existentialism is depressingly good in its way. But I take it that you are more interested in her as the author of a series of modish and facile novelettes?'

'I think Simone's sort of made my point for me,' said Dora. 'The women who did do anything themselves just got endless sneering and sniping. People said the most incredible things about Iris, and Brigid too. They were scared stiff of them, of course.'

I am quite happy to admit that I disliked Iris Murdoch on sight. But for the first time in my life, as I listened to these brainless bitches massaging one another's egos, I felt truly and profoundly sorry for her. I could not begin to imagine how it would feel to a person of her genuine intellectual gifts to find herself an object of patronising pity from the likes of Ms Chapman, let alone Dora. I allowed myself a vision of the pair of them up for a logic tutorial in Professor Murdoch's Oxford study: things would go very ill with them.

Perhaps fortunately, Ms Chapman changed the subject. 'What have you done since then, Dora? Do you think your youthful optimism, the sexual fizz and idealism we were talking about, did anything for you in the long run? Or was it all a bit of a trap? I'm also interested to hear whatever you feel you can tell me about your relationship with Simone. I'm just reading the body language here, but I gather you two haven't stayed together? Can you clarify the situation for me?'

I was as interested as she to hear how Dora coped with this one: while she was annoying the hell out of me, I had to admit she was putting up a superb performance – she had picked up my lead with more flair than I had anticipated, and was playing to little Chapman's preconceptions like a good 'un.

'I've had a scrappy sort of life,' she admitted. 'You've got to remember, Janice, that careers were the last thing on anyone's mind in those days. We all thought you could skip university and go to India for a couple of years, pick up work here and there when you needed it, stay free and uncompromised. Now of course, you look back, and realise that you ended up with no qualifications, and all the jobs were dead-end, and the State doesn't look after you any more. Of course, we never thought about pensions and things. You just didn't. I don't think we even expected to get old. Do you remember The Who? "My Generation?" Roger Daltrey singing "hope I die before I get old"? That's *my* generation he's talking about.'

'But Simone didn't feel like that . . . ?' prompted Ms Chapman.

'I think he did a bit,' said Dora, damn her impertinence. 'But he got bored. He's always had that Italian side, you know? People talk about Latin lovers, but actually, it's us who are the romantic ones. He was never one of the really reckless types, even when he was young. He was always expecting to do something, when most of us were just content to be, to live in the moment.'

'So you drifted apart? The fact that you're here tells me you never really quarrelled?'

Dora laughed a little, her expression a nauseating blend of matronage and sentiment. 'We had plenty of rows, I assure you – we both had hot tempers then – but none of them were terminal. Then Simone was offered this job in Italy. I didn't want to go, there was some other stuff I was doing at the time, and it didn't fit. I was going to go out after a while, but you know what it's like? A few months go by, and you're both living totally different lives, then after a while, there doesn't seem to be any point. But we kept in touch, and when Nigel died, and Simone realised what an archive he'd built up here, he asked me if I'd give him a hand sorting it out.'

Whatever anyone might have thought of to say at that point was short-circuited by the doorbell.

'That'll be the photographer,' chirped Ms Chapman, and went off to let him in. I smiled encouragingly at Dora, who was sitting there with a dazed expression on her face.

'You're doing splendidly,' I hissed. She looked at me desperately. 'It's all right,' I insisted, 'she's eating it up.' There was no time for more. The door opened, and Ms Chapman came back in, followed by a hulking figure in jeans and leather jacket, with an arsenal of equipment. He sucked his teeth, sizing up the room and the pair of us.

'I'll just have a look around,' he said. 'Don't mind me.' It had not occurred to Ms Chapman to introduce him: it seemed best, therefore, to connive in the fiction that he was a mobile item of furniture. The remainder of the conversation was necessarily somewhat interrupted. We posed for some shots in the dining-room, with reference books and photographs littered artistically: misleadingly so, since I had insisted throughout on tidy and disciplined work habits, the only possible way to reduce such an archive to order. Then, after some lengthy fiddling with reflector screens and other tiresome apparatus, we were set up for conversation pieces in the sitting-room. Dora's nervousness markedly increased, but fortunately, expressed itself mainly in a sulkiness which was easily readable as bloody-mindedness. The photographer, having evidently reached a technical impasse, fished in his pockets for cigarettes, and held out the packet.

'Want one, love?'

'Oh, I don't. Not any more.' It was a complete mystery to me. As though a switch had been thrown, Dora emerged from somewhere the other side of panic, securely in possession of her borrowed persona. She became quite friendly, even a little flirtatious. I exerted my charm, such as it is, and despite the essentialist suspicion of the Latin *mentalité* expressed earlier, both Dora and Ms Chapman appeared adequately susceptible to its appeal. Since I had begun to suspect that Dora had had quite enough excitement for one day, I shifted the conversation to the contents of Daddy's letters, etc., and told some of the stories we had found. This, as I had hoped, went down extremely well: I began to see an acquisitive gleam developing behind Ms Chapman's big round spectacles. With murmurs of 'an American library . . . but things are still very much at the discussion stage', I then proceeded to fob her off and bring the interview to a close.

Once the door was firmly shut behind the journalist and her anthropoid sidekick, I turned to Dora once more.

'Thank you, my dear,' I said simply, 'that was superb.' Manners dictated that I should take the woman out; but I could bear no more of her company.

'When will it come out?' she asked.

'I really don't know. You should have asked Ms Chapman that. Since it's not tied to a particular occasion, they may keep it for a while, especially if they need to check the copyright on some of the photographs.'

'Oh.' With the excitement over, she was returning rapidly to her old self, refusing to meet my eye, mechanically straightening items disturbed by the photographer. She seemed, I was relieved to see, as disinclined for more of my company as I was for hers.

'Dora, my dear. Would you think me frightfully rude if we called it a day?' She flushed: something in her pose suggested the imminence of tears before bedtime.

'Actually, I'm tired too,' she said. I fled, without further delay.

After this episode, life in the flat returned to normal. For another week or so, we continued to sort, file and catalogue. But the effort of mounting the deception we had perpetrated on Ms Chapman had somehow taken the remaining bubbles, such as there were, out of the project. I was sick of the whole thing. Dora, as ever, kept her own counsel: I was somehow both touched and repelled to observe that she continued, each day, to make up her face in the style recommended by Harvey Nichols; though she was forced, during working hours, to surmount this work of art with her awful glasses. Then I received a letter from Sofia, who had returned from the jaunt with her sisters some time before, and was back at home. It opened, '*Tesoro mio*. My greetings to your ugly mistress, who I hope, continues to charm you,' and continued in the same vein of agreeable banter. This was not, of course, the first letter that she had sent since our separation, but it was the first to hint, however indirectly, that she felt my absence to be unduly prolonged. It also served to remind me forcibly of how much I prefer my wife's company to that of any other woman. When I got to the flat, and saw Dreary Dora already at work, a wave of the most profound annoyance rose in my gorge like heartburn. I wanted to hit her, for being boring, fat, commonplace, middle-class, English and dowdy. For being my secretary, and not my wife. I knew this to be both unfair and discourteous, and masked it as best I could. I worked through the morning somehow, almost unable to sit still, trying not to look at her. We got through to lunchtime, with minimal interaction. As usual, I prepared to go out. Equally according to routine, Dora produced a packet of crisps, a sweet but calorie-reduced yoghurt, and a chocolate bar from the depths of an elderly vinyl bag. I stared at this primitive feast, and thought, 'I cannot endure this woman one moment longer.'

By the time I returned from lunch, I had evolved a plan.

'Dora, my dear. We must have a council of war. Let me put on some coffee, and we can drink it together in the sitting-room.' I was not, let me assure you, making coffee in order to redress an imaginary slight to Dora's forgotten predecessors. I was making coffee because no Englishwoman of my acquaintance, past or present, can be trusted to do so. When I carried the pot through, she was sitting on the sofa once more, looking vaguely alarmed. It seemed best to reassure her.

'Dora, this is all taking rather longer than I anticipated. Can I just check with you that you don't have a future engagement that I will have to treat as a deadline?'

'Oh, no. Nothing like that.' Her colour returned to normal: I had been right, I think, to surmise that she feared she was about to be dismissed.

'That's splendid. I think it may be hard for you to appreciate it at this stage, but we have come a very long way in the last three months. In particular, I do appreciate the magnificent effort that you have made. You have familiarised yourself, in extraordinary detail, with an entire world of people and experience. You have performed miracles of empathy as well as of organisation. I am hardly flattering you when I say that you are now dealing with this material as well as I could handle it myself.'

'Thank you, Simone,' she murmured, eyes modestly downcast. 'Professor Strachey' had fallen victim to the ineffable Ms Chapman and her ridiculous interview; which, I rather think, is one of the reasons poor Dora had come to irritate me so much.

'I realise, of course, that my life in the present day is somewhat vaguer and less visible to you than my life in the nineteen-sixties. However, let me assure you that I have one, and that it cannot be put on hold indefinitely. My poor father's demise coincided with the end of the Italian academic year, which is to say, the time when I am most free.' Actually, as I mentioned earlier, Daddy had contrived to die some weeks before the end of the teaching year, bless him: there was a lot of my summer still to come. But I was trying to give Dora the broad picture. 'I am expected to write a book from time to time. My publishers, naturally enough, neither know nor care about my personal problems, and as you might imagine, I am now well behind schedule. I also have to write a conference paper to be delivered in Turin in September, and I have a couple of contributions to journals which have been left on hold. In short, Dora, I am not a person of infinite leisure, even though I have considerable flexibility in organising my own time-table.'

'Yes . . . I see.' She was looking confused again. 'What do you want, then?'

'I have a proposal to put before you. Having worked by your

side for weeks and weeks, I have every confidence in your ability, your organisation, and of course, your diligence. As time has gone by, you have needed me less and less. From director and assistant, we have gradually transformed, with the passage of time, into co-workers. How would you feel if I left you to finish the job on your own? You already have keys to the flat and the building. My father's executors have been instructed that no attempt can be made to sell the place until this archival work has been completed, and are content to wait for my instructions in the matter. Mrs Pettigree is happy to go on taking care of the flat itself for the foreseeable future. You would therefore have no additional job to do – it is just that you would be coming in here to work on the papers on your own. Do you think you could do it?' Her brow knitted: she was always an easily frightened creature. 'All I would want from you', I tempted, 'is to send me any bills that eventuate, not just your salary, but electricity and so forth, and a monthly summary of your findings. I do, of course, recognise that even given your remarkable efficiency, work will proceed more slowly with one than with two. Reckoning roughly from where we have got to, I should think that the Strachey papers will give you continued, and reasonably congenial, employment till the end of the summer, which may perhaps be a consideration?'

'All right, Simone. I'll do my best.'

'Excellent. Then, if you have no objection, I will spend the afternoon making arrangements for my return to Italy.'

I strolled out into the London sunshine, heading for the Alitalia office, with a light heart. The bleak picture I had painted for Dreary Dora was, I am happy to admit, less than wholly accurate. My book could wait: fire would not come down from heaven merely because its arrival at the publisher's was delayed by six months. The conference paper I intended to write in a week. What was actually on my mind was my summer vacation, which I proposed to take in a leisurely and civilised fashion, in the company of Sofia, at some place of resort infinitely more agreeable than my father's pathetic flat. But first, I wanted to go home. I had not a shred of conscience in abandoning Dora. Had I remained in her vicinity for many more days, I fear that it would all have ended in her dismembered parts being left out for the bin-men. No, it was better thus.

The following morning, I settled up with my dismal hotel and flew back to Florence, well pleased with myself: I took the first opportunity which offered to purchase a nectarlike espresso from an ordinary coffee-stall, and knew I was home. Sofia had come to meet me, so I was in a mood to forgive even the impossible Florentine traffic-system, and sat silent and contented while she piloted us efficiently out of the city and down the valley of the Arno. The roads were thick with tourist traffic as we passed through Tuscany: it was July. But once we reached Foligno, and swung west, zigzagging up into the Apennines, as we left behind the vineyards and olive-groves, so we also left the crowds. The peace of the Marche's endless woods descended on us. On these winding mountain roads, made with the matchless skill that comes from two thousand years of continual practice, there went only ancient Cinquecentos, farmers' trucks laden with maize or potatoes, the occasional private car, almost never one with a foreign numberplate. We had returned to a land of mighty hills, most of which bore, like Cybele, a mural crown: a citadel, secure behind ancient and lofty walls. Caldarola. Tolentino. Home. We live in the *centro storico*, in part of a discarded ducal palace built and briefly occupied by Francesco Sforza, surrounded by a happy mélange of the fifteenth and the eighteenth centuries, memorably precipitous of access even by local standards. Our Alfa slipped up the winding street as if it knew its own way, up to the Palazzo Sforza perched in a corner of the clifflike wall of the castello, with a sheer drop below down to the valley of the Chienti, and a stupendous view across the blue and breathless distance.

Evening was falling. I bathed, and changed completely, enjoying the simple pleasure of inhabiting my own space, which has more than sentiment to recommend it. The Corsi furniture inherited from my mother was mostly neoclassical, and fine, disposed rather sparsely and formally in big, high-ceilinged rooms. The only point where we achieve actual grandeur is in the *salotto*, where neo-classicism blends harmoniously with the classicism of the Renaissance: the walls are decorated with an Arcadian fresco of nude grape-pickers, painted towards the end of the fifteenth century. Every muscle is as distinct as in an anatomist's study, and they are deployed in postures safely imitated from the best models: the Discobolos bends not to throw his discus, but to capture a low-slung bunch; Graces temporarily separated from one another's embrace reach their soft round arms up into the branches, while a rustic Farnese Hercules broods over the weight, not of his club, but of a heavy-laden basket. This work of art delights me: for its competence within carefully defined limitations, its elegance, and its inadvertent comedy. The room is completed by a set of First Empire chairs in the Greek taste, arranged in file along the walls, a big Baroque mirror, and a cool tiled floor contemporary with the fresco. It gave me indescribable pleasure, after months spent between my father's overcrowded flat and the timid vulgarity of the hotel, to walk through a space so big, so bare, and so entirely coherent in spirit and content.

Sofia was waiting for me in the loggia, as I had expected, elegant in mint green, and contrasting agreeably with the vibrant yellow satin of the neoclassical daybed on which she was sitting and reading *Commentari d'Arte*. In a moment, we would go out for the evening *passegiata*, and sit for a while in a café with perhaps a Cinzano or a Martini. Then we would stroll home again, and have a simple little meal free from excess, preciosity, or chef's selection of baby vegetables. Then we would talk, and some time later, we would go to bed and make love. A simple programme, in which one thing perfect of its kind would follow another. Sofia came and took my arm, and we went out into the town. We conversed agreeably, of the things of that moment. My wife asked nothing about London, aware that, if I wanted to talk about it, I would certainly do so. It was only when we had consumed *spaghetti all'antica*, grilled chicken and a *contorno* of bitter greens, and were sitting at leisure over pears and pecorino, that I felt in the least inclined to shift my attention beyond the innumerable pleasures of my homecoming, and address a subject outside our immediate environment.

'Tell me, *carissima*. Where would you like to go this summer? I think we should go somewhere nice, we have had a very trying few months.'

Sofia looked thoughtful. 'I should like to go to Geneva. We could perhaps take a house by the lake? There is art, and also, we could ski in the Alps. Now we have the money coming from your father, God rest him, we can perhaps endure the Swiss franc.'

It sounded like a fine idea to me: we agreed to go to Switzerland. We looked at some maps, and some works of art history, and I ended the day in the arms of the woman who is for me, the only woman in the world.

Once I woke the next morning, the London jaunt seemed as remote as the palace of Armida. I went to my office, answered my accumulated correspondence with uncharacteristic zest and promptness, worked a little on my book, beamed at any colleagues I happened to encounter, and allowed the peculiar pleasures of provincial Italy to wash over me. A couple of weeks later, Dora sent me the *Sunday Times* supplement. Distance had lent no enchantment, but it had at least blessed me with detachment: the ineffable Chapman had netted herself a good five pages, nearly three of which were occupied by photographs. I was delighted for her sake to see that in the photograph of myself and Dora in the flat, she had come out as well as she could ever have hoped to look. It had been taken after the moment when she had come to life, and had caught her gesturing, in mid-utterance: she looked lively, and indeed almost pretty in a raddled sort of way. The actual text fascinated me. Dora, of course, had said almost nothing: but what a world of supposition and inference Ms Chapman had woven around her Sybilline clichés! She came out of the whole thing rather well; I, inevitably, as the brutally indifferent child of privilege, born with a silver spoon up my nose. It was all most entertaining. No doubt poor Dora would cherish it; but so would I. As an exercise in creative reading and misreading, it held possibilities beyond Janice Chapman's wildest dreams. I could certainly use it as the starting-point for a book: the memory of journalistic man (and woman) being extremely short, it seemed to me fair to assume that the unveiling of this wholly successful deception in a couple of years' time would cause the young woman no more than passing annoyance.

'What is amusing you, *tesoro mio*?' enquired Sofia. I explained what I had done, and what I intended to do with it. To my considerable surprise, my wife was disposed to take a rather stern view of the whole *jeu d'esprit*.

'I think you have been unkind to this poor ugly Englishwoman,' she said austerely. 'It is not good or right to play with people's dreams.'

'But my darling Sofia, you have entirely missed my point. I brought her dream to life. However dreary her future, and it is probable that it will be dreary beyond our conception, I have given her something to look back on.'

Sofia arched her fine eyebrows. 'Simone, you are not God. It is not for you to meddle with the lives of others.' She got up – we were sitting over our coffee, surrounded by the morning's post – and took the *Sunday Times* from me. Returning to her own seat, she studied the photograph of Dora with concentration.

'She's not so very ugly,' she observed, after a couple of minutes' intent scrutiny.

'I can assure you, Sofia, that what you see before you is the result of a near-miraculous transformation which took an entire afternoon and cost a great deal of money.' My wife waved a dismissive hand, sweeping aside Harvey Nichols and all their works.

'There is vitality here, Simone. This is a woman who has had no education, and no opportunity, but there is great strength. I would have been afraid to do as you did, *caro*.'

'What rubbish, Sofia. You are afraid of absolutely nothing.' She stood up, collecting together her own letters, and spoke tartly over her shoulder as she left the room.

'My dearest Simone, I do hope you have not been very foolish.' With which Parthian shot, she left me, and went about her own business.

It is an inevitable feature of even the most harmonious marriages that one's beloved spouse may be detected, from time to time, in preparing the ground for the utterance of the dread words 'I told you so' should these at any point prove necessary. I was not disposed to let Sofia worry me. For one thing, the day before me was quite a busy one, and I had other things on my mind, including a PhD student whose examination I had to fix. Also, while I was prepared to admit that my behaviour had perhaps been a little tasteless, or incongruent with the ethics of true politeness, it seemed to me that the intellectual value of the book which I proposed to write needed to be set in the scales against the possibly dubious morality of gratifying the fantasies of a dreary and ageing spinster, a point which Sofia, of course, did not concern herself with. I dismissed Dora and the whole idiotic business from my mind, and went about my work.

I did not stir out of Macerata again until the beginning of August, when we betook ourselves to Rome, from whence we would fly to Geneva. We spent a couple of days in the city itself, to allow Sofia to pillage the Via Condotti, and this achieved, we bought another suitcase in which to stow her loot, and took ourselves off to Ciampino. We had allowed a fair amount of time for checking in, and, as things turned out, there was some delay to the plane itself. Resignedly, we settled down in the Departure

Lounge, where we seemed likely to remain for some time. I dislike flying, on the whole: Sofia loathes it. I do at least find that I can read in airports; but as she has explained to me, she finds the experience too stressful to allow her to concentrate. It is the one context in which one can be certain that somewhere at the bottom of her bag, a rosary lies coiled, and probably, just to be sure, a miraculous medal or two. Having spent as much time as possible lingering among the duty-free perfumes, she left me to guard such baggage as we had not checked, and prowled up and down the concourse unhappily, looking for something to do. All of which explains why, after one of these pointless excursions, she returned to my side carrying a copy of *Hello!*, a magazine which would make no demands on the intellectual resources of a gerbil, and settled down to look at the pictures. After a peaceful half-hour, in which I continued to read Goldoni, there was an explosion at my side.

'*Dio mio*!'

I jumped, losing my place, and turned to Sofia. 'What is it, *cara*?'

Sofia folded the magazine carefully, and handed it to me, her expression grim. I studied it in some puzzlement: she had directed my attention to one of those double-page spreads depicting the slightly famous disporting themselves at parties which are a feature of the magazine. Then, after a moment, I saw it too. There, in conversation with a once-modish interior decorator of faintly familiar appearance, was Dora. She had lost weight, and was wearing a decolleté dark-blue, sequinned dress which I could never have imagined her having the nerve to put on: in the caption below, just in case I might have thought I had made a mistake, was the name 'Dora Strachey'. I stared at the thing in amazement. It was probably the most sudden and unexpected peripety to occur in Rome since my regrettable namesake got the wrong side of the Apostle Peter. I was so angry that I could not trust my voice. Sofia was glaring at me, with that air of righteousness justified which is one of the most irritating postures a wife can adopt.

'And what are you going to do about it, eh, Simone?' Up above us, the loudspeaker began to announce that the plane for Geneva was now boarding. I got to my feet, and dropped the magazine in an adjacent bin.

'As soon as we touch ground again, I am going to sack her.'

I was feeling no more forgiving by the time the plane decanted us in the city of John Calvin. In due course, we met up with the agent, took delivery of the keys, and established ourselves in a commodious villa out towards Cologny, with an excellent view of Lac Léman. Then, in the course of our first reconnoitre of our new environment, I provided myself with some Swiss stamps from the Hôtel des Postes, and wrote a curt note to Dora, dispensing with her services from the end of the month. I no longer cared if the job was completed: far and away enough sorting and editing had been done to convince the Americans, since I had expected Dora to be finished by the end of the summer in any case.

Between the mountains, where we exercised periodically, the Musée d'Art, the concerts, and the resources of the Grand Quai and its environs, our time in Switzerland passed very pleasantly. It is true that, like another of Geneva's best-known, though fictional, denizens, I was uneasily conscious that somewhere in the world beyond, there stalked a monster of my own construction, set in motion not by grave-robbing, vivisection and van der Graff generators, but by a team of maquilleurs, hairdressers and modistes, operating not in the depths of some workshop of filthy creation, but in the perfumed inner sanctums of Harvey Nichols department store. Victor Frankenstein, fleeing with abject loathing from the hideous object he had brought into being, was the only individual in fiction or fact who would in the least have appreciated my feelings about the dreadful Dora. It is most unclear, in Mrs Shelley's sweet romance, what her Victor (who surely recognised the unaesthetic qualities of his creation even before he threw the fateful switch?) imagined that he wanted his monster to *do*, after it had vindicated an experimental hypothesis by drawing its first breath. I had at least been quite clear on the subject: I wished Dora to step momentarily into my life, for perfectly good and sufficient reason. Then I wished her to have the extreme goodness to step out of it again, after her little moment of glory, and go about her own concerns, whatever those might be. Clearly, on the evidence of the cretinous *Hello!*, the woman had contrived to insinuate herself into a party under false pretences: what else might she have done? Never mind, I said to myself, there are such things as lawyers in the world. Once I am back on my own territory, a series of injunctions should consign the miserable woman to the darkness from whence she emerged. With that happy thought, I was able to spend the rest of the vacation agreeably, without thinking about Dora at all.

One of the most depressing things about coming back from a holiday is dealing with the mountain of correspondence which accumulates in one's absence. The morning after our return to Macerata, Sofia and I arranged ourselves, with a large wastepaper basket on the floor between us, and began opening letters. I was mildly surprised, working down the pile, to come upon a missive with an English stamp, written in a large, splashy, unfamiliar hand. Light dawned when I looked at the letterhead, which indicated that my correspondent lived in the environs of Covent Garden. It was from an amiable old queen of my early acquaintance, who in an earlier life had been one of the newly enfranchised, post-Wolfenden gay-boys who had so markedly increased the resemblance of Swinging London to the Cities of the Plain. He had attended Daddy's funeral and come on to the subsequent reception, where he had exchanged fragments of biography for ten minutes, and asked for my current address. We had never had much in common in the old days, not least because he had so clearly regarded social intercourse with any man whose flies remained securely fastened as a waste of his valuable time, so I was surprised at first that he was so keen to renew what had been a distinctly minimal contact. It then struck me suddenly that since his queer friends, one may reasonably assume, must by now be dropping in their tracks, he might be getting a little lonely. The letter opened, obviously, with 'how nice to see you again/hardly look a day older,' etc. etc., which were to be expected: I was coasting through the remainder, alert principally to whether the old sweetheart was angling for an invitation, which I did not propose to extend to him, when a sentence literally struck a galvanic thrill through me: 'I was dining at Roger's the other evening, and ran into your charming ex, who is looking very well these days. To be frank, I have no very clear memory of her in the old days – all the doe-eyed popsies looked alike to me, and of course none of them ever *said* anything – but she has grown up into a most amusing woman. She had us absolutely in stitches with some of her stories – if you found your ears burning last Fri., it was probably *us*!!!'

'*Caro*, have you got indigestion?' asked Sofia, solicitously, 'you have gone quite pale.' I asked her to make me a tisane, in order to remove her far too observant eye, and give me time to compose myself. I reread the letter frantically, trying to extract yet more meaning from it; but it was all too clear. Stories! It was only too obvious what sort of stories Dora might be telling. I realised, with sinking heart, that I had left the woman in sole and unsupervised charge of an enormous literary archive, which she had been at complete liberty to pillage for a good two months. In the nature of things, not every story told, or hinted at, in the privacy of my father's diaries, the family's private correspondence, and the rest of the collection, was calculated to reflect credit on all concerned: what on earth had she found? Sofia, looking worried, gave me my tisane; I put the letter aside, and drank it, beginning as I did so to regain my perspective. I ripped grimly through the rest of my letters, and escaped to my office. In the privacy of the University, I phoned my English lawyers, who were, it seemed to me, unnecessarily unhelpful, and wrote to Mrs Pettigree, organizing the changing of the lock on the door of Daddy's flat, then debated with myself what to do next. There was no point in taking out an injunction against *Hello!*: however irritating it was to me, the editor could perfectly reasonably claim to be acting in good faith. My man of law, to whom I had put the problem in somewhat hypothetical terms, told me that legally, there was no objection which could be made to a woman's choosing to use the name Strachey: indeed, she could adopt it by deed-poll if she wished: I would only have a case against her if I could demonstrate that she was posing as my wife, thus implicitly libelling me as a bigamist. As far as the wretched man knew, there was nothing whatsoever preventing a woman claiming to be my *ex*-wife, as long as her alleged tenure of my affections did not overlap with my current marriage to Sofia, and as long as she was not using this to extract money under false pretences.

It was the false pretences idea that seemed to me the most promising one. There was also the little matter, if she was drawing on literary material from Daddy's archive, of intellectual property. But there, I was reluctantly forced to admit, she had me. With the Hell-begotten *Sunday Times* article available as evidence to the contrary, I could not unmask her without making an abject fool of myself. My expensive idiot in High Holborn had made it abundantly clear, through his hummings and ha-ings, that in the circumstances, I could hardly sue her for libel, especially if I did not know precisely what stories she was choosing to tell. All right, I thought to myself, let her. I will never set foot in London again: let her reign in that tedious city, the queen of an alternative reality, deceiving a gradually shrinking band of drink- and drug-sodden survivors. What did I really care? Occasional scraps of evidence, such as the morning's letter, could be filed and put to good use in my own book, and the fact that London café society, unknown to itself, had just drifted off at a slight tangent to reality was something which concerned me little, if at all. Instead, I got on with a job which I had not expected to start till Dora was quite finished: preparing a digest of her professional activities, and beginning to assemble my pitch for Austin, Texas. Selling a collection of this magnitude is a delicate matter, and deserves full and undivided concentration. It also represented, as far as I was concerned, a more important, and indeed more interesting, problem than whether a number of elderly alcoholics cherished the illusion that I had once been married to a woman called Dora.

In the course of the next few months, my posture appeared to be vindicated. Having played Austin with the delicacy appropriate to a twenty-pound fish which you have hooked on a fifteen-pound line, I had the immense satisfaction of bringing them safely to shore: that is, I persuaded them to take the 'Strachey Archive' off my hands, and for a handsome sum. They were a little puzzled, I think, that I chose to complete our negotiations in Texas rather than London, and to employ my lawyers (at considerable expense) as agents to oversee the packing and transhipment of the material, but they appeared content to imagine that this represented some kind of scrupulosity on my part. Once the whole collection was out of the flat, I put the latter on the market; and with a value now securely established for the literary material, looked forward to the final administration of my father's will and (however reluctantly) to handing over a depressing proportion of the total in death duties. At least, as Sofia reminded me, my parents had had the sense to give me a great many valuable items while they were both above ground – we could also console ourselves with our private knowledge of the exceedingly valuable drawings which my wife had so deftly liberated before any inventorising took place. At remote intervals, London correspondents such as Roger reported sightings of Dora: since I answered none of these letters, the intervals became greater and greater. The whole ridiculous episode seemed safely buried in oblivion.

My life resumed its normal tenor. I got my book finished, and began a new university year. In November, I received a courteous note from Polity Press, reminding me of something which I had almost forgotten: aeons ago, they had undertaken to publish an English version of one of my books, doubtless on account of Ecomania, but the translator had got ill, and the whole thing had ended up on hold for three years. The translation had finally come through, and they had a window in their publication schedule, so could I read and return the proofs which were coming my way in about a fortnight? This is absolutely typical of academic publishing, by the way: you hear nothing at all for years, or in some instances, decades, then they expect you to be able to drop everything and make an instant response. I read the thing, wincing at the style, suggested one or two improvements, and returned it covered in blue and red ink. That, again, was followed by total silence, then in late May, the arrival of a parcel containing six copies of my work, which I was mildly interested to see: one's own writing acquires a strange and exotic air in a foreign language, even one which is very familiar. I was also interested to see what English-speaking readers made of a work which emerged so entirely out of an alien tradition of discourse. Thus it was that, almost exactly a year after my father's death, I was to be found skimming through the *London Review of Books*. I turned the page, to find a review article, called 'Theories of Sixties Style', featuring four recent books. Might one of them be mine? I stopped dead, my heart slamming against my ribs. The third item was *Look Back in Anguish*, by Dora Strachey. I looked at the title for a long time, as if I was trying to will it out of existence. I could hardly make myself believe the evidence of my own eyes. How on earth had she done it? Dora possessed not a hundredth of my mental agility, or verbal skill. It is a great deal less easy to write a book than those who do not write books assume: on one level, I was simply astonished that she had achieved more than a few thousand words of leaden prose before collapsing in self-doubt, fractured syntax, and general technical incompetence. The next question which occurred to me was scarifying. The world's appetite for tripe about the nineteen-sixties was astonishing, but probably not insatiable. What, posing as hanger-on to an indisputably minor figure such as myself, could she possibly have offered which had got her past any editor's slush-pile? At that point, my squirrelling thoughts were thankfully interrupted by my secretary. I was due to go and give a lecture. I bundled the *LRB* into my desk drawer, and left. I thought it better not even to look at the article until I had some time to myself.

One thing leads to another. It was not until the middle of the afternoon that I was able to return to my room, lock the door, and, reluctantly, get out the *LRB*. What I read was the following:

> Dora Strachey's book is a very different cup of cold poison. Like some other recent biographies, it makes something of a virtue of being 'unauthorised'; an odd concept to apply to an autobiography, but Ms Strachey makes the perfectly valid point that women's recollections are subject to all kinds of censorship, from within and without. Her authentication is her own memory, her own perceptions. With sometimes incredible frankness, she dives into the wreck of 'Swinging London', to produce a spirited, grotesque, insider's view. It comes as no surprise to learn by the end of the book that she is no longer married to the elegant Simone, who provides some of the book's principal highlights. Now a semiotician, he will doubtless find his ex-wife's balefully comic portrait offers much grist to his professional mill. This is Dora Strachey's first book, with a first book's virtues and vices: a fast, funky, feminist flood of passionate, urgent revisioning combined with a very '90s sense of irony. Worth reading for sheer entertainment, it may yet become a minor classic of postmodernism.

And what would your reaction have been, dear reader? In the state of fury which gripped me, I experienced all the symptoms which Sappho assigns to passionate love: my heart fluttered, a pale fire seemed to run beneath my skin, my ears roared, and I was awash with cold sweat. I could not move for some time. When the phone rang, I jumped about a metre, screamed at whoever it was to leave me alone, and slammed it down again. When I had calmed a little, I began to try and think what to do. My first impulse was to see if I could make contact with the Red Brigade, or perhaps the Mafia, and arrange for the kidnapping and assassination of Dora, her publisher, and everyone remotely connected with this diabolical enterprise. I allowed myself some strenuous minutes of vengeful fantasy before dismissing this as impractical. It was vital, of course, to get hold of a copy of the book: little as I wanted to see or even think about it, I would have to know what it contained. I scribbled a fax to my bookseller, and bypassed my amazed and affronted secretary to send the thing myself: I did not want the name 'Strachey' to trigger any impulse to curiosity. Then I rang my English lawyers, only to discover that they had gone home: it would have been perhaps 4.30 in England, but the legal profession does not overexert itself. Then I went and had a drink, brooding furiously. An injunction? A writ? A summons for libel? I could do nothing, obviously, until I knew what the fiend Dora had said about me; but oh, how I wanted to. Seized by a random bright thought, I got a pocketful of change from the barman, went to the phone-booth at the back of the café, and rang International Interflora. They refused point blank to send a wreath of poison ivy, even when invited to name their own price. Nor were they prepared to consider poison-oak, squill, garlic, or nettles. The conversation became acrimonious, and Ms Interflora slammed the phone down. My voice, I came to realise, had risen during the course of this discussion, and everyone in the bar was listening in: I turned to see a ring of interested faces.

'Women are the devil', opined an old man, clearly speaking for them all. I paid my bill, and hastened away, pursued by a barrage of sympathetic glances.

For the next week, I was, I know, impossible to live with. I became a prey to nervous indigestion, I could not sleep at night, and I was liable to bouts of sudden and disproportionate rage. Sofia eyed me with justifiable apprehension, dosed me with a variety of revolting liver-tonics, and began muttering about spas – it was clear from her manner that if she did not manage to persuade me into some such institution, she would retreat to one herself in order to get away from me. I did not want to share the latest bombshell with her. I had not the slightest desire to add a wifely sermon to the many other irritants which I was enduring; I could not think of any way in which she could be positively helpful, and finally, I was desperate to keep her free of this mess. It was bad enough for me to be embroiled in the demon Dora's fantasy-life; I wanted her well out of it.

After a difficult eight or nine days, the book arrived, and I locked myself in the office with it, first unplugging the phone. The cover promised the worst: on the front, was the Bailey 'Simone and Dora'; on the back, there was a recent portrait study which I was hard put to it to recognise as my ex-assistant. She was still thinner, leaning with one elbow on a bridge ('over troubled water', doubtless), looking as portentous as an eggbound hen, in austere semi-profile. Her makeup had acquired a more Sixties flavour, as had her hair, though within the bounds of contemporary taste, and she was wearing a simple Chanel jacket of the kind described as 'dateless' over a plain knitted top. I could hardly bear to look at it. She had certainly improved, to any eye but mine; to me, the plausibility of this monstrous woman's impersonation was the more horrid for its very resemblance to the thing it imitated.

Academics usually turn first to the Acknowledgements: the most revealing page in the book if you know how to read it. This one was no exception. Fulsome acknowledgements to that rabid Minnie Mouse, Janice Chapman, 'who stood by me at every point during the creation of this book'. Acknowledgement of the

Dulwich Writing Workshop (members listed and thanked individually, for everything down to 'extra strong mints and encouragement'). Acknowledgement of the London Library, the Hulton Picture Library, and so forth, the cunning bitch. Abject acknowledgement of 'my wonderful agent, and my marvellous editor' (at which point I was sick in the wastepaper-basket). Acknowledgement – Oh, God! Oh merciful God! Oh, fucking hell! – of the help and co-operation of the Harry Ransom Humanities Research Center at the University of Texas at Austin in allowing her to draw on material held in their priceless archive! It had never for one moment occurred to me that she would have had the *nous* to cover her back in that way. And finally: 'It would be appropriate to end by acknowledging the help and assistance of Professor Simone Strachey, if I had received any. There are many things in these pages which Simone might choose to quarrel with, if he ever reads it. I want to make it clear that they were *not* checked with him, and that I make no claim to speak for him. I am giving my own view, as I see, and saw it. Let this stand as one woman's perspective on the past.' At which point, I nearly choked on my own bile. Some fiendlike lawyer had been over this introduction with a microscope. It began to look horribly as though she had me where she wanted me. On the face of it, she had made no mistakes; but could she get through a whole book without putting her bunioned foot in it up to the hip?

I read on. 'It was the best of times, it was the worst of times' – oh, write the bloody thing for yourself. It was a new dawn, it was the same old darkness, there was continuity *and* change, what a turn-up for the books. Metaphors mixed till they seethed and bubbled, like Dr Hyde's magic potion; we were not spared the Chatterley ban and the Beatles' first LP. From the horrible *olla podrida* which was Dora's prose, there emerged the slimy skeleton of a narrative. We began, inevitably, with Dora's flowerlike youth, so soon to be betrayed: she hurried over this, for understandable reasons, and progressed as rapidly as possible to her late teens, when she met her Svengali (me), and began a Candide-like progress through Sixties London. She had at her disposal, do not forget, letters, including my own letters to my parents, diaries, and other personalia. She was well positioned to reconstruct my life from week to week, to identify my friends, acquaintances, enemies, mistresses, and employers. The horrible thought also struck me, at about page sixty, that the version of her past she had given Janice Chapman might not, apart from the central fiction of her connection with me, have been entirely inaccurate.

With respect to myself, one effect, doubtless intentional, of inserting herself, as 'wife' into a life adequately stocked with women, was to turn my sexual career into one of persistent infidelity bordering on rampant satyriasis, something which she revealed, rather than glossed over, by showcasing it in a mass of pop sociology on the importance of 'going on the pull' to Sixties Man, and the general erotic psychology of the Latin races, as the English understand it. Some of my mother's acerbic, though of course amused, comments on my erotic adventures, paraphrased in English by my father in his diaries, were quoted completely out of context, to give the impression of dark, unhealthy undercurrents. Dora, of course, knew nothing of the discourse of affectionate raillery in Italian; translated more or less verbatim, I have to admit it can sound a little strange. I had better come clean. What I hauled dripping to the surface, after dabbling in this sink of filth, was a portrait along the following lines: a boy who loved his mother, like the late king Oedipus, not wisely, but too well. My mother, dissatisfied with my father, encouraged the intimate attentions of her only son (how intimate? Dora took great care not to say, but the Common Reader has a mind like a cesspool). Prevented from consummating this one true love of his life – this, at least, Dora conceded – the young Simone took up a career of frantic, arid Don Juanism, unable, due to this irretrievably warping adolescence, to form a relationship with an adult woman.

At which point, I really was sick. I mean, I ran to the washroom, clutching a handkerchief to my mouth, and vomited into a sink. Waving off the well-meant assistance of various concerned colleagues, I blamed a perhaps ill-considered *fritto misto* at lunch, accepted aspirin and mineral-water as the shortcut to peace, and locked myself in my office once more.

Wearily, I returned to *Look Back in Anguish*. It got worse. I had come to realise, of course, that the hag Dora felt herself to have just cause of vengeance against me (for what? For employing her for a few months? For buying her a dress costing nearly £500? For giving her Mr Warhol's statutory fifteen minutes of fame? I will never know). In building on and elaborating the picture I had allowed her, with my full connivance, to present to the *Sunday Times*, she was fulfilling narrative expectation. Since I had allowed this to develop in the first place, and everyone, including my Sofia, seemed to take the view that I was not entitled to occupy the moral high ground, I was therefore obliged to take my medicine like a gentleman. If Ms Strachey, speaking for the Silent Scrubbers of the Sixties, felt obliged to erect a leering cardboard cutout of my young self and to throw mud at it, I had, by my own action, forfeited the right to object.

But I felt quite differently about the vengeful fantasia which was her portrait of my parents. As I read, I began slowly to realise that Dora had mastered the conventions of the genre to lethal effect. The modern literary biography masquerades as history, but formally bears more resemblance to a Greek tragedy or a modern musical. In such works, as the principals go about their business centre front, they are, apparently, uninhibited in their expression of mutual emotion by forty-odd hoofers clattering on for the big number. Similarly, in a modern literary biography, the presence of an invisible chorus of legal eagles, beadily watching every move that is made in search of actionable statements, must be assumed at all times. In consequence, certain intrinsically anodyne statements have acquired a violently alternative significance, especially in combination. My mother was wholly charming, though I do not wish to imply by that that the dial was permanently set to 'sweetness and light'. She lived in the present with the completeness and style of a Siamese cat, she loved many people, and things, including Daddy and myself, without sentimentality. She could be brutal, but not dull – in short, she had almost nothing in common with an Englishwoman of the same generation and background. Dora's portrait of this woman, whom she was less equipped to comprehend than an orang-utan, made use of such deadly phrases as 'excitable, nervous and highly strung'. Which in this context, is inevitably read as alcoholic, or crazy, or both. She made Mamà sound like Elizabeth Taylor, or possibly the degenerate scion of Transylvanian nobility.

Daddy fared no better. Dora, of course, had gleaned the information that at various times, my parents spent as much as six months apart, he in London, she in Rome: it was assumed in her disastrous narrative that such separations were a symptom of a failed marriage, and also, of course, that both were habitually unfaithful. Daddy's principal sobriquet was 'aloof', though he also copped 'detached' and 'peremptory' (read, domestic tyrant and probable sexual weirdo): he was a cold-blooded, lobotomised victim of upper-class male education; a disastrous match for a passionate Italian contessa; incapable (again!) of forming a relationship with a woman; a man who had turned to heroism as another might have turned to heroin, as a distraction from Inner Emptiness, and had gradually shrivelled into the mere husk of a man once he was no longer able to fly, race, etc . . . I was pondering this travesty, when part of the reason for it occurred to me (textual scholarship, once acquired, is a skill which seldom deserts one even in extremity): my parents had corresponded in Italian. My father's letters to me, which open with 'My darling', and maintain a tone throughout which would astonish Dora, were of course not in his files, but in mine. Vast chunks of the inner life of my family had been completely inaccessible.

And this, of course, was being represented as 'the truth' about the Strachey marriage. I was not going to be sick again: it is only surprise which will force such a visceral response to the written word, however repellent. I was, however, so angry and upset that I was far from feeling in control of my reactions. Another trip to the washroom, for more ordinary purposes, revealed that I was grey, crumpled and sweaty: if I went home like that, Sofia would think I was stewing up for a heart-attack. I did what I could to straighten myself out, invented a meeting with a colleague, and rang home: I intended to appear before Sofia late, and slightly drunk, hoping that alcohol would cover up all other symptoms. I still had not got beyond Chapter Five. I began to wonder if I ever would. Before leaving the office, I riffled the remaining two-thirds of the volume. Her account of Mamà's death was something which I resolved to spare myself: I caught a word or two, and my eye winced past in self-protection. As the book developed, Dora disgorged a quantity of part-digested theoretic perspectives, which (at least in her own view), allowed her to have her cake and eat it; to revel vicariously, fantastically, in description, dresses, hairdos, and portraits of the once famous, and to 'deconstruct' them. In a way, I could see what the *LRB* meant about the literary quality of the text: the effect of building idols only to cast them down again had a sort of manic energy, as if the monstrous Dora was wrestling with herself. Having achieved a level of calm which permitted this analysis, I shut the book in my bottom drawer, and locked it.

By the time I returned home, after midnight and smelling of grappa, to face Sofia's justifiable wrath, I was at least back in my own life, as it were. One of the saving aspects of the academic community, in the present context, is its parochialism. Few Italian scholars are read outside Italy, other than the Big E, and Italian scholars, on the whole, return the compliment. It was exceedingly unlikely that any of my colleagues would pick up that *London Review of Books*, or any other London-based review: Dora was phenomenally lucky to have got even one review in a major journal, and was unlikely to get others. If I allowed myself to think about it, I was profoundly angered by the libel on my mother, but distressing though all this was, it was at least with reference to the past. I would allow no more translation into English. In future, I would live my life entirely within Europe, which is, God knows, big enough to keep anyone occupied.

The goddess Nemesis cares nothing for such optimism. I came home one day and found Sofia on the phone, screaming at some unknown individual. Sofia, being a real Italian *contessa* and not one imagined by Dora, does not scream. She does not have tantrums at hairdressers, upholsterers and so forth. So I was immediately alarmed, and hurried into the drawing-room to see if I could help in any way. She spotted my entry from the corner of her eye, said, 'Simone's just come in,' and slammed the phone down. Then she turned to me, incandescent with rage.

'Simone, you stupid bastard, how could you be such an idiot?'

'What? What?' I gibbered, gazing around wildly for clues. Sofia picked up a copy of *Marie Claire*, which was lying by the telephone, and threw it at my face. It opened up as she hurled it, and came tumbling through the air, pages fluttering, I caught it automatically.

'Read that,' she snarled, 'and tell me where we can go to live it down.'

The doorbell rang, followed by a cheerful shout of 'Taxi, signora!' Sofia picked up the case which, I suddenly noticed, was standing by the end of the sofa, and marched out. Moments later, I heard the door slam. I sank into a chair, filled with the direst foreboding, and looked at the bulky object in my hands. *Marie Claire* is the magazine read by women who don't think of themselves as magazine-readers. Sofia bought the Italian edition regularly; so did her sisters, and so did the wives of most of the people I knew. Its three hundred-odd pages are largely devoted, naturally, to sex'n'shopping, but the recipe is varied with sex'n'shopping'n'social concern (mostly sex-related), 'n'sociology (also mostly sex-related). I began to have a doom-laden feeling that I knew what the problem was. I turned to the contents page. 'Four minutes of fame' struck a nasty, reminiscent bell. I flicked frantically through the magazine with trembling, sweaty fingers – why, in these magazines, do they only print the page-number on about one page in ten? Is it deliberately intended to prevent you from finding anything? – once located, by finding page 143 and counting forwards, it turned out to be some crap about would-be fashion designers. Mystified, I turned back to the contents page. A sort of light began to dawn. There were *two* contents pages, with subdivisions – who designed this fucking magazine, St Thomas Aquinas? – I had been looking at Fashion. Under Features, I found an article under the heading LIFE STORIES. You can guess the next bit; I already had. 'DORA STRACHEY. The seamy side of "swinging London".' *Marie Claire* had obviously decided that Carnaby Street, etc. still rang bells with an international audience. Oh, dear God.

Brandy. I went and got myself a very large drink, and turned misgivingly to page 285. LIFE STORIES is the feature at the back, just after the small ads, which virtually guarantees that everyone will read it. The article, I realised in horror, was written by Janice Chapman. Its tone was survivalist: Dora, a victim of the Stracheys and their corrupt lifestyle – at this point, the extraordinary fantasies of *Look Back in Anguish*, crudely paraphrased by the woman Chapman, took on a surreal life of their own, and turned the Strachey family into something more like the House of Usher – had yet lived to fight another day, write a book, and Become Her Own Woman. It was illustrated, of course. On the first page, there was another shot of the new-look Dora, with the front cover of her book superimposed in the bottom righthand corner. Later in the article, *Marie Claire*, whose budget I did not even want to think about, had reproduced 'Spring in the Bois', treating it in the mode of tragic irony; as a comment on the future development of its subjects' lives. They also printed a quite flattering, if vampiric, and undeniably recognizable photograph of myself in my late twenties.

I drank quite a lot of my brandy, and sat staring at page 285. The phone began to ring. I ignored it. It stopped after some time, then almost immediately, began to ring again. I was devastated. I could guess who was on the telephone. It was almost certainly Maria, Laura, or Giulietta. The sisters would be running out to buy *Marie Claire* (which of them had bought the first copy?), ringing round, exchanging impressions with each other, then ringing Sofia to check on her version. In the next few days, my colleagues' wives would visit hairdressers and beauty salons. The phone lines would once more be busy. By the end of the week, every single woman of my acquaintance would have read this article, and shown it to their husbands. Not all my colleagues love me: most of them would invest a few thousand lire in Dora's book. There was not the slightest point in issuing denials. My life was irrevocably touched, flyblown and compromised by this fabulating hag.

Thinking about Sofia's sisters, and the sort of cooing *schadenfreude* with which they might greet such a social disaster, led me on to further thoughts about families, and another, dreadful thought struck me: sooner or later, someone would ring Sofia's parents. My wife and her sisters were Catholics in the pagan sort of way which comes so naturally to well-born Italians; but her parents were *molto Cattolici*, deeply traditionalist, and neither of them were possessed of the faintest sense of humour. When Papà got to hear about this, the fat would truly be in the fire. The distinction between wife and what was politely called 'common-law wife' in the Sixties was a blurred one, both publicly and privately. The Monster had never actually flourished fake wedding-lines; repute, and the use of the name 'Strachey' had been quite sufficient. But Papà would not see it like that: there are wives, and there are mistresses. Dora had claims to be a wife; since

the floor, or some other childish crime has been traced to its origin by the grown-ups, they say: It wasn't me, it was – whoever; Peeky, Poo-Poo, 'bears'. I had no need of such an invention. Throughout our childhood, it was Florian who dared, and I who hung back. It was not my hand which scrolled luxurious spirals of Mammie's lipstick down the length of the newly painted hall. It was not I that boiled the goldfish; or I who destroyed the outboard motor on Pappie's boat. He was always so sure of what he was doing; while I watched, often horrified, but always unable to resist the sheer force of his personality. Our childhood was punctuated with the inevitable inquisitions on outrages of one kind or another, and a sort of parental litany gradually developed for use on these occasions: 'Hendrik, why on earth didn't you stop him? You're supposed to be the one with your head screwed on. Honestly, the pair of you are as bad as each other,' and so on, and so on. Even children have their pride. I preferred to be thought an accomplice rather than the helpless onlooker I in fact was. And now, when the mark of Cain sits, visible to no one but me, upon Florian's smooth brow, I find myself no more able to stop him than I ever was in the past, and with no better idea of what to do about it.

We lived in The Hague as children, in a house of some elegance, and led the orderly lives of privileged children. We were good at most of the same things, though by our early teens, we deliberately chose to differ in areas of no importance. I learned the violin, Florian the piano. He fenced, I rode. But we did all the same subjects, graduated with an almost identical academic profile, and (predictable little rich boys that we were) went on together to enter the Law Faculty of the University of Leiden. Pappie was delighted, and I think relieved: there is something about the basic nature of twinnishness which makes even your parents perceive you as rather unaccountable. And while they were fairly sure of me (was I not the boring one?) I think they both feared that Florian's habitual brinkmanship would somehow lead to disaster.

The flamboyancy of his behaviour at school somehow prevented anyone but me from observing that, in fact, he studied hard, long and successfully. Anyway. Pappie had a great deal to say about the usefulness of a law degree as a foundation for a professional career, and, by any reasonable standards, too much about the social advantages of a few years in Leiden. In particular, he waxed sentimental about the student corporation called the Athena.

'Sooner or later, some pack of do-gooders will demolish it as an offence against dullness, but it's still there, thank God. They'll spot you for the right sort. When they offer you membership, for goodness' sake accept, and in the next six years you'll meet everyone who'll be anyone in twenty years' time.' We looked ironic, doubtless, since it was Pappie telling us this, but the idea had more appeal than either of us was prepared to admit. We were not natural democrats. We were also comfortably aware that the Athena selection committee would indeed recognise us at sight as 'bulls' in the making. We already wore the uniform as to the manner born – clean jeans and an English-cut navy-blue blazer (universally known as a *ballenjas*), and the indispensable final detail, a signet ring on the little finger of the left hand, discreetly bearing the family *wapen*. We also had the manner, something which is best summed up in a very Leiden joke which Father had already passed on to us. There were three students in a room, when in came a mouse. The Amsterdammer jumped on his chair and began frenziedly trying to form everyone into a committee for mouse-management. The Delftenaar began putting together a technological mousetrap out of paperclips and biros. The Leiden bull merely looked at the creature, and said languidly, 'I say, mouse. Miauw.' Mouse flees. An idiotic story, but it expresses a sort of ideal which was far from unattractive to us.

I can now remember little of our arrival at Leiden. I know we suffered the traditional hazing of new students, who must make a circuit of the town canals, suffering whatever is thrown down on them from the many bridges, but strangely, my memories of assaulting our successors from the bridges in the following year is very much clearer. There must have been a time when the streets of Leiden were strange to us, but I cannot now imagine it. As Pappie had predicted, we were duly approached by the Athena, and elected as new members without dissent. Athena was all that Pappie had said, and more. While it owned property in various parts of the town, and its essential function was accommodation, it also owned a clubhouse: a large and graceful eighteenth-century townhouse on the Rapenburg. It was enough to make a good housewife lay down her broom and burst into tears, but I loved it for its combination of comfortable, male shabbiness and intrinsic elegance. From its windows, one looks across the canal (with grebes punting busily up and down, and tall-gabled houses reflected in the dark water), at the house where Spinoza once lived, and a few doors down, at another currently inhabited by the Crown Prince. Leiden is a provincial little place, even by the standards of The Hague: we were five minutes' walk from anything of the slightest significance, including our lodgings (somewhat further down the Raap, at the shabby end), the Frisian bakery with its delicious marzipan fruit-bread, and both the Law Faculty buildings, the stripey brick affair on Hugo de Grootstraat, where teaching basically takes place, and the magnificent structure called 'sGravensteen (the Count's Castle: a relic of less democratic days), one entrance of which is on to a square called Righteousness, under the great Gothic shadow of the Pieterskerk.

My only unequivocally clear memory of our initiation into Leiden life was the *openingscollege*. Again by custom, the work of one's student days begins with a general lecture to all new members of the Faculty. As we crowded into the Faculty's biggest lecture hall, I fully expected an extremely dull occasion on which some old professor, weighted down with learning, would spend forty minutes or so uttering platitudes about law and justice. The introduction, by the President of the Faculty, was all that I had feared; but to my surprise, the figure which stood up and briskly made its way to the platform was relatively youthful. Professor Balder van Aldegonde was then fifty-six, and could easily have passed for ten or even fifteen years younger than he was. He was dark, on the short side of average, pale-complexioned and slim, dressed with unobtrusive elegance in a dark suit. At first sight, he appeared rather ordinary. He laid a slim sheaf of small white cards carelessly down on the lectern, stood in silence for a moment, collecting his thoughts, then raised his eyes and addressed us. From that moment, it was plain that he was someone of real distinction, both physically and intellectually. The first remarkable thing I noticed about him was his eyes, so light in colour they seemed almost silver. The effect, when he looked directly at you, was disturbing, and even shocking, a fact which he clearly understood, and exploited with skill. His other great beauty, I came to realise, was his hands; long-fingered, very beautiful hands, with which he gestured only seldom, but extremely effectively. The distinction of his person was matched by that of his address. His voice, also, was attractive, not loud, very patrician, but clear enough to carry to the back of the hall.

He began, I remember, more or less as follows. 'For the first two hundred years of this University, its Law Faculty educated the lawyers of half the countries of Europe. As an institution, we have been of incalculable importance to the development of Western thought and culture. You, ladies and gentlemen, are the latest recruits to an aristocracy of the intellect.' His silver eyes flicked across our faces, coolly assessing, pausing momentarily here and there. 'You must always remember that democracy and aristocracy are not terms in opposition. As Plato made quite clear, the greatest good of the greatest number is not opposed to the excellence of the talented few, but correlative with it. You are of this élite, with the burdens and privileges that entails.' We were all, I think, puzzled, shocked, and intrigued in varying proportions. The lecture hall was completely silent, not a cough or a scuffle anywhere. 'Law,' he continued, 'is an art. Justice belongs to heaven; but since Cain first smote down Abel, fallen man has needed law. It is the single greatest construction of civilised man, beside which Great Walls, or great books, are mere ephemera. In its arena, its theatre if you will, the art of the novelist and that of the actor meet and embrace with the wisdom of the scholar and the priest. The local manifestation of this greatest of all arts, which you are about to begin studying, is a worthy child of Themis, with a distinguished history. In the legal practice of our own Courts, Cicero himself would find much that is familiar. It is the direct descendants of the Roman forum; for the legislation that Cicero illumined with such consummate art was in time codified by Justinian, greatest of Byzantine emperors. And even after the barbarisation of Europe, Justinian's *Digest* formed the basis for what is called Roman Vulgar Law, the law of European nations from the Dark Ages to the present. Our law, therefore, bears the hallmarks of Imperial Rome. Which is to say, it is orderly, logical, and internally coherent. The individual, in his or her passage through life, is supported by a mutually interlocking complex of rights and duties. If any of you is so rash as to commit a major crime, you will discover in the course of the months that follow that as citizens, however iniquitous, the power of the State over you is strictly limited by the legal code which you are about to discover. If you are honest young persons, this might strike you as foolishness on the part of the State. It is not; or if it is, it is a folly that lies deeper than wisdom. You do not even have to imagine the alternative: all you need do is glance at our neighbour across the Channel, where the social effect of institutionalising prejudice, in the form of a legal system based on precedent which leaves the individual entirely without protection against the State, is clearly and depressingly demonstrated. *Civites Romani sumus*, like St Paul, who despite the fact that he was quite evidently a dangerous little virus in the body of the Roman state, was nonetheless able to point out to a justifiably irritated governor that he was a man with rights. We are citizens under the law, and each one of us can claim its protection against the malice, stupidity or prejudice of our fellows.' He spoke with a well-controlled passion which was as disturbing as it was exciting. It had never occurred to me that the study of law might be anything but useful; the thought that it might also be interesting was a welcome one.

In subsequent weeks, I found out quite a lot more about Professor Balder van Aldegonde. Though he had written some distinguished books, and had an international reputation as a scholar of jurisprudence, he still contrived to be an ambivalent and controversial figure. This was partly simple jealousy. Most of our professors were extremely boring, and he so evidently was not. As a teacher, he was outstanding. His lectures were models of clarity and elegance, so much so that I do not think I have forgotten anything of importance which he taught us. Other aspects of his personality, however, raised eyebrows. One foible in particular caused a good deal of gossip: his habit of taking up a small number of students in each year. This caused a great deal of tut-tutting, especially among the women. The life of a first-year law student is necessarily an anonymous one, since it is seldom that you find yourself in a class of less than a hundred; and most of our learned preceptors made not the slightest attempt to distinguish one of us from another. Van Aldegonde, on the other hand, held court for his chosen few, either in the café opposite 'sGravensteen, or occasionally at his home. Invitations to join this group were an accolade, both socially and intellectually, since they were extended only to young men who were both intelligent and of good family.

Like everyone else at first, I assumed that he was homosexual. The truth which emerged was almost the opposite: his sexual reputation was extraordinary. It was widely known that he never kept a girlfriend for longer than six months, but he was something quite different from your average shit. He had somehow contrived to make himself into a challenge, a fashion, or perhaps a *rite de passage*; it was as if he asked, 'Which of you is woman enough to keep me?' My countrywomen are obstinate, and optimistic. Also, all his rejects agreed that he was an excellent lover. As a result, he strolled among the first year as if he was at the flower-market, choosing whom he wished. I observed, incidentally, as time passed, that he never took up with a girl of his own class. Overhearing him with them in the café, I wondered whether the Annemeiks and Ritas he selected ever perceived the delicate nuance of contempt hidden beneath his silky, indefatigable courtliness.

But all that was later, of course. I must go back to the beginning. Florian and I met him some time in late October of our first year. We were walking down a corridor after a lecture, when he came round a corner, and almost bumped into us. He stopped, of course, with a murmured apology, then did a double-take, as people do when twins walk together. He looked us up and down comprehensively, with a single raking glance, then smiled charmingly.

'I teach you, I think? I'm almost sure I've seen those two blond heads bent over their notebooks.' We hastened to assure him that he was quite right, and introduced ourselves, since the occasion seemed to demand it. When he heard the name Barnevelt, he became positively cordial. 'You aren't rushing off, are you? I wondered if we might have a little cup of coffee together.' Florian told him that we were at his disposal, and not without pride, we followed him out of the building and down the road to the café on the Gerecht. It was too cold by then to sit comfortably at one of the little tables shaded in summer by the now-leafless avenue of pleached limes, so we took our coffee into the comfortable little snuggery where the newspapers are, and ensconced ourselves on a dark-oak settle opposite him. What I expected, at this point, was a more or less direct inquisition on our parentage and upbringing; but as I came to realise much later, van Aldegonde was far too subtle a creature to do anything of the kind. Instead, he took a cue from the arts page of the *NRC*, which lay discarded on the table in front of us, and turned the conversation to music. We admitted, shyly, to being reasonably competent instrumentalists, and in a few minutes, he had us arguing about *The Magic Flute* (which he disliked) as if we had known him for years. The best part of an hour later, he sighed, and fished a pocket watch from the inside pocket of his jacket. 'I'm sorry, gentlemen; I'll have to go. I have some kind of ghastly committee in about ten minutes. I've so enjoyed our little chat. If you aren't otherwise engaged, perhaps you'd care to call on me on Saturday?' We said, of course, that we would love to. 'Splendid. I have a little house on the Vliet; number six, left side of the water. I'll expect you around three.' Shaking hands briskly, he picked up his briefcase, and departed with economical swiftness. Through the window, I saw his elegantly tailored back retreating across the square, and vanishing through the tall wrought-iron gates of 'sGravensteen. I turned to Florian, who was idly reading a review in the *NRC*.

'Well, we seem to have made it.'

He shrugged. 'It was only a matter of time. From what everyone's been saying, we're just his type. Actually, though, he was more interesting than I expected. I wonder what his house is like?'

We found out on Saturday. Florian and I met after lunch, and went up the town to the good flower-shop, where we argued for a while what would be most suitable. Finally, we settled on white alstromeria and eucalyptus, with a few long-stemmed white freesias: a combination which we hoped would seem tasteful and reasonably masculine. Under our direction, the florist made up the bouquet, rolled it in grey tissue paper, and bound it with matte, dark-green ribbon.

'It looks like something for a funeral,' grumbled Florian, as the man handed it over.

'Shut up. It's too late now, anyway. I think it's fine.' Holding the flowers, with which we were no longer pleased, we crossed the little, hump-backed bridge at the bottom of the street, and turned off for the Vliet, which is literally a backwater, a quiet little cul-de-sac of seventeenth-century townhouses, not large, but of great elegance, built on either side of an offshoot of the canal. As instructed, we went up the lefthand side and found number six, where van Aldegonde opened the door to us.

'Florian. Hendrik. How nice to see you. What charming flowers.'

Since it was Saturday, he was not wearing a suit; but he was not a man for slopping about: he was in grey flannels, with an impeccable cashmere jersey. He stood back, ushering us in, and vanished off to the back quarters to find a vase. We looked around with interest. The room was dominated by a square piano, clearly in regular use, and a pair of eighteenth-century sofas heaped with very lovely petit-point cushions. There were few pictures, but those that there were, were good. Van Aldegonde came back in with our flowers in a plain glass vase, and caught us looking at the half-length portrait of a lady in a pink, Empire-line dress which hung over the mantelpiece.

'My grandmother's grandmother,' he observed. 'Sidonie von Braunschweig-Lüneburg. Unlike some of our countrymen, I have never attempted to conceal the fact that some of my relations are German.'

'Oh,' said Florian easily, 'we've got the odd filthy Hun dangling off our family tree too.' I looked at van Aldegonde with misgiving. It is true that if you are going to use the word '*Mof*', it is almost impossible *not* to put '*rot*' in front of it – they go together like bread and butter – but I still thought Florian should have been more careful. However, if our host was offended, he chose not to show it. He stepped behind us without comment, and set the vase carefully on the piano.

After we had talked for a while about paintings, while consuming the ritual cup of coffee and some excellent little biscuits, van Aldegonde stood up and moved to the side of the piano, from where he looked down at us, a couple of metres away.

'Tell me,' he said to Florian, 'do you care for Schubert at all?'

'Some of his stuff's not bad.'

'Do you know *Winterreise*?'

'Of course. I haven't played it, though.'

'Would you think it might be within your technical range?'

That was always a dangerous sort of question with Florian, who couldn't resist a challenge. He looked up, lounging in his corner of the sofa, meeting our host's pale eyes deliberately. 'Oh, I should think so.' He got up, without haste, and went over to the piano, where the score already stood, and opened it at random. Having studied the page with complete concentration for a couple of minutes, he flexed his fingers, and began to play without any preliminaries or hesitation. To our considerable surprise, van Aldegonde proceeded simply to open his mouth and sing. He was, we rapidly discovered, a very considerable artist. He had a flexible, silvery tenor, with no real depth, but he phrased the vocal line with such genuine musical intelligence that the effect was something very out of the ordinary. Florian, after the first shock of an unexpected voice at his right ear, settled down to play his best. Van Aldegonde put his left hand casually on my brother's shoulder. I looked at the long, strong white fingers unfurled across the dark broadcloth of Florian's *ballenjas*, and though they appeared not to move, I was aware from the winking of his signet ring that minute signals about phrasing and tempo were being transmitted economically and effectively. Before they reached the first repeat, he and my brother were completely in rapport.

They went through three or four songs in succession, one straight after the other, so when it ended, it came as a shock. At the end of '*Frühlingstraum*', Van Aldegonde dropped his hand from Florian's shoulder, and took a step away. 'Bravo,' he said, just a little too lightly. Florian was furious; his eyes kindled stormily, and his lower lip stuck out ominously. I could see that he felt he had been patronised, and also that he was angry because he had been made to betray something of his inner self to a man who was in no way an intimate. The professor regarded him with cool interest. To my surprise, Florian, who was seldom meek when he felt his *amour propre* had been slighted, dropped his eyes, and submitted to van Aldegonde's authority. 'That was delightful, Florian,' said van Aldegonde, urbanely proffering a small olive branch. 'You play with real feeling. I enjoyed it very much, and I would very much like you to play for me again. But we must not exclude your brother for so long.' He turned to me, and I felt his charm curling towards me like a perfume. 'I'm sorry, Hendrik. I'm afraid it is hard to find a place for the violin in this domestic setting.'

'That's all right,' I said, 'I like to listen.'

I recall nothing else of significance from that visit. We talked for a while longer, on indifferent subjects, and left at half-past five, like the well-brought-up boys we were. Florian was excited, and against his will, impressed. I had expected him to abuse van Aldegonde all the way back to the Rapenburg, but he did not.

'I'm going to have to do some practising,' he said suddenly, after we had walked along in silence for a bit. 'There's a piano at Athena, but it's absolutely buggered. I think someone said once there are instruments at the Music School you're allowed to book.' I made no reply. 'I want to surprise the bastard,' he added. 'Wipe that smirk off his face.' We had come to a crossroads, and stopped to let a couple of bikes go by.

'I'll have to go up to the Breestraat and the long way round,' I said, 'I've got some laundry to pick up.'

'Okay. See you later, then.'

As the year went on, we became established members of van Aldegonde's circle, particularly Florian. But while he moved more and more into the centre, I found myself impelled in the opposite direction. The principal reason for this, or so it appeared to me at the time, was that I had acquired a fairly serious girlfriend, Jorien Coomans. Since it was made very clear that Jorien would not be welcome even to join us in the café, I sometimes chose to go somewhere else where we could be together. Florian, meanwhile, made no moves towards any of the girls we encountered. They all laughed at anyone who attempted to imitate van Aldegonde's *grand seigneur* ways, so celibacy was effectively the price of membership of his inner circle, one which my brother was willing to pay. I did not drop out altogether, of course. Jorien is not the kind of woman who likes to make a show of her power, and she understood that among my anxieties at that time was not growing too far apart from my brother. But apart from wanting to be with Florian, the 'Professor's Boys' were quite interesting enough to make associating with them a pleasure as well as a privilege. The group's conversation was invariably interesting and sometimes even instructive.

I remember one meeting in particular, in the café, towards the end of our first year. The papers, which were as usual lying about, were dominated by foreign news: some suspected members of the Irish Republican Army had been traced to Amsterdam, and the British government was loudly demanding their extradition. We had been sitting talking among ourselves for a few minutes, when van Aldegonde came in. 'What do you think of this stuff, Balder?' said Maurits, indicating the headlines. He was a tall, dark, tough-looking man, considerably our senior, since he was then entering his fifth year. The oldest and most authoritative of our group, he was the only one of us who dared to use van Aldegonde's first name.

'The advocate's told them to piss off, hasn't he?'

'Yes.'

'Quite right. Florian, will you get me some coffee?'

'But don't you think the judicature should be doing something about international terrorism?'

'My dear Maurits. The situation is quite a plain one. The English, as far as anyone can judge from what they have chosen to reveal, have a chain of suppositious inference which they believe links these people with crimes which have been committed. We may assume that more lies beneath this than is known to the *NRC* and the *Dagblad*, but the case as it has been made public is so thin that I assume it depends on informers of some kind. This is extremely problematic, since of course, sources which cannot be revealed cannot be checked – the fact that informers are often malicious and untrustworthy is a principle which was accepted even by that notoriously illiberal organisation, the Spanish Inquisition. What all this adds up to is that under the terms of Dutch law, as you should certainly have understood after four years of instruction by me, there is no case to be brought against these unfortunate Irish persons. The English have not even attempted to indicate *why* any of these people should have performed the actions they are accused of. All they allege is that they are Irish patriots, and may have been in the right place at the right time. But a person cannot be convicted on mere inference, and to do so is hardly a step beyond lynch-law. The English, I know, cherish the belief that a random collection of strangers can decide such matters by the operation of collective prejudice, but I entirely fail to see why we should oblige them in this matter.'

'But professor,' objected Florian, 'there are such things as terrorists. What about the Baader-Meinhof gang?' Van Aldegond raised his eyebrows wearily.

'The fact that some individuals make war on their fellows at random in pursuit of some private theory or belief is covered by the law as it stands. The underlying principle is that unless you can advance a reason for a deed, you cannot attribute it, but the reasons do not in themselves have to be those of the average citizen. However senseless the activities of Baader-Meinhof might seem to us, they certainly had their reasons, according to their own lights. So, of course, does the army of Irish liberation. But to move from the proposition that some Irishmen believe it is necessary to murder Englishmen, to the thesis that Mister Patrick O'Something sitting in the corner over there is a murderer because he is Irish, is indefensible. To be precise, it is a syllogism defective in the second term. A nation cannot be held collectively guilty, and a suspected terrorist is entitled to the protection of the law just as much as a suspected murderer of a more ordinary kind.'

'Don't you think the seriousness of the problem makes a difference?'

'Absolutely not. Once the law starts to respect persons, positively or negatively, a central principle has been broken.'

I wondered where the discussion was going to go, but I could see Jorien through the window, walking up and down the square: we were due to meet for lunch. It was good of her not to come in and get me, but I could hardly abuse her tact. With some reluctance, I excused myself, and slipped out.

'Hi,' she said as I came out, 'let's go to Camino.'

'Fine by me.' Hand in hand, we wandered out of the square and across the bridge to the Doelensteeg. Jorien liked Camino, which is bright, high-ceilinged and contemporary, and I had come to like it too, at least when I was with her. The clientele often look as if they're working a bit too hard on looking cool, but it has its virtues, one of which is that it is too pricey for students' everyday lunch, and therefore it is not usually crowded. It was early summer, so we took our beers and went to sit in a sort of private little vine-hung arbour at the end of the walled garden. We talked about this and that for a while, avoiding the central subject which I knew we would sooner or later have to discuss. Jorien wanted us to go on holiday together, but I had at that time never gone anywhere without Florian, and the idea filled me with an emotion which I can only describe as obstinate panic. The waiter interrupted our exchange of inanities by bringing us a plate of *bitterballen*.

'*Dank U wel*,' said Jorien, accepting it with automatic politeness. Once he was out of earshot, she turned to me.

'Hendrik, do you think Florian's ever going to get a girlfriend? Or a boyfriend, maybe?' This was not the angle of attack I was expecting, and I could not think what to say, so I took a *bitterball*, and nibbled it thoughtfully, concentrating on the smooth, meaty flavour, contrasting agreeably with the crisp outer shell. One thing about Camino, they always employed good cooks –

'Hendrik?' Jorien was not deceived, she never was.

'Oh, I don't know. He put it about quite a bit when we were at school. Maybe he's got bored.'

'He's not gay though, is he?'

'Oh, no. One thing about being a twin, I think, you don't find your own sex much of a thrill. Such a lot of things men do together, we just always do with each other, you see? But the sex thing, there'd be no point. Like wanking. Girls are a lot more interesting.'

'Well, he's not going the right way about meeting anyone, then. I don't think I've ever seen him on his own. He's either shadowing that awful Maurits, or he's got a bodyguard of loudmouths from Athena.'

'Oh, for goodness' sake, Jorien. I'm just his brother. I don't own him.' (Am I my brother's keeper? echoed in my head.) 'Tell you what. If you've got a cute friend who's looking for someone, just say the word, and I'll set her up. I'll even sneak her into his bed, if you like, and if she can't manage the rest for herself, she's not half the woman you are.'

'Hendrik, do stop clowning, and think about what I'm saying.'

'Okay, okay. But I don't think Florian's your business, Jorien.'

'You're my business, Hendrik. And I can tell you something. You're trying to pretend you're just brothers, but you're not. You've got to care about what he's doing.'

'I'm going to get some more beer. Want another?'

'No more *witte bier*, thanks. Can I have a Dommelsch?' We didn't usually drink so much at lunchtime, but the conversation was clearly getting heavy. When I came back, I realised it was time to come clean.

'You're right, Jorien. We're in trouble. What do you think?'

She considered the question carefully, as she always did. 'I don't think I really *know* Florian,' she confessed. 'It seems funny to say it, when I spent weeks trying to work out ways of telling you two apart. Actually, he's always been so polite, in that sort of urbane, Hague-ish way you can both put on when you like, he's never really said anything to me at all. Let's look at this the other way up. Okay, to me, and maybe ninety-five per cent of the population, you're just a nice, normal, polite, upper-class boy, and Florian's really quite strange. But it's clear that he's always been the leader, not you, and anyway, people like you don't care about the other ninety-five per cent. So, why is it that he was seduced by that creepy Professor, and you weren't?'

I was desperately uncomfortable. What I really like about women, especially Jorien, is that they don't see things the same way you do, but sometimes, it is also what I really hate.

'Jorien, this is like open heart surgery, you know. I don't see how I can talk about this stuff.'

'You've got to. You're still tied together, don't you see? Either he's going to pull you in, or you're going to pull him out, or you'll have to cut the tie. Whatever happens, you need to know what you're doing.'

'All right, then. The truth is, Balder doesn't really want me. Florian's the golden boy, I'm just the shadow that tags along behind. If he'd put half the energy into charming me he's put into Florian, I'd still be sitting in the Gerecht. He's really a wonderful man, you know. I know he's ridiculously sexist, but he's the most amazing conversationalist, and he's got a really extraordinary mind. It sounds peculiar when you say it, but he's sort of dazzling. Like Socrates. What does he look like to women? Do you fancy him?'

Jorien shrugged. 'Sort of. There's a story he's very good in bed, and he's got that sort of energy, that intensity, which makes you think it's probably true. But I'd never really fancy someone I couldn't talk to. I don't mind all that old-fashioned courtliness, it's better than the piglike way some of the others behave, but if you actually listen to him, you realise you're being quietly put in your place. And I don't think the likes of van Aldegonde have the right to decide what my place is.'

'I think that's very fair.'

'Actually, he's much more seductive to men than he is to women. And works a lot harder at it, too. But what do you think he's doing? Is it just that he likes the feeling of power?'

'I think he's lonely. He's very isolated from his colleagues. Maybe he started picking up the more intelligent *bollen* just to have someone to talk to.' Jorien received this in a silence I could not interpret, and resumed only after a pause, and the thoughtful consumption of a now cold *bitterball*.

'Hendrik, what do you know about his politics?'

'He doesn't really talk about politics. Just law.'

'My father was a bit worried when I told him I was auditing lectures from van Aldegonde. He remembers when he first came to Leiden. My parents used to live in the Professors' Quarter, you know, before they moved to Warmond, so he knew a lot of university people. There was quite a lot of fuss at the time.'

'What about?'

'Well, his family did awfully well under the Nazis, you know. That bit *too* well. His father was an architect, something like that, and his mother was a musician. They were quite prominent, well-known people. My father said what he heard was that after the war, there wasn't quite enough of a case for trying them as collaborators, but there was a lot of unpleasantness all the same. I think they ended up going to South Africa.'

'But that's completely unfair. Van Aldegonde can hardly have been ten when the war ended. No, younger. It's got nothing to do with him.'

'Well, it has and it hasn't. It was his attitude, really. He sort of pushed them in people's faces, how talented they were, a lot of stuff about the aristocracy of genius, and the duty of the genius to his art, ta-ti-ta, ta-ti-ti. If he'd just had the sense to shut up, no one would have minded.'

'But they'd have known.'

'Oh, of course.'

'Well, then he could hardly do anything else, could he? He's incredibly proud.'

'It still wasn't sensible.'

'Jorien, darling, we're talking about the other five per cent here. He's *not* sensible. He's honourable. It's completely different.'

Jorien is highly intelligent, sensitive, and well travelled. But as I looked into her clear blue eyes, it was appallingly obvious that she understood not a word of what I was saying. I have noticed before that even people who are genuinely sophisticated about the mentality of French or English acquaintances have a complete blind spot for the concept that all Dutch are not, fundamentally, much alike. She sat puzzling over my reply for a while, then changed the subject.

'Well, are we going to France this summer, or aren't we?'

When we were quite little boys, Florian climbed the tall cabinet in the back drawing room, and dared me to follow him. He made it down unharmed, but I slipped, and came down in a shower of Delft and Venetian glasses which, looking back on it, must have broken my mother's heart. The important thing at the time was that I fell among the glass, and cut myself very badly. Mammie rushed in, hearing the screams, bundled me up and took me straight to Casualty. When we got into the surgery, Mammie put me on the table, and the doctor turned round, with his hands held up in shiny gloves, the way they do, and with long, glittering steel claws, some kind of forceps, I suppose, looped over his knuckles. I was so terrified I went berserk. Mammie had to grab me, and hold me down by main force while he picked glass out of my legs. What I remember very clearly was the expression on her face; stern, remote, beyond pity. Jorien's expression had something of that terrible mercy as she looked into my face, willing me to reply.

Such a simple question, I thought numbly, to be a key moment of my life.

'Let's go down to the Breestraat, and talk to the travel agents,' I said, getting up. I couldn't look at her.

We left Camino in silence, and walked for a while, still unspeaking. By consensus, we avoided the straight way, which would take us back through the Gerecht, and instead went left along the canal, under the extraordinary military fantasy of the Doelengracht arch, and up towards the Galgewater. Finally, Jorien said,

'It's going to have to be a split, isn't it? You can't start taking the lead after twenty years.'

'It's worse than that. You're talking as if all this is rational, and it's not. Here's something which might help you understand. The last time I was at the Vliet with the gang, Florian started playing "*Der Erlkönig*". He's got very good, you know. Van Aldegonde was singing, also very well, and I looked at him and thought, you *are* the Erl-king.'

'So if he's the Erl-king, I suppose you're saying that you're the man who's trying to escape, and Florian's the child who knows he's surrendered? I've always thought they were meant to be two different bits of the same person. Id and superego, maybe. It could be about drug-addiction, or something like that.'

'You're probably right. But I suddenly felt it was very personal to the three of us. I'm the one who's riding like hell, and there's a bit of Florian saying, go faster, get me out of here, and another bit that knows for certain that all the Erl-king has to do is put his hand out and take him.'

' "*Erreicht den Hof mit Müh und Not; in seinen Armen das Kind war tot*",' quoted Jorien. 'Brrrh. But you're attracted to van Aldegonde too. You're not simply riding away.'

'That's the problem. We're both the rider, and both the child. Only I'm mostly the rider, and Florian's mostly the child.'

Once we had made our plans, I wandered around Leiden for a

few days in a state of tight-stomached misery, trying to avoid Florian. I dreaded breaking the news to him, and finally spat it out one night at Athena when we were both a bit drunk. He received my news in complete silence.

'Have you any plans?' I asked, a bit too casually, when I could bear his lack of response no longer. He shrugged, slumped indifferently in his chair.

'Dunno.'

'If you liked, we could –' He sat bolt upright, galvanic with anger. '*Flicker op*, Hendrik. I'll not be patronised by that smug little bourgeois bitch.'

'Keep your tongue off Jorien.'

'*Und wie*! I wouldn't touch her with a bargepole. She's splitting us, isn't she? That's what you get when you mess with the *burgerij*.'

'I'm not listening to this,' I shouted, scrambling to my feet.

'Bugger off then,' he shouted back, as I slammed my way out.

We didn't speak properly for quite a while. The end of term was coming, we both had exams, we were very busy. When we met in public, we nodded: neither of us wanted to advertise the situation. I continued to be one of the 'Professor's Boys' at least as far as anyone else could see. I am not sure that even van Aldegonde, clever though he was, quite divined what was going on between us. I even went along to the Vliet one more time, with Florian and Maurits. It was a Sunday afternoon, a lovely summer day. People had taken their sofas out of their front doors all over the town, and were sitting amiably about on the pavements, wearing shorts and drinking beer. Naturally, this air of general relaxation and cosy public coexistence did not extend to number six, where standards were always maintained. Van Aldegonde greeted us attired in linen trousers and a blue and white striped shirt worn with a tie, the sleeves rolled just so, revealing unexpectedly hairy and powerful forearms.

After we had had some tea, Florian went automatically to the piano. His talent as a pianist had made a bond between him and van Aldegonde from the beginning, and over the year, he had consolidated this advantage by working very hard on his technique. It was, I suspected, a way of establishing an ascendancy over Maurits, who was, obviously, older and more sophisticated, and had known van Aldegonde much longer. Van Aldegonde was passionately musical – I remembered Jorien saying his mother had been a professional musician – and they had worked together until they had reached a virtually recordable standard. In particular, van Aldegonde had a profound feeling for Schubert, who suited his voice mysteriously well. I had always heard Schubert sung by people who brought a full, romantic tone to the work; but the professor's cool, silvery voice and great musical intelligence found new meanings in the often rather simple-minded words, and gave them a resonance which fitted only too well the bleak passion of the music itself. *Winterreise* was something they came back to again and again, so I was not surprised when Florian began '*Gute Nacht*'.

I sat on the sofa with Maurits, listening and watching. Van Aldegonde no longer put his hand on Florian's shoulder. He stood with his hands loosely at his sides, upright and relaxed, and sang like a fallen angel. If you translate the words of *Winterreise*, which I once had to do at school, there's nothing to them, just simple-minded romantic tweeting and male self-pity. As set by Schubert, and sung by van Aldegonde, they become the end of all hope, a turning away from life and beauty into the dark. When that cold, desolate voice uttered the words, '*Ich mußt auch heute wandern vorbei in tiefer Nacht, da hab ich noch im Dunkel die Augen zugemacht,*' I found the hair rising on the back of my neck. It was bright summer, with sun sparkling off the water in the canal outside and setting up complex, marbled refraction patterns on the white ceiling, yet we were all rushing on a journey into the dark, riding the music. At some point, I became aware of Maurits, out of the corner of my eye. He was listening, or appeared to be listening, with his big hands loosely folded in his lap, and he was watching Florian intently. I could not guess what he was thinking.

They went through the whole of *Winterreise*, which takes more than an hour. When they got to the end of '*Der Leierman*', they both looked dazed, as if they no longer knew quite where they were. We stirred, and sighed, avoiding each other's eyes; and after some moments, Maurits offered to go and make fresh tea. When it arrived, the atmosphere began slowly to return to normal. Watching the other three, I found myself remembering Jorien's father's hints about van Aldegonde's background, and I was curious; I wanted to find out more about what he felt. And music was over for that day. He had shrugged off Schubert's inconsolable Wanderer, and reverted to a more public persona, playing Socrates with his clever young friends.

'Professor van Aldegonde,' I said, 'I was thinking about what you were saying on the Gerecht a couple of weeks ago. About individual and collective guilt. We were talking about the Irish and the English, and you were saying that the law doesn't let you accuse a single individual who fits what is really a collective accusation.'

'Mmm. Not exactly what I meant. But what point are you making?'

'I was wondering how this idea fitted the special case of war crimes?'

Van Aldegonde did not react directly. Instead, he leaned forward, deliberately, and poured some more tea.

'Ah. That's quite ingenious of you. If we are still talking about Irish patriots, it doesn't. The Irish Republic and the United Kingdom have not declared war. Part of the difficulty with the current situation is that the Irish Republican Army, who are not of course an official body, have declared war unilaterally, and the British Government have refused to accept this.'

'I see,' said Maurits. 'If the British Government insists that members of the Republican Army are merely criminals, then they are entitled to the protection which the law gives to citizens even if they are suspected criminals. If they demand the right to treat them according to the rules of war, then they must accept the declaration of war, if only by default.'

'Precisely, Maurits. At which point, of course, the Geneva Convention applies, and these malefactors come under a different set of protections.'

'But more generally,' I persisted, 'wouldn't you say that the whole question of war crimes has to do with individuals answering for collective guilt?'

'Oh, yes. Indeed. That, of course, is because law is made by victors. In fact, it is probably true to say that war crimes tribunals have very little to do with law as it is ordinarily understood. Actually, I suspect they may operate on a principle borrowed from the synods of the Roman Catholic Church: the retrospective criminalisation of activities which were perceived at the time as unexceptionable.'

Van Aldegonde normally maintained a detached, dryly witty tone through such expositions, but on this occasion, his voice was acid. Maurits flushed darkly, and it struck me that he was probably a Catholic; again, van Aldegonde was not normally careless of such details.

'So,' said Florian, speaking to cover Maurits' obvious discomfort, and of course unaware of what Jorien had told me, 'with a war crimes trial, what you basically have is a whole lot of atrocities somewhere down the line, a group of people actually in front of you, and a pretty random process for connecting them. Like, if we were talking about Holland, there were a lot of suspected Nazis and collaborators whose connection with known crimes was generic, not specific.'

'Yes. Most of whom should have been released at once, if the whole thing had not turned into a vast international circus.'

'But you couldn't do that,' persisted Florian, with innocent unwisdom. 'Surely people were entitled to some redress, after all they'd been through?'

'Redress?' said van Aldegonde contemptuously, his voice cold with rage. 'My dear Florian, "redress" is lynch-law. Tell me, how do you imagine it might soothe a woman whose whole family has been shot by the Germans to know that some innocent stranger has been hanged by the British?'

'Well . . . ,' he floundered, 'it's cathartic. Something had to be done.'

Van Aldegonde flung up his long, white hands in theatricalised despair. 'And I teach you! We're back to religion again, are we? It is meet and right for one to suffer for the sins of the people? For heavens' sake!'

I was beginning to panic: Florian was scarlet with embarrassment and fury, Maurits was sulking and it was my fault. Desperately, I wondered how to shift the conversation on to safer ground.

'Can we turn the whole thing the other way round?' I blurted, realising I was quoting Jorien. 'The conversation's got on to crimes which are randomly attributed. I was actually thinking about crimes that are properly attributed, and randomly *committed*.'

'Go on,' said van Aldegonde, while the others subsided in relief, and reached for their teacups. My mouth was dry with nervousness, but I stumbled ahead.

'Well, isn't that what war's all about? For instance, a soldier sees a movement, and thinks it's a sniper, so he fires. Later, he finds it was a little boy looking for shell-cases or something. Well, in this case, obviously, he's a soldier on sentry duty, and his duty is to fire. But there must be all kinds of things which happen during a war which amount to random acts of gratuitous violence. Resistance booby traps, for example. Somewhere at the back of it, there's a theory, killing Nazis in this case. But in practice, that kind of thing must have often ended up as a sort of *acte gratuit*. So, has a crime been committed, or hasn't it?'

'Bravo, Hendrik. You've hit on something genuinely interesting. In the specific arena of war, of course, the definition of criminal or not criminal is simply dependent on who wins. In the last war, Resistance incidents of the type you describe would have retrospectively been perceived as sad accidents. But in the context of ordinary law, the *acte gratuit* is a logical impossibility which cannot be covered. The perfect crime, in fact.'

'How come?' asked Maurits, interested.

'Remember the maxim, "unless you can advance a reason for a deed you cannot attribute it"? The State, before it brings you to the bar, must establish first that you could have committed the deed, and secondly, that you had some reason for doing so. It doesn't have to be a good reason from anyone else's point of view – let us say, for example, that someone is shot while wearing an Ajax shirt. If the prosecution could demonstrate that the sight of an Ajax supporter drove the suspected man into uncontrollable paroxysms of rage, then an adequate case could be made. What's more, of course, if a good suppositious case could be made, but no reason, however eccentric, could be advanced, then the police would look very hard into the question of whether the suspect was some kind of psychopath. But if they came up with a clean bill of mental health, they would have to let him go.'

'Doesn't that create problems?' asked Florian.

'Not half as many problems as the alternative. Imagine a fairly ordinary case. A lady is found strangled in her flat, the outer door of which is locked. No one is known to have a key but the woman herself, and hers is in her bag. Suspicion therefore falls naturally on the concierge for the block, who has a pass-key. The police turn his life inside out, and find that he has no connection with the victim, no evidence of a sexual interest in strangulation, and no signs of any pathology which might lead him to commit an act of random violence. At that point they of course let him go, and we take it for granted that they do, but the fact that they do is in deference to the maxim we have in front of us.'

'So, if an otherwise sane person committed a completely random murder, as long as he wasn't actually caught with the gun in his hand, the police would have to let him go?' Florian seemed to be fascinated by this point. I was merely relieved that we had returned to the plane of abstract argument. Van Aldegonde shrugged elegantly.

'I should think so. Certainly, if I were the individual's lawyer, I'd be telling the *commissaris* that in no uncertain terms.'

'It's got a certain irony,' observed Maurits. 'I mean, random violence is what society most fears. Think of all those people out there, sitting in the sun, chatting to neighbours and strangers. If anyone thought for a second that another happy sun-worshipper might whip out a gun and kill someone at random, the whole social fabric would collapse.'

'It is ironic, but it is true. We can build in no redress against genuine randomness, without destroying the premises on which law expresses mankind's social relation to itself: first, that humans are social animals, and second, that they can be trusted to act roughly in accordance with their own and the collective interest.'

After it reached this point, the conversation began running out of steam. It was about six, and manners dictated we should go: also, we had revision to do. After a bit of desultory chat, van Aldegonde politely dismissed us. We went out into the balmy evening, the light just beginning to fade and turn golden, all rather silent and busy with our own thoughts.

That was the last time I visited the Vliet, and just about the last time I appeared in the guise of one of the 'Professor's Boys'. Exams were upon us, and afterwards, of course, van Aldegonde was busy with assessment, so he had no time for us. I started to discover, to my grief and alarm, the extent to which Florian had taken my defection to heart. Since everyone was too concerned with their own affairs to notice much, he no longer bothered to keep up a front: his acknowledgements of my existence became ever colder and more curt. I just went doggedly on with my life, as best I could, and spent as much time as possible with Jorien. When the vacation came, I took her to meet my parents, who liked her very much, and then we went off and had an idyllic holiday in Normandy, staying in a little auberge with a landlady who looked like Gertrude Stein and cooked like an angel, where I was quietly, utterly, miserable. When we were in The Hague, my mother mentioned innocently that Florian was in Prague with a couple of the chaps, assuming I knew all about it. Later in France, lying in Madame's coarse, well-laundered sheets with Jorien snoring faintly by my side, I endlessly pondered this scrap of information, trying to extract some juice from it.

It was during that vacation, after some long talks with Jorien, that I decided to switch out of law, and into history. I found some of the work I was doing interesting, but all the same, I was less and less convinced that it was what I really wanted. When we got back to Holland, she went off to Warmond to spend some time with her parents, and I went home to The Hague. After a while, Florian showed up, in no communicative mood, though I divined that his companions (as I had suspected) had been van Aldegonde and Maurits. He kept an extremely low profile, and did almost nothing but play the piano, read, and exercise. No one really noticed, because for a change, the entire household was occupied in shouting at me rather than him. My father's reaction to my decision was unexpectedly atavistic: in essence, it boiled down to the idea that it was for the likes of us to make history, not to study it. Mammie tried to mediate, with predictable lack of success. Florian's reaction was more complex; on the surface, he confirmed family expectations and annoyed my father by backing me up, but I think that at bottom, he felt confirmed in his rejection of me. We were saying so little between ourselves at that point that I really have to guess, but I think that the rift which arose from Jorien was of such significance between us, that this further symptom of treachery made nothing actually any worse.

In the autumn, things were very different. I kept my room on the Raap, but Florian moved out to another Athena house round the back of the Pieterskerk. We no longer saw each other at lectures – in fact, we started our days almost literally moving at ninety degrees away from each other, since the history faculty has part of the new University complex on the Witte Singel, while Florian of course was still going up to the law faculty building on Hugo de Grootstraat, near van Aldegonde's house on the Vliet. It was no longer natural for me to drop into the café on the Gerecht; it was so much more obvious for me to go to Camino or the Great Bear. Obviously, I could have gone on going to the Gerecht just to see him, but I was so very far from sure he wanted to see me that I did not do so. I got some news of the professor and his boys, of course, from Jorien, who was still in the law faculty, and naturally kept her eyes open. She reported, for example, that van Aldegonde, having discarded a girlfriend in October, had made no move to replace her: when he was seen in company at all, it was generally with Maurits and Florian: the outlying 'boys' seemed to be getting considerably shorter shrift.

I puzzled about this news, but was unable to bring any focus to the disquiet which it caused me. In particular, I began to review what I knew about Maurits Crommelin, which was not a great deal. He was from the South of the country, Eindhoven or somewhere like that (which is basically why I had assumed he was Catholic), a region not at all familiar to me. He was reputed to be extremely clever and academically ambitious and it was clear from what was said generally, that before the arrival of Florian, he had been van Aldegonde's undisputed best boy. It began to occur to me to wonder what he thought about recent developments. To get a post-doctoral position, which he clearly wanted, one is entirely dependent on the sponsorship of a powerful professor: it was very clear that in this respect, Maurits had put all his eggs in one basket, and his future as an academic rested solely with van Aldegonde. How did he see my brother? – as a threat to be neutralised, which would in a way be natural? – or were they in fact friends, or were they merely thrown together by proximity? I saw no way of answering these questions, but they disturbed my sleep and got into my dreams, which increasingly featured images of Florian drowning, or receding rapidly in a dark, snowy landscape, where I knew he would freeze to death, and even more disturbingly, very incoherent nightmares in which Florian strangled Maurits, but as the death took place, the figures reversed, or the dead Maurits wore Florian's face.

It was very cold that term. The long-range forecast was for a hard winter, so everyone was getting excited about the weather, which became a regular topic of conversation. There was even a hope that it would be a year when the inter-town long-distance skating race in Friesland could be held, which had not happened for a few years. I remember experiencing quite a different kind of chill, though, when Sander, one of my Athena friends, said something casually about meeting my brothers at a late-night showing of Mürnau's *Nosferatu*.

'My brothers?'

He looked at me as though I was mad. 'Florian and Maurits.'

'Maurits is not my brother.'

'Excuse me. I really thought he was your older brother. It's funny, though. He looks terribly like you.'

'He doesn't!' I was unreasonably upset, and Sander was understandably offended.

'I'm sorry,' he said stiffly. 'I saw them together, and the resemblance was very obvious.'

I answered him somehow, I must have, and kept the conversation tucked into the back of my mind. The next time I saw Florian and Maurits at Athena, I saw exactly what he meant. It was all in mannerisms, of course, the tilt of the head, expressions; there was no real physical resemblance, but resemblance is not simply a matter of the physical reality, as I had cause to know. Florian had exercised the transformative power of his will on the physical world, as he had always done, and out of his own need and desire, he had contrived to make himself another twin, or to make himself into the twin of another: in that moment of visceral outrage, it was hard even for me to see whether he had modelled himself on Maurits, or persuaded Maurits into resembling him. He turned his head, saw me staring, and stared back. He knew what I had seen, and how I felt about it. Even as I stood there, my heart swelling, dumbstruck with humiliation, I admired his brilliance. I had to concede it was the most perfect revenge he could have taken. It was only after I had walked out that it occurred to me to wonder if it was he that had thought of it.

Of course, I took the whole thing to Jorien, whose reaction, to my everlasting hurt and astonishment, was unnecessarily cruel.

'Of course he's tried to turn himself into a twin again. So have you. You've wrapped yourself round me like a *verdomde* porous plaster.'

'I'm sorry, Jorien. I had an idea you cared about me.' I was so upset, I was nearly in tears. She sighed, and put down her pen.

'Oh, Hendrik, of course I care about you. I love you lots and lots. But I'm beginning to worry about the way you treat me. We've known each other just about exactly one year, and we're pretty close by normal standards, but normal standards don't make sense to you, do they? I'm sorry, but I don't *want* you to tell me everything you're thinking. From my end, it feels as though you're trying to educate me into being a twin, and I can't, you know? I don't understand that sort of closeness. You don't know who my best friend was at kindergarten, or who I first went out with, or if I was ever scared of spiders, and actually, I don't want you to. I don't think you realise you're being pretty hard on me. You've been talking at me for a solid half hour about Florian, and maybe this and maybe that, and I've got a pile of work to do by tomorrow.'

'I'm so sorry to have taken up your time,' I said coldly.

'Hendrik, don't take it like that. Just try and think about what I'm saying. You're just about as much loved as a nice, decent, attractive boy deserves to be, but ultimately, you're still all alone. People are. You'll have to try and get used to it.'

'But I can't, Jorien. This is unendurable. Don't you know how I feel?'

'Of course not. I guess, and because I care about you, and I'm quite bright, sometimes I guess right. But has it ever struck you you don't know how *I* feel?'

'I suppose I never quite expected to,' I said sulkily. 'Women are mysterious.'

'Oh, for Christ's sake. You've got a logical mind. Even you must see how silly that sounds. If you think I'm some sort of alien creature, how can you believe I've got any basis for understanding you at all?'

'Because you must,' I said, and burst into tears. She hurried over and put her arms round me, and we wept together for a bit, then the whole thing ended in bed, as you might expect.

Later, when I had calmed down and had a chance to think a bit more rationally, I went home and tried to digest what she had said, and it struck a chill to my heart. Lying alone on my own bed, staring at the ceiling, it became clear to me that for his sake and mine, I must mend fences with Florian. Somehow, we were going to have to learn how to live separate adult lives, but in a way which did not actually deny the peculiar quality of our relationship. From the days when we had lain curled together in our mother's body like Yin and Yang, we had breathed in unison; we had been one person for most of our childhood, and that person had been him. I could not believe that all this could be shattered by a single incident, however symbolic. What Jorien had said also bore another interpretation: I was prepared to admit I had been frantic to manufacture a twin-substitute, but did not his parodic relationship with Maurits bespeak equal desperation? Was he waiting for me to reach out to him? That night, unsurprisingly, I dreamed of him, as I often did. He was rushing, with mysterious swiftness, through dark, snowy woods, as if he was running away from some invisible enemy. I was moving even faster, in some kind of vehicle, something like a car, only it seemed to be open. Swiftly, easily, I came up with him as he fled obliviously into the dark. Florian! I yelled, it's me. Hop in. I was leaning out of the vehicle, which seemed to be looking after itself, holding out my hands, while he stumbled on, his breath sobbing and panting with terror. He tripped over a root and fell huddled in the snow; I stopped the car, and he scrambled up, turning on his knees to face me. The hands which he reached up, blindly grappling for mine, were fleshless bundles of sharp steel claws, with nothing human about them. As these horrible hands rose towards my face, predatory and automatic, I jerked back in total revulsion, and woke, drenched with sweat.

After that, I had to see him. The next day, I went over to the house behind the Pieterskerk, and looked up at it. His curtains were open: he was either in working, or already off somewhere. I was debating what to do, when I heard a voice behind me. 'Hi, Florian. Forgotten your key?' I turned: the man who was grinning at me had evidently been out for his breakfast: he was clutching a pint of milk, a packet of coffee, and an enticingly fragrant paper bag from the baker's. He was, I remembered, the warden of the house, someone I had barely met. I smiled back at him, and on the spur of the moment, decided to lie, as I had sometimes done in my childhood and teens.

'Fraid so. They must be in my other jacket.'

'Yah. I've not seen you in that one. You don't wear it often, do you?' He fished for his own key, and let us in. His name, I recalled suddenly, was Jan something.

'Thanks, Jan,' I said, following him into the hall.

'I suppose you want the pass-key? Do remember to give it back, like a good lad, or we'll all be in trouble. Just in my pigeonhole is okay, but don't forget.' He vanished into his own ground-floor flatlet with his morning goods, and came out again a moment later, holding a key.

'Hey, thanks. Sorry to be a nuisance.'

'*Als je blieft*,' said Jan amiably, handing me the pass-key, and disappeared, doubtless to make his breakfast. I went up the stairs slowly, my heart banging against my ribs, and paused for a long moment on the landing before knocking on the door. There was no reply. I inserted the key, and slipped into Florian's room.

It smelt of him, faintly of course, but to me, so perceptibly it brought tears to my eyes. It was pretty neat, much as usual. A shelf of lawbooks, and a couple of shelves of light reading; computer on the desk with a box of disks, paperwork reasonably under control, a hefty pile of the Peters editions of Schubert's *lieder* and other music . . . all much as expected, and none of it very revealing. I began looking a little harder, for some kind of evidence of Florian's current mood. Neither of us had ever kept a journal, and I couldn't imagine he'd have started one. I started up the computer, but a quick look through the directories revealed nothing that was not, on quick inspection, some piece of work, or impersonal stuff like letters to banks. There was no correspondence headed 'Maurits', or 'Balder', which I hardly had a right to expect, since they saw each other regularly. I didn't want to read everything, since I didn't want him to catch me at it, but it was pretty obvious that document titles like essay1 were unlikely to hide anything very revealing. I turned the machine off again, and thought hard. Any personal letters he kept would be in his box – an old, rather beautiful box, from Surinam, made of some dark tropical wood, carved with leaves and fruit, and inlaid with little pieces of mother of pearl – he had had it for years, and loved it. If there were notes from van Aldegonde, or from Maurits, they might tell me something. The box was not immediately visible, but I was certain it must be somewhere about. After a bit of searching to and fro, I found it under the bed, and slid it out. Sitting on the floor, I undid its little brass catch, put the lid carefully back, and reached into it to take out the bundle of letters it contained. When my fingers touched cold metal under the paper, I froze, unbelievingly, thinking, in some confused way, of my nightmare. But lifting out the pile of letters, I found I was looking at a new nightmare of a quite different kind. At the bottom of the box, lay an old German army Luger, and a handful of cartridges. I could not imagine what Florian might be doing with such a thing.

One thing was clear: with secrets like this to keep, Florian must not catch me in his room. I looked at my watch; I had been there for about twenty minutes. I couldn't assume he was out for the day. I put the letters back, closed the box, and put it back exactly where I had found it. I looked round the room: everything was as he had left it. I had touched nothing but the box and the computer. Rapidly, I slipped out of the room, and hurried down the stairs, automatically sticking the key in Jan's pigeonhole, as requested – it was only once I was on the pavement outside, with the door shut behind me, that it struck me I might have done better to hang on to it. No: if Jan then blew Florian up about it, he would know I had been there . . . Hopelessly irresolute, I wandered away from the house, and down towards the Saturday market, where I could lose myself in the crowds. The carillion player in the Town Hall steeple, another feature of Leiden Saturdays, was improvising with great skill on a theme by Bach, the sweet, chiming notes spiralling in the thin, clear air as the happy shoppers bustled and chattered on either side of the Nieuwe Rijn. I was terrified by the unknowability of people. The leather-lunged, bawling stallholders, the beady-eyed housewives, the sloppy blondes in bright down jackets eating frites out of paper cones; they all looked like people whose lives you could guess at, more or less. But what could I know of any of them, if even my own brother could have a secret like that?

I could not force myself to linger among jostling citizenry whom I could no longer bring myself to trust, and fled back to the relative security of my room, where I tried to think. One obvious thing, of course, was why, if he was going to have a gun at all, he should have had an old Luger. Even today, those who buy houses from dear old ladies may find, when they start to make over the attic into a playroom for the children, or take the floorboards up for rewiring, that a mummified corpse in German army uniform is trussed up tidily behind the cold water tank, or tucked in between a couple of joists. Tidiness is a national virtue, after all, and it has been abundantly demonstrated since the last war that a dead man, handled in a sufficiently organised way, can take up remarkably little room. A surprising number of the keen and zealous Moffen who came into Holland as an army of occupation walked down our cosy little streets on private errands, and silently, unobtrusively vanished. Which is to say, of course, that their guns also vanished: some of them are doubtless now rusting at the bottoms of canals, but others are hidden in greenhouses and potting-sheds in case of emergency, or quietly and discreetly in circulation.

My immediate instinct was to blame Maurits, probably unfairly, since he had never, in my hearing, expressed an interest in guns. On the other hand, he was certainly the person whom Florian was spending most time with, and therefore the likeliest suspect. He also kept his hair very short, and had faintly military manners: I had assumed in the past that this was pure affectation, but was it actually an expression of inner predilection? For once, I did not immediately think in terms of rushing off to Jorien. She had given me my warning, and I had taken it, with all the damage that went with it. But more fundamentally, I realised, in this extremity I could not trust her. She would be horrified – nothing wrong with that, I was horrified myself – and because she was female and sensible, she would insist on doing something. Unfortunately, there was not a single thing to be done which would not put Florian at risk of being thrown out of Leiden, damage our relationship beyond any possibility of repair, or both. If Florian stood against the world, or the world against Florian, I stood at his side. I could do nothing else, even if I was privately resolved to kick seven kinds of shit out of him once the emergency was over.

I resolved, therefore, to try to keep an eye on him. What this meant, in practice, was that I adjusted my routines to allow more chances for our paths to cross. With the usual perversity of things, it was a couple of weeks before this decision bore fruit. Meanwhile, the weather had finally obliged everyone by freezing hard, which sent everyone's routines into a spin. Around the beginning of November, the Council announced that the canals had been passed safe for skating, and everyone went crazy. Leiden looked ridiculously beautiful and archaic, with few vehicles in the streets, and the people in brightly coloured ski-suits tacking to and fro on the ice below a leaden, winter sky. From a distance, their modern dress did not call attention to itself, and the whole composed itself into a series of Breughelesque pictures, softened by the snow which fell in fat, soft, feathery flakes from the dark sky. I finally caught up with Florian in the place which was rapidly becoming one of the key rooms of our private memory-palace, the café on the Gerecht. I had been walking up from the Rapenburg, when I spotted him twenty metres or so in front of me, scuffing unconcernedly through the snow. I shadowed him, as if we were playing Cowboys and Indians, and was unsurprised when he disappeared into the café. One important thing about the place is that it has two entrances. The one opposite the back of 'sGravensteen, which Florian had gone in by, and another, which is to the sandwich-bar end of the place. Inside, there are three bits in enfilade: the sandwich room, a sort of horse-box which holds about six people, and the snuggery with the newspapers. I detoured round, therefore, and went into the sandwich-bar. I bought a cup of coffee, and began drifting cautiously towards the front of the café, listening hard. Standing behind the connecting door to the snuggery, I heard the click of the café door, and moments later, van Aldegonde's voice, greeting Florian, and shocking me rigid by addressing him as '*je*'. Concealed in the darkness behind the door, I tried to digest the implications of what I had just heard. Van Aldegonde was the most formal of men. The only people to whom I had ever heard him use the familiar '*je*' rather than the formal '*uw*' were his little girlfriends, in which context, it held unavoidable overtones of patronage and contempt, at least to my ears. All his best boys, even Maurits, invariably got '*uw*'. What on earth could this signify?

Florian, who had gone to the counter for coffee, returned, and they sat down together. They were ensconced in the corner settle, which is to say, up against the wall I was leaning on the other side of. I could move quite far within earshot without their spotting me, by sliding cautiously forward into the horse-box and sitting in the corner leaning forward, since the projecting corner of the settle would block any possibility of their noticing movement behind. The only problem would be if the proprietor asked me what the hell I was up to, but fortunately he seemed to have retreated into the back half of the café, which was considerably busier.

'The snow's getting very thick. You can hardly see across the square,' observed Florian.

'Mmm. Rather lovely, don't you think? It has a simplifying effect. The townscape is at its best in grisaille.'

'I wouldn't know. Ask Maurits. Art's his thing.' Florian sounded wary.

'My dear Florian. I know perfectly well it's music which is your "thing", but you are supposed to be a gentleman, not a trades unionist. You are perfectly entitled to have an opinion about the aesthetics of townscapes without the help of Mr Crommelin.' Van Aldegonde's voice was silky, reasonable, merciless.

'Balder, I don't think I've got opinions about anything any more. It's all second hand.'

'Of course. You're extremely young. Originality only becomes a virtue when one has thoroughly mastered one's cultural inheritance. Which, against the spirit of the age though it be to say so, is not characteristic even of very clever boys of twenty.'

'I feel such a fraud sometimes.'

'You aren't. Think of it as practice. Remember, when you were learning the piano, how long it took before you mastered a piece? When something stopped being a meaningless collection of problems and key-changes, and suddenly acquired meaning? By lucky accident, you have found yourself in a milieu with people considerably further ahead of you. I have to say, Florian, that choosing to match yourself against Maurits Crommelin does more credit to your courage than your prudence.'

He spoke with indulgence; a lightness which to someone like my brother, was a challenge. From where I was, straining my ears in the dim café; much was ambiguous. I could not know how they were physically related; what expressions or gestures accompanied the words. I heard the landlord's step; and moved back reluctantly, pretending I had stood up to look at a picture. The acoustics of the room immediately silenced Florian and van Aldegonde as completely as if a felt curtain had come down. A group of people clumped in, their hair and shoulders spangled with loose snow, pink-cheeked and laughing, and settled themselves around me with tea and applecake. I admitted defeat, swigged the last of my coffee, and left. One thing was quite clear to me. However else things might appear on the surface, Florian and Maurits were rivals for van Aldegonde's – what? Love, you could hardly call it. Esteem, regard, whatever. Whatever it was, the professor was undoubtedly encouraging it. The little scene I had just witnessed with Florian was doubtless reproduced, with artful variation, when he was with Maurits. No wonder he hated

The Magic Flute, I thought irrelevantly, he would make the most sinister of all Sorastros.

The following Saturday, I was woken early by Jorien.

'Hey, Hendrik! Come on. Get up.'

'Urrr.' I burrowed under the duvet again, but she was inexorable.

'Come on, *schat*. I want to get stuff for Sinter Klaas, and the market will be heaving unless we get in early.'

She had a point. My family hadn't paid much attention to the feast of St Nicholas since Florian and I got to the stage of our teens when we thought chocolate initials uncool, but since most people made a thing of it, I thought I had better lay in some stuff for ritual exchange, some tubes of Droste *flikjes*, and so forth (I drew the line at actual chocolate letters), and the market would certainly be cheaper than having to buy it all in Vroom & Dreesman. Jorien, I vaguely remembered from the previous year, took the whole thing a bit more seriously, and bought sweets for sisters, cousins, aunts, the lot. The previous year, she had even bought me the first chocolate H I'd had since I was thirteen, though we didn't yet know each other all that well at that time. I conceded defeat, and got up. While I was shaving, she made us some coffee, then we put on boots and ski-jackets, stuffed carriers into our pockets, and ventured out into the cold.

With Jorien by my side, the mysterious horror that had gripped me on my last visit to the Saturday market was completely dissipated. The day was cold and crisp; the sky a pale, clear, winter blue, with a watery, determined sun, which had melted the top millimetre of the ice on the canals, giving it a slick, wet, black surface, and blurring the myriad curving scars left by ice-skates into Art-Nouveau arabesques. The stallholders were all bundled up like Mother Courage, with huge, clumsy moon-boots, and fingerless gloves; they had the cheerful air of anticipating a good day's sales. The thin, sweet notes of the carillion floated over the market chatter. We were approaching the Korenbeursbrug, when an enticing waft from a small white caravan parked by the river reminded me that we had not had breakfast.

'Hang on, Jorien. I'm going to get us some *loempias*.' Three for me, two for her. I handed up my five guilders, and the little Vietnamese lady efficiently swaddled five nice hot *loempias* in paper napkins, and handed them down to me. I squirted sambal-sauce over mine from the plastic bottle on the counter, and leaned against the corner of the *loempia*-van to enjoy my breakfast. There is a certain art to eating *loempias*, without either spilling the mixture of beansprouts and chopped this-and-that from the crisp shell, or getting chilli all over yourself; one which students master quite rapidly. I loved *loempias*; the fact that my parents insisted eating in the street was vulgar only added to their appeal. Once we had finished, we wiped our fingers off with the napkins, and dropped them in the handy bin. The good cheese stall was immediately to our left, so we headed down that way, picking up general shopping, and working our way down to the big sweet-stalls at the bottom end of the market. Jorien had various nephews, nieces, godchildren and so forth, besides a number of friends, and what with one thing and another, she ended up with quite a few bags of goodies besides the bread, cheese, oranges and general marketing which we were doing as we went along.

The morning was advancing, and as she had prophesied, the market was getting very crowded. The weather was worsening too: the sun had gone behind a cloud, and the wind had risen in little, chopping gusts, not blowing a gale, but producing an occasional spiteful little rattle of hard, pellet-like snow. I was beginning to get tired of the whole expedition, but when I shouted this into her ear, Jorien was inexorable.

'You're always saying you'd like us to spend more time together,' she shouted back, rather unfairly in my opinion, 'well, for once, let's spend time together doing what I want to do.'

'Jorien, that's cheap.'

'Oh, yes, I know. But I do want you to help me carry stuff.

Let's just get it all over in one go. It'll save a lot of time and trouble, really.'

'Why are women so bloody practical?' I moaned, admitting defeat.

'Look, there's the *stroopwafel* man,' she said suddenly, ignoring my capitulation. 'I'll get you some *stroopwafels*, to cheer you up.'

'I haven't got a hand free to eat the bloody things.' She darted off, and came back with a packet of fresh syrup waffles, tucked them into my pocket, where I could feel them against my right hip-bone radiating warmth, and looked at me ironically. 'You can eat them later, *schat*. You're full of loempias now anyway.' I had a sudden vision of what Jorien would be like as a mother.

We had worked our way round as far as the flower stalls – where the blooms were swaddled, like newborn babies, to protect them from the weather – when I spotted the dark, bare head of Maurits Crommelin rising above the crowd, and immediately felt sick. Jorien was buying a pot of forced hyacinths, and not looking around her.

'Jorien!'

'What is it? There you go' – to the stallholder, as she handed over her money, and received her pot of bulbs, wrapped in pink tissue – 'Thanks.'

'Look. Over there, on the bridge. Between the second and third arch.'

'It's Maurits, isn't it? Oh, look. Florian's there too.'

'Jorien, what should we do?'

'Go and meet them? Suggest we all go off for a coffee?'

'I don't know that we can.'

'I know you don't. That's why I think we ought to ask, don't you see? Is this an artificial barrier, or is it something real? It strikes me you'd better find out.'

We were standing practically nose to nose, in everybody's way. 'Scuse me', said a fat woman, elbowing past with a baby-buggy and a trail of older children, in a tone which meant practically the opposite. Even the stallholder was looking daggers: the market only worked if everyone kept moving, even brief pauses tended to break up the flow.

'Look, Jorien. I know it's a lot to ask, but can I go on my own?'

Jorien is tall enough to look me straight in the eye. She did so now, her cheeks and her fine rather aquiline nose pinked by the spiteful little slaps of the wind, her blue eyes furious.

'Do what you bloody like. But remember to bring me my shopping.' She turned on her heel, and vanished into the crowd, leaving me standing there like an idiot with six carrier-bags of assorted junk. The flower-man was just opening his mouth to comment, an inescapable tendency of the *burgerij*, when I forestalled him by seizing a couple of bunches of forced red tulips, and thrusting them into his mittened hands.

'These, please.' They were very expensive; inevitable, at that time of year. He handed them back to me, wrapped up, with a hoarse, conspiratorial chuckle.

'It'll take more than that to get round your young lady. Judging by her expression. There's some nice pink roses. Good, long-stemmed ones, fresh this morning.'

'Thank you. I think these will do,' I said with hauteur, and stuck them in the top of the least full of my horrible bags.

Loaded with my undignified burdens, I began trying to catch up with Maurits and Florian. This was a nightmare process. Traffic round the stalls was continuous, but slow. Coming to a dead stop inconvenienced everyone else, but trying to move faster than the crowd was agony. I felt like a pinball, apologising continuously as one or other of my bulging bags rear-ended some respectable *vrouw* leaning forward to scrutinise the chicory, or clumped a snotty, snowsuited infant round the ear. The snow was thickening fitfully, reducing visibility with occasional gusting whirls of white.

The bridge, thankfully, was a bit clearer. Sometimes dodgy

antique-dealers display their wares on it, but in this uncertain weather, they had decided to stay home. I stood at the highest point, straining my eyes, and spotted my brother moving off rightwards. I plunged after them with determination. Through the jostling shoppers, I could see Florian and Maurits strolling ahead of me, with an air of almost married intimacy, buying nothing, and looking in the windows of shops; Florian in a ski-jacket which I remembered from our last family holiday, Maurits dapper in a Loden coat which must have cost a bomb. I caught up with them at the bookshop, where they had come to rest, considering the display of new second-hand stock. It's one of those rather old-fashioned-looking shops, mostly jewellers, that has two display windows facing inward, with the actual door of the shop two or three metres in. Maurits observed me out of the corner of his eye.

'Well, well. Hendrik. Haven't seen you in a while,' he observed lazily, turning round to look at me. His shrewd, assessing glance measured me up and down, taking in my gaily-coloured carrier bags with faint mockery.

'Good morning,' I said, with dignity, or so I hoped. 'Hello, Florian.' My brother dragged his gaze away from the vitrine, which appeared to be more than normally fascinating, turned round, and looked at me with flat, opaque eyes.

'Hi'.

I considered this stranger who was almost myself, and the gambits available to me. Nothing reproachful, that would be worse than useless. I was almost intimidated by them, standing side by side, their hands in their pockets: how well I knew, how often I had exploited, the little trick of mirror-movement with Florian to catch others off-balance; how could it be that I would fall for it myself? Fortunately, literature wasn't the first thing on the Leidenaars' mind; between the windows of the second-hand bookshop, we were out of the stream of human traffic, which flowed busily past, unheeded by us. I was able, therefore, to put my bags down, and put my own hands in my pockets, a deliberately copycat gesture; when I did, of course, I encountered Jorien's *stroopwafels*, which I had forgotten. Both Florian's and Maurits's pockets seemed to be similarly distended, I was glad to see: they may have been putting altogether too much energy into looking cool, but clearly, they had not been able to resist ruining their silhouettes by picking up lumps of nice cheese and suchlike goodies.

'Hi,' I said, keeping my voice as casual as I could. 'It's been a while. I was wondering if we might meet up some time. Dinner, maybe.'

Maurits gave me a courteous, distant smile. 'Thank you so much for the offer, Hendrik. But you know, I really don't think it's a good idea.'

I looked at him again, sharply: beneath the superficially relaxed air, I was almost certain he was as tense as a spring. I glanced across at Florian: with him, I was certain. He looked the way he did when he was about to play the piano in public, keyed up, a huge amount of energy and excitement and commitment concealed beneath a façade of carelessness, even bloody-mindedness, which regularly fooled my father, but had never deceived me even for a moment. I looked straight at him, trying to catch his eye.

'Bro, it was you I was talking to.' Florian shrugged one shoulder, keeping his hands in his pockets.

'Piss off, Hendrik. It's too late for that.' His voice was quiet, bleak: was he in despair? He was hidden even from me, and I did not know how to reach him. On an impulse, I fished my ridiculous tulips out of the nearest of the toppling bags, and held them out to him.

'For St Nick's, Florian. If we're going to be strangers, we might as well do it properly.' He looked me in the eye for the first time since I had waylaid them. I had hurt him; but how, and to what extent, I could not know.

He swallowed hard, still refusing connection. 'We've got to go,' he said harshly. They whirled, with a single movement, and were out of the shop and moving away before I was able to bend and gather together the many plastic handles of my bags. By the time I made it out of the shelter of the doorway, they had vanished into the crowd. Something caught my eye, between the fish-stall and one of the vegetable stalls, and I braved the bustling crowd to get nearer the canalside and see. My bunch of tulips, lying forlorn on the black ice of the Nieuwe Rijn. He must have tossed it away as they left the shop.

Grimly, I plodded back to Jorien's room. She was out, which hardly surprised me in the circumstances, but I was able to get the house-warden to let me in with the bags. I left a note on the pad on her desk, simply saying 'No Go. H.' Let her make what she could of it. Wasn't she always insisting that she wasn't my keeper? On my lonely walk back to the Raap, through the thickening snow, I detoured off to the nearest grocer, and bought a bottle of rum. Despite the fact that national patriotism (among other considerations) keeps genever rather cheap, I have never really liked the stuff, and I intended to get quite drunk. I don't make a habit of this, but there are times when it is absolutely the only answer.

I shut myself in my room, with the curtains open so that I could look at the snow against the black sky, put on tracksuit trousers and an old blue sweater my mother knitted for me, and put a CD in the player. Schubert I could no longer listen to; I chose some Mozart, I think. Then I opened the rum, and began drinking, trying to think as little as possible. The room was warm, going on stuffy, and I had been out in the cold for a long time. It did not take very much rum to send me off into a doze, perhaps even to sleep. Certainly, what drifted into my mind, absolutely uninvited, was the end of the nightmare I have already mentioned – my brother turning on me, with grasping, metal hands. In all the strained, false conversation of the morning, I had not seen my brother's hands. It came to me then, with sick certainty, that if he had taken his hand out of his pocket, it would indeed have been metal. It was not cheese or *stroopwafels* which had distended his pocket, but the old Luger I had seen in his room. And Maurits had one too, I did not doubt. Locked as they were in a dreadful, covert, competition, what were they doing with these guns?

I hadn't actually drunk very much, maybe a centimetre or so of spirit, to judge by my glass. At any rate, I suddenly felt most unpleasantly sober. I recalled with horrible clarity the conversation in the Vliet which had turned on the concept of the *acte gratuit* as a perfect crime. Was it possible, could it be possible, that my own brother and the very intelligent and able Maurits were actually stalking the jolly bustle of the Saturday market, daring one another to murder a total stranger at random? It was hard to believe, but I was also having trouble with not believing it. I got up, and padded restlessly round the room, as one does to shake off a nightmare. Was I just being paranoid? Where does the line lie between twinnish intuition and fantasy?

Pausing to stare out of the window, it occurred to me that the most important question to ask was what van Aldegonde was doing in all this. But what could a student in my position really find out about a secretive and isolated professor? I already knew what everyone thought of the man; and none of it helped. It seemed to me, as I put the top back on the rum-bottle and made myself some strong coffee, that some part of the problem lay in the particular combination of three unusually talented and strong-willed individuals: that the rivalry between Maurits and Florian, the deadly seriousness with which they competed for him, was something which van Aldegonde had not been able to resist exploiting until, perhaps, things had escalated beyond anything even he had actually imagined. I tried to think it out, leaning my forehead against the cold window-pane until I felt as though my actual brain was hurting.

With one corner of my mind, I almost felt sorry for him; it seemed such a waste. We went to the sort of school which does Classical Greek; we had been route-marched through a couple of Plato's *Dialogues*. Of course, these are held up to you, as a schoolboy, as a sort of totem of civilisation. Looking back, thinking about the horror I was engulfed in, and the profound admiration which – in spite of everything – I still felt for van Aldegonde, the *Dialogues* came to mind. Not Socrates the pre-Christian saint, dying for justice and the people, but Socrates the conniving bastard, the deft, powerful manipulator of relationships between his dazzled crowd of youngsters. The way that people of the sheer stature of Plato and Aristotle were reduced, in the last third of the dialogue, to the beaten whimpers I knew so well, because they were so easy to guess – stumbling through as one was, one was safe to assume that the replies meant either 'If you say so, Socrates', or 'That would seem to follow logically'. Knowing van Aldegonde as I did, I began to wonder how the relationships between Plato, Charmides, Phaedo and so forth had actually worked. What happened when they weren't sitting under a plane tree in a respectful circle round the Master? What happened when Charmides met Plato, buying fish? It seemed to me, it still does seem to me, that if Socrates was a totem of civilisation, then van Aldegonde was entitled to a lot of respect. Something was going wrong; but it was going wrong because he had been *made* an enemy of the people, for reasons which were only too obvious; his pride, his aristocratic arrogance, his talent, had put him crossways-on to a people whose instinct is profoundly levelling. If half of what I suspected was true, van Aldegonde was crazy, or wicked, or both, but there was enough in my own heritage to give me a sort of shamed sympathy with him. Pappie, thank God, had never been in a position where he or his family could have been accused of collaboration, but it could easily have been so, with the hindsight of history, you could see that. This sort of reflection gets you precisely nowhere. The only useful idea which I had all night, apart from going and making my peace with Jorien, was that it might be an idea to go to Warmond and talk to her father. Fortunately, since it was Sunday the next day, even a doctor was likely to be home.

The next morning, accordingly, I walked down to the station, and took a bus out to Warmond. I suppose the place once had some kind of separate identity, but it's now very purely a suburb of Leiden; one of those achingly prosperous, immaculately kept little enclaves of big houses in a sort of pseudo-Scandinavian taste which represent the pinnacle of bourgeois aspiration. Looking out at the endless succession of watered-down De Stijl and bogus Larssen flowing past the window of the bus, I could not imagine living in such a place, or being brought up there. Nearly there. I hopped off the bus, and turned up the street (Crocusweg, or some such damn-fool name) for the Coomans' house, which I had visited once or twice before. When I rang the bell, Jorien's mother greeted me warmly, and took me through to the back, across a vast acreage of immaculately polished parquet, explaining that Theo would certainly be in the greenhouse. Mirjam is one of these women who are so well preserved that's all you notice about them, though she's perfectly nice in her way. It explains a lot, I think, if I say that she was wearing high heels and three diamond rings, even though it was Sunday, and when I had rung earlier, she'd said they weren't going anywhere.

Out the back, there was the sort of garden which looks a picture in summer, though in late November it hadn't much to offer but a frosted lawn and a lot of bare twigs. There was also a substantial, timber-framed greenhouse, with someone working in it. Mirjam knocked on the door, and after an answering shout from within, stood aside to let me pass. Theo stood at the far end, making leaf-cuttings from begonias with a scalpel. He was a substantial figure, silver-haired, in much-worn jeans, an old Breton smock, and clogs; his big hands moving with deft authority. He did not look up as I came in.

'Hendrik.' His voice was a rather light tenor, with a pleasant timbre. 'I'll just get these done, then we can have a chat.' Then his attention returned completely to his plants; it was as if I were no longer there. I leaned against a section of greenhouse staging, content to watch him. Mami always contended that doctors by definition had no manners, they get too used to people jumping to it all around them, and looked at thus, Coomans was a prize example of the species. Paradoxically, though, I found my respect for him rising. I'd always found him perfectly pleasant, though not exactly fascinating. The deftness and skill with which he was handling the plants brought into better focus a person I had previously seen only wearing company manners, or through his daughter's eyes: not, perhaps, a complex man, but a man of integrity. Eventually, his tray of plantlets was completed to his satisfaction: he dusted a little loose compost off his fingertips with automatic fastidiousness, and turned to me.

'Now, lad. Let's go through to the conservatory, and you can tell me why you've dropped in.'

I followed him back to the house, and into the conservatory, which even at that time of year, was lush with foliage plants, with flowering this-and-thats in jardinières, which presumably zipped in and out of the greenhouse on rotation. The air smelt pleasantly of damp compost, with a peppery tang of geranium. We sat down on spindly, wrought-iron seats, comfortably cushioned, and looked out at the winter garden. A moment or two later, the house-door opened, and Mirjam click-clicked in with a tray of coffee and biscuits. I thanked her, and she smiled graciously, and tittuped away. Theo poured coffee.

'I'm assuming,' he said, 'you haven't got Rien pregnant. Sugar?'

'My God, no', I said, confused. 'I mean, no to both. No, it's nothing about Jorien, nothing about us at all. I wanted to ask you about Professor van Aldegonde.'

Coomans put down the coffee-pot rather abruptly, and gave me a long, hard look. It was the first time I had felt myself being actually weighed up by the man, and it made me realise that he was, in his way, formidable: I found myself blushing idiotically.

After some long moments, which felt even longer, he sighed, and handed me my cup.

'What's he done to you?'

'It's difficult. He hasn't done anything to me, or at least, I don't think so. It's my brother. You know. Florian.' I was finding it very difficult to say anything at all; it was as if something was actually stopping me, an ox sitting on my tongue, as the Greeks used to say.

'Your brother's one of van Aldegonde's Junkers, I take it?'

I nodded, and took a swallow of coffee, which seemed to have a liberating effect on my voice. 'It's worse than that. Last year, when I was knocking around with them, there were about seven or eight of *de jonkheren*. It was fun. I mean, it was interesting. You learned a lot. But now it all seems to be different. There's just two. Florian, and a man called Maurits Crommelin. The others have all drifted away, or been given their marching orders, I don't know. I've been worried. But I'm trying to keep it in perspective, you see? I thought I'd come and ask you, because you've known van Aldegonde, or known about him anyway, for a long time. I mean, does this happen quite often? A whole gang one year, a couple of "best boys" the next?'

I trailed off, hating myself for my incoherence. Theo Coomans rested his chin on his big fist, and visibly thought. When he returned his attention to me, his expression was alarmingly stern.

'Hendrik, I think you had better tell me a great deal more.'

Stumblingly, I told him what I knew of the relationship between Florian, Maurits and van Aldegonde, apart, of course, from what I knew or suspected about the guns. When I had said all that I could, he bowed his head, and brooded in silence for a while before pronouncing.

'You are right to be extremely concerned. You knew that, of course, you aren't a fool. As you suspect, it's out of pattern. Up to now, there's always been a praetorian guard; it's been a little foolish, perhaps, but not positively unhealthy. Some of the lawyers, I know, thought positively well of the habit, since it sharpened up a lot of very talented and able students – van Aldegonde's young gentlemen have always done extremely well in the final examinations. But two, and the kind of relationship you describe . . . I have to say, I find that very alarming. I'm not formally a psychiatrist, as you know, but the situation is one which rings professional alarm-bells.'

'But what can I do for my brother, sir?'

Coomans spread his hands, a resigned, rather helpless gesture. 'Keep channels open, as far as you can. Make it clear there isn't a problem on your side. That's all. He's a free agent. You think, and I agree with you, that he is in a situation which is potentially dangerous to him. But no drugs are involved, as far as anyone knows, apart from perhaps Schubert. I'm afraid, lad, you're in the classic position of the parent who finds his child has become a Moonie or a Krishna-worshipper. You see a personality alteration, you are convinced that this is not on some level the child's "real self" speaking, but you have not the shadow of a right to intervene.'

'But –.' All this awful stuff about guns, my real fears – or were they real? Had I invented most of it? – it was all hovering on the tip of my tongue. Would it make a difference to point out that my brother had at least committed one civil misdemeanour already, to wit, keeping an unlicensed firearm, improperly secured? Loyalty, as ever, sat on my tongue, as hard as the Greek poet's ox. Theo Coomans raised a big, magisterial hand.

'Try not to worry unduly, Hendrik. He's your identical twin, so it's safe to say he's got his fair share of brains and common sense. If you want an off-the-cuff diagnosis; it's my belief that van Aldegonde's the one who's cracking. He's been brilliant, but not exactly stable, for a good few years. This all sounds like the early warning of something I saw coming years ago. I'd guess that in a year or two, you'll find a note on his office door one morning saying that he's retired "on health grounds", no mail will be forwarded, collect essays from the secretariat, etcetera. The young are tough, Hendrik. Your brother will pull himself together.'

'Thank you, sir. You've been most helpful.'

My tone gave me away, I know. He gave me an ironic, but not unkindly look, and nodded politely. I got to my feet, and he walked me to the front door.

'I know, Hendrik,' he said unexpectedly, from behind me, as we walked through the hall. 'Everything I've said sounds completely beside the point. I was young once. All I can say is, experience suggests I'm about ninety per cent certain to be right in the long run.' We shook hands at the door, and he patted my shoulder. 'Thank you for coming, lad. I value your confidence.'

'Thank you,' I replied, and set off down Crocusweg, Jorien's remarks about 'the other five per cent' ringing in my ears, miserably aware that I'd failed on all counts. I had completely failed to reassure myself, and I had made a fool of old Coomans by causing him to theorise on insufficient data. All I'd really got out of my bus-trip to Warmond, apart from an increase in respect for Jorien's father, was a conviction that I was for all practical purposes on my own.

I took absolutely the point which he had made about Moonies: in some ways, it was indeed a cognate situation. All I could think of to do, at that point, was to take a look at the enemy; so I went to see Jorien to ask if I could take a look at her law faculty lecture list.

'Did you get any help from Dad?' she asked, as I came in. She was sitting on her bed, wearing only a tee-shirt and a pair of knickers, painting her toenails, looking ordinary, lovely, and desirable. I sat down in her armchair where I could look at her.

'Not really. He thinks van Aldegonde's probably going crazy. I think he's right. But it doesn't help.' Jorien put the top back on the varnish, and sat with her legs straight out in front of her like a doll, rolling her ankles gently to dry the nails. We stared at her slim, freckled shins and moving feet.

'You know what I really hate about all this,' she burst out suddenly. 'It's all been going round and round between the four of you. You and Hendrik, and Maurits, and the Professor. It's so arrogant, as if the rest of the world doesn't exist. All this doom and doubt, like something out of Schiller or Goethe. I know you're all quite posh, but there's really no excuse for it. You think of yourself as the sensible one, but the way you go on, it's as if there's nothing outside the city walls except snow and pine-forests, when you know perfectly well there isn't a hectare of land without nice little houses on it between here and Scheveningen. I just wish that wretched man would make himself realise he's only a state servant with a salary and a pension! If he'd just start thinking like that, he'd have to come off stalking around the Count's Castle like bloody Dracula.'

How right she was. And how wrong. I could see it from both sides. Jorien's was the voice of reason, no doubt of that, but she was also the voice of levelling mediocrity. It took more than *burgerlijk* virtues to make Holland out of nothing; and it seemed to me that the something more which we represented still had value, even if it was an intangible one, hard to quantify. Jorien was casting up profit and loss, debit and credit, like the good bourgeois she was, but I could not make myself feel that the sum at the bottom was the beginning and end of everything.

'Rien, darling. Can I have a look at your lecture list?'

'Of course. It's on the desk there. Under the blue folder.'

I looked through it: good. If I cut one of a desperately boring series on the Rampjaar next Tuesday, I could catch van Aldegonde's two o'clock lecture on legal history.

It was a strange experience, joining the crowd streaming into lecture room six in the law faculty building. I had done so legitimately for the whole of the previous year, but so volatile is student life, all that now felt as if it had been someone else who did it; I 'belonged' on the Singel. The room held about two hundred people, and was pretty full. I chose a position quite high up and to one side, and was pretty sure that I would not be spotted by van Aldegonde: if Florian was there and saw me, he would just have to make what he could of it.

Van Aldegonde walked in, abruptly, with his usual flair for entrances: he was suddenly there, at the lectern, as if he had popped up through a trapdoor. He said nothing, but as his blank, silver gaze swept the rows of student heads, the usual chatter and gossip abruptly ceased. He was talking, I think, about Grotius's theory of Natural Law: certainly, 'Natural Law' was the basic theme, but typically, his treatment of the subject involved everyone from Moses to Mozart, and for once, I was not listening with enough attention really to follow. Or rather, I was listening to the man, not the words. I began to see what Theo Coomans had meant in predicting a breakdown. He was as brilliant as ever; me aside, the audience was rapt in attention, but there was a terrifying intensity in his discourse. His hands were as well controlled as ever, but his sparse gestures had a suppressed violence that was alarming. He was a man in whom almost nothing appeared on the surface which he did not intend so to appear, but to someone like me, who knew him reasonably well, the ease, the control, seemed increasingly fictitious. But would the collapse come soon enough? Could one engineer it? It is dreadful to have to say it, but the wild thought of painting swastikas all over his beautiful white house did cross my mind – for Florian, I would even have done such a thing, if I could have been sure I would drive him crazy. As I sat there, listening to his elegantly turned, witty sentences, I was bleeding inside for the way that we were all, even me, being forced out of the social contract. He could not be resisted, within the law; in fact, he was what he had called St Paul, a dangerous virus within the body politic. But where law was powerless, was lawlessness the answer? I was, in his terms, a mere callow child, but I was helpless within civilisation. Van Aldegonde was in some respects a profoundly civilised man, but he was armoured by anger and contempt in ways which made him more of a menace than any mere psychopath. Would it help, I wondered, if I stole Florian's gun, with the assistance of the idiot Jan, and shot him? No, I thought numbly, as the lecture came to an end and people started clattering to their feet all around me, because I could not do so. I could see exactly what would happen: he would open the dark-green door of the house on the Vliet, take one look at me, and hold out his long, beautiful white hand. And I would give him the gun. As a civilised person, in the absence of identifiable crime, I was condemned to doing absolutely nothing.

They had all gone. I was sitting on a worn oak form, polished by generations of student bottoms, looking blankly down the well of the empty auditorium, with a new lot of people already clattering down the stairs from the top. I pulled myself together hastily, and left before I found myself trapped in some Godforsaken lecture on maritime law, or worse. I wandered out of the building, without meeting anyone I knew. Blank with misery, like a cow following a familiar path, I found my feet taking me up Hugo de Grootstraat and round to the Gerecht.

It was too cold to sit outside, really. The café proprietor left his light aluminium chairs out practically all winter, in the hope of the odd days of sun, but today, the metal was furry with crystals of frost. There was a little sun, indeed: my side of the square was still in shade, but the light struck the Baroque façade of 'sGravensteen. I sat down anyway, in one of the furry chairs, my hands dangling between my knees, exhausted with futile emotions.

There was light, as I say, on the façade of the Count's Castle. The windows were, mostly, blazing squares of blue and gold. But despite the cold, one sash was raised, in a window on the top floor, on the left hand side, and in the room there moved a shadow which, even at a distance of about a hundred metres, I knew. Twenty years ago, Florian and I had swum like blind fish in the cave of our mother's belly; and like the blind, white fish that swim in caves, we had developed some sort of physical awareness of each other's existence. I knew it was Florian up there, though I had seen nothing but a glimpse of blurred movement. Blank, tired, as I was, I was no longer sure where I was, who I was. Was it my hand, my clever, muscular, pianist's fingers wrapped round the squat butt of the Luger, my eye, sighting down my arm, taking aim at Hendrik's red jacket in the square? Did it matter? It was an end, whatever. I raised my head, and looked directly at the window where I knew Florian stood. Our bond held; never, in all our life, had I shopped him. Did he know?

I thought it was just the two of us, or rather, the two of us was all I thought about. Jorien's right; I can be so stupid, sometimes. There was me, and there was Florian, and though I hardly noticed her, there was also a woman walking by, a very ordinary woman. She was wearing one of those absurd padded coats which make you look like a boiler, dingy brown, and tatty grey boots with embroidery round the tops. Her perm was growing out, and she was pushing one of those shopping baskets on wheels. She was pottering across the Gerecht, maybe heading for Vroom & Dreesman or somewhere, when suddenly her head exploded. There was a fountain of red across the gritty snow, and the rest of her fell forward over the absurd trolley, the grey boots still twitching and drumming, while I sat paralysed. Behind me in the café, someone began to scream.

The Colonel and Judy O'Grady

Judy O'Grady ceased to exist the moment she got on the plane for India in 1961, that much was certain. Twenty years later, it was a completely and entirely other person called the Venerable Sri Ananda (no connection with any previous firm), who told me about the Colonel in Princes Street Gardens.

We met when Ananda was working in the University library. I was wrestling despairingly with the writings of Tacitus, an author of such devastating sophistication that I was beginning to feel I would have to turn into Ronald Firbank to do him justice, and she was cataloguing the Sanskrit and Tibetan collections. What we had in common at the outset was simply poverty. Ananda, of course, was committed to poverty as a life-choice, while I was a graduate student, and thus tended to associate with people who could be relied upon not to suggest doing anything expensive. Moreover, Ananda was exotic, and the exotic was in short supply at Edinburgh University. She wore dark red robes and thick grey socks, and had a shaven head marked by six ritual scars. She was met, on the whole, with quiet consternation and acute social embarrassment. Grown men cringed in their chairs as she passed silently by on sandalled feet. Somehow, the blue eyes and pink cheeks made it all worse rather than better.

She seldom spoke of the past, though, vigilant for hints, I once heard her say that she had started off in life with the name Judy O'Grady. Other clues: she retained a faint but perceptible Dublin accent, and had been heard to mention casually that her parents had hoped she would go to University College. But she took the passage to India, instead, her mind already made up. Why? How had she known? If she felt the call to be a nun, why not a Catholic nun, for Pete's sake? I thought about Mr and Mrs O'Grady (pillars of the church? parents of twelve?): weeping, pleading, running round in agonised circles as parents do when they find they have inadvertently hatched a saint. Like St Columbanus, stepping over the prostrate body of his weeping mother, like St Patrick, like half the saints of Ireland, she did what she felt she had to. At least St Columbanus didn't have to raise the air-fare – how had she managed it? I looked at Ananda, basking in the meagre northern sun, and began spinning fantasies: perhaps she'd sold her grandmother's string of pearls, given her as a first-communion present . . . St Mary of Egypt had worked her passage to Jerusalem as a ship's whore, but that wouldn't have washed with BOAC . . . Ananda, smiling and serene, was clearly not about to tell me.

Back in 1961, when Ananda was newly hatched, Tibet-in-Exile had settled itself down in Simla, just the other side of the Himalayas from home, and had busily set about recreating the loved and familiar patterns of religious life. They were not the only exiles in Simla. In the days of the Raj, any Europeans in India who could possibly do so escaped the boiling heat of the Punjab and the Ganges delta and moved up to the hill stations in summer. A series of unnaturally British resort towns composed of white and veranda'd bungalows decorated the cool and salubrious lower slopes of the greatest mountains in the world: Simla, Srinagar, Naini Tal. After Partition, these had become the homes of a strange and pathetic group known, collectively, as the Ancient Britons. Children, grandchildren, great-grandchildren of the Army and the Indian Civil Service, born, bred, and brought up in India, sometimes for four or five generations. Yet they were not white Indians; they thought of England as 'home', though they were, in many cases, dimly aware that this abstract conviction would hardly survive the briefest visit. When the tumult and the shouting had died, and the captains and the kings had departed, the Ancient Britons, left helplessly stranded by the receding tide of the British empire, took their pensions, their half-pay and their collections of silver-framed photographs up to the hills, and stayed there. High above them, clinging to the slope of the Siwalik Range, the Tibetans' new *gompa*, Yamdrok-Tso, arose, and behind and higher still, fifty miles off, hanging like silver shadows behind the wooded slopes of the hills, towered the austere and pitiless peaks of the Greater Himalaya, the outer ramparts of holy Tibet. The shaven heads and the Panama hats met periodically in the bazaars, like animals at a watering-hole, with an entire lack of mutual curiosity.

Reading between the lines, it must have been a considerable shock to the introverted and self-sufficient little community of the Ancient Britons to observe, amongst the brown-leather, flat-faced ascetics, a bald head which, under the scorching sun of India, had turned pink as a wild Irish rose, and blue eyes set in a small, freckled face. Ananda's narrative style was ingenuous, immediate, and focused on physical realities. She seldom evoked an emotion or a stance, her own or anyone else's. But Ananda, in the early eighties, was still beautiful in her own peculiar way. In 1961, she must have looked like the Colleen Bawn with a shaved head. Punks were a long way in the future, even beatniks were still a pretty rare breed, and in any case, the Ancient Britons probably thought even bobbed hair was a little fast. What could they feel about a pretty girl's spoiled beauty, but outrage, shame and pity?

Sri Ananda was as untouchably serene as a statue of Buddha.

She rose at four a.m. to meditate, never ate after midday, avoided all stimulants except tea, and did a full day's work on it. She radiated the serene, unquenchable gaiety of the born religious, and had the patience of forty saints, of whatever denomination. Simple chronology indicated that she must have been about fifty at the time when we were closest, but meditation and contemplation combined with imperturbable physical health had done their work well: her freckled face was as smooth as a girl's, unmarked by passion, tension or worry. Since it was barely the case that she was passing through the stages of woman's life except in the most abstract, physiological sense, she did not look any age in particular.

Increasingly, I found thoughts of Ananda haunting every waking and sleeping hour, and took to prowling about the Manuscripts room (where I was supposed to be spending some, but by no means all, of my time) in the hopes that I might bump into her. It was, I reflected in a moment of lucidity, a bit like falling in love with a fish. Ananda's life and personality were extraordinarily complete and coherent. There was no wound to close, no hole to plug, no loose-hanging tag of hair or clothing to tangle her life with another's. I was as yet too young to realise that it was precisely this quality of wholeness which made Ananda so attractive. I have to admit that, if she had been capable of falling in love with a boundlessly self-indulgent postgraduate haunted by fears of unemployability, she would probably have lost her charm for me.

Naturally, I sought unconsciously to protect myself from this melancholy truth. I became increasingly curious about Ananda's twenties: what she had been like when she was still imperfect, still looking for answers to impossible questions. I hardly dared think of Judy O'Grady, the name which Ananda had once, casually, mentioned. Judy was a closed book, lost, gone, forgotten. It was impossible to ask Ananda questions when she didn't want to answer, they seemed to slide off her. In any case, I had a wholly justified terror of becoming a bore and a nuisance. Like every graduate student who was ever spawned, I was a tiresome neurotic, making life hell in roughly equal proportions for myself, my friends and (when I could find him) my supervisor. I will give myself the credit for feeling, unlike many, that I was perhaps not always as charming as I might have wished. But, although Ananda had buried Judith O'Grady full fathoms five, she was sometimes more forthcoming about the early days of her novitiate. Baby Ananda, as it were, Ananda the novice, was still a part of the person she had chosen to become – and what she was like must surely, in some unimaginable way, have grown out of what she had once been like? I desperately wanted to know Ananda, because I loved her so much, but I needed a bridge between my ordinary self and her shining, enigmatic, strangeness. The only common ground there could potentially be must be in the past, in the process of her self-formation. Thus when, with the cunning of obsession, I stalked Ananda's history, it was her early life in India which I had in my sights.

'What was it like, going to India for the first time?' I asked, as we sat facing each other in the dubious, grudging Edinburgh summer, cross legged on the grass in the shade of a plane-tree. Distantly, the notes of 'McCrimmon's Lament' drifted over the roar of the traffic: some tartan twit was presumably strutting his stuff on Princes Street to impress the toories.

'Oh, gosh. Well, it's hard to remember now. It was the first time I'd been out of Ireland, even, and there was so much to absorb at once. Travelling by plane was quite exotic then, you know. It took a terribly long time, and we had to stop for refuelling at Djibouti. There was a wonderful electrical storm, and the plane was bouncing about with lightning flashing through the windows . . . I remember how hot it was, when I came out of the plane. Somehow you don't really believe in hot climates, not what they're really like, till you actually get there. I took trains from Delhi to Simla – it was a bit overpowering, though everyone was friendly. Because of the Anglo-Indians, there were lines all the way, even the last bit from Kalka, which is really steep. The little train goes puffing through the foothills, over the most amazing viaducts, and through lots of tunnels. It's got to get up about seven thousand feet in the last bit, so it feels a bit as though it's clinging to the track with its fingernails. It was such a relief when it started climbing though, that I do remember, because it started to leave the heat behind.'

'What about the monastery?'

Ananda's face, earnest with memory, was abruptly transformed by a reminiscent grin. 'Well, there's one thing I *wasn't* expecting!'

'Mmm?'

Ananda absent-mindedly pulled a blade of grass, and tied it in a knot. 'Er. Well, there's one difference between Tibetans and Europeans. They don't wash. Not at all. And they rub butter into their skins, to protect themselves from the weather. I mean, you read that kind of thing in books, and it doesn't make any impact. But the *am-tse* – that's the novice-mistress – and the other seniors were sort of patinated. Goodness knows what colour they were, really, under the ground-in dirt. I nearly fainted when I met them, though they couldn't have been nicer. It was months before I could get through a lesson without sort of unconsciously trying to hold my breath. And you feel a bit funny about the food, for a while.'

'Did it make it hard to take them seriously?'

'Well, no. Not really. I was scared stiff of them. But there was a lot of unlearning to do. You're quite right. You do think of madmen and tramps, at first. People you'd talk at, and not really listen to. We aren't used to human filth any more.'

'It's a very modern affectation, washing,' I said, absently. 'Most of the saints thought it was a dangerous luxury.' I wasn't really thinking about what I was saying. I was thinking about filthy hands, with grimy, broken, blackened nails, plunged into a basin of flour, kneading dirt energetically into greying dough. The cook turns towards you with a beaming smile: See! I'm making something delicious for us all to eat. Could you smile back? Could you, when the pile of bannocks, buns, whatever they were, was handed to you at last, take one, and bite into it? I was fastidious; I hated even to share a glass, I could never have used a lover's toothbrush or handkerchief. How long, I wondered, before you stopped caring?

'It doesn't really matter,' said Ananda, who was watching my face. 'But it's funny how your conditioning stays with you, with something like that.'

'What did you eat?'

'*Tsampa* and tea, mostly. It's roasted barley-flour. You make it into a sort of stiff porridge with butter and a bit of the tea, and roll it into little balls. It's actually quite nice sometimes, though that depends on the butter. There's a Scottish thing that's quite similar, isn't there?'

'It's called *drammach*. Raw oatmeal and water. It's what people lived on when they took to the heather in the Forty-five.'

Ananda gave me a faintly ironic glance.

'It just goes to show that peasant food is much the same wherever you are. The thing about Tibet is it's basically a pre-modern culture. Living on *tsampa* and tea only looks odd by twentieth-century standards.'

'You got used to it?' I persisted.

Ananda laughed. 'I won't say I was never dying for a good potato! Irish folk love their praties. But that's really just trying to get back to what's familiar. You learn to cut loose, in the end. It's partly why I was there.'

The day was wearing on, I was dying for a drink, and the Doric, that watering-hole of Edinburgh arties, is not that far from Princes Street Gardens. But I was dubious about offering to take Ananda to a pub. I found myself curiously squeamish about asking Ananda precisely what her vows committed her to. Would she or wouldn't she? Safer not to ask.

'How did you get on with the English community?' I asked, thrusting the Doric determinedly out of my mind.

'Oh, goodness. Of course, they were very set in their ways, even for the early Sixties. Do you know, I even met someone who still gave little lectures with a magic lantern? I must say, though, they did try very hard to be kind. There was one person there, the Colonel, who rather took me up.' She paused, looking at me with some affection, indecision written all over her face. Perhaps, in retrospect, she was wondering how much privacy you owe the dead, especially the long-dead? She realised, maybe, that I could only have been a toddler at the time – that to me, it would all be ancient history. 'It's rather a strange little story.'

I was insatiably curious about anything capable, even momentarily, of ruffling her serenity. What is more, I have to confess that at that time, I would cheerfully have sat still and listened to Ananda reciting pages from the phone-book, as long as it meant she was talking to me, and letting me look at her. So I said, 'I'd really like to hear it, if you wouldn't mind.'

This, then, is the story Ananda told me. Or at least, the story I understood her to have told, which may not be the same thing. In it, you will see the things that happened; the appearances, and some of what was on the surface of Ananda's mind – guesses on my part, glossing. Even then, I was well read. Because of Ananda, I had been reading about the East: I had pictures in my head of India and Tibet. I knew some history. I even knew something about being a woman, or so I thought. But I knew absolutely nothing about being a nun, and I have to admit, I did not want to. Ananda, if she had had access to my version of events, might very reasonably have said that all I could picture were the bits that didn't really matter. Perhaps so: but unlike Ananda, I am committed to the world of illusion.

Ananda met the Colonel a couple of weeks after she first came to the monastery, the first time she had ventured out of Yamdrok-Tso since the excitement and confusion of her arrival. The expedition was one which she had been putting off, and the view of Simla as she came down the mountain road was not one which suggested that it would yield any incidental pleasures. Viewed from the height of the Hindustan-Tibet Road, it was unimpressive. If God had tripped coming down the Himalayas and dropped His tea-tray, the result would have been something very like Simla. A mass of ramshackle jerry-built structures, which cascaded down a precipitous cleft in the Siwalik hills like a tumble of broken crockery. But once Ananda had negotiated the dismal peripheral slums and had emerged on to the Mall, there was a far clearer sense of being somewhere in particular; though precisely where remained moot. The tall buildings were Victorian fantasy architecture, breaking out capriciously in balconies, verandas, half-timbering, and bizarre pointed roofs which they seemed to wear like pixie-hats. The General Post Office, towards which she was heading, was a massive structure somewhere between a Swiss chalet and a Mississippi steamboat in appearance. She entered it with some hesitation. When she pushed open the door, it took a moment for her to adjust to the relative darkness of the interior, so it was the voice she registered first, light, hesitant, clipped, slightly stuttering. Then she noticed his ears. He was a dapper, smallish man, sparely built, with hair of an indeterminate sandy fairness, shading to grey, but cut so short that it was hard to tell where it begun and ended. Its extreme shortness made his ears very noticeable, largish, with long, pendulous, creased lobes. Only the day before, looking at Ananda's own pretty, round little ears, Tsering had told her that long ears were one of the signs of a saint, one of the first things to look for if you suspected a child was a reborn lama. She wondered if he knew. The little figure had 'military' written all over him. He was dressed with pernickety freshness in immaculate white ducks, and carried a short cane. He was involved in an intricate discussion in Hindi with the postmaster, in the course of which a dingy piece of paper was pushed back and forward between them on the post-office counter, an argument so engrossing that at first neither of them heard her enter. His voice gradually rose from a base-position of patient reasonableness to some kind of rhetorical climax, and he tapped the counter smartly with his malacca, saying, '*Chulo*, *chulo*, *chulo*!' The postmaster blew through his moustache and shrugged, pushing the creased chitty back towards his tormentor with a resigned gesture. Straightening up, he spotted Ananda standing quietly in the middle of the room. He emitted a grunt of surprise, put the tips of his fingers together in a brief gesture of courtesy, and addressed her in Hindi.

'I'm sorry,' said Ananda, 'do you speak English?'

The Englishman swung round abruptly and looked her up and down, his eye travelling incredulously from her face to her robes and back again. Slowly, he removed his Panama, tucked his cane under his armpit and made her a formal little bow.

'Mornin', m'dear. Colonel Hatherton. Take it you're new here? Can I be of assistance?'

'Oh, hello, Colonel. I'm, er, Ananda.' She stumbled a little over the name: it was the first time that she had had a chance to use it to an outsider. 'I'd be glad of a little help. This postcard's got to get to Dublin, you see, and I'm wanting to be sure it's got the right stamp.'

Hatherton digested the name without a flicker. The faded eyes remained steady and kindly, while his brick-red countenance (faintly reminiscent of the Queen-Empress in her later years) remained a mask of impenetrable courtesy. 'Only to happy to help, Miss Ananda.' He took the card she held out to him, and glanced at it. 'Had a troop-sar't O'Grady once, salt of the earth. Splendid fellow. Any connection?'

'I'd doubt it. I'm the first person in the family to set foot in India, that I've ever heard of.'

'Shame.' He flicked the card with a fingernail. 'This should go all right. I'll just make sure that Khan puts it in the right bag.' He turned away courteously, and addressed the postmaster again. The man nodded and bowed, took the card obsequiously, and whisked it away beneath the counter. Ananda watched it go. Duty done, the end of an old song. Hatherton turned back towards her, touching the brim of his Panama with the tip of his cane to set it at a jauntier angle.

'If you're walking back up the hill, perhaps you might indulge an old buffer with your company? Don't often see a pretty girl here, that's a fact.'

Ananda looked at him in disbelief. It seemed as if, faced with the irreconcilable, he had reconciled it by the simple process of blanking out the half which didn't fit. The goodwill, however, was absolutely unmistakable. She remembered her teacher Tsering saying, 'Do not refuse kindness.' More distantly came an echo of Father Doolan's voice, all the way from Sandymount, 'Offer it up as a mortification, Judith.'

They walked out together into the clear, crisp air. The sky was very blue, and in the distance, impossibly far up the sky, the high peaks shimmered.

'Got a bit of a flap on,' confided Hatherton. 'Been expecting some stuff for months, home comforts, y'know. The crates got to the docks all right, old Khan double-checked with the telegraph. They'll be marooned in a siding somewhere between here and Bombay, no doubt about that.'

'But you don't know which?'

'Good girl! That's precisely the point. I was trying to ginger old Khan up to ring round the stationmasters. There's only so many possibilities, after all. The man's just making difficulties. No initiative, not a scrap – which, my dear, you will find is the problem with the native outlook, splendid fellows though they are in many respects.'

He ambled serenely on, unconscious of offence. I mustn't let this touch me, thought Ananda. *Maya*: illusion. It's just noise. I mustn't go carrying that kind of thing around with me. She thought of the meditation hall instead, the *am-tse*'s face, bronze-dark in the half-light of dawn; the sense of freedom, letting the chatter of the world blow away like dust on the wind. Hatherton broke into her thoughts after a while.

'Of course, your lot. *Quite* another kettle of fish. Not a military bone in their bodies, of course, but fine chaps all the same. Not like Orientals at all. I saw your what-d'you-call-him, your Dalai Lama, on a newsreel once. Dashed impressive little fellow.'

They left the Mall behind them, and wandered up the road out of Simla. Beyond the confines of the town, the hill road meandered up the slope, the ground falling away dramatically to the right, shaded with deodars and gigantic rhododendrons. The road was stony and dusty, but the shade of the trees was cool and pleasant.

After a pause, Colonel Hatherton broached a new subject, with some hesitation. 'Harrumph. One thing I've never been quite clear about. Tell me, Miss Ananda, are you all ladies up there? Or is it some kind of mixed outfit? It's dashed hard for an outsider to tell, what with the bundles of old clothes and the shaved heads.' Ananda glanced at his reddening countenance in some amusement. 'We're all women,' she replied, watching him blush, then took pity on him. 'It's quite unusual, actually. Women are pretty second-class in the Buddhist system – a lot of monks argue that nuns don't count. Just like the Church, really. But the thing about Yamdrok-Tso is that our leader's a female reincarnation of a Bodhisattva.'

'Like the Dalai Lama?' interjected Hatherton, grasping at known facts.

'That's right. Quite a few Tibetan monasteries have "Living Buddhas", but all the others are men. It gives us a lot more status than ordinary nuns. Generally, women just seem to have little communities sort of hanging on to the skirts of monasteries, as far as I can see.'

'Jolly sensible choice, then,' commented the Colonel. 'What put you on to them?'

'Luck. I just wrote to His Holiness at Dharmsala and said I wanted to join a female community, and the fellow who wrote back suggested I get in touch with Yamdrok-Tso. I didn't know very much about it then, and I suppose it sounded the most like what I had in mind because it's the most like a Catholic convent. Not that it is, really.'

Hatherton, meanwhile, had drifted to the side of the road, where he snapped a couple of small branches from one of the rhododendrons that hung low over the revetment of the road.

'Don't know if you care for flowers,' he said, proffering them shyly. 'They're one of the high points at this time of year. Don't get them like this at home, I'll be bound.'

'There's a good few rhododendrons round Dublin,' said Ananda, 'but not at this kind of size.'

'They're by way of *congé*,' explained the Colonel. 'I'd better turn back here, you see. My wind's not what it was. I'm at 15 Jubilee Road, by the way, down by the Lakkar Bazaar. Any time you cared to call, I'd be delighted to see you. And if I can be of any help, you know, don't hesitate a moment. I don't see a lot of people, these days.'

After the Colonel had turned back, Ananda turned off the Tibet road and trudged on up the hill path to Yamdrok-Tso. What had begun as a pleasant walk became, by imperceptible degrees, stonier, rougher and steeper. She tucked Hatherton's flowers into her sash, then was forced to hitch her robe up indecorously through it, while her calves began to burn as though she were climbing an endless flight of stairs, and sweat trickled down her back. Toiling up through the trees, she was momentarily startled by the crashing of a heavy body in the underbrush. She thought of bears (which, she had been told, still roamed in the mountains), and was therefore relieved when some moments later, one of the community's cows, shaggy, wilful beasts who foraged as they pleased in the woods until dusk, heaved herself out of the gully by the side of the path and strolled across the road, udders swinging insouciantly. Shortly after the cow had taken herself off, Ananda caught sight of the *chorten* which guarded the immediate approach to Yamdrok-Tso, and moments later, the complex of monastery buildings loomed above her, enclosed by its wall. Prayer-flags fluttered gaily, stuck in the ground on either side of the gate.

The medieval constructional methods and primitive solidity of the *gompa* made it hard to believe that the complex was less than two years old. It already looked as though it had been there for ever. The monastery dogs, great, chestnut-coloured, mastiff-like beasts with leonine ruffs and white feet, danced and raved at the ends of their chains as she approached, then, catching her scent, flopped back into the shade of the wall, where they panted and grumbled. She stopped at the gate by the prayer-wheel, and gave it a push while she caught her breath, let down her robe, and tried to shake it back into seemliness. The dying flowers fell to the ground, and she pushed them under the drum of the prayer-wheel with her toe.

As she entered, she saw the *am-tse* emerge from the dark, cavernous mouth of the novice's quarters and hesitate on the threshold, looking round the courtyard.

'*Yai*!' she exclaimed, spotting Ananda, who hurried over, fishing for her few words of Tibetan, and sketched a respectful bow.

'Am I late, mistress?'

The novice-mistress looked down at her from her vantage-point on the steps, her expression, as so often, jovial yet bullying, like a big dog which probably won't bite, but might. She smiled, exhibiting a vast array of blackened teeth, though her eyes remained opaque and watchful, and spoke, loudly and exaggeratedly, as if to an idiot. It was a courtesy, to a student whose Tibetan was still rudimentary, but somehow gave the impression of an insult.

'Great Precious . . . want . . . see . . . you. Hokay?'

'Dear God,' said Ananda, reflecting irrelevantly on the ubiquity of the word 'okay' in even the unlikeliest mouths. The *am-tse* continued to stare at her, a broad, powerful figure poised on wide-planted, sturdy legs, formidable. As novice-mistress, she was fully able and entitled to make any student's days a living hell if she so chose. Ananda wished devoutly that she could detect some clue as to how the senior woman felt about this summons to their latest and most unorthodox recruit. After a moment's stillness, the obsidian eyes flickered, and the *am-tse* jerked an unceremonious thumb towards the courtyard.

'*U-cho*, she come.'

Well, thank goodness for that, thought Ananda. The teacher of the novices, Tsering, was the only member of the community to have a fair grasp of English. It was she who had corresponded with Ananda at the outset and stood as her sponsor, she who added to her other duties a Tibetan beginners' class of one, she who was, inevitably, the nearest thing Ananda had to a friend. Slight and wiry, she came chuffing across the sunny courtyard like a little train, and gave the *am-tse* her characteristically jerky bob, before turning to Ananda. Tsering seldom smiled, and approached everything from Tibetan grammar to the problems of the day with humourless intensity, but there was, despite the vehemence, a warmth and friendliness about her wholly lacking in the bigger woman. Ananda saluted her as gracefully as possible, saying '*U-cho*' with becoming reverence. Her teacher's eyes brightened behind her smeary, wire-framed glasses at this symptom of a grasp on civilised behaviour and she nodded encouragingly, while the *am-tse* slipped off about her own affairs on broad, noiseless feet.

Tsering whipped a carefully folded white silk scarf from that universal Tibetan carry-all, the bosom of her robe, and handed it to Ananda.

'When you greet Great Precious,' she warned, 'you give her this *khatak*. Is for respect. Use both hands.'

'Yes,' said Ananda, taking the cloth uncertainly. Her teacher promptly took it back from her, and demonstrated.

'You kneel, okay? Hold it on both hands, like so. When you

lift your head, you hold it out. Don't worry.' She turned, and set off again across the compound.

'Why does the Rinpoche want to see me?' asked Ananda, trailing behind her across the dusty courtyard.

'Great Precious very progressive. She think now she need learn English.'

They had reached the temple itself, and began climbing the steep wooden stairs to the first-floor audience room. With their eyes adjusted to the clear blaze of day in the courtyard, it was a journey into darkness, though the window-shutters were in fact open. Ananda found her heart beating jerkily. She was at last going to meet the central *raison d'être* of the entire community: a Living Bodhisattva in her eighth incarnation. Someone who had known who, and what, she was from her first breath.

As her eyes adjusted to the gloom, Ananda realised with a start that the high throne on the dais at the end of the room was already occupied by a slender figure, so still that in her dark-red robes she was almost invisible in the gloom. She stumbled forwards, clutching her silk scarf, to pay her respects. The Rinpoche Palden Lhamo acknowledged her bow gravely, and, leaning forward a little, presented her with another scarf closely similar to the one she had just been given. Ananda, slightly at a loss, stuffed it into the front of her robe and bowed again. That seemed to be all right, or at any rate, it would do. The Great Precious gestured her to be seated, so she assumed the lotus position. When she dared to look up again, she found herself gazing up at a smallish, painfully thin, round-shouldered girl in her twenties, with an un-Tibetan air of physical fragility. There was a long, angry-looking scar across her cheek and the bridge of her nose. The damage it represented apparently forced her to breathe through her open mouth, displaying bluish, irregular, slightly protruding teeth. Her eyes were large, filmy and too wide-set, like a hare's. She was neither beautiful nor impressive. On the wall behind her cavorted a stupendous, six-foot high representation of her other self, Palden

Lhamo, the Adamantine Whore, one of the avenging goddesses of the Tibetan Buddhist pantheon. She was a snarling, blue-skinned, full-breasted deity, seated on an insubordinate white mule with a mad look in its eye, bejewelled, skull-bedecked, and lifting a skull-cup filled with blood and entrails to her distorted mouth. Beneath this overwhelming image, which seemed to vibrate with energy held in tension, her earthly avatar sat as still as a trapped animal, with no movement but the liquid shifting of her eyes.

The Rinpoche Palden Lhamo stirred finally, and gave Ananda a tired smile, then leaned forward to address Tsering, who replied at some length. Ananda caught very little of the ensuing discussion except for the word '*Ingilisi*', which recurred at intervals, and sat on, her knees beginning to ache, as they always did after a while. She passionately looked forward to the day when her hamstrings would have lengthened enough to make the position a comfortable one, and meanwhile, surreptitiously refolded her legs into a more natural position.

The Rinpoche cleared her throat, and unexpectedly addressed Ananda in halting English.

'Zhou ar-re Ingilisi?'

'Dear God, no,' said Ananda, before she could stop herself.

'You are not English?' echoed Tsering, puzzled. Ananda wanted to fall through the floor. Oh, Jesus, Mary and Joseph, I've done it now, she moaned to herself.

'I'm Irish.'

This was relayed to the Rinpoche, and as she had anticipated, shed no light whatsoever.

'Where is Ireland?' came back, via Tsering.

'It's in the West.'

'Near Amelika?'

'No, near England.'

'So you *are* English,' concluded Tsering, in triumph.

Ananda fought down her temper. The words, 'The same way you're Chinese' hovered on her lips. She looked up at the impassive face of the Rinpoche again, and the anger drained out of her, leaving embarrassment behind. In Tibet, as they were beginning to hear, all religious were being treated with brutal savagery, but the Chinese were reserving special torments for living Buddhas, whose importance they had understood all too clearly. Ananda reconsidered the passive-looking, youthful figure before her. She had escaped, and what is more, she had reformed her community round her, so she had managed to escape with money. And how had she acquired the dreadful scar across her face? It occurred to Ananda suddenly that the eighth incarnation of the Adamantine Whore must have had more adamant in her own right than had seemed initially to be the case.

'The Great Precious need English,' said Tsering. 'She must speak with many, many people, maybe in India, maybe even Amelika.'

It was one of the ironies of history that English had ended up effectively the *lingua franca* of independent India, but the fact was undeniable.

'English very good people' – in the process of selling the Dalai Lama down the river rather than upset Peking, thought Ananda bitterly – 'she very glad you here. It not our way for strangers to see Great Precious. She very, very precious, so she very hidden, like pearl wrapped in silk. You come to us just when we need you.'

To teach a language the English made all of us speak, thought Ananda. It's almost funny.

'When do you want me, Rinpoche?' Ananda asked, through Tsering. The living Bodhisattva replied the same way.

'Come in the afternoon work period. If I have time, there can be a lesson.' The Rinpoche Palden Lhamo settled back on her cushions, and her gaze went blank. The audience appeared to be over.

Left to herself at last, Ananda went thoughtfully through the novices' study-hall, and climbed the stairs to her first-floor room.

It was a small, squarish space with a rough, beamed ceiling and wooden shutters, still standing open to catch the cool, and framing the celestial blue of the evening. There was a low, square work-table at the window end, and three thick, square cushions which, pushed together in a row against the wall, made her bed, or could be dragged about separately to use as chairs. There was also a chest for her quilt, and a small bookshelf. She lit her lamp. The Great Precious, in consultation with the *am-tse* and the bursar, had reluctantly recognised that the new Yamdrok-Tso, unsupported by pilgrims and offerings, could not possibly afford electricity, but the superiority of paraffin over butter-lamps for reading in the evening had not been lost on them. She sighed, adjusted the wick, and opened the book which Tsering had given her to study. It was a massive, archaic-looking affair, with inch-thick, carved wooden boards, block-printed on fibrous, clothlike Tibetan paper. Its name, according to her *u-cho*, was *The Solace of Bees with Young Minds*, or *Summary of the Thirty-Five Ornaments of Truth*. She also had Sir Charles Bell's optimistically titled *Grammar of Colloquial Tibetan* (a relic of the friendly contact between His Majesty's government and Lhasa in the thirties which, as she had found, seemed to have had a considerable effect on Tibetan perceptions of the outer world), and Jaschke's *Dictionary*. With their assistance, she could make out perhaps one word in five.

Ananda gave up, shut the books, and looked out thoughtfully, scratching her ribs through the coarse robes. She had adjusted successfully to many features of life at Yamdrok-Tso, but not to the fleas which had (or so it seemed) declared a festival of their own at the arrival of a new flavour in their little world. She was positive she must have more than her share. Sometimes, particularly at night, it felt as if there were tiny feet moving all over her body.

Far below, the lights of Simla glimmered, yellow and friendly-looking. It was a relief that the Rinpoche seemed to have thought of some useful purpose for her. She had not been in the community for more than a couple of weeks when it became clear to her that finance was one of her seniors' most pressing preoccupations. Any member of the community with the slightest trace of artistic ability spent the afternoon painting *tankas*, mostly of their fearsome patroness, according to ancient and minutely prescribed rules. Ananda had at one point tried to convince the nun in charge of this enterprise, a stout, pockmarked woman inappropriately named Lend-zema ('good and beautiful') that their efforts would probably command a higher price if they used traditional Tibetan earth-pigments rather than the shrieking pinks and sickly chemical greens they bought in the Lakkar bazaar at no little expense, but Lend-zema, intoxicated both with the power and brilliance of Indian gouache, and with the exotic ease with which it came obediently and consistently out of its nice little foil tubes, entirely failed to see the point. So, to her disappointment, did Tsering. Those nuns who were not painters spent all the hours not otherwise committed weaving simple carpets and hangings on huge, archaic looms. But Ananda could not be trusted to paint in an appropriate style, and a loom, with her hand on the shuttle, turned into a torture-rack possessed by independently active demons. While her fellow-nuns earned their *tsampa* and tea, Ananda helped with the chores. Though the work, the hours of meditation, the intensive language study, and the sheer culture-shock left her tired from morning till night, she still felt like a freeloader.

It was not for some weeks that Ananda was able to take the Colonel up on his invitation. Tsering, in addition to redoubling her efforts on Ananda's Tibetan and Sanskrit, took her up to the audience-room for an English lesson every afternoon. Gratifyingly, the two-way process seemed to be speeding up her own language-learning, though she felt, increasingly, that she was little or no use as a teacher. Both Tsering and the Rinpoche were formidably learned, and had a highly educated apprehension of the structure of language which she could in no way meet, and it depressed her how often she had to return 'I don't know' to obviously sensible questions. When, one Thursday morning, Tsering announced after their own lesson that the Rinpoche was withdrawing from them for a period of private prayer and meditation. Ananda felt guiltily relieved. After the end of the morning's teaching, she walked out of the compound and headed down the hill, with an agreeable sensation of playing hookey. As she walked, the release from constant pressure allowed her, for the first time in weeks, to gauge the depth of her exhaustion.

Once she had reached town, she began searching for Jubilee Road, which was rather harder to locate than Hatherton had led her to believe, mainly on account of Simla's sudden changes of level, which cause streets to peter out unexpectedly into rubbish-choked gullies. The Christ Church clock had already chimed twelve by the time she turned the corner into the road itself, which turned out to consist of a row of pleasant, trim, whitewashed bungalows, dating perhaps to the nineteen-twenties, and set in reasonably substantial gardens. At the far end of the lawns, the ground fell steeply away, so that the sharp-pitched roofs of the Lakkar Bazaar seemed to rise like tents beyond it. The area round number 15 was laid to grass, with a few shade trees at a discreet distance from the house. She went up the carefully raked gravel path, and rang the bell.

Hatherton was patently delighted to see her. His red face glowed even redder, and he waved her in with some ceremony.

'My dear young lady! Come away in. We're in the sitting-room, at the back.'

She followed him through a nondescript hall adorned with bad watercolours and a few improbably shaped native weapons, into a pleasant, medium-sized room looking out over the lawn, furnished with a suite of low chairs in white-painted rattan. There was a woman in the chair opposite Hatherton's own, a washed-out-looking, elderly gentlewoman with finger-waves in her grey hair, wearing a lilac print frock and white buckskin shoes. She arched painted eyebrows as Ananda entered, and looked as though she was in two minds about extending her hand.

'Miss Ananda, midear. Allow me to present you to Mrs Babbage. Alice darling, Miss Ananda O'Grady.'

The temperature in the room dropped to freezing-point. Mrs Babbage's faded, bluish eyes looked her up and down, and the pinched nostrils flared forbiddingly. Her thin lips primmed in a hostile little smile. 'How very unusual.'

Ananda, grey eyes kindling, pressed her fingertips together, and made *namaste*, replying (with elaborate, false humility) in Tibetan. 'I'm damned if I'll give the old bitch the satisfaction of hearing my accent,' she thought, furiously, eyelids virtuously lowered.

Hatherton looked from one hostile countenance to the other, and interposed manfully to retrieve the situation.

'Miss Ananda's a new recruit for the lama-esses up the hill,' he explained, unnecessarily.

'So I had imagined,' replied Mrs Babbage with sweet self-restraint.

'Harrumph. Now, ladies. A spot of something before lunch? My wretched boxes turned up at last, you know, and there's some decentish Amontillado.'

'No, Colonel. I won't stay.' Mrs Babbage rose to her feet, and picked up her gloves and sun-hat. 'I'll leave you with your new little friend. Goodbye, Miss O'Grady.' Hatherton ushered her out, then returned, voluble with apologies.

'Sorry, midear. The old acid drop hasn't had a pleasant word to bless herself with since her man died – which, between you and me, she drove him to. I've half a notion she's been setting her cap at me since then – ghoulish thought, ain't it? Sherry? My dear, what's wrong?'

'No one's *ever* to use that name to me,' growled Ananda, between clenched teeth.

'What name?' said Hatherton, completely at sea.

'O'Grady, you blind, bloody fool. I thought I'd got shot of it at last.'

Ananda dropped into a chair, and burst into tears of rage, frustration, and sheer tiredness. The colonel's consternation was total. He patted her shoulder awkwardly, and began puffing to and fro between the sitting-room and his private quarters, bringing her, successively, a clean white handkerchief, a glass of sherry, a bottle of aspirin and some eau-de-cologne.

'Oh, my dear,' he said blankly, as she sobbed herself to a standstill and blew her nose damply on the hanky. 'I *have* put my foot in it, have I not?' He looked so indescribably contrite that Ananda, despite her justifiable ire, gave him a watery smile.

'I'm not wanting any of that,' she explained. 'We don't use surnames. Ananda's what I've chosen, and that's what I'll be.'

'I see. I'm sorry to have presumed on information from your postcard, which I shouldn't perhaps have seen. It's difficult for an old buffer like me, you know: we were brought up to do things a certain way, and old habits die hard. Is there anything I *can* call you?'

Ananda considered. '*Rapjung*, maybe. Roughly the same as "novice". They don't use it as a title, but I don't see why you shouldn't if it makes you happier.'

'*Rapjung* Ananda. That should do quite nicely. If I see the lady canine in question, I will endeavour to make this clear to her. You haven't touched your sherry. Would you rather have orange squash? Or tea, perhaps?'

'We're not allowed to drink alcohol. Tea would be lovely.'

'How silly of me. I'll just go and put the kettle on.'

After a couple of minutes' polite immobility, Ananda got up and tracked a distant sound of clattering and banging to the kitchen. This turned out to be a tidy but antiquated establishment with an ancient, blackleaded range, refreshingly clean after the monastery. The kettle sat on the hob, the beginnings of a wisp of steam rising from its spout, and the colonel, magenta with effort, was on his knees in the middle of the floor trying to get the top off a tea-chest with a hammer and a cold-chisel.

'Can I help?'

'Oh, my dear. You shouldn't have troubled. Just let me shift . . . this . . . *wretched* thing . . .' The last nail gave way with a screech of tortured wood, and Hatherton fell backwards, still clutching his hammer. 'Damnation!' He picked himself up again, puffing, and began rummaging in the case which, Ananda observed, was stencilled with the name of Fortnum & Mason, scattering wood-wool prodigally over the floor. 'If I hand you things, could you just put them on the kitchen table for the time being? Tongue . . . no . . . tinned pears . . . no . . . patum peperium . . . no . . . aha! Gotcha.' Triumphantly, still kneeling on the floor, he handed Ananda a tin of Bath Olivers, a tin labelled Best Devon Butter, and, using both hands, an entire Stilton, wrapped like a mummy in miry bandages. The kettle whistled, as if in acclamation, as it appeared. 'Excellent,' he panted, scrambling to his feet, and taking a battered but well-polished silver pot over to the stove. 'That's lunch dealt with. I rather thought the cheese was in that one.'

Hatherton proceeded to make tea using – Ananda observed – tea from a Fortnum & Mason caddy, and carefully diluting evaporated milk from a Fortnum & Mason tin for the silver jug that went with the pot. Putting pot and cups on an old Sheffield plate tray with a plate of petticoat tails out of a tin, he led the way back to the sitting-room. With pleasure, she watched the clear brown liquid running into her cup, gradually clouding as it hit the pool of milk in the bottom. After months of thick Tibetan tea with butter, it tasted like nectar. She gave herself up to appreciation.

'D'you get everything sent?' she asked after a while.

'I do. Saves trouble in the long run.' She received this statement in dubious silence, and after a few moments, he explained further. 'If you start buying stuff, don't you know, they never leave you alone. Give one poor devil your custom, and all the others come screaming round you with apricots and eggs and God knows what. You never know what you're getting, either. Now, the thing with stuff from home is, you know it's all right, and you *do* know what you're getting. I've dealt with Fortnum's since I was a subaltern, and they haven't let me down yet. Well, there's been the odd packing-case dropped in the river and rust in the sardines and short commons, but you can't blame Fortnum's for that.'

'It's a strange thing, now,' observed Ananda, 'to fetch a pound of tea from India to London, and fetch it all the way back again.'

'Oh, well,' said Hatherton vaguely, and let it ride. They sat in companionable silence for a little, watching the jays quarrelling on the lawn.

'How are you getting on, up the way?' he enquired at last.

'Oh, fine. Actually,' she added, struck by a sudden bright idea, 'there's just one thing I meant to ask you about. They've asked me to give English lessons to the Rinpoche Palden Lhamo – that's sort of our Mother Superior, or maybe it's best to think of her as a living saint.'

'Good for you.'

'Well, and it would be,' said Ananda frankly, 'if I weren't making a pig's ear of it.'

'I'm sure you're doing very well.'

'And I'm sure I'm not. They're demons for analysis, and I didn't even do Latin at school. You can't think of anything which might help? Did you have to teach people English when they joined the army?'

Hatherton stroked his chin pensively, and brooded. 'No,' he said finally. 'Not my world, I'm afraid. Hang on a minute, though, I know someone who might help. Excuse me one moment.' Heaving himself to his feet, he lumbered over to the telephone, which was quarantined in an alcove, on a little table by itself. 'Hello? Hello? Alured? James here. Are you at home this afternoon? Excellent. And Etheldreda? That's absolutely splendid. If I were to call after luncheon with a young friend, would you have a moment? See you later.' He replaced the receiver, and turned to Ananda, eyes twinkling with suppressed triumph. 'And now my dear, once we have discussed our nice Stilton, prepare to meet as queer a pair of coots as you'd find in a month of Sundays.'

After lunch, they set off together into Simla. The Colonel led her back to the Mall, and then headed off in the general direction of Annandale, and turned up a street of large, three-storey houses.

'Pukka houses you get along here,' observed the Colonel, gesticulating with his little malacca cane. 'Quite a bit older – as you can see for yourself, I've no doubt. These were built for pukka sahibs, the real government-wallahs, ICS types. Most of the building material was shipped from Europe, in the days when ships still carried ballast.'

They turned in at a rusting, wrought-iron gate which bore the name Waverley Lodge. The house had once been white stucco, but was flaking and peeling to such an extent that it could no longer be said to be any colour in particular, and the ground floor was made gloomy by a badly overgrown shrubbery, which Hatherton surveyed with a critical eye. 'Bad practice to let stuff grow up so near the house,' he muttered. 'Encourages vermin, and puts temptation in people's way. Far too much cover.' They came up to the peeling front door, and Hatherton rang the bell firmly.

The door was opened by a tall, elderly Hindu, dressed in spotless white, with his long grey beard divided in the middle, twisted round itself along his jawline, and looped back tidily behind his ears.

'Ah, Moti Lal. Keepin' well? Master and Missy Dark upstairs?'

'Yes, sahib,' replied the servant with grave courtesy, standing back to let them enter. 'They are in the study.'

'We'll announce ourselves, Moti. Don't trouble yourself about us.' Ananda followed the Colonel up the uncarpeted stairs as the Indian disappeared soundlessly into the back quarters of the house. 'He used to be Dark's *syce* in the old days,' whispered the Colonel breathily as they toiled upwards, 'but now I think he does just about all that gets done in the house.' He led the way across the landing, and knocked on the door of what appeared to be a first-floor drawing-room. A fluting, elderly voice called, 'Enter.'

It had been a fine room, once. The proportions, with the two tall french windows opening on to a veranda, were those of a London town-house, and the walls had once been hung with a fine Regency striped paper. But that had been long ago. The only other relic of past grandeur was a large painting over the fireplace: two blonde children, in starched white frills, posed with a native servant and a leashed cheetah. Their expression was friendly, candid and enquiring, and the little girl held a branch of frangipani. Now the room was lined with bookshelves, which rose nearly to ceiling-height, and behind them the remains of the once-lovely paper hung in strips. More books, bristling with tabs of yellowing paper, lay in dusty heaps on the floor. The room was dominated by what had once been the great mahogany dining-table of an era of heroic eaters, now piled from end to end with heaps of spidery copperplate manuscript, gradually turning as brittle as dried leaves. A lectern was set by one of the french windows, to catch the best of the light, and at it stood a tall and bulky figure, in silhouette, his fluffy white hair standing out like thistledown and forming a silver halo round the big head.

'James, my dear fellow.' The voice was high-pitched, Oxonian and pedantic, but markedly friendly. 'Long time no see.' He left the lectern, closing his book on yet another marker, and led the way to a pale blue brocade Victorian drawing-room suite grouped round the fireplace, the seats of which were sagging nearly to ground-level through their prolapsed webbing. One, as Ananda observed, was actually built up from below with a pile of folio volumes, and looked exquisitely uncomfortable. This, it seemed, was Dark's own chair. Taking his position in front of it, he gestured his guests towards the sofa. 'Who is your charming young friend?' he enquired.

'Ah. Alured, the *Rapjung* Ananda. Ananda, Mr Alured Dark.'

'Delighted,' murmured the old man politely. Ananda's fingers were taken and briefly engulfed in an enormous, clammy hand. 'Allow me to present you to my sister.'

'Etheldreda, my dear,' exclaimed Hatherton, startled. 'I didn't see you there.'

Lost in the depths of the wing-chair on the other side of the fireplace was an elderly lady, as thin as her brother was gross, hands folded in her lap, her expression so similar to that of her baby portrait that her stiff white curls and withered skin looked somehow like fancy dress. 'How nice to see somebody young,' she observed.

Hatherton took charge of the conversation.

'Miss Ananda, as you'll have realised from her costume, no doubt, has joined the ladies up the hill.'

Both Darks nodded gravely.

'You are affiliated with the Gelukpa sect, I believe?' offered their host, politely. Ananda nodded. 'A most interesting development. The establishment of an autonomous female community –'

'She's in a bit of a quandary,' continued the Colonel, interrupting firmly as if his host's penchant for abstractions was a known phenomenon requiring the application of stern measures, 'and thought you might be able to help.'

'We will certainly be happy to try,' said Miss Etheldreda, smiling at Ananda.

'The problem is, as I understand it, that the ladies have asked Miss Ananda to teach their head lama-ess English. Now, I find this hard to believe, personally, but she tells me she's struggling a bit. They're a very brainy lot up there, and she needs some bigger guns. So, when she told me her troubles, I got my thinking-cap on, and asked myself, now who do I know who's absolutely bulging with info about languages and things? – well, you can guess the rest. I tucked her under my arm, and shot her straight along to you.'

Alured Dark's eye kindled, and he sat straighter in his chair. 'It's a question of structures, I take it? Grammar.'

'Yes,' replied Ananda.

'Well,' rejoined Mr Dark, striking the palms of his big, soft hands together slowly and relishingly, 'I think we can help you there.'

Ananda, in her *naïveté*, had thought when she entered that the room was untidy. Twenty minutes later, it was indescribable. Hatherton had retreated actually within the fender, as the only space in the room where a book was unlikely to fall on him. Dust swirled thickly in the air as both Darks panted to and fro, building a new tower of Babel for Ananda's special use. Sanskrit grammars, Tibetan grammars, *Chips from a German Workshop*, comparative philology of all kinds, books of great age and obvious value were triumphantly unearthed, each new find accompanied by a self-deprecating narrative of triumphant acquisition – 'picked this up in Calcutta for five rupees. Not bad, eh?' – and both her kindly hosts began to look as if they had spent the afternoon coal-heaving.

'You're from Dublin, are you not?' enquired Alured. 'Thought I recognised the accent,' he continued, with innocent satisfaction. 'The pater knew Whitley Stokes, you know, when he was out here codifying Sanskrit law for H.M.G. *For*-midable scholar, formidable man. Pa dined out on Whitley Stokes stories for many a long year. You don't have Irish yourself, do you?'

'Just a bit of the Government Irish,' said Ananda, deprecatingly.

'Well, there you go then,' said Alured Dark, amazed that there should be any further problem. 'Irish is very like Sanskrit. Quite different branch of the family of course, but nearly as archaic. I have Myles Dillon's paper on similarities between Irish and Hindu traditions here somewhere . . . Ethel, my dear, have you seen it?'

'I've just found Dr Binchy on sitting *dharna*,' replied his sister, standing on a hard chair to search a high bookshelf with her stockings coming down round her thin ankles, 'so it ought to be here somewhere. Here we are.'

'There is a great deal of correspondence at the linguistic level, also,' pursued Alured implacably. 'Compare, for example, Sanskrit *raja*, Old Irish *rí* . . .'

Ananda cast a look of appeal at Colonel Hatherton, standing in the fireplace with his hands clasped behind him. Poker-faced, he gave her a solemn wink.

'The poor girl hasn't got a pantechnicon with her,' he observed. 'Can you not find her some sort of general grammar-book and leave it at that?'

Alured looked hurt. 'It's a highly technical subject,' he protested.

'*Please* don't go to so much trouble,' said Ananda imploringly. 'Unless it's very simple, I won't understand a word.'

Alured Dark rubbed his lower lip thoughtfully. 'I'll tell you what. Take Max Müller – he at least sets out the basic principles of comparative philology – and perhaps Skeat. Between them, they should give you some inkling of Indo-European grammatical structures.'

'I'm so sorry to have put you to so much trouble,' she said, as he laboriously released the books he had just mentioned from the mountain of miscellaneous learning on the floor.

'Don't mention it. Always happy to be of service to a fellow student.'

'Apart from the Colonel, it was the Darks that I got to know best,' concluded Ananda. 'They were very kind-hearted, and quite incredibly learned. Neither of them had ever had a job. Their father had been something on the Viceroy's legal staff, I think, and a bit of a philologist on the side, hence the names. He sent Alured to Oxford in about nineteen-ten, I suppose, but it must have been obvious he wasn't cut out for a career. When the parents died, they just carried on in the old house, living on less and less by the year, as happy as sandboys. They went on trying to educate me for the next three years, bless their old souls, till I had to go.'

'I was never very clear why you left,' I commented, pouncing on this cue.

Ananda laughed gently. 'The usual reason. Money. I don't know if I've been quite clear what a financial shoestring the whole place was on? It's not what anyone wanted to think about, of course, but you do have to think about economics a bit or the whole thing collapses.'

I called to mind the only convent I had known, the Sacred Heart at Kilgraston, where the nuns, to my cynical schoolgirl eye, had seemed to have had an excellent grasp of the cruder worldly realities, for all their Sunday homilies about starving Africans. But they were a teaching order: Catholic parents of the professional classes paid through the nose so the likes of me would came out with three 'A' levels, good deportment, lovely manners and Grade Eight piano. None of the above, presumably, applied to Yamdrok-Tso.

'What was the financial basis, actually?'

'That's part of the trouble. The original Yamdrok-Tso was a very special place. It was on the shores of a sacred lake a couple of hundred miles south-east of Lhasa, where you could see visions of the future. It's sacred to Lhamo, the bodhisattva. Actually, she's a goddess really. A group of senior lamas always come up from Lhasa when they're looking for a new Dalai Lama, and seek a vision in the water, and of course, ordinary folk consult it for their own problems. There's a very well authenticated story that the search committee saw three letters, Ah, Ka, Ma, a monastery with a green and gold roof, and a house with turquoise tiles, when they were looking for the current Dalai Lama in the thirties, and all three visions turned out to be absolutely right.'

'Your Rinpoche's the incarnation of the goddess Lhamo, isn't she?'

'Yes. And it's the only monastery on the lake. I'm sure you can see what that means. What with questioners, and pilgrims, and visiting bigwigs and one thing and another, they'd done very well over the centuries. And of course, there was a fair bit of land, so even though it was a big place, they were pretty well self-sufficient in barley and dairy-stuff. They'd just been able to get on with being holy for ever such a long time.'

'Then you went to India.'

'Then we went to India,' agreed Ananda. 'The senior nuns hadn't ever had to think about money, and they really didn't have much of a notion of how to manage. All their specialness was tied up with being in that particular place, you see? Somehow, I think, they must have got some portable wealth out with them, gold maybe, or jade; I can't think how they'd have got started otherwise. The Indian government was very generous, and labour and wood are cheap up there, but even so, it all had to be paid for. It was only a skeleton community, of course. Thirty or forty nuns and lay-sisters, and a handful of novices. There'd have been hundreds of all sorts at the first Yamdrok-Tso.'

'It's amazing they got out at all,' I remarked, trying to get my mind round this combination of the practical with the other-worldly. 'Do you think someone saw something in the lake?'

'I wouldn't be surprised,' said Ananda, quite seriously. 'And you have to remember that the Eighth Palden Lhamo was really a very exceptional person. She was highly intelligent, and where they were, with important people coming to and fro, she'd have been well placed to pick up news and rumours. I never asked, you know, but it must have been her who led them out into exile. No one else would have had the nerve.'

'What do you think happened to the people who got left behind?'

'What happened to any religious, in Tibet?' countered Ananda, sadly. 'No one knows. The Chinese are still keeping very quiet about those years, but some terrible stories came out over the mountains. Most of them must be dead, and I'm sure Yamdrok-

Tso isn't a monastery any more, even if the buildings are still standing.'

'Didn't the core community have terrible problems with guilt?' I asked.

'I don't know,' said Ananda thoughtfully. 'Buddhists handle all that sort of thing better than most. We spend a lot of time thinking about pain. The whole idea of the Buddha and the bodhisattvas is that they turned back from their own happiness to help with the troubles of the world, you know. But on another level, everyone has their own karma. You can't know whether, if people you knew were killed by the Chinese, there isn't some kind of benefit in it, in the very long term. There must have been an element of "why me?" for most of them – they wouldn't have been human otherwise – but they'd have had ways of dealing with it.

'Anyway. It was the money problem I was telling you about. Everyone did what they could, but they could only get about tuppence-ha'penny for their *tankas* and things – they were mostly wanted by other Tibetans, who didn't have any money either. I think the bursar was getting near her wits' end by '64. We couldn't even be self-sufficient, because we had hardly any land, just enough to graze some cattle.

'It was Alured who came up with a good idea, after I'd been telling him about our troubles. He got in touch with the Edinburgh University librarian – they'd acquired masses and masses of Oriental books some time in the fifties, when they'd hoped to set up a really ambitious Oriental studies faculty, and he'd been corresponding with the man, who was an old friend from Oxford days. Anyway, he suggested that they give me a job, and talked me up like nobody's business, bless him, though I'd only had about three years of training by then. The Rinpoche leapt at it, of course. I keep what I need to live on, and the rest goes straight to the community. It gives them some hardish currency coming in regularly – not exactly a fortune, but you'd be surprised how far it goes, up there. And I'm entitled to sabbaticals, I'm glad to say, so every six years I join them again for a few months, and when I retire, I can go back full-time.'

'It must be very sad for you, though. Surely you didn't want to leave?'

'No. It's much nicer at home. But I go on working on my own, you know. And I don't just catalogue the stuff at the library. As long as I work the hours of my contract, I'm allowed to read it as well. My teacher's very helpful. She's not a great letter-writer, but even if it's just a few words, she always manages to put me on the right track. It's been slower, working on my own, but I've had the equivalent of a doctorate for quite a while now.' Ananda swung her legs under her, and prepared to get up. 'Goodness, it's got quite dark. I'll see you in the library.'

In the days that followed, we did not meet. Term was approaching, and my own work was, for once, going quite well. I was supposed to be putting together a paper for a graduate seminar, but Ananda and her stories were not far from my mind. Even in the insulated world of the university, the rumblings of greater events were to be felt. Labour had gone down fighting; and what would the landscape look like now it was laid to rest?

'Tacitus,' I typed, 'is underestimated as a comic writer.' I paused for thought, marshalling my evidence. I'd have to use unsinkable Agrippina, bobbing up triumphantly like a plastic duck when her mad son tried to drown her. Then there was the whole business of the Emperor and the Senate; Tacitus's monstrously comic portrait of gauche, gloomy Tiberius, a hypocrite with two left feet, and a whole Senate full of alleged Fathers of the Country, falling over themselves to sign away their power. It's funny. He's got to have meant it to be funny. Everything about the style, his deadpan, disturbing wit, is potentially comic. 'If his writing were not so difficult to translate,' (I typed on, beginning to translate this vague thought into the language of the academy) 'we would now find it easier to see that he is rightly classed with satirists such as Juvenal rather than with the historians.'

What can one do with a dictator? I was wondering. The Romans, as Tacitus so immortally demonstrates, pandered to their lightest whims, surrounded them with obsequious placemen and positively encouraged them to lose all contact with reality. And what was their reward? – A series of raving lunatics, Caligula, Claudius, Nero. Tibet-conscious as I had become at that time, because of Ananda, I could see that the same was all too clearly true of Mao-Tse-Tung's China: Mao had loomed over China in the fifties and sixties like a swollen god. When was the last time anyone dared to contradict him, I wondered. Do you have to be a raving loony to become a dictator in the first place, or do they go mad from lack of opposition? Thoughts along these lines inevitably took me in the direction of Mrs Thatcher, who seemed, in those days, to be making up policy unilaterally as she went along, her Cabinet cowering abjectly at her feet while she laid about her with her handbag. And that, whatever I might have been thinking about similar events two thousand years ago, or three thousand miles away, didn't seem funny at all.

I got up, and ranged round the room, coming to rest in front of the window where I could look out over India Street. I couldn't use any of that last bit, people would just think I was trying to be clever. A chilling thought struck me: how do you tell when you start living in a dictatorship? When Augustus seized power, he spoke endlessly of 'restoration', of repairing a lost balance, getting back to basics. When did the Romans realise that, actually, everything had changed? When did the Chinese, who had wanted and been promised a revolution, understand that they were more or less back where they'd started, but with a new set of oppressors? I very much wanted to talk to Ananda, and I very much wanted not to put any of this in my paper, though I was beginning to despair of keeping it out. With some relief, I heard my aunt (with whom I was living at that time) moving around in the kitchen, so I abandoned my work and went down to talk to her instead.

A suitably dull and correct forty minutes on Tacitean humour had been written, delivered and received with polite lack of interest before I met Ananda again. Ananda had not, of course, attended the paper, since I had been too bashful to tell her I was giving it (I think I hoped she would somehow divine it, or come across a poster somewhere about the university). It was a week or so after the graduate seminar had come and gone that I found myself in the grip of an emotion so powerful and uncharacteristic that instead of hanging about abjectly in the manuscripts room hoping that Ananda might appear, I actually went up, for the first time in our acquaintance, to the minute broom-cupboard on the top floor of the library labelled 'Edinburgh University Oriental Languages Project', and knocked on the door. Hearing Ananda's voice answer from within, I opened it and found her in front of a computer screen, surrounded from floor to ceiling with stout brown cardboard box-files neatly labelled in a variety of languages.

'Oh, hello,' said Ananda, 'I was just thinking of going down to the tea-room. Would you like to come?'

'You wouldn't like to come out for a walk, would you?' I asked, cunningly realising that I was virtually certain to end up raising my voice. 'It'd be nice to get a bit of air.'

Once we were out of the library, it was easy to steer Ananda where I wanted her to go. 'Have you seen the papers?' I asked, gesturing at the headlines on a news-stand, which we just happened to be passing. The *Scotsman*'s banner read, 'Rifkind unveils plans for new tax.'

'I don't usually get one,' confessed Ananda. 'I find it rather expensive, and it takes up so much time.'

'I don't, but my aunt does. I saw the *Scotsman* this morning. That greasy toad Rifkind's announced that they're going to be piloting a new tax system here in Scotland. D'you know, it was

Malcolm Rifkind that drove the final wedge between me and my father?'

'How was that?'

'Dad agreed to paint his portrait. He's been doing horribly competent bravura daubs of oil-barons and provosts and industrialists for decades – and getting bloody well paid for it, as he likes to remind me – but agreeing to do the Secretary of State for Scotland was the last straw.' Ananda looked a little sad, but held her tongue. It was restful: one great thing about her was that you were certain to be spared homilies on family togetherness.

'What's the new tax?' she asked, carefully moving the conversation on to more impersonal territory.

'Oh, it's outrageous. They're proposing to dismantle the rates and raise local government revenue with a poll-tax. It's absolutely criminal lunacy. There's nothing more regressive than a poll-tax. It was poll-tax that brought down the Roman Empire.'

'Really?'

'That and other things. But the *capitum* was crucial. Why hasn't anyone told them?'

'People never do.'

'That's what I wanted to talk to you about, Ananda. Do you think anyone could have stopped Mao doing what he did?'

'Tibet, you mean? I'd doubt it. As far as we can see, he'd created a situation where his inner circle could do nothing but agree with him. Think what happened to Liu Shao-Chi.'

'Who? Oh, never mind. What I wanted to ask you is, knowing what you know, and seeing what you've seen, could anyone stop Mrs Thatcher?'

Ananda shot an unexpectedly stern, teacherly glance at me. 'This is a democracy, Kirsty. It's not the same thing at all.' Her tone was superficially mild, but I experienced a moment of profound awareness that I was talking like an idiot, which I ignored. I knew perfectly well, intellectually, that there is a difference between experimenting with taxation and sending the tanks in, but even so, trainee academic that I was, I was too much in the grip of my own rhetoric to dismantle the well-turned sentences which I had been rehearsing since breakfast time.

'Oh, yes? Do you know how many seats the Tories got north of the border in '83? They got hammered. The Tories have not the vestige of a trace of a mandate left in Scotland. And do you know how long it's been since they've dared to let a Scottish regiment have a tour at home? They're all patrolling up and down the bloody Rhine like bloody Roman soldiers. This isn't a democracy, Ananda, it's a fucking elective dictatorship. Okay, we might get Thatcher out at the next election, but what happens *till then*? Who's even raised a voice of opposition, except Scargill, and look what happened to him? The papers ended up making him out as some kind of mad socialist werewolf.'

'I didn't know you felt that strongly about Scotland, Kirsty,' observed Ananda, a little surprised.

'I didn't,' I protested. 'I went to Cambridge, and I thought I was a citizen of the world, as they say. I don't even *sound* Scottish, except to the trained ear. It's taken Mrs Thatcher and bloody Malcolm Rifkind to get me talking like this. Do you know what they're doing?' I was, I realised, beginning to enjoy myself, a fatal problem for the analysis- and rhetoric-prone.

'I think you'd better tell me,' said Ananda patiently, tucking her hands into the opposite sleeves of her robe as we turned at the far end of the Meadows.

'They're trying this tax out on Scotland first, before they do it in England. And what that means is that they're just about to break the terms of the Act of Union, and they don't seem to think it matters.'

'Does it?'

'Of course it does. The Act of Union is the only legal entitlement which the English have to political authority north of the border. It's a masterpiece of early eighteenth-century legislation, and it's got fail-safes built in. The relevant one is that if any tax is imposed in Scotland which isn't imposed in England, the treaty is automatically voided. Do you see? They're just about to break it in cold blood, and when they do, I think we should be trying to take the whole thing to the International Court in The Hague.'

'Kirsty,' said Ananda gently, 'it's only law. The English are a pragmatic lot, as you very well know. They aren't going to be looking that far back.'

'Law is law. It doesn't come with a sell-by date. I suppose I'm making a twit of myself. Power is above the law, which I ought to know from Tacitus, and if I didn't, I'd have learned it talking to you. But isn't it interesting? You grow up in a democracy, with constitutional rights, and say you're not a political animal, and don't vote, and the minute you find that your rights are being taken away, suddenly you want them after all. I've spent most of my twenties so far worrying about nothing worse than being the daughter of a portrait-painter to the rising scum, and I've suddenly been reminded that if you leave my old man out of it, I'm the descendant of hordes of bloody-minded legalists. Do you know, I've nearly found myself uttering the dread words, "it's a point of principle"?'

Ananda laughed, and looked at her watch, a little pointedly, shooting back her cuff to do so. 'I'd better get back to the library now. It's been nice to get out for a bit, but I've got to get on with my catalogue.'

After this sudden eruption of white-hot nationalist sentiment, my emotional universe gradually cooled to its normal temperature. Worrying about the state of the nation takes time and energy, especially when I was already committed to full-time worrying about the state of my thesis (which, in broad theory, I was supposed to be able to do something about), and additionally haunted by a lot of things which I could do nothing about at all: the basic state of being a Kirsty, the imminent bankruptcy of the University of Edinburgh, and the total absence of academic jobs in the arts being advertised anywhere in the country, or perhaps, the world. Even the Americans – and in earlier years, people in my then position had repeated like a mantra the soothing words 'there's always America' – seemed to think they had imported enough Brits to be going on with. There's nothing quite like the sensation that you're spending whole years of your life to prepare for a future that doesn't exist to generate passive despair. Should I (I often wondered, usually about halfway down the bottle) think about becoming a Buddhist nun? It seemed to solve a lot of problems, and would have the additional benefit of annoying my father.

The next time I saw Ananda was entirely by accident. She was standing on George IV Bridge, looking strange and exotic as people often do when you see them out of their usual context, and also, as I realised, coming up to her, looking almost upset. It was nothing very specific; no creased brows or bitten lips, more the temporary absence of the generalised, forty-watt cheerfulness which she seemed to radiate in the ordinary course of events. It made her seem suddenly older.

'What's wrong, Ananda?' I asked gently. Ananda did not reply immediately, but led the way across the road to the stone bench under the statue of Wellington, where she sat down, making room for me beside her, and stared at the traffic.

'It's the collection. Do you know, I was counting back in my mind, and I've been cataloguing and analysing and sorting those books for more than twenty years, even counting sabbaticals?'

'You haven't finished, have you?' I asked, horrified.

'Oh, by no means,' said Ananda, amazed at the idea. 'It's terribly complex. There should have been a team of us, really, with different linguistic specialities, and there's only been me. But I've got whole sections of it really nicely under control now. There's some unique stuff in the collection – I've never really tried to tell you about it, because I know it all sounds much the same until you know quite a lot – but there's quite a few things

I've found which we seem to have the only copy of in the whole of the Western world. Actually, with the Chinese and everything, maybe the only copies that survive at all, anywhere. The librarian told me this morning that they're going to start selling it off.'

'Oh, Ananda, I am sorry.' I could well appreciate the enormity of this tragedy from Ananda's viewpoint. The full bibliographic history of each separate book, in some cases, the result of weeks of painstaking research, would of course go with it, and would in that sense never be lost. But the *Catalogue*, the monstrous summary of all this effort piled up in its cardboard box-files, would never exist now. As Ananda added to one end of it, the University would be taking stuff away again from the other. A frustrating, joyless state of affairs. At the same time, I reflected that only someone as unworldly as Ananda wouldn't have seen this one coming.

'They're selling everything that isn't actually nailed down,' I pointed out. 'Pictures, real estate, bits of the library, you name it. The Secretary of State for Education is threatening to make an example of us for gross financial incompetence. We're actually bankrupt, if you read between the lines. I think the government would have closed us down if they hadn't been afraid of the political consequences. It's one point where being Scottish has actually done us some good. If we'd been Reading or Durham or somewhere we'd all be out on the street by now.'

Ananda looked completely bewildered. Clearly, as she flitted in and out of the library beaming with ecumenical goodwill, no one had ever told her anything.

'I suppose it's very stupid of me,' she said sadly, 'but I've always thought of a university as a kind of monastery. It made things easier, you know, when I first left Yamdrok-Tso. It's made me blind to a lot of things, I think.'

I sighed. 'Universities certainly used to *sound* more like monasteries than public limited companies. What I gather from the idle professorial sodomites who got us into this mess is that there used to be this great rhetoric of the disinterested pursuit of learning. I suppose that's what you're talking about. As far as I can see, they used to make elaborate public statements about it any time a taxpayer had the nerve to ask what they were doing for their money, and then went out and played golf. All this bottom-line-at-the-end-of-the-day stuff they're spouting now is new since the Blue Reich got under way, but I have to say, it's the senior academics who've brought it on us. Now I suppose we'll suffer for the sins of the fathers, as usual. They're not actually axing your job, are they?'

'No,' said Ananda, 'I don't think they can. My salary's paid by some kind of a trust, I believe. I don't think it's money they could put to any other use.'

'Just watch them,' I warned. 'They call it "virement", these days. Actually, Ananda, you're quite safe as long as you're still cataloguing. I mean, how can they ship the stuff off to Christie's Oriental until you've given them the information to assess its worth?'

Ananda looked genuinely stricken, and I was sorry. The trouble with studying Tacitus is that after a while, bleak, black humour and wounding irony start to seem like the only viable responses in a crisis. 'Me and my big mouth,' I said, as lightly as possible. Ananda did not answer and an awkward silence lengthened between us as we sat side by side. After a while, I got up and slunk away. Ananda vulnerable, upset, was, I realised with self-loathing, not something I wanted to deal with at all. I re-crossed the road, with due care and attention, and looked back unwillingly from the other side: the upright little figure sat on, staring unseeing in front of her.

In the days which followed, Ananda was temporarily driven out of my mind by my mother. Although I was not on speaks with my father, diplomatic relations were warily maintained among the women of the family. My mother and her sister were close, and a couple of times a year Mummy engaged in mighty feats of baking and shopping (lest Dad, poor fragile flower that he was, might have to think for two seconds about his own maintenance) and came up to spend a few days in India Street with her sister and daughter. She generally timed one such visit to coincide with something she wanted to catch at the Festival, which we, as full-time Edinburgh residents, assiduously ignored: a characteristic form of local snobbery. My mother, Lilias, was and is a tough-minded, humorous woman, not without talent, and when she was not entirely occupied in pandering to my father and his monstrous, tumid self-importance, we got along very well.

Like most students, I came down rather late in the mornings, and generally expected to find Mummy and Fiona gone about their business. When I slopped down in my dressing-gown one such morning, a day or two into Mummy's visit, and pushed open the kitchen door, I was surprised to see them both still sitting at the table, with faces of thunder.

'Good morning, darling,' said my mother automatically. So it wasn't anything I'd done, then. I went to put the kettle on.

'What's up?' I asked, switching it on, my back to them.

'Look at this,' said Fiona grimly. She unfolded the *Scotsman* with a brisk shake, and laid it on the table between them. The kettle burbled unheeded as, with dawning bewilderment and anger, I stared at the front page. It was completely blank, empty, except for a small notice in a box, like a death announcement. 'The Government has ordered the suppression of news which we believe to be in the national interest. We have accordingly printed no news at all.'

'They can't do this,' I said, after a while.

'I think this is going to have to stop,' agreed my mother, and I, who had heard that deceptively mild phrase often enough in my infancy, gave her a wary glance. 'This is an insult. Dear knows, I've never concerned myself with politics, but we can't have this sort of thing.'

Fiona caught my eye. 'And thus spake the voice of the Scottish professional classes, the length and breadth of the land,' she murmured.

'I hope you're right, Fiona.'

'Dear God,' said my aunt, 'the final revolt of the articulate. What d'you think they'll put on the banners, Kirsty? Something uncompromising but grammatical. "Even if the Government were to oppose us, we should stand firm"?'

'None of your nonsense, Fiona,' said my mother.

'What about the Rifkind portrait, Mummy?' I asked, innocently.

She favoured me with a reproving stare. 'There will not be a Rifkind portrait, Kirsty. It's a point of principle.'

'I'd better get on with my work,' I said, and fled. The vision of Mummy talking down my father was a rare and precious one, which I wanted to savour on my own. I was still euphoric after the entire process of dressing, dragging a comb through my hair, and getting myself off to the library. It was the shapelessness and gradual attrition of my life which had got me down as much as anything. The morning's outrage was clear and definite, a Rubicon. An awful lot of people, of whom my mother was no bad sample, who had never 'been political', had suddenly been pushed a tiny bit too far. Something would come of it, not at once, maybe, but a turning point had been reached.

Thinking this, I thought of Ananda again, and my own bad conscience. Betrayal. Ananda had her own ways of dealing with bad stuff, goodness knows, but how was she reacting to the idea that she was colluding in the destruction of all she had worked for? Brooding thus, I climbed the library stairs and, for the second time in our lengthy acquaintance, knocked on Ananda's door.

'Come in.' She looked tired, I could see, but the serenity was back.

'I'm sorry, Ananda. I was acting the goat that day. Rhetoric gets the better of me sometimes.'

'Oh, it's all right,' replied Ananda. 'Do sit down.' There was a second chair in the little room, a hard one covered in brown leatherette, piled high with bits of paper. I removed them carefully on to the floor, and sat, looking at Ananda, and past her, at the computer screen.

After a pause, Ananda spoke. 'I've thought about it quite a bit, and it suddenly struck me, what does it matter? If the books all go off to other libraries, they'll still exist. They're valuable, they won't be destroyed. And so the ideas will still be there, which is all that really counts.'

'But your catalogue!'

'Oh,' said Ananda lightly, 'that's just me. I'm not an academic, you know. It doesn't matter to me if I get my name on the spine. That's vanity. *Samsara*.' She sat, very upright in her typist's chair, smiling. She gave every indication of meaning what she said. To me, her point of view seemed inconceivably remote. Ananda looked back at me. In her own way, I think she was also concerned to pick up the frayed threads of the relationship. Though it was not an aspect of the overall situation which struck me at the time, as I look back, I realise that the recent developments must have upset Ananda greatly, since they demonstrated the moral and intellectual gulf between her own world-view and that of the people she worked among. Perhaps even she had come to feel a little lonely. Certainly, there must have been some reason why quite suddenly, and quite uncharacteristically, she began telling me about something which had once happened to her without my offering her so much as a cue.

'You know,' she said, 'I realised the other day that I never told you the end of the story.'

'What story?'

'About the Colonel. I found it out when I went back for my first sabbatical. 1970, that would be.'

It was a very different Ananda who went back. For one thing, she was heading for thirty. She had lived on her own in Scotland for six years, she had studied both Tibetan and Sanskrit for nearly ten, and she expected, and hoped, to be allowed to present herself for her first examination. It must also have been apparent, even in the relatively short journey from Delhi to Simla, that she was returning to a very different India. She had left (just) the India of Mr Jawaharlal Nehru. She had returned to that of Mrs Gandhi, whose large, saurian eyes and white-streaked hair now seemed to be everywhere – still, in the eyes of India's poster-artists, Durga, invincible, eight-armed goddess, riding high, still secure in her seat on the tiger. Not yet Kali, the destroyer.

When she paid off her taxi and toiled up to Yamdrok-Tso, panting uncontrollably in the thin air under the weight of her newly-acquired rucksack (the Hindustan-Tibet road was marginally better made than it had been, but the track up to the *gompa* itself was still impassable for motor vehicles), she found things looking, superficially, much the same. The same, or similar, dogs raised the same hideous protest against intruders, the same prayer-wheel, now painted blue, stood at the gate. Someone came out to see who she was, and did not, at first, recognise her: Dondrup the cook, older, stouter, incongruously bespectacled.

'Ananda! Welcome.' Soon, all was joyous bustle. With some ceremony, she was shown to a new room, in the nuns' quarters, no longer on probation. The room, in itself, appeared to be much the same. Much tea was brewed, and the revolting, oily, furry Tibetan biscuits she remembered only too well were produced in her honour. Her spoken Tibetan (which had been excellent by '64 but which was rusty with disuse), began to come back. She had brought two pounds of tablet and some toffee from Scotland, and these reciprocal gifts were ecstatically received. As the nuns and lay-sisters crowded round, enjoying the fuss, she looked about her curiously. Her teacher, Tsering, looked much as she had always done: like many wiry, hardworking little women, she would almost certainly look much the same, getting a little thinner and greyer maybe, till the day she keeled over in her tracks. Ananda noted with interest that hers was no longer the only alien face. A

German woman had joined the community, and there were also a few Indians. She felt a curious sadness. India had taken them to her generous heart, and there, slowly but surely, they would dissolve in her equally generous digestive juices. She wondered how the older nuns felt about it.

'Where is the *am-tse*?' she asked, by a natural association of ideas.

Tsering looked sad. 'Dead. Long time ago. She was just as always one day, then something burst in her heart.' A stroke, maybe, thought Ananda. 'She was the first of us to die here.' A strange notion and – my goodness! – quite a problem, come to think of it. 'We put her for the birds,' continued Tsering, confirming her thought, 'and the authorities were very upset. There was much discussion, the Rinpoche wrote many letters. Then they said it was okay.'

'How is the Great Precious?'

'Not good. She works too hard.'

The next day, Ananda was summoned to the high room where the goddess Palden Lhamo cavorted, bright and fierce as ever, on the wall, and was able to confirm this for herself. The fetid odour of unwashed women, butter and incense, which she was gradually reacclimatising to, was, in the audience chamber, underlaid by something truly appalling, a cold stink of the grave. As she entered, she could hear the Rinpoche's rasping breathing from the door. Once too thin, she was now skeletal: as they exchanged courtesies, the hands which presented Ananda with the ritual white silk were as white, thin and cold as if she had already been picked over by the birds, and she settled back into her cushions as if any effort exhausted her.

Cancer, thought Ananda: not long to go, either. The Rinpoche pulled herself together, and the large eyes, now sunken in their sockets, focused on her guest. Clearly, she could read Ananda's thought, and a weary smile flitted across the thin face.

'Have you seen a Western doctor?' asked Ananda, baldly.

The Rinpoche lifted her hand slightly, in a little gesture of denial. 'I will die soon', she promised. 'It is good. I am very tired.'

Nunc dimittis, thought Ananda. She had feared what she might find on her return, but the community was thriving: not much larger, but consolidated. She was more and more aware of the extent to which it was the driving force of Palden Lhamo's will which had brought this about.

'I am from the past,' confided the Rinpoche, 'from the first Yamdrok-Tso. I will die, and then there will be Number Nine. She will be born in India, and then there will truly be the new Yamdrok-Tso.'

Ananda was astonished, and rather disturbed: the Rinpoche seemed to have picked the thoughts of the previous day from her own mind.

'But it will be something very different. Do you not mind?'

The Rinpoche, unexpectedly, smiled. She had lost most of her always-poor teeth, and the effect was ghastly.

'We are in the world. We must change, or die. Number Nine will make us live again. We old women from Tibet are only ghosts.'

Sobered by this encounter, Ananda let the routine of the monastery close over her gratefully for a while before she excused herself for a day and went to visit her English friends. There was still no telephone at Yamdrok-Tso, so she simply took herself off. To her distress, she found that the house in Jubilee Road was empty, and clearly had been so for some time. The windows were boarded up, and the lawns rank with rampant growth, while the once trimly whitewashed garden wall was plastered with posters and graffiti. Unreasonably disturbed, as she had not been even by the Rinpoche, she went to look for the Darks. It took her some time to walk to Waverley Lodge. There was far more traffic on the roads than there had once been, and what had remained of the English flavour of Simla was gradually melting in the sun. It was clear, too, as she walked up towards Annandale, that such of the big, old houses as survived were now occupied by Indians: the severe, eighteenth-century stucco was painted in a variety of bright pastels, picked out with contrasting woodwork, in a wholly un-English fashion. Several had been torn down, and four- or six-storey blocks of flats occupied the sites. The sound of competing transistor radios drifted tinnily from open windows.

Waverley Lodge, though more ruinous than ever, was unaltered in any significant respect. Ananda rang the bell, and when nothing happened, knocked. The sound echoed hollowly in the cavernous hall. She stood there for some time, then knocked again. Finally, she heard a slow shuffling approaching the door. It opened, with a rattle of chains, and Alured Dark, now a mountainous old man, wrinkled and baggy as an elephant, stood blinking against the light, trying to make out her face.

'My dear Ananda! How perfectly marvellous. Ethel will be so pleased.'

'I'm glad I haven't missed her,' replied Ananda frankly.

'Indeed not. She's in famous form, actually. We lost poor old Moti Lal, you know. *Anno domini* and overwork, God bless him. Well, as you can see for yourself, I'm a useless old hulk these days, what with arthritis and fat, but Etheldreda's as spry as she ever was. She turned to and rolled her sleeves up, and now she looks after us both as if she'd been born to it.' He shuffled painfully back, and Ananda went in. The hall, as ever, was dark, the one light-socket dangling bulbless in the middle of the ceiling – which, from the look of the frayed, ancient wire, was probably just as well. As the door shut behind them, she could hear Miss Etheldreda calling,

'Who is it, darling?'

'Ananda, Ethel dear. She's come back,' roared Alured.

'Top-hole!' Miss Etheldreda appeared from the back quarters with surprising speed, wiping soap-suds off her thin arms with a linen hand-towel. 'Ananda, my dear, dear girl. What a surprise.'

She swept Ananda into a hard, bony embrace, and kissed her on the cheek.

'Sound notion, that,' said Alured, mischievously. 'Wonder I didn't think of it myself.'

'Get along with you,' scolded his sister, swiping at him with her towel.

'I've moved into the breakfast room,' explained Alured as he opened the left-hand door off the hall. 'Can't manage the stairs these days. Etheldreda hired some chaps to bring a bedstead down, and I'm as happy as anything down here. If I want a book, she goes and fetches it, but to be honest with you, I'm just as glad to sit and think most days.'

The breakfast room was large and square, full, inevitably, of piles of books, to the extent that the tall mahogany bedstead was almost lost against the far wall. The smell of leaky old gentleman hung pungent in the air, but Ananda, used as she was to the Tibetans, was not disturbed by it, and the Darks had quite obviously long ceased to notice it themselves.

'This is very nice,' observed Miss Etheldreda. A round table stood in the front window, covered in a dusty red plush cloth edged with chenille bobbles. She removed the books from it, added them to the tottering piles by the wall, and proceeded to clear three chairs. Alured watched this ruthless process with respect, but did not offer his assistance. 'Do sit down,' she invited triumphantly, when it was at last possible to do so. Ananda sat; whereupon Miss Ethedreda whisked out again, intent on hospitality. Alured took the chair opposite – a sturdy mahogany affair, with a barley-sugar back, well equal to his weight – and seemed content, for the time, just to look at her. His breath wheezed gently in the quiet room.

Some little while later, Miss Etheldreda reappeared, out of breath, but triumphant, carrying a mighty tray on which reposed three exquisite old flute glasses, a cheerful glass jug painted with colourful daisies and containing fluorescent orange squash, and an ancient black bottle with a wired cork.

'My God, Ethel,' said Alured, amazed. 'You've found a bottle of the Pater's champagne.'

Miss Etheldreda ignored him, and smiled at Ananda very sweetly.

'I know you're not allowed to drink, my dear. But I doubt that we still have that many occasions to look forward to. Perhaps you wouldn't mind opening it for us? Neither of us has the strength in the fingers, these days.'

Ananda took the dusty bottle from the tray, and struggled with it inexpertly. 'I've never done this before,' she apologised, carefully undoing the wire, and looking at the ancient cork with apprehension.

In fact, it gave very little trouble. Rather than popping, it eased out of the neck with a tiny, regretful sigh. Ananda poured the wine, which was almost beige in colour and did not foam, though it was pearly with tiny bubbles. Even to so inexpert an observer as herself, the wine was quite obviously senile, but as she helped herself to the lurid squash, the old couple took their glasses with perfect satisfaction.

'Here's to us,' said Alured, raising his glass in turn to his sister and their guest.

'Cheers,' replied Miss Etheldreda.

The civilities thus observed, Ananda drank a little of her squash and opened the subject most on her mind.

'Miss Etheldreda, you can't tell me what happened to Colonel Hatherton, can you?'

To her surprise, both the Darks looked sad, and rather uneasy. Alured swirled the wine in his glass, whistling under his breath. Ananda's disquiet increased. 'He wasn't murdered, was he?'

'No,' said Alured slowly, 'er, he wasn't.' He appeared to come to a decision. 'Your story, darling. It's you who was the ministering angel.' Etheldreda sipped her wine.

'It must be two years ago, now.'

'Three. It was just before Mrs Gandhi got herself elected again.'

'Good Lord. Yes, you're right, dear. Three years. The Colonel started going down rather suddenly – you know how it is, with people who are never really ill? There just comes a time when – well. It's difficult to put it into words. James started getting thinner and thinner, and very breathless, and refused to go to a doctor. Said he didn't hold with them. What with never buying anything – you knew about that, didn't you? – and not keeping a servant, there was no one coming to the house regularly except the dhobi-wallah, so all us ancient fossils started getting jolly worried. He wouldn't admit it, but you could see his heart was giving out, he had all the signs. I took to calling, on Wednesday afternoons.'

'Because,' put in Alured, 'that was the day that ghastly old cat Mrs Babbage had her mah-jong afternoon. Still does, for all I know.'

'Yes, indeed. Ministering is one thing, but I saw no reason to submit myself to unnecessary unpleasantness. Alice Babbage always had a soft spot for the Colonel, and he was too much of a gentleman to quarrel with her.' Alured made a deprecating, gobbling noise, and his sister gave him a quelling glance.

'*Gentleman*, I said. He was, you know. Anyway, this went on for some months, and there was nothing to show it wouldn't go on for years.' She took another sip of geriatric champagne, and looked sadly out of the window. 'Then one Wednesday, I went along, and found the dhobi-wallah's laundry bundle in the porch, and I knew something was up.

'I had the key. He wouldn't have given it to me, I know, but I asked him for it point-blank, and he could never refuse a woman. I went in, calling out, just in case, and there was no reply. I went into the bedroom, and there he was, lying dead in his bed.' Her eyes brimmed, and she blinked the tears away fiercely before she could continue. 'Sorry. I'm a silly old fool, sometimes. Anyhow.

He looked very peaceful – must have just gone in his sleep, without waking up.' She looked at Ananda directly. 'Now, you mustn't be shocked, my dear. You get very queer and homely when you're as old as we are. And I went for a VAD in the War, you know – Alured already had his dicky heart and couldn't go, and I was quite determined we would do our bit, one way or another. I saw a good many chaps then the way you wouldn't see them in a drawing-room, and I laid a good few out in my time. Now, as I was saying, James was a terribly, terribly private sort of fellow, and he'd always steered clear of the blacks. So what I thought was, someone's got to look after him. Would he want some darky funeral-wallah poking him about, or would he rather have an old chum? Put that way, I think you'll agree I saw my course clear. I heaved out the best sheets and a lovely clean white shirt, put some Lysol in a bucket, and set to.' She paused. 'Well. When I got his jamas off, I got the shock of my life. He was a her.'

'What?'

'I'm sorry, I perhaps didn't put that very well. I mean, Colonel Hatherton was a lady all along. I had to sit down, I remember, and all I could think was, what a sell for Alice Babbage! Anyway, I got on with it, as one does, and I made up my mind that no one must ever know.'

'But how could anyone get away with it?' asked Ananda, bewildered.

'I have no idea. But they have, you know, more than once. There was a woman in the Army in Pa's time, I think: my memory is that she ended up as a Medical Officer somewhere in Africa. Terrible stink there was, when that came out. It's amazing how much people go on what they think they're seeing. Anyway, James had had us senile old coots properly fooled for the best part of twenty years. He must have had a dashed convincing act, in younger days.

'I got him – her – no, I'd better say him, it's too confusing otherwise, and anyway, it's what he wanted – I got him sorted out, nice clean bed, fresh linen, jaw nicely tied up, and so forth, and rang my own doctor, since James didn't have one, and got him to turn out. Then I got hold of a reasonably pukka-looking funeral service, and when they came, my dear, I have never come the mem so hard in all my born days. "He died in his sleep," I said, frightfully on my dig, pukka burra-bibi, just like Mama, God rest her, "and he has been prepared for burial. I'd thank you not to disturb him further." They talk, these people, there's no stopping it. Anyway, the doctor backed me up, and after a lot of argy-bargy they let us away with it, and boxed poor old James up without a murmur.'

'I'm not surprised,' said Alured, 'with you standing there glaring at them like a ruddy owl.'

'Well they did. Then I locked up the house, and came home to Alured, and after I'd had a good cry, I told him all about it.'

'Then we decided it must all go no further,' said Alured.

'I won't tell anyone,' promised Ananda.

'It'd hardly matter if you did. We'll all be dead soon enough. Tell you what. Keep mum while we're still above ground, and tell who you like thereafter. It's a jolly good story, I do see that. If it had happened to friends of mine, I'd have dined out on it for years.'

Miss Etheldreda picked up the thread again. 'I have been to a great many funerals, some more harrowing than others. But James's interment was in a class of its own. It was a proper military do, of course. The Last Post, you know, and volleys fired over the grave, and a lot of stout old boys in their best khakis saying the right thing. I was frightfully sad. I'd always been fond of James. But then I caught sight of the Babbage, giving herself widowed airs in figured black silk, and do you know, I nearly made myself ill trying not to laugh? It was the most terrible experience. I really couldn't explain, except to Alured, and I'd have set him off too, so I didn't dare. I had to pretend I'd been overcome, and bundle myself off home in a *jhampan*.'

Miss Etheldreda paused, and refilled the glasses. 'Here's to James, God bless him. I'm sure he'd have understood.'

'She left everything to the Regiment,' commented Alured sadly. 'I don't think anyone ever quite made her understand that it doesn't really exist any more. That's why the house is still standing there empty.'

For once, Ananda had left me speechless. One of the few things in the world that I was absolutely sure of is that she would not lie, and I doubted that she would even improve on a story to any significant extent. For one thing, she showed very little sign of having any imagination whatsoever – further, and more importantly, the events of the material world did not interest her enough for her to waste mental effort on sorting them into patterns. 'What an amazing story,' I said feebly, cursing myself for my own banality.

'Not really. Miss Etheldreda was quite right. If you believe in yourself enough, you can get away with the most extraordinary things.'

'When would the Colonel have been born, do you think?' I asked, my mind niggling at practicalities.

'I think her age must have helped. To judge by appearances, she'd have been just a bit young for active service in World War One, and too old for World War Two. She had a lot of desk jobs, maybe. I don't really know what people do in the Army.'

'Perhaps she wasn't *in* the army,' I suggested (I was a keen reader of detective fiction). 'She might have had a twin brother who died in an accident or something, and taken his identity.'

'Yes, I suppose so. She didn't have any old regimental chums that I knew of.' Ananda was clearly uninterested; the logistics of deception had no grip on her mind. Unsurprisingly, I reflected.

Anyone who had reinvented herself as thoroughly and comprehensively as Ananda was unlikely to find the process very surprising when it was detected in someone else.

The silence lengthened, friendly in the little room. Ananda seemed to be in no hurry to throw me out.

'What's happening in the world?' asked Ananda suddenly, breaking the quiet, as if she had just remembered that I was interested in that sort of thing.

'Change,' I said, cryptically.

'What sort of change?'

'Can't tell yet. But there's that feeling, suddenly, that we're moving into transition at last. Cracks appearing in the Blue Reich. Do you know what I find really creepy about your friend the Colonel? It's not pretending you're a man instead of a woman, it's living three thousand miles from London on stuff out of Fortnum & Mason hampers. Like a little girl in a Wendy house, with a lot of crisps and stuff she's nicked from the kitchen, saying she's really on a desert island.'

'Most of the Anglo-Indians were a bit like that. Colonel Hatherton just took it further than most. I suppose we were just as bad.'

'Who's "we"?' I asked, confused.

'Yamdrok-Tso. What you were saying about desert islands made me think suddenly. Most of the community was living in India as if it was really Tibet. The *am-cho* certainly didn't seem to think there was a world outside the gates. She didn't like me. I didn't know why at first, but I can see now that I was a symptom of change.'

'It's not quite the same,' I protested, very far from wishing to upset my idol again.

'Well, you know, I really think it isn't. The *am-cho* may have been focused back on Tibet all the time, but the Rinpoche herself believed in change and progress.'

'She died, didn't she? I suppose you've got a new one?'

'Yes, of course. She's about twelve now. She was born in India, and I think a lot of things will change once she's old enough to take over. It was different with the Ancient Britons. They really were just waiting to die.'

I could not simulate an interest in the Ancient Britons, or even the Ninth Rinpoche. My mind was elsewhere. Something was niggling at me; something which I could almost remember ... some kind of jingle. Kipling. Kipling and women. What on earth had Kipling to say about women? 'The female of the species is more deadly than the male.' No, it wasn't that . . . Got it! Something like, anyway. 'The Colonel's a Lady, and Judy O'Grady's her sister under the skin.' I began to laugh. The Colonel and Judy O'Grady had been sisters, all right. How he'd have hated Ananda's story. She was looking at me quizzically, smiling, waiting for me to explain the joke, and the atmosphere was warm between us: she had just given me a gift, a story, of her own free will.

'I do love you, Ananda,' I blurted. 'I hope you don't mind.' It felt very strange actually to say it, but liberating.

'No, of course not.'

Strange and heretical thoughts seemed to be slipping about beneath the surface of my mind. It was a morning for coming clean; an exhilarating sensation, but alarming. I found myself wondering what was going to pop out of my mouth next. Meanwhile, my mind was still vaguely engaged, on the surface, with Kipling and nineteenth-century determinism; East is East and West is West, men are men and women are sisters under the skin, a leopard can't change his spots . . .

'I've just realised something,' I announced. 'Don't worry about the connection, there isn't one. You and the Colonel between you have finally put me off Tacitus.'

Ananda laughed, incredulous. 'Oh, dear!'

'No, *not* oh, dear. It's two things coming together, I think. Your story, and this morning's non-news, which I haven't told you about yet. Don't worry about it. What I've realised is that I've been spending the whole summer thinking like Tacitus, and it's just not good enough. Irony and despair are attractive in their own way, that's the trouble. Then you realise suddenly that the old prune hasn't a shred of any kind of positive agenda. It's totally negative. The dreadful thing about irony is it assumes that nothing can ever really change.'

'I don't think I've ever understood irony,' confessed Ananda.

'Ananda, you wouldn't know irony if you met it in your soup. There's nothing negative about you, and what's more, the whole of Buddhism is anti-ironic. It assumes that practically anything you can't get right now gets sorted out some other time. But your story's even better than that; it's about sorting stuff out *now*. I've just realised Tacitus is absolutely wrong. Irony's not tragic, it's just a deeply seductive way of getting you to waste your own time. Just think, if the Colonel had ever heard of irony, she'd have drooped around Piddling-in-the-Marsh or wherever, feeling she was born for great things and doing sweet fuck all, like Dorothea Thingy in *Middlemarch*. As it was, she said "Bugger this for a lark", handed in her liberty-bodice, and stamped off to join the army.' I was laughing, but I had never been more serious. Ananda began to giggle.

'Oh, Kirsty. You do say some silly things.'

'True, but not in this case,' I retorted. 'I'm talking about life strategies. What you've been telling me is that the world quite often changes to fit what you want if you're clear enough about it. If it doesn't, you can always go mad.'

'What do you want yourself, Kirsty?' asked Ananda.

What did I want? Well, first of all, I wanted to think of a way of telling her that I didn't just love her, I was in love with her. Or did I? A sort of terror gripped me at the bare idea of exposing myself that much. What on earth did I want her to do about it? In a moment of panic-stricken clarity, I realised that I was much happier with things as they were.

'It sounds to me as if things are beginning to let go of you at last,' commented Ananda, watching my face, when I failed to reply.

'Growing up at last?'

Ananda laughed at me, with an expression I had often seen on my mother.

'Oh, no. I wouldn't say that.'

She was wrong. That was the moment when I cut loose from trying to make my life work – Tacitus, unrequited love, the University where I'd spent far too long, Dad, everything – and actually made myself understand that there are such things as alternatives. Time passed. I found a job, I started falling in love with the sort of woman you can get into bed, I stopped worrying what my Dad thought of me. This is a work of history; a true story in its way, but it's about things that happened in the early eighties. I was a good ten years younger, then, and there was a lot I did not understand. Centrally, of course, I did not understand why I had become so obsessive about Judy O'Grady, and I certainly did not understand Ananda, or how completely a woman can be finished with her past.

When I was a little girl, Dad let me stay up to watch the first moon-rocket on TV. Ancient history itself, now. It went up, so unbelievably slowly, like a weird, self-powered skyscraper balanced on a column of white fire. Then it came to bits. About two-thirds of it fell off: no one said what happened to it, or if they did, I've forgotten. Then a bit later, most of the rest fell off too, leaving just a slim little metal pencil, going all the way to the moon. Ananda was like that, I think. Sandymount, being Judy O'Grady, Catholicism, all the rest of the stuff I was so obsessed with finding in her, had powered her up, given her impetus. It must have. But then it had fallen away. I can understand that now, better than I did, at any rate, now that I am nearly forty. I remember tiresome little Kirsty, as she was in the mid-eighties, but she is no longer who I am.

Crossing the Water

I

Towards dawn on the ghastly night which I am about to describe, Claudia, my beloved wife, chose to remark that I wouldn't be able to stop talking about myself long enough to announce the end of the world. Despite this vote of confidence, I feel I must make some attempt to describe what happened in Suffolk in September 1982, the day my life came to an end. Oh, it started again. Claudia saw to that. But I must try to put some sequent account together in my mind, because I have never entirely ceased to be afraid that some fine night, Sock Holderness will put two and two together and smash his gun-butt against our tasteful front door, asking for explanations. Quite frankly, I am scared stiff of my dear old chum, whom I recently heard has returned once more from a prolonged sojourn in Mogadishu, Mozambique or some such hell-hole: a superstitious terror which the passage of time has done nothing to diminish. 'It's not guilt you're riddled with,' Claudia observed, busily ironing her black cap the other day, after I had been fool enough to open my mouth on the subject. 'It's oceanic self-pity, thickly disguised as masochism. What you really want is for Sock to tie you to a tree in a moonlit clearing and shoot you slowly with a rook-rifle.' Thank you for this penetrating aperçu, my darling. Just call me Sebastian.

Since the events of that night have scattered the circle of my friends beyond recall, it would be morbid to give any account of our society in its more fortunate days. I was at Durham with Adrian March and Colin Johnson, where I read History of Art in the company of the unspeakably beautiful Georgiana Stradling, who was later to take as her husband a well-born thug known as Sock Holderness. I first met Sock at a dinner party to which he had not been invited, and at which he was perfectly sober and breathtakingly rude. There you have it: I have begun to tell Holderness stories already. All his acquaintance told them, which was I think inevitable, since he fascinated all of us, but none of us had the faintest idea where he came from, who he was, or what he did. Thus, invention and anecdote gave us something to say about him. He did not encourage speculation about his profession. All one could guess is that it was military-ish (emphasis on military, or ish?), and required frequent absences from England.

It is all too easy to see why the icy and brilliant Georgiana married Sock: he is, literally and metaphorically, a handsome bastard. He showed up uninvited to some dance or other one winter evening, and that was that. Eyes met across a crowded room, à la Barbara Cartland. In the summer after our graduation, Georgiana (as pale and determined as ever) took Michael Luke Holderness as her husband in the Catholic church at Aldeburgh, in the presence of Adrian, Colin, the priest, and the plaster saints. Georgiana is, like the rest of her family, *molta Cattolica*, though I might add that Sock has never manifested any religion before or since, unless one counts a grudging admiration for the designer of the Lake District and the Highlands of Scotland. That same summer, I contrived to inherit a repulsive sheaf of drawings by a neo-classical ancestor (though most unfortunately, no money with which to keep them in the style to which they were accustomed), failed to get my job at the Courtauld, threw the *crise nerveux* of all time, and found that, when I came to my senses, I had gone through a form of marriage with my elegant and heartless Claudia.

In due time, a son was born to Sock and Georgiana (just the one, as things turned out), and Sock christened him Josiah on some ancestral impulse out of the Black Country and the factory towns. Georgiana, gripped by some patronising desire to creep 'real life' up on me by degrees, insisted that I should act as the little brute's godfather. I was too drunk to remember much about the ceremony, but I am informed that it has left me theoretically responsible for the brat's moral welfare until the good fathers of Ampleforth take him out of my hands. Anyway. When the child was three or so, Georgiana's father died, and her mother decided to go and live near her sister in Buxton. Sock and Georgiana therefore established themselves at Georgiana's family house, Jordans in Suffolk. There is little more to be said about this happy household, except that with the passage of time, Sock's mysterious job took him abroad more and more.

Adrian, meanwhile, worked on in London, his eye riveted always on the main chance: drawings and reviews, articles about him and by him in the *Sunday Times*, a fine house in the slums of Spitalfields which he bought for virtually nothing because all his neighbours were West Indian or Bengali. I have often wondered about his reasons for living there – rent boys, cocaine, or organised crime? – but on the only occasion when I dared to voice any speculations, Claudia kicked me hard under the table and Adrian came back snappily with the riposte that I existed principally to remind him of the complete futility, considered as a lifestyle choice, of disorganised crime.

Colin, the most conventional of our happy band, got a job, and camped out in a decent house at Malton, with a gazebo in the garden, lecturing (doubtless) with dull conscientiousness on Art History at York, hoping to make it to Senior Lecturer, and living in sordid bachelor squalor which a succession of young women from the university seemed only too happy to clear up for him.

And I, meanwhile, did nothing worth shouting about. A bit of lecturing on the London extramural circuit and selling some neoclassica far too cheaply secured me the ripe purgatory of a year at Yale, which entirely failed to lead to anything. On my return, I inaugurated my career as a kept man, following my wife Claudia in and out of a diversity of expensive Bedlams and a succession of equally costly rented flats. The whole untenable charade ended sharply in an apocalyptic row in the sculpture court of the V and A, followed by a silent and furious walk around the ceramic galleries, and I found myself out on the town again earning my living through an honest and ghastly summer. The noise and heat were tempered only by the funds which I got by flogging off two ancestral sepias; so I was all too happy when Georgiana invited me to Jordans in September.

This brings me to a part of this narrative which I would rather avoid: the description of a house which I can never hope to visit again, but which haunts my imagination because it represents all those qualities which our generation has lost, spoiled, and thrown away. Baldy Pevsner dates it, dismisses it as 'Noddyland', and tells you nothing important: nothing about the placing of the house on the estuary, the graduations of flame in the bricks of the garden walls, the honeycomb of bedrooms and dressing rooms, the heartbreaking and innocent carving of a harvest cart on the drawing-room fireplace, and of course, nothing about the most haunting thing of all – the faint smell of cedar smoke, tobacco and lavender.

Georgiana and Sock took possession of the house without developing any of that selfishness which is so common in the newly propertied. In the summer, on the odd occasions when he was there – less often towards the end – Sock was out all day, his forehead burnt brick-red like a cricketer's, while Georgiana weeded in the shade, and looked after her loathsome son with an unfeigned contentment. The evenings were the best part of those days: a smooth sequence of archaic pleasures, reading Horace in the bath, putting on a clean shirt, going down for gin and tonic. The house was full of books in English and Latin in leather-bound, gilt-edged editions: the school and college prizes of that generation of slaughtered great-uncles whose sweaters (cable-knit as for a race of giants) still filled the chests in the spare bedrooms. Sock rather tended to come the country gentleman on the strength of all this, somewhat more than their kitchen garden warranted, but I was happy to eat my nice Ashmeads Kernel, Ribstone Pippin, whatever, count my blessings, and say nothing.

I can't stop myself from spinning fantasies about the last gathering of my friends. Adrian would have come on from the house in Cumberland where he had spent the best part of two years decorating ceilings and designing meretricious little pavilions, driven through the September weather across by Hexham and the Roman Wall, lunched at the Wig and Mitre in Lincoln, and then come over the flat fields by the smugglers' churches. Colin would have evicted the shag-of-the-month, slammed his Georgian front door on the squalor within, and hammered down the A1 with whatever was newest and nastiest screaming from the car radio in quadraphonic sound. I merely suffered the Liverpool Street train in damp irritation, where, since First Class was now beyond me, the horrible children of the people reminded me of my godson's tough hostility. I changed trains at Ipswich, thinking about my folly in ditching a rich wife and, by gradual degrees, of the unobtrusive efficiency with which farmers and soldiers dispose of surplus partners, and grew calmer as the train passed through those East Anglian stations whose names freshen with the approach of the sea. At Wickham Market, Georgiana was on the platform, turning from picking one of the stationmaster's roses to offer her satiny, expensively nurtured cheek for a kiss. She was thirty-two, as were we all, and clearly well aware that she was more beautiful than ever. I opened the car window as we drove into the woods, and smelt in the rush of air familiar pine trees and sour water.

She told me that Sock had been away all summer. There had been a phone call at the end of April, and he had left the next day. He'd sent various primitive postcards, but had given no hint as to when he might return. I amused myself as we drove through the wood with fantasies about Georgiana's life when her husband was away. Perhaps she endlessly made and unpicked a set of petit-point chair-covers behind half-drawn curtains, waiting for Master to come back. Her profile was ironic and self-sufficient. Did it still conceal the abject, canine devotion which she had once so nakedly displayed?

We were alone that night. The child, thankfully, was staying with a friend: the thought of playing mummies and daddies revolted me. Adrian and Colin were to arrive when they could. Conversation didn't wither completely as we discussed the weaknesses of our common friends, but I felt that we were hunting each other in circles. She trailed her beauty, her charm and her sympathy before me like the most adroit of fly-fishermen, but I flatter myself that I gave little away. If I learned nothing new about Sock, or their way of life, she certainly can have learned nothing about Claudia, or the circumstances of our estrangement. I went up to bed reflecting that I no longer liked darling Georgiana in the uncomplicated way in which I like Venetian windows or *oeufs Florentine*: I appreciated her beauty and I admired her determination, but she had ceased to charm me.

The noise of moths softly battering the window disturbed me, and I was strangely upset to find a piece of one of Sock's shirts (a shirt which I had once touched with fear when his hard shoulders were in it) worked into the quilt beside the silks and flannels of the long-dead uncles whom the Flanders mud had swallowed one by one. The next night was better, because Adrian had arrived, and in reversion to our undergraduate days, he left the door between our rooms open. I remember holding forth, answered by noncommittal grunts, until I drifted into sleep without, for once, dreaming my nasty and familiar dream about riding and drowning, about Sock's departure and return. In the morning, Adrian drifted into my room massaging essences from Trumper's into his sleekly shaven chops, and opened the case for the prosecution.

'Oliver, are you all right?'

'I have disposed of Claudia,' I replied austerely. 'I had the horrors the night before last. Otherwise, I am quite well.'

'I don't follow. Don't you realise Claudia really loves you?'

'Those are precisely the last two words I would use.'

'Well, I can tell you this. I was in Covent Garden a few weeks ago, and I saw Claudia at Tutton's. She was making a bit of a scene.'

'I'm glad to hear it. I imagine she'd taken her dinner in liquid form. Did she do something predictable? Chuck up on the waiter? Throw an omelette at some pinheaded publisher? Or lose a shoe on the way to the Ladies and fall into Terry Wogan's lap?'

'Christ, Olly, don't be silly. She looked a bloody sight more dignified than you do, lying there sneering as if you'd done something to be proud of.'

I snuggled down deliberately, and lay in comfort for two minutes to punish him for being over-familiar. He wandered restlessly round the room, fiddling with my silver-backed hairbrushes, and staring out of the window. He began again, from an obliquer angle.

'You never used to be like this, Oliver.'

'Are you surprised? We used to be golden lads and lasses, remember? And look at us now. As you so tactfully remind me, I've done nothing to be proud of. Have you? Look at what you're doing, Adrian: rag-rolling walls for cretinous used-car salesmen, and arselicking the Meejah for the next contract.'

He didn't like that, so predictably, he went on the offensive.

'Haven't you been selling off the ancestral art at a bit of a rate? I saw two of them at fast-food Sotheby's last month.'

'If you're asking whether I've run out of money, the answer is yes. The *Burlington* didn't take my last piece, and the V&A job came to an end in July. Anyway, the fucking drawings went for tuppence-ha'penny. All the dealers were in Brighton.'

'I bought one.'

'Dirt cheap, if I remember. A bargain.'

'Don't be horrid. I bought it to keep for you, you idiot.'

'If you bought the "Return of Ulysses", you can bloody well hang on to it. I don't like it. He looks like Sock in a paddy, and he gives me the creeps.' It was perfectly obvious that Adrian was keeping the ancestral little nasty up his sleeve as a reunion present for when I got around to crawling to Claudia, bless his sentimental heart.

'Well, I like it.' Another characteristic from earliest youth: a stubborn determination to get value for money.

'Then keep it.'

He stuck his lower lip out, and frowned at the brush he was holding. 'You shouldn't have sold the other one. It isn't decent.'

'I've spent the summer living in a hovel in King's Cross without enough to drink. It was a straight choice between selling a picture, or the use of my various orifices. I thought on the whole I'd rather sell the piccer.'

Adrian ignored this, choosing to believe that I was not wholly serious.

'But Oliver, it's a marvellous drawing. Don't you realise that the butterfly at the window is the boy's soul departing? Don't you see that the dead athlete is a self-portrait? Hasn't Claudia ever told you that he looks just like you, you old throwback?'

'If you go on like that, I'll burn the lot, and chuck the ancestral diary on top. That'll teach you art historians to mind your own business. Aren't you going down to breakfast?'

'See you down there.'

A surly truce had been declared.

Colin arrived soon after I got downstairs, his flash car chewing up Georgiana's drive, and his thoroughbred vowels distinct at thirty paces. God knows what they made of him at York. After he'd kissed Georgiana, eaten some cold toast for the look of the thing, and made small talk for a few minutes, the work of the day began.

It is a truth universally acknowledged that any man not in possession of a slipped disc who is invited as a houseguest, especially when the house has extensive grounds and an absentee master, is expected to earn his keep by doing endless buildings and works in the vegetable garden. As soon as was decent, if not sooner, Georgiana shooed us upstairs to change into our oldest clothes, and stood by the back door like the Mother of the Gracchi counting us all out. She was ill pleased to discover that Adrian had eluded her vigilance and disappeared with his paintbox. Colin was set at a herbaceous border which needed cutting down, while I was chivvied forth to pick peas and trim the box edging in the kitchen garden. She, meanwhile, fooled about in the kitchen, keeping an eye on us through the window, and uttering occasional piping cries of encouragement. At some point in the course of the morning, she also took delivery of my repellent godson, who emerged headfirst from a Range-Rover stuffed to bursting with a pullulating mass of juvenile delinquents, accompanied by a barrel-shaped and malodorous hound named Taggart who was, strictly speaking, Sock's, but who condescended to chaperone the son and heir when Master was otherwise engaged. We were graciously permitted to come in for lentil soup, bread, and cheese at midday, and once this simple collation was over, we were swept out again.

Adrian reappeared apologetically, clutching a soggy watercolour, and was firmly set to work. I am not wholly sure I did not see Georgiana lock the back door and pocket the key as she brought up the rear. Perhaps I malign her. She assumed a position of command in a wicker chair on the lawn in front of the house, armed with my trug of peas, a colander, and a white china basin. In the afternoon, I managed a full ten minutes of staking chrysanthemums (horrid flowers which the French, quite rightly, consecrate to the uncomplaining dead) before I invented a headache and retired to the shade of the chair where Georgiana sat unzipping pods. It was perfectly obvious from the look Georgiana shot me over the top of her dark glasses that she was cross with me, but at that moment I couldn't have cared less. I pinched the current *World of Interiors*, with which she clearly proposed to vary the diversion of watching us all work, and laughed myself to sleep.

It is unpleasant to wake suddenly and realise that something has happened. Georgiana jerked upright in her chair, Adrian dropped the shears, Colin leaned on his scythe like the Grim Reaper, and the child stopped rolling about on the grass with the dog. No one was expected, but there was no mistaking the noise of a fast car grinding to a stop on gravel. Through the still, late-summer air, a sequence of sounds came which seemed to threaten my smooth and sleepy afternoon: a car-door slammed forcibly, a rattle of keys, quick and confident steps marching over the gravel.

My heart lurched unpleasantly. Georgiana scrambled to her feet, very white, as the man came round the side of the house, her mouth forming round a sibilant. Against the light, his build and carriage suggested Sock, but he hesitated as Sock would never have done, and remained silent till he was very near to us. I studied him as I rose smoothly to my feet, swallowing to reduce the sudden dryness of mouth which a moment's shock had given me, and assumed the welcoming smile which has earned me a number of hot dinners. Army man, good haircut, neat blazer and striped shirt, fine, hard profile like one of the cameos which had delighted my neo-classical ancestor. Like Sock Holderness, and yet unlike. An able and energetic boy. Sock was a man.

He almost bowed in front of Georgiana, pulling his shoulders straight and half-ducking his head.

'Mrs Holderness? Sorry to burst in on you like this. I'm

Edward Horsfall. I promised Sock that I'd look in on you.' Her expression was glazed, tigerish: she looked as though she might eat him. I realised suddenly that she must have thought he was bringing her the news of Sock's death. Then she smiled, holding out her white, white hand: the warmth of relief lit her face like a flame. Adrian and Colin scampered up from the garden, wiping their muddy paws on their bottoms and fluffing up their hair. They both took one look at him, and reverted to their schoolboy selves. Why is it that the eruption of one reasonably good-looking Lieutenant into a company of aesthetes produces such distressing symptoms of inadequacy? Adrian and Colin virtually barked their surnames, and shot out their right hands. I bided my time.

Then he came towards me as Georgiana murmured my name. I put my hand out, unable to read him. What was I going to be? 'a man among men', or 'everybody's favourite nephew'? In that moment of hesitation, his dry, warm hand closed firmly over mine, and I knew that his eyes had marked my lack of decision, and guessed at its cause. Well, it would have to be the nephew; the wrong choice. It came to me quite clearly in that second that I would never feel easy in the man's presence, for much the same reasons that I can never relax with Sock. Splendid they may be, but there are gulfs of affinity which can never be bridged.

Needless to say, my pernicious godson came tumbling up from the lawn with his dog, took one look, and worshipped. The infant is very much his father's son, at the caterpillar stage. He drew himself up to a height of approximately four foot six, and put out his hand.

'Josh Holderness, sir' (as though that fact were not perfectly obvious). The hound meanwhile obtruded himself, and poked the newcomer in the testicles with his moist black snout, inhaling with every appearance of satisfaction. Was I dreaming, or did a faint suggestion of envy flit across Adrian's boyish countenance?

'That's Taggart, sir,' the brat volunteered (do they have cadet corps at prep-schools in these troubled times, or had he picked all this up by osmosis?) 'Oliver's my godfather, but he's scared of dogs,' he continued, smugly communicative. The man Horsfall held his grubby little paw a moment. 'Edward Horsfall. Edward to you, laddie. I'm a friend of your Pa's.'

I turned aside to retch into a few late hollyhocks, and tagged on to the end of the party as they wandered towards the house. I caught up with Adrian, who was owed a home truth or two after the morning's amateur psychology, and gave him the works.

'Well, well,' I said pleasantly. 'A Gainsborough Master of Hounds. Doesn't Sock know how to pick 'em?'

'Shut up.'

'I thought the eighteenth century was rather, um, your thing. Lace frills and dirty hands, and all that. Claret and silver candlesticks, pissing in the same chamberpot. Out with the hounds in the crisp dawn light. Just your sort of world, really. And who shall tell the horseman from the horse?'

I collected a prize dirty look as my reward for that one. Does Adrian ever find himself wondering, in the stilly watches of the night, whether the trade of art historian is quite manly enough?

I had little time to rile him further as Horsfall was already accepting an invitation to stay the night, stripping off his blazer, rolling up his sleeves, and insisting to Georgiana that he liked doing a bit of heavy work in a garden. Or elsewhere? Time would tell.

I watched for the rest of that blazing and doomed afternoon: Horsfall heaving and shifting earth, the godson in bliss grubbing after him picking roots and stones out of the soil, Adrian and Colin spurred to unusual activity, and Georgiana gazing at the man with reminiscent pleasure. It was only when the sun was going down and gin-time (mercifully) approached that Horsfall leaned on his spade and announced that Sock was pretty likely to show up soon. He had finished his business abroad, and was on his way home.

II

While Adrian was still cheerfully occupied sucking up to Horsfall in the hall, I slipped into our shared dressing-room and abstracted a goodly quantity of his Extract of Limes, which made my bath smell pleasantly of the fortunate islands in the southern seas. My ideal bath happens at about six in the evening, and involves cologne, vast amounts of hot water and the perusal of an auctioneer's catalogue. I had these requisites of happiness to hand, having very prudently nicked a Sotheby's catalogue from Sock's sacred and shuttered study earlier in the afternoon. It was only a catalogue of firearms, and the sale was long past, but it is the principle of the thing which matters.

I lay in the deep enamel tub, stirring the scent of limes up with my toes, and decided regretfully that a pair of shotguns by Holland and Holland would be of little use to a solitary aesthete in bachelor lodgings above the pub in Swift Court. I may, perhaps have fantasised about disposing of Claudia; but accidental shotgun wounds are hard to contrive in an urban environment. Moreover, the smell of cordite and the noise of guns evoke excitements which have but little to do with wives.

For a minute or two, I amused myself by watching the slanting light on the red brick of the window-frame, allowing myself to travel in imagination over the shimmering marshes which surround the house, but I must confess that aesthetics bore me in the end. I fell to more delightful meditations; wondering where the brute and throwback Sock might be at that moment. At what café table in what foreign town might he be waiting for a train, and dreaming of the whisky and decent bitter of his native land? How would he return? By day, tramping into the garden like Horsfall his lieutenant? Or by night, with the house ablaze, and Georgiana in a white dress coming down the lawn to meet him? Adrian was scrabbling at the door. I remembered the various passages of arms between us that day, and so ran out the last of the hot water, leaving him to find this out in due course. It crossed my mind that perhaps, given the way he had been eyeing Horsfall during the afternoon, a cold bath would be good for him. I did not then hurry down to the drawing-room, because I guessed that the presence of the comely lieutenant would prevent the discussion of anything amusing. So I lay on my bed for half an hour, watching the light at the window, before I dressed.

Nobody actually dresses for dinner these days, but in the country-house circles on the fringes of which I then moved, a certain effort is expected. I donned cleaner corduroys, the regulation striped shirt, and an unattractive plain tie. I hesitated for a moment about a jacket, but settled for a striped seersucker souvenir of my sufferings in America, thinking that, with any luck, it might irritate Horsfall.

I composed my tie and descended; but as I reached the threshold of the drawing room, I found myself pausing, sensing at once that something was up. For a moment, feeling sick at the top of my stomach, I thought the general silence within was the result of something dreadful on the six o'clock news, but Colin looked too smooth and relaxed for it to be anything like that, lolling in the window seat and letting the light catch his hair. Adrian (I do hope that he had enjoyed his bath) sat upright in an armchair, looking simply bad-tempered, as though a patron had promised him lunch and then fobbed him off with a glass of milk and a Bath bun. Horsfall was perched on the club fender in full undress uniform (blue blazer, grey flannels, stripy shirt, foulard tie) looking keen and alert; but that is an attitude which I believe is taught at Sandhurst in the deportment class.

The drawing room at Jordans is, in its way, not unattractive. It has three long windows looking over the estuary, dim green walls, a fine chimneypiece, squashy and faded sofas and everything you might expect. Somehow it was Georgiana who took my eyes, stretched out on the sofa in a dark blue dress with a Cavalier collar, one pale hand resting on the receiver of the telephone.

'Pour yourself something,' she said, 'and sit down. You're about to get a nasty shock.'

Claudia on the phone? One of my less creditable bits of horsetrading bobbing to the surface? Or other things? Who knew how to find me at Jordans? I headed for the drinks table and poured plenty of gin, almost forgetting the tonic.

'Do your worst,' I said. 'Astonish me.'

'You know the house on the other side of the estuary?'

'Of course. It's called Blackwater, it's by Soane, and it looks a bit like Norwich gaol. I assume you're asking whether I'm aware that it belongs to friends of my ex-wife's.'

Georgiana gave me an automatic Papist grimace for using the word 'ex-wife', and continued: 'It belongs to my cousin.'

'So? I see at once that everyone in this room except the handsome Lieutenant has some connection with the place. Adrian is bound to know if they want someone to colour in their hunting prints. Colin is bound to know who did the drawing room fireplace. I trust you to know your family, within reasonable limits. What, or who, is making the lot of you look as if you're by Coward out of Terence Rattigan?'

Georgiana gave me one of her calling-to-order, head-girlish stares.

'My cousin,' she began quellingly, 'is called Stephen Gibbs. I don't think he's ever done anything worth mentioning except contract a disastrous marriage. I pushed him in the mere once when we were children, and I wish I'd done it more often.'

I remembered all too clearly that someone called Stephen Gibbs had married a friend of Claudia's. He came to dinner with us more than once in the days of our joint ménage: rich, dim and pompous, but harmless.

'Well,' I said, 'and how is he taking his revenge for the cold dips of yesteryear? I assume that he is, since you've mentioned him?'

No straight answer was available. Adrian and Colin, infected by the tight-lipped military air which pervaded the room, muttered something which might have been 'it's a bit much'. Horsfall rolled his shoulders and all but growled. Georgiana sighed.

'It's his wife I object to,' she said. 'There are limits.' Since I did not wish, in this context, to air the fact that I had met the lady on several occasions, I asked if anybody knew her name.

'Florabella,' Georgiana said with malice. 'Theresa, Immaculata – oh, the kind of name you'd expect from the worst sort of mix of New York and South America.'

'Isabella,' Adrian said firmly, 'as if you didn't know.'

'Fine,' I said. 'We have now established that the lady is called Isabella, and that she is, in your opinion, a low Dago who oils her hair and substitutes heavy perfume for frequent baths. Let me have another little drink, and you can tell me what she's supposed to have done.'

'She's just invited herself and her friends to lunch tomorrow!' Adrian gave me a hard look, as though he knew something which would pay me back for his nasty cold bath. I was on my guard at once: the dear boy should know better than to give advance warning that way.

'She lives five miles away,' continued Georgiana.

'Less by water,' put in Horsfall, whose professional instincts had evidently led him to study the terrain.

'She is married to my cousin, and not once, since she succeeded in dragging Stephen into some registry office in the Fulham Road, has she had the decency to ask us to anything at Blackwater except gatherings of London perverts and kept women. She makes cheap remarks about us at parties all over Suffolk. What she's done to the house is nobody's business. And she has just had the cheek to telephone me, all sweetness and light, commiserate with me for not having Sock here, and ask herself to lunch tomorrow.'

'I imagine,' I said, 'that what they really want is to get Adrian off his guard and get him to rag-roll their lavatory at family rates. I can't see why else she should want to come.'

'Leave me out of this,' said Adrian automatically. He has never been a man to stand idly on the platform while a gravy-train pulls out of the station.

'I think you're being deliberately stupid, Olly. The man is a cousin of sorts, wet though he is, and I found I'd invited them before I knew what had hit me.'

'Don't you worry, ma'am,' contributed Horsfall. 'Have game pie for lunch, and let me pump a couple of extra cartridges into the rabbit before you cut it up. Never fails. No narg ever comes back for more.'

'How sweet of you, Edward,' said Georgiana. 'But, much as I like the idea of honest lead playing hell with their expensive dentistry, I don't think it's as simple as that. I do feel, quite seriously, that they need a lesson. You wouldn't believe what they've done to the house – my family house, if all had their own. And they haven't even got any children. Oh, if only Sock were here, he'd sort them out.'

'Well, ma'am,' piped up the ineffable Horsfall, 'if I can do anything to hold the fort till he comes . . .'

Georgiana looked him over with an analytic and considering eye. Adrian and Colin seemed to be simply thrilled at the implication that they couldn't hold a fort between them. My mind began to rove idly over the possibilities thus suggested. Sock, after all, had apparently proffered this bright-eyed, cold-nosed puppy as a sort of *locum tenens* till he should choose to reappear. What had he meant by it, and precisely which aspects of his domestic role had he had in mind? I began to perceive that a little fun might be had out of what had looked like being a dismal evening.

At this point, the godson came into the room looking intensely washed and scrubbed, with the dog lolloping at his heels. He said 'Hello, Mummy' to Georgiana, ignored everyone else in the room, and made a bee-line for Horsfall. Seating himself on the other end of the fender, he ordered the animal to lie down, and said 'Hello, Edward' with becoming and nauseous shyness.

'Have an almond, Josh,' replied Horsfall, offering the brat the silver pot of salted nuts which should have been reserved for his elders and betters. Georgiana, meanwhile, had clearly not finished with Stephen and Isabella. She made a peremptory gesture towards Colin, indicating that he should refill everyone's glasses. Her eyes roved consideringly over the company, collecting everyone's attention, and came to rest on Horsfall and the boy, who were engaged in a mutually agreeable game of pushing each other along the fender.

'Now, Josh, you've got to be grown up. We're talking about people you know, so you mustn't repeat what we say.'

'Who?'

'Uncle Stephen and his friends.'

The child smirked, and whispered 'They're wets' quite audibly to Horsfall, who nodded seriously.

'Promise, Mummy.'

The words were barely out of his mouth before Georgiana returned to her resumé of ancient grievances. 'Everything they've done in the past might have led me to expect this. They've simply no notion of civilised behaviour. Of course, Stephen's grandfather snitched Blackwater from us in the first place. I can't say I mind terribly about that now, but to think of the house being systematically ruined is quite another matter.'

I have often reflected that art historians from old families are a menace to society. I'd heard this particular *récit* before, so I let my attention wander, playing at catching the blue light in my gin, thinking how much Horsfall and the child looked like two dogs painted by Landseer, and noticing the way the white flowers were beginning to show up against the box hedges in the garden as the day abated. There can be few English county families who do not have a story about being done out of a house with lawns going down to a river, and Georgiana's was no exception. The matter of the history is simply told, and the responses of Horsfall, Adrian and Colin were entirely predictable. For three whole weeks in

1917, Georgiana's grandparents had been the undisputed owners of the cheerfully-named Blackwater, on the other side of the river. Then the grandfather had been killed in France, and Stephen's grandfather, 'a rabbit of an M.P.,' according to Georgiana, had made some faintly shady settlement with the widow and taken possession of the house with indecent swiftness. Personally, I would not have minded being given the amiable Jordans as a consolation prize, but neither Georgiana nor her audience were in the mood to view the matter in this sensible light.

'Rough luck,' said Horsfall emphatically.

'If Blackwater's ours, why don't they give it back? Then I could have a proper boat,' piped the child, fixing his gaze on Horsfall as though he expected any army man worth his salt to organise a raiding party immediately.

'Things don't happen like that in England nowadays, Josh,' said Georgiana, 'more's the pity. Uncle Stephen doesn't go in for giving anything back to anyone.'

Whence the high moral tone, madam? I wondered to myself. Is there any English county family whose motto, at bottom, is not *prendere et tenere*, grab it and keep it? It was the lust for acquisition, after all, which had kindled in the eye of the infant Josiah, a chip off the old block if there ever was one. I thought it would be fun to keep the ball rolling, so I said, 'You wouldn't really want Blackwater anyway. You know that perfectly well.' At which point, as I had hoped, every single person in the room except the dog turned on me and uttered a pleasurably indignant sentence which included the words 'a matter of principle'.

(So far so good.)

'You could never afford to heat it,' I continued, with infuriating reasonableness. 'I for one would be quite happy to let principles look after themselves if I was as comfortable as you are here.'

'Oliver,' said Adrian, on his best behaviour in front of Horsfall, and rising to the bait like an exceptionally thick trout, 'we all know only too well that you have never let a principle interfere with your comfort for a single second.'

'I'm just trying to be faintly practical. It seems to me that a house with six or seven bedrooms, even leaving the attics out of it, is probably adequate for one man, one woman and one child. Or should I understand that this sudden interest in Blackwater implies that Georgiana has finally taken her Holy Father's precepts on board, and intends to present young Josiah with a dozen or so siblings?'

'Shut it,' said Horsfall and Adrian simultaneously. You can take the boy out of the prep school, but you can never take the prep school out of the boy. Good old, soggy old Colin made a feeble attempt to pour oil on troubled waters, and invoked the returning demigod. 'Sock likes this house,' he observed. 'He always says he feels comfortable here – you know – that he can do the garden and come straight in for a drink, without worrying about getting mud on the marble.'

Everybody's eyes travelled together to the painting above the fireplace (Adrian's inexpensive wedding present, his own rather limp pastiche of John Nash, heavy on ochres, madders and grey) which showed the garden at Jordans with Sock's well constructed and unmistakable back vanishing through the gate to the estuary, spade on shoulder. I remembered now how I'd been told to shut up when I first observed that it was an intensely sinister effort, suggesting generally that Sock was some sort of unpleasant Classical god trading between the living and the dead. Poor old Colin waded on oblivious, doubtless wishing he was safely back at York being frightfully keen at meetings of the Civic Trust.

'Anyway, in this house, you know you can manage quite well with Mrs Thing coming in in the afternoons. You'd need proper staff to keep Blackwater going. And Jordans is lovely. I can't imagine anyone's ever been really happy in the place over the river. It's pretty grim.'

'Oh,' I said (slightly misjudging the state of play), 'it might have its uses. Sock could always take his shirt off and strike attitudes in the hall, just like a soldier's tomb by my horrible old ancestor.'

I copped a round of offended stares. They don't altogether like being reminded that, for all my little faults, I did not crawl out of the darkness the day before yesterday. Horsfall was showing a pleasing impatience to chuck any traducer of the British Army into the nearest bit of still or running water. I smiled at him, and sailed on.

'The real trouble would be the' (pause) 'art historians. Can you imagine what Sock would do if young inverts kept phoning him up and telling him what colour to paint his study walls? I don't suppose the old hero's even so much as heard of the Royal Commission for Historical Monuments, and my goodness, I wouldn't like to be in the room when he found out.'

Was it only my imagination, or did my little godson whisper 'Sick him' to the dog Taggart at this point? Georgiana was too preoccupied by her theme to take any notice of this interruption. We might never have spoken.

'Blackwater,' she went on, earnest and touching, 'is only horrid because horrid people live in it. If it could ever be put back together once Isabella has quite finished with it, it would be perfectly all right.'

'I don't think they've done anything to the fabric,' Adrian volunteered.

'Don't be too sure,' said Colin darkly. 'I heard somewhere that they'd got everybody's least favourite modern architect to put a melamine chimneypiece into the dining room.'

'The locals tell me,' said Georgiana, 'that seven different baths in different shades of avocado green went into what used to be a perfectly lovely Pompeiian dressing-room before Isabella was satisfied. And they've painted the panelling in the library sludge brown.'

'So that's where the Soane pier-glass at Architectural Salvage came from,' said Adrian, with the zeal of the detective.

Honestly, as a taxpayer, I am horrified that the Civil Liberties people don't shove the entire art-historical mafia in the slammer, for their flagrant interference with the right of every householder to wreck his historic house in his own good time. Horsfall, meanwhile, who had followed this conversation very much as if it had been held in Serbo-Croat, made a prodigious intellectual effort.

'You mean they've rotted the show? Londoned it up?'

'Of course they have.'

'Rough.'

'Oh, I don't know,' I said, irritated by the way that this inanity was reverently received, 'if everybody left their houses alone, what would you all have to talk about? And where would Adrian earn his honest crust?'

'Don't be silly,' Georgiana said at once.

'Oh, let him talk,' snapped Adrian. 'Well, Oliver, you may as well practise on us. You're going to be discussing the whole thing tomorrow with your wife.'

'What?' I said stupidly, feeling the usual sick qualm.

'Claudia's staying there,' said Georgiana, with satisfaction. 'I could hardly not invite her. We try and keep up some standards here, whatever Stephen and Isabella might do.'

III

A moment of silence fell on the merry little gathering, while I watched them all watching me. I was blowed if I was going to give them the cheap thrill of a response (thank you, Adrian, for the inadvertent warning of storms ahead). I walked over to the window to look at the twilight falling on the garden trees, coming up like mist from the river, and let the silence gather. I could, I suppose, simply have left; but I could not bear the thought of sitting in the train thinking about the whole lot of them sitting around the Jordans dinner-table listening to what Claudia had to say about me.

Georgiana, remembering at last that she had set herself up as the last guardian and inheritrix of civilised standards of conduct, broke the silence by asking if anyone wanted anything more to drink. I made my first bit of history for that evening by replying, 'No thank you, my dear. A splash of tonic water, but don't let me stop anyone else.' And while they filled their glasses (third round, more than their habit) I reflected that that was that, and that I would make history out of them if it was the last thing I did. One cannot spend three years as the husband of a woman like Claudia without gaining a very thorough grounding indeed in unobtrusive techniques of social mayhem. It occurred to me that they had not yet realised how very capable I had become, under my wife's expert tuition, at self-defence. In the meantime, I went into one of my very best acts, the manly and grieved husband chastened by private sorrow and incapable, thus crushed by recollection, of keeping up his usual misleading front of brittle, clever banter.

Since Adrian and Colin were coming the public school hot and strong for Horsfall's benefit, they had to fall into line. They obviously decided that the only way out of the pit they had dug themselves was affectionate teasing, sealing their fate by so doing. I can hardly claim to be much of a success in the world, but even so, I find I have a certain aversion to being patronised. Even as I studied them adjusting their expressions, I could hardly fail to observe that Georgiana's eyes were lingering on Horsfall, as (I do hope) she thought of her returning husband. The brat, meanwhile, took advantage of the grownups' inattention to slip his brute a salted almond, which he champed with noisy satisfaction. My own position suddenly hardened with absolute clarity and completeness. The lunch party was not going to happen: somehow, it must be prevented. At whatever cost, I was not going to sit passively at Georgiana's table the next day, and make agreeable small-talk with my wife under the eyes of my oldest and dearest friends. For the present, I was prepared to smile and let traces of my old stammer creep back into my diction, until even Horsfall might begin to like me.

'Poor old Oliver,' Adrian began, wading in with all four feet. 'We should have told you at once, but I thought it would be kinder to let you top up your gin-level first.' Adrian knows full well that I drink like the proverbial fish, and is seldom above making pointed little digs about it. What he does not know is that it is when I put the cork back in the bottle that you have to watch out.

'Lovers' meetings,' said Colin, always the least verbal of our old foursome, giving utterance to the first cliché that floated into his head. He could hardly be expected to have realised that I was even then racking my brains in order to arrange a very different sort of meeting that very night. Horsfall, being the virile and unmarried sort, had nothing to contribute, but I wasn't disposed to forgive him anything for that. Georgiana tried to matronise, damn her impudence. She came over, and put her arm through mine, looking up at me with her Madonna expression.

'Oliver dear, dear old Oliver, it's probably all to the good. After a week with that cow Isabella, she'll probably be so relieved to get back to civilisation that she'll fall on your neck the minute she sees you.'

If one reflects that, by the tenets of her Church, Georgiana is tied to the thug Holderness not merely for this life, but for eternity, one might forgive her such trite observations. But if she was doing her bit for the sanctity of marriage, she should not have let her gaze (still set at clement, loving and sweet) drift past me to play about Horsfall's elegant profile in quite the way it was doing. I had her number, and my plans for the evening began to mature. I gave her arm a little fraternal squeeze of inarticulate gratitude.

'I don't know,' I said with becoming modesty. 'She's probably well rid of me. *Parlons d'autre chose*, m'dear. I wouldn't want to cast a blight on the evening. We have so little of the summer left now, after all.' I affected to shake off my depression in a profound sigh. My godson was watching like a hawk, open scepticism written all over his blobby, freckled countenance, but who listens to children in traditional households? I slipped my arm out of Georgiana's, sat down again with my tonic-water, and revived the topic of the hour to demonstrate that I had accepted the rebukes of all concerned and was prepared to be sweet and good.

'Georgiana, did they get Blackwater with contents, or did your Grandmamma manage to get all the best stuff over here?'

Weren't they all relieved that the topic of my marriage had been laid (as they thought) to rest, and that they could get back to class solidarity and sniping at the enemy? They all brightened up no end.

'They copped the lot,' Georgiana declared, with genuine indignation.

'Pictures, furniture, frescoes and all?'

'Don't talk about the frescoes,' Adrian groaned. 'They've tacked hardboard over the Pompeian room.'

'And covered it in Laura Ashley wallpaper with roses on,' Georgiana added. 'The decorator in Aldeburgh, decent man that he is, told me for a fact. Bless him, he didn't like doing it. According to him, Isabella seemed to be under the impression that it gave a really Oldee-Worldee-Englishee air to the room. May she be forgiven.'

'I heard,' said Colin, 'that they simply slapped vinyl paint over the grotesques in the dressing-room, because some bloody London interior designer thought they were spoiling the colour scheme in what la Señora Gibbs doubtless calls "the bedroom suite".'

'There really ought to be a law,' growled Adrian. 'Why didn't English Heritage get an injunction?'

'Oh, they know all the right people,' said Georgiana bitterly. 'Do you know, there's wall-to-wall shagpile carpet over the painted floor in the saloon, if local sources are to be believed? And glass coffee tables, and spotlights over the pictures.'

'You mean they copped the ancestral pictures?' said I, with pretty indignation.

'Portraits, that sort of thing?' asked Horsfall, with exceptional brightness.

'Oh yes, Edward,' said Georgiana gently, 'the lot.'

'I can't remember,' I said (I could, though). 'Was there anything special?'

'A Devis, quite a nice one of the family, in the drawing room,' Adrian chipped in.

'Really?' said Colin, the eager young professional, 'it's unusual to find him working so far south. I'd like to see that.'

'They weren't sporting enough to lend it for the exhibition, of course,' said Georgiana sweetly.

'If you really want to see it, Colin,' I said sadly, 'we'd better all eat buckets of humble pie along with Georgiana's lovely luncheon tomorrow. Do the soggy dog act, like dear old Taggart' (Josh shot me an unusually hostile look, even for him). 'We've all had to do it in our time. Oh, I say, Mrs Gibbs, Isabella, I mean, do you really have a Devis? Gosh, I'd love to see it. Pant, pant, slobber, slobber.'

'Oliver's scared of dogs,' remarked the godchild to Horsfall, with unerring grasp on the irrelevant. 'Ed-Edward, have you got a dog?'

'Black lab., old son,' replied the Monosyllabic Marvel. 'Good enough dog. Wish I had him as well trained as your Taggart.' Well aware that he was being discussed, the animal thumped his tail, and placed his damp jowl on Horsfall's knee. Incidentally, just to put the record straight, my detestation of dogs is not, as the infant Josiah naively assumed, based on fear. Beyond the obvious facts that they are uncomely, malodorous, intrusive and boring, dogs irritate me profoundly by offering a distorted, cretinous parody of human desires, emotions and interactions. Taggart's winsome act nauseated me precisely because it so closely paralleled that of Adrian and Colin.

'Slobrador,' said Horsfall, administering a friendly clout about the ears, 'go to master.'

Would the dear child not have followed his father's lieutenant to the ends of the earth at that moment?

I noticed that the conversation was straying into unfruitful channels, and steered it back on to course.

'I seem to remember that they were foolish enough to invest in my ancestor,' I remarked diffidently, 'but I think they had the sense to stick it in the shrubbery well out of sight.'

'There's a very good statue by the landing-stage, if that's what you mean,' Georgiana said. 'It looks very nice there, but I believe its days are numbered. Isabella has been heard to talk about swimming-pools.'

'Blast her,' said Colin, who likes the ancestor so much more than I do.

'But didn't you Stradlings buy some rather good stuff in the eighteenth century?' Adrian said, showing off (having obviously forgotten that Horsfall would award no brownie points for an unmanly knowledge of the visual arts).

Georgiana rose suddenly from her chair and walked to the window, her blue dress stirring as she moved. She stood for a moment with her hand resting on the shutter, looking over the dim water towards the other house.

'Hell and darkness,' she said quite unexpectedly. 'I forgive them for swiping the house, but they could have left us the Stubbs.'

IV

She stayed at the window for a moment, not moving at all, then shook herself out of it and turned back into the room. Horsfall was looking both rattled and excited, a look which I once saw on the face of Sock Holderness. On that occasion, Claudia and I invented a dental appointment, packed our bags and did a runner. You don't mention Stubbs to a company of art historians without generating a certain amount of excitement, so Colin and Adrian charged in quite oblivious of the fact that a child of ten could have seen that Horsfall had started to smoulder. The child of ten present, let it be recorded, did indeed notice and grew excited, doubtless by a sudden recollection of his dear Papa.

'I'd heard there was a Stubbs!' said Adrian. 'Any good?'

'What's it of?' Colin broke in.

Georgiana had recovered her calm, and oddly, her cool voice doubled the force of her words.

'It is a proper Stubbs, and I would quite literally give the whole house for it, this house too, almost anything. It's a man with a black horse. Marvellous thing.'

'What,' said Adrian, half-rising from his chair, 'not that one? The one that's only in the old book – of course, it must be! "private collection, Suffolk" – bloody hell.'

'Come on, tell me,' said Colin.

'D'you mean it's a really good one?' I asked innocently, seeing immense possibilities, and having every reason to keep the temperature good and high. Adrian was so excited that he forgot the cold bath.

'Simply the best,' he said. 'Well, as far as I can tell from the old photograph. I thought it had been lost somewhere round the first war – of course, everybody knows there's supposed to be some kind of Stubbs at Blackwater, but I always thought it was just any old painting of a horse, and the attribution was wishful thinking. Why on earth didn't I put two and two together? Georgiana, are you really telling us that your awful cousins have got "The Horse-Tamer" on the ghastly glazed, dragged and sponged walls of their saloon? Good Lord.'

'Oh yes, they've got it all right. It's been away for cleaning, trust them, but it's back there now. I haven't seen it for years, but it's not the sort of painting you forget in a hurry.'

Just for once, Adrian appeared to have nothing more to say.

'What is it?' Colin asked. 'Come on.'

'I can't remember everything about it,' said Georgiana. 'I was still doing my A levels when I last saw it, and when you do see it, you're so knocked sideways anyway you don't take much in. There's a man holding a rearing black horse.'

'That's right,' Adrian put in. 'A jagged storm just clearing, and a magnificent silvery light on the trees. The horse is simply beyond description, a thundering great beast in every sense of the word, it somehow looks as if it's made out of cloud itself. I can't describe it properly, but it's absolutely one of the greatest Romantic paintings there is. Oliver, do you remember the two Stubbses at Yale?'

'Of course I do. Lovely things. I used to go and weep the tears of exile in front of them every day at about noon, before I crept out and gnawed at a hamburger.'

'Well, it's streets ahead of them. It really is a scandal that it should only be known by one spotty photograph where you can hardly make out the man's face.'

'Well I for one,' Colin said, 'want to see this wonder, and I want to see it soon. It's never been shown?'

'Not a chance. Isabella and her little insurance man are like *that*, and he wouldn't like her drawing attention to it. It's all very well for all her yummy decorator friends to gaze at it as much as they like since they're too pig-ignorant to know what they're looking at, but no one with an education's meant to cross its path.'

'Georgiana, would it be too awful to suggest that we might be rather nice to them tomorrow, and get ourselves invited for tea to have a look at it?'

'Do what you like,' Georgiana snapped. 'Edward and I will have the decency to stay here and wait for Sock.'

'Given the circumstances,' said Adrian diplomatically, 'it might be more useful to look for the book. You don't have a copy here, do you, Georgiana?'

'No. There's a book about Stubbs somewhere, a paperback thing of Sock's, but it's much more recent. "The Horse-Tamer" isn't in it, of course.' Georgiana spoke absently, her thoughts elsewhere. Adrian was still on the scent, and keen to display his expertise. 'The catalogue of the big Royal Academy exhibition doesn't have it, as I remember, not even the old black-and-white photograph.'

'There's a second-hand bookshop in Aldeburgh, and one in Saxmundham,' said Colin. 'They might just have the old Stubbs book. We couldn't possibly ring them up?'

'What about the library at U.E.A.?' I suggested.

My godson was evidently too fascinated by the situation to agitate for his long-delayed supper, and was making up for it by champing his way through all the salted nuts with mechanical persistence. Horsfall seemed absorbed in the discussion, having realised two essential facts: that it was a picture of the sacred animal, and therefore worthy of his notice, and that it was of burning interest to his lovely hostess.

'U.E.A.?' Georgiana asked vaguely. 'I thought they made dishwashers.'

'No, darling,' said Colin, 'it's a new university. Not a bad thought, Olly' (ah, Colin had registered that I was trying to be helpful) 'but the campus is actually in Norwich, and that's a good two hours. More likely that someone we know in Aldeburgh might have a copy.'

I observed a sudden outbreak of alertness from the dog. A

whispered consultation was in progress between Horsfall and the child.

'Well,' the boy said, with appalling, bell-like clarity, 'why don't we just go and take it? It's ours anyway, and they're wet.'

Georgiana looked rather pleased at this unmistakable proof that Josh was his father's son. Meanwhile, my godson continued with absolute confidence, 'Ed-Edward would do it. So could Daddy. Couldn't you, Edward?'

Horsfall, sensing that the dignity of the British Army was at stake, replied, as he was bound to, 'Well, a quick take-out mission might be a possibility.' At which point Adrian shook me rigid by saying, 'At least we'd see it if we half-inched it.' It was not merely the sentiment, but the Spitalfieldian vernacular popping into Adrian's usually precise speech which was worthy of remark. I realised that I would have to do very little to get them all involved in a distinctly discreditable rag, provided that alcohol continued to flow freely. Horsfall was beginning to look keen, and Colin took up the ill-fated role of the Voice of Reason.

'Breaking and entering,' he said amiably, 'equals six months without the option. We're pillars of society these days. I have students. Adrian reviews books in the *Spectator*.' He grinned a grin which was patently intended to offset the dismal, middle-aged caution of this remark. It was clear to me that he was fatally compromised between two positions, the desire to look as if he was still ready for any boyish lark, and the hope that the matter would go no further. I foresaw little trouble from him.

'It would show them, oh, it would show them,' Georgiana said, perfectly seriously. 'Would anyone like another drink?'

I shook my head, the others didn't.

'Georgiana,' Colin said reasonably, 'this is not a novel by John Buchan. Judges take dim views of this sort of thing. People end up in the slammer.'

'Only,' she replied with a fatuous air of logic and sweet reason, 'if they're stupid enough to get caught.' She proceeded to play her art-historical trump card.

'It's the painting I'm worried about. It's not just that my cousin is a ghastly little man who doesn't deserve it. Even when I was a schoolgirl, I noticed that it was on panel, and the varnish was beginning to wrinkle at the bottom. Now the swine have had it cleaned, it's got less to protect it. Dry, hot rooms, Colin: central heating on a thermostat, on and off every day. How long would you give an unvarnished painting on wood? It'll be lucky to last another year before the paint starts flaking off . . .'

'On to the shagpile carpet,' I couldn't resist adding. I was ignored.

'Scum,' said Adrian, very distinctly beginning to show the effects of the gin. 'That settles it. They don't deserve it.'

Colin made his last effort, uneasily aware that Horsfall was already regarding him with an officer's eye.

'We aren't undergraduates. It might be rather hard to pass it off as a joke. The picture must be worth a very great deal. What are you going to do with it – keep it in the cellar?'

'They can see it here. They can be told to look after it. Then they can have it back.' Horsfall was firm. Did he imagine for one moment that Georgiana would give it up, once she got her hands on it? Tosh, sir. Just look at the expression on the woman's face. I thought it best to raise the temperature by objecting.

'And supposing,' I said, 'that alarms don't ring in every police station from here to Colchester – and I'm sure they would – what is poor old Horsfall going to say when he's caught in the saloon with gilt all over his hands? It's all a jolly frolic, and he's looking for the way back to the boat-club dinner, please? Forget it.'

'You could do it without getting caught, couldn't you, Edward?' Georgiana was openly pleading, almost quivering with her passionate desire to get her own way, regardless of the cost. She locked eyes recklessly with Horsfall, who flushed slightly.

'I could.'

Her lips parted in a little sigh, her whole face soft and hungry. Georgiana, do not forget, was a very beautiful woman, but never had I seen gin and acquisitiveness combine to such astounding effect.

'Might need to take a man or two with me,' he continued. 'How big's the thing?'

'I can't remember exactly,' she answered. 'It's not vast. Four foot by six-ish?'

'Two men could lift it,' said Adrian. How drunk was he? If he had been functioning normally, he would have squashed this ridiculous conversation, not urged it on. Still, if he wasn't stopping them, I had no plans whatsoever to do so. Quite the reverse.

'I'll come to keep watch,' Colin volunteered, infected by the Saturnalian atmosphere which had overtaken the whole party.

'Good man,' said Horsfall. (Are all burglaries planned as casually as picnics?)

'Shall we have dinner,' I said, 'so that the chaps can build up their strength? They really ought to have beefsteaks and porter, since they obviously plan to go rowing.'

'Who said anything about rowing?' Colin said defensively.

'Good thinking,' yipped Horsfall.

'It seems obvious,' I said modestly. 'I'm sure they'd hear a car miles down the drive, and there's probably gravel at the front.'

'It'll be much quieter by water,' Adrian agreed. 'There's still a boat, isn't there, Georgiana?'

'There is.'

'I can steer it,' the brat volunteered. Adrian looked obscurely relieved.

'Dinner,' he said decisively, offering Georgiana his arm.

'Josh should have had his hours ago, poor little chap,' said Georgiana quite calmly, as though everything was settled. 'You'll just have to have it with us, Josh.'

Horsfall rose from his crouch on the fender in one swift movement, not using his hands. He assumed command.

'Did I see a map in the hall? Twenty-five-inch? Excellent. We'll take it in with our scoff, and have a good look at it.' They passed into the hall. I took a moment to catch my breath, trying not to laugh, to explode. I resisted the temptation to do any private business with the drinks tray.

It was dark outside the house, and the tide was coming in.

V

On that evening at Jordans, planning a burglary had already made dinner so late that, when I had composed myself and joined the others I found that they were surrounded on three sides by the staring and intrusive night. There were candles on the table in honour of the past, and their watery reflections glowed on the polished wood. Portraits of Georgiana's ancestors gazed down with what looked like an active lust for blood at the silver game-birds on the sideboard. Georgiana went out and came in again, setting a place for her son with the metal kitchen cutlery.

I took a moment to look at them all. A pretty sight, especially in the context of my private agenda. Georgiana was at the bottom of the table, leaning forward, one white and rounded elbow on the mahogany already. Adrian and Colin sat side by side with their backs to the window, their reflections behind them like the ghosts of footmen. In the odd, reflecting light, Horsfall sat at the head of the table, strangely like Holderness his master, handsome and unpredictable.

I slipped into my place on the other side of the table beside Josh, murmuring apologies.

'Olly can never resist a final go at the drinks tray,' Colin said amiably. Old friends are entitled to comment on one's tiny weaknesses. I smiled at him, and then at Georgiana.

'Georgiana, dear,' I said to her, 'is there any chance of a little water with my lovely dinner?' Adrian asked if I was sickening for something. I ignored him.

'Josh,' said Georgiana, 'be good, and get your godfather some Vichy water from the sideboard. While you're at it, you can go downstairs to daddy's cupboard, and get, um, let's see, four bottles from the claret end for the men. Edward can open it.' She gave me a smug look, as though I was to be hanged, and she had plaited the noose from her own hair. Why should I care that she had set me among the impotent?

A notional first course, involving a half-avocado and a dry quarter of lime, was consumed and taken away. Georgiana then fetched some school-sized white enamel dishes from the Rayburn, and plonked them down in the middle of the table.

'Cottage pie!' Adrian said, with every appearance of satisfaction. 'God bless Mrs Thing, and confusion to the Boroughs of South Kensington and Chelsea and mucked-up foreign cookery practised therein.' A bit clumsy and over-elaborate, but his audience was not critical.

The child returned with the bottles and put them down beside Horsfall, then fetched him a silver corkscrew from the sideboard, giving an altar-boy's half-bow before returning to his seat. Where do well-bred children pick up these antique habits?

'Good man,' said Horsfall, thus sealing the brat's devotion for ever. 'Gosh, good show,' he continued, grappling efficiently with the first bottle. Georgiana looked at the label in well-concealed horror as the bottle passed round the table.

'Josh, darling,' she said sweetly, 'you have rather brought the best there was. But I think the occasion deserves it. I'm afraid you'll just have to warm the mugs in your hands.'

'Good idea, silver mugs,' pronounced Horsfall from the top of the table, 'warm up well.' Another bottle was immediately sent in the wake of the first.

'Mind how you go, Edward,' said Colin to Horsfall. 'I don't want a pint of the stuff, and neither do you.' The cretin Horsfall, naturally, took this as a challenge, and very deliberately filled his mug to the brim.

Adrian made a discreet noise indicating that, while he would not like to be taken for a greedy drunk, he had a healthy capacity for claret, especially twenty-one-year-old Lynch-Bages for which he was not paying. He took the bottle from Colin, and topped up his mug. Horsfall held his mug up before he drank, catching candleflames in the silver. All in all, it was just like one of those Regency prints of a hunt dinner in the grass shires.

'Drink, puppy drink, and let every puppy drink,' I observed cheerfully, with intention to annoy, since I saw the brat holding up his mug and mouthing 'ego', 'that is old enough to lap and to swallow . . .'

'A splash, darling, since it's a special occasion,' said Georgiana, busily ladling out cottage pie and peas, 'and ask your godfather for some of his fizzy stuff.' She sent the last of the plates on its way, and rose to her feet. 'A toast.'

Horsfall rapped the handle of his knife on the table.

'Confusion to Isabella Gibbs and all who sail in her.'

'And to all gentrifiers, improvers, and muckers-about with houses,' Adrian added.

They all drank with a nasty, ritual slurp. I swigged at my water with a will. Colin, I noticed, was beginning to get cold feet again. He only took a mouthful, and put his mug down carefully.

'Confusion to all nargs,' said Horsfall wittily, taking a long pull at his wine. Colin, again, merely touched the rim of the mug with his lips. I thought a little joke might help to keep things humming along.

'What's the matter, Colin? "He that will this health deny, down among the dead men let him lie." ' He didn't bother to answer me, but instead made a touchingly inept attempt to change the subject.

'I don't like it when it gets dark before dinner. It reminds me of Sunday evening blues at school.'

This seldom fails to open the floodgates of reminiscence, especially when all those present are anxious to make it quite clear to one another that they personally went to the right sort of school. Cathedral bells, letters home, gothic windows lighted on the far side of the rugger pitch . . . This time, nobody rose to the bait at all.

'Proper claret,' Adrian said with satisfaction, refilling his mug.

'Good scoff, this,' said Horsfall with appreciation.

'Better than you'd get over the water,' said Georgiana with smug malice. 'Dinner's practically at midnight by the time they've finished putting vermouth in the sauce and sauce on the plates and meat on the sauce, and found the cherry tomatoes, and snipped up the basil. Anyway, the sauce always gets burned while Isabella has a *crise* over the soufflé.'

'Kiwi fruit with everything,' Adrian added. 'The horror.'

'Mango gloop and slices of radish, and *fromage blanche*, and the whole ghastly mess is on octagonal plates. "Ees taste," as Isabella says. I'm sorry to say she did one of those fearsomely expensive cookery courses, and she's been steadily starving that poor sap Stephen into an early grave ever since. Monica Lucas told me she and Clive had dinner at Blackwater, with a sliver of this and a shred of that, and ended up in their own kitchen at half past one in the morning making themselves bacon sandwiches out of sheer, ravening hunger.'

'Sounds bloody,' Horsfall said, stoking with a will. 'We're better off here. Good solid scoff.'

'I wonder what Sock's eating tonight?' said Georgiana.

'Classified info,' said Horsfall, gallantly. I had a surreal vision of Sock ripping piles of computer printout into chunks with his strong, white teeth, and gulping them down wolfishly.

'Cabbage and sausages,' Adrian guessed.

'Wild boar,' Colin said with an effort. I noticed that since he had failed to cool the party down, he had been applying himself steadily to his mug, and was getting back into hero mode.

'Raven stew,' I suggested, 'in honour of the dark and bloody-minded gods of the north.'

'Steak pie and chocolate pudding,' the brat said, missing the point absolutely. 'That's what Daddy likes. So do I.'

'And so say all of us,' Horsfall said, leaning over to bestow one of those boyish punches on the upper arm with which grown-ups remind the young that they were boys once themselves.

'Eat up, Josh,' he went on, 'we've a stiff night's work ahead of us.'

Radiant with contentment, the child reached out to punch Horsfall back, and then ate up his dinner as though his life depended on it.

'When we've got it,' said Georgiana excitedly, 'we'll see the horse properly. I'm sure it's got something to do with bringing in a new strain of Arab blood. It couldn't have been the first, could it, Adrian?

Adrian knew, of course; his omniscience was legendary. I sometimes scrounge dinner with some friends in Hampstead who keep a list of things he doesn't know: it is short, and peculiar.

'Darley and Godolphin were the first to bring them in, I think. Wasn't there a Stradling who was a friend of Lord Darley's?'

'The Byerley Turk, the Godolphin Barb, and the Darley Arabian,' recited Horsfall dreamily. Even real men are allowed to know a little history, if it is the history of the Noble Animal.

'Quite right,' said Colin. 'Blunt the poet had them all over the shop, didn't he?'

'Whereas,' I remarked, 'Blunt the art historian did not.'

'Shut it,' said Horsfall irritably, jerked from his romantic haze.

It was necessary at this point to annoy them, just a little.

'Shut what?' I asked plaintively. 'And talking of shoving one's oar in, I do hope that one of you knows how to muffle oars. You'd look pretty silly arriving with a splash and a shout of "Stroke!" like the boat race. It's obvious that you all know John Buchan's beautiful works by heart, so someone must remember. Of course, if you don't there's not much point in carrying on, I should say.'

This little speech succeeded beyond my wildest hopes. Colin had got over his moment of indecision, and Georgiana and Horsfall needed absolutely no encouragement. I was having slight doubts about Adrian, who seemed disposed to hang back a bit.

'I understand,' said Colin, falling straight into it, 'that you tie cloths round the blades of the oars so that they don't make a splash when they go into the water.'

'Tosh,' said Horsfall, his voice rising as if he were drilling a platoon with the wind against him. 'All you need to do is give a thorough greasing to the rowlocks, bung a sock or something round the bit of oar which actually touches them, and feather carefully when you pull out for the next stroke.'

'There's plenty of gunge for the mower in Sock's shed,' said Georgiana. 'It should do for the rowlocks.'

'Good stuff,' said Horsfall. 'Gun-oil does quite well too.' Gun-oil: a smell I have somehow always associated with Sock.

'I seem to remember,' I said innocently, 'that Colin did a bit of messing about in boats when he was an undergraduate.' And why did he give me such a filthy look? It is my fate, alas, to be misunderstood when I am only trying to help. 'We all have pasts, old son,' I said pleasantly.

'Yes,' said Adrian. 'You more than most.'

I smiled forgivingly.

'All this meat,' I explained to Horsfall, 'seems to have gone to his head. All that the poor chap usually has of an evening is a swift banana and a spliff with his Rastafarian lodgers.'

'Oliver,' began Adrian ominously, 'now look here . . .'

'Cut it out, will you,' Horsfall snapped. 'We've got better

things to do than listen to you being clever-clever.' Good. Good. Good.

'Listen, chaps,' said Georgiana, 'let's ignore Oliver and get to the matter in hand. As you were saying, Edward, before people started trying to be funny . . .?'

'Sound idea to muffle the oars. We can't be doing with giving the enemy advance warning. What we need to aim for is a quick take-out. In and out, no fancy stuff.'

My godson was drinking this in with ecstasy. He looked as if he was memorising every word for repetition in the dormitory as soon as he got back to school. I was memorising it also, just in case it ever needed to be repeated in front of a magistrate. Sadly (I reflected), if they did all end up at the local Assizes, the magistrate would probably have gone to school with Georgiana's father, and they might just swing it as a family joke, ghastly, foggy and class-ridden island that this is. A furious discussion started on the subject of muffled oars, in the course of which Georgiana, Colin and Horsfall displayed an extensive knowledge of Boy's Own fiction. Dornford Yates was quoted, Buchan was extensively referred to, 'Sapper' was cited as an authority. Through all this, Adrian remained disturbingly quiet. I made sure that the fourth bottle was shoved in his direction as often as possible.

'What larks,' I observed to the darkness and the clustering ghosts outside the windows, 'so many theories.'

Horsfall looked hard at me, taking the measure, just as he had done when we first shook hands. 'If you came with us, laddie, you'd find out.'

'Just what I was thinking,' Georgiana said, closing her hand over mine and squeezing it hard. 'It would be very good for you. It might help to chase away the cobwebs and anyway, you don't take nearly enough exercise, Olly. We worry about you.'

'When did you last pull an honest oar, then, Olly?' asked Colin with offensive, drunken jollity.

The words 'not since I married' rose to my lips, and were ruthlessly suppressed.

'It'd sort you out,' Adrian muttered, and relapsed into his sulks.

'I intend,' I said firmly, 'to do nothing tougher this evening than retire to the kitchen and watch a programme about elephants on Mrs Thing's television. Bad luck, chaps.'

'You're coming, my lad,' said Horsfall grimly, 'like it or not. When there's a weak link in a unit, you're a hell of a lot better keeping him under your eye where he can't rot the show, than leaving him at base to cause trouble.'

'It'll do you a power of good to have to keep quiet for an hour or two,' said Colin, with a cretinous schoolboy guffaw.

'Poor old Olly can't keep quiet for ten minutes,' observed Georgiana maternally, tightening her grip on my hand, 'but he'll just have to try. Won't you, darling?'

I saw at this point that they were going to do it more likely than not, and that very little would be needed to tip the balance. A policy of continuing to annoy them looked like my best bet.

'Why on earth should I come?' I asked plaintively. 'I live on my wits in two rooms above the pub in Swift Court, between the tarts and the Tonbridge Mission. My father drank the family house before I could toddle, not that it was anything to shout about. Ancestral piles and pretty horses have absolutely nothing to do with me, and what's more, all this public-school bloody heartiness gives me a bilious headache. Forget it.'

'I've taken men out for saying less than that,' said Horsfall menacingly, taking a long slurp of his claret. So I was very sure of my effect when I answered, in my very best pansy drawl,

'Quoth the bloody son of bloody Belial, flown with insolence and wine.'

Georgiana came down on me like a ton of bricks. 'Oliver, apologise at once. I'm not having you being beastly rude to a guest at my table. And what the hell d'you think's insolent about all this? All we're trying to do is get back my own family property, for God's sake.'

'Frightfully sorry,' I said to Horsfall. 'I promise not to quote out of a book ever again. I'll even promise never to read one, if you like.'

Horsfall, who had no ear for sarcasm, muttered 'fair enough' in an orthodox way, unclenched his fist, and devoted his mind to the mission in hand.

'Now, men,' he said. 'Do we agree that there's no point tackling this one by land?'

'Think so,' Colin agreed. Adrian nodded, looking a touch less miserable.

'Edward,' piped up the infant Josiah, 'please, I mean, sorry, but hadn't we better do it soon? Daddy would. The tide's probably almost in now.'

VI

This timely little piece of relevant local knowledge from the brat won a moment of respectful silence from all, broken only by Horsfall's predictable murmur of 'sound lad', and the noise of Georgiana's taking away the plates and returning with rhubarb crumble. The child was sent away to get a bottle of pudding wine. I did hope, though not aloud, that Sock, who has a roaring bad temper, would agree that his best claret and Barsac had disappeared in a good cause.

'Right,' Horsfall said. 'We cross the water. We stroll in, and hoist the thing. Simple stuff.'

'What about the people in the house?' Colin asked.

'No trouble,' his captain replied. 'They're bound to be at dinner. Georgiana says they dine late.'

'It's getting awfully late, though,' said Adrian. No doubt about it: he was having second thoughts.

'From what I hear,' said Georgiana, 'they eat at Latin hours. I wouldn't imagine they sit down to dinner much before ten.'

'Good show,' said Horsfall. 'Better do a recce. Let's have a look at the boat.'

Adrian looked a shade more cheerful at the mention of the word 'boat'. No doubt about it: he had had second thoughts, and unless I was very much mistaken, he had thought of a way to put a damper on the whole thing.

'Splendid idea that it is,' he said seriously, 'I'm not at all sure we can work it. We've agreed that it's mad to try and do it by land, what with noisy gravel and all the rest of it. And I've got a nasty feeling we won't be able to do it by water either. You see, I was out painting down by the estuary this morning, and there was about as much water in the whole thing as Oliver puts in his whisky. And we all know that it's stupid to get mixed up with the mud-flats, because half of them are quicksand. Georgiana, I'm right about that, aren't I?'

''Fraid so,' she said, none too pleased. My charming godson looked at Adrian with pretty thorough hatred.

'And also, I don't think that salt mud is absolutely the best thing to drag a major work of art through, especially when it's also an object of immense value belonging to somebody else.'

With joy, I recognised the badge on Horsfall's blue blazer, and added my modest contribution.

'Quite so,' I said solemnly. 'And whatever the players of Rugby football may think, mud all over a chap's shirt doesn't make him look particularly manly. It just makes him look as if he'd been pushed off his punt.'

Splendid. Horsfall's eye flashed, and he was spurred into thinking hard about how to show me where I got off.

'So,' Adrian concluded with becoming regret, 'be that as it may, it's simply a stupid risk to take. Call the whole thing off.' He sat back, having, like Dr Johnson, done his bit for reason. The child looked at Horsfall with something like desperation. Horsfall was obviously thinking very hard indeed. Georgiana began to say 'Edward,' but thought better of it.

Horsfall, whom Sandhurst had evidently taught everything a chap really needs to know, fished out his pocket diary, and grinned.

'You know what, men?' he said, 'We're in luck.' A shade of unease flitted across Adrian's countenance.

'It's the third week of September, which means it's the equinox, and there's a new moon. Low water's at its lowest, which is what you saw, Adrian, but we're all set for the highest high tides of the year. Josh, nip out like a brave lad and see which way the wind's blowing.'

We all stared at each other while the brat dashed out, and returned to report breathlessly that the wind was blowing off the sea.

'Great work,' said Horsfall. 'Couldn't be better. Solid insurance. In about an hour, the estuary will be as full as it ever gets.'

'You mean we could get a boat across without any risk of grounding?' asked Colin, with simple faith.

'Exactly,' said Horsfall. 'Must be one of the best nights of the year for it.'

Adrian looked decidedly cross with life. But Horsfall knew what to say to him.

'Adrian' (the bark of a man who doesn't go in for first names himself), 'you're well up on all this stuff, and you must have a pretty useful memory. D'you reckon you could draw us a rough plan of the house if you put your mind to it?'

Adrian looked a touch more interested, but I thought it might do no harm to make sure. 'He could do it in a flash,' I said. 'He's an absolute whizz on Soane.' I kept to myself the suspicion that

Adrian spends half his waking life in Sir John Soane's museum with a very firm intention of being the director some day, and has long since measured the stairs to ensure that his Empire desk will go up them when that brave day dawns.

'Dear Adrian,' Georgiana said, meaning it.

'Only my job,' he muttered, managing a reasonable smile for her.

'You're such an asset,' she said, meaning that too.

'Right,' I said firmly. 'You've got yourself a cultural attaché, so may I repeat, loud and clear, that I'm not going. Quite apart from any other considerations, I might meet my wife. Thanks, but no thanks.'

'It's the one way of making sure you don't rat on us,' declared Horsfall in his ringing English tenor. 'We haven't forgotten that there are such things as telephones, y'know.' (Banners of old battles hanging in cathedrals . . . Sorry, my mind wanders.)

'No thank you, brother,' I said firmly.

'What makes you think you've got options?' said Horsfall, still trumpet-toned and military. He stood up, scraping his chair. Colin and the brat were on their feet in a second, Adrian was a bit slower. Horsfall motioned the child in the direction of the port decanter on the sideboard, let him pour some into all the glasses, and then took the decanter away, getting another altar-boy's bow.

'A toast,' he said, 'to the success of this mission. Bumpers, gentlemen.' Adrian and Colin did as they were told. I took an ostentatious sip of flat Vichy water. Horsfall allowed the child to touch the rim of his glass. 'And to Sock Holderness coming home, safe and soon.'

Business with the decanter. All, Georgiana included, drank to that. I didn't, reflecting that Sock's homecoming might be more fun than any of us had bargained for. Adrian sat down abruptly, studying the rhododendrons outside the window as though he were planning to eat them. The others stayed on their feet.

'Now,' said Horsfall, 'we're going to need some other kit. It's going to be a shiny night, and blazers and shirts will show up bright and clear. Pigeon-shooting drill: dark kit. Georgiana, your good man must have a Barbour or two about the place?'

'There are plenty of Sock's clothes upstairs,' said Georgiana immediately. I noted that an invasion of the sacred study was planned. Good. Horsfall chose at this moment to have a romantic afterthought, and sent the decanter round again.

'Men now dead or overseas.' They drank that one all right, in a haze of Great Game nostalgia.

'Let's go up,' said Georgiana. 'Sock's got the proper map up there too.'

'Lead on,' said Horsfall gallantly, and swaggered out after her, followed by Colin and the godson. The little brute was keyed-up and quivering like a lurcher, and three sips of port had done him no good at all. It was not impossible that he might be sick with the sheer excitement of it all. An agreeable thought.

Adrian stared at the shrubbery and his own reflection until the door had closed behind them. He turned to me, just as I was wondering if I might allow myself a small and hard-earned glass of port, and gave me a nasty smile.

'Oliver, you really are the cleverest of us all. I'd go so far as to say that you're as clever as sin, and in happier circumstances, I'd find it a pleasure to watch you at work. But on this occasion, you can cut it out. We're supposed to be your bloody friends, remember?' I had been expecting this. Adrian is not stupid.

'Adrian, I'm not following you. Are you feeling all right?'

'Oliver. A straight question: do you ever feel at all ashamed of yourself?'

When we were at university, they always told us that you shouldn't bring *ad hominem* questions into arguments. But standards slip, over the years.

'Sorry, Adrian. Not with you.' He was at least a bit drunk, and I doubted if he was in complete command.

'I know all about Roy Sutler and the sale at Sotheby's.'

'So does half London. And that's not cricket, Adrian, to borrow the idiom of the cretinous Horsfall. To judge by the ominous way you've introduced the topic, you're intending some rather clumsy attempted blackmail. Letting the side down, don't you think? Conduct unbecoming.' And if it is a crime to have played a tiny practical joke on one of the most obnoxious men in creation, that was not what Adrian had thought at the time.

'I see from your little performance tonight just how you did it – no, don't interrupt.' I didn't dream of it. When dealing with a drunk, it is an excellent policy to say nothing at all and let him run on till he runs out of steam.

'I worked it out afterwards. You must have got poor old Roy well oiled at luncheon, and then proposed a little wander through Sotheby's, just to have a look-see. You were surprised to see there was actually a sale on, weren't you? But you stopped him at the back, just to watch. Had you swiped a catalogue in advance and made plans? – anyway, you kept him there till some seriously bogus statuary turned up. I'm right so far, aren't I?'

I smiled the forgiving smile of a wise don who knows that lads have to learn how to hold their drink, and preserved my understanding silence. He blundered on:

'Then you ran downstairs for a catalogue, if you didn't have one. You stuck your dagger-hand in the air at regular intervals, while you gabbled some out and out lie to poor old Sutler. The version I heard was that you were almost ready to swear you'd seen the bloody things before in the attics of some palazzo in Venice or Lucca or somewhere. Anyway, you got poor, greedy old Roy to jump in and offer ten quid more, and folded your arms and grinned, just like you're grinning now, while you watched him spend more money for a ghastly nineteenth-century fake than you've earned in the last three years. They said the thing was half gesso and half woodworm.' Lies: some of it was dry rot.

'Adrian . . .'

'Shut up. Just remember, I've got your number. So run along

like a good boy, and put a stop to it.'

'Adrian, you're not yourself. I've been trying to stop them all evening.'

'Skunk.'

'In fact, it was you who started it, remember? If you've got cold feet now I don't blame you, but don't imagine for one moment that Captain Horsfall and his Swallows and Amazons will listen to reason. I would think that, as so often in life, your best course is to lie back and enjoy it. Take a long pull at the decanter, and let it all carry you along. At least if you go, you can keep an eye on things. Try and stop them dropping the Stubbs into the estuary, and that sort of thing. Jolly useful, I'd say.' That foxed him.

'Come on,' I said, pouring him a perfectly lethal shot of port, 'let's join the others before Captain Horsfall court-martials us at the drum's head. He'll be wanting you to do the plans by now, and I imagine he regards art historians as disposable commodities.'

He may have murmured something about settling my hash later, but he drank off his port like a lamb and led the way upstairs. Oh, I was so clever, then; drunk, dizzy, intoxicated with my own ability. It is sickening, looking back, to realise that never in my whole life have I deployed more concentrated intelligence, and to better effect, than in wrecking everything I ever cared about.

VII

Under the bleak light of a central, hanging bulb in Sock's study, Georgiana, Horsfall and Colin were standing round the map table in the window with the blinds open to the dark. The brat was sitting in Sock's big armchair, his feet barely reaching the edge of the seat. It is a hard, estate-manager's room, with a bare parquet floor, a big and ugly desk, and framed photographs of mountains on the walls. Half-empty bookcases reach up to the ceiling, with some old Penguin detective stories and Wainwright's guides to climbing in the Lake District carelessly disposed on the upper shelves. The lower shelves hold only the random litter of Sock's life: boxes of Eley cartridges, stacked packets of Navy Cut, two heavy tumblers, and two partially full bottles of whisky (Jameson's and The Famous Grouse).

Sock had left the room as he found it, and this indifference made it the more his own. The dressing-room beyond was also lit by a bare bulb. An iron bedstead was piled with folded clothes, and there was a pile of rods and sticks in the furthest corner. A canvas gun-case leaned against the wall. I took stock of the position. The four already in the room were no trouble, they were dead set on making the raid. All I needed to do was to keep them simmering nicely by making one sarcastic remark every other minute. I was much less sure of Adrian; unsure whether he was drunk or no, whether he'd really spotted my game, and how I was playing it, and unsure, finally, of how he stood regarding the whole enterprise. I did the most practical thing I could think of. I unscrewed the cap of the bottle of Grouse and put it on the table within everyone's reach. Few men who are just about to go off on an adventure can resist a manly swig from a convenient bottle of whisky. In the event, they topped themselves up nicely without any further encouragement.

Adrian, oddly, took one tremendous pull from the bottle and forgot his second thoughts. He seemed, in fact, to get genuinely interested in doing the thing efficiently, since it had become perfectly clear he hadn't a hope in hell of stopping it. Georgiana and Horsfall got him to the table in short order, and in a couple of minutes, he was drawing a predictably accurate plan of the ground floor of Blackwater, even sketching in an elevation for Horsfall's benefit. He was unable to resist adding a bit of shading round the roofline to hint at the moon breaking through clouds, and a faint light on treetops. I withdrew myself from the group around the table and paced the room, giddy with suppressed laughter. Lovely words drifted across to me: 'terrain', 'landing', 'mission', 'synchronise'. Georgiana was making very sure of Adrian, and was also keeping the others up to the mark. I felt superfluous. I really couldn't have done it better myself.

While nobody was looking, I opened the top drawer of Sock's desk, knowing full well that I would never have the chance again. I found more packets of Navy Cut, a huge stapler which looked like a revolver, and one of those booklets of tide-times which they sell in seaside towns. This gave me a useful line with which to re-enter the comedy. It was perhaps getting chilly, and there was a smoky hint of autumn in Horsfall's convenient east wind. Grey flannel, clean linen and so forth do indeed show up well on a shiny night. Neither of these considerations, however, justified the tremendous game of dressing up which was starting in the further room.

I approached Horsfall, just as he was struggling out of an enormous cricket sweater, embroidered 'DJM 1907', and presented him with the tide-table. He dropped the sweater on the pile of their jackets, and was kind enough to thank me.

'Good work. Here we are: high water at Yarmouth, 22.24, Southwold, an hour and ten minutes later. A shade sooner than I'd thought. Right, men, we've got half an hour.'

The fun in the dressing room proceeded at high speed. I was reminded that Jordans was a house which threw nothing away when I recognised two pairs of worn but clean corduroy trousers which Georgiana had chosen for Sock while we were in our last year at University. All the clothes piled on the bed were Sock's: heavy cotton shirts, striped like mattress ticking, thick sweaters, peaty jackets, all permeated with his musky, tigerish odour. Any of them would have done, since they were dark and warm, but the assembled company turned as one to something more romantic. Georgiana flung open one of the two prehistoric wardrobes which flanked the door.

'What's wrong with Sock's stuff?' I enquired curiously. 'Are you afraid to leave mud in his turn-ups? Or are you proposing to blame the burglary on the dead?' The opened doors revealed dim ranks of tweed and flannel. There was a flash of grey here and there, as jolly as a peil-tower on a grouse-moor. 'We're heading for All Soul's night, after all.'

'Shut up,' remarked Horsfall over his shoulder. 'Don't be sillier than you can help.'

'These are more suitable,' Colin said seriously.

'They'll smell the mothballs from the bottom of the garden,' I said. 'They'll smell them in Aldeburgh if you get a following wind.'

'Listen, you barrack-room lawyer . . .' began Horsfall.

'The magistrates will convict you on the smell alone,' I went on. 'May I assure you for the last time that I am not coming?'

'Oh, but you are,' Horsfall said firmly, throwing me an antique shooting-jacket. 'Put that on, and belt up.' I dropped it neatly on the floor.

'Thank you,' I said austerely, 'but the clothes which are good enough for New Bond Street are good enough for the Assizes, and at a pinch, for the scaffold. I have a dark coat and a scarf downstairs.' Adrian had one hand on a braided blazer. I turned on him. 'I would prefer not to appear in court looking like a provincial revival of *Salad Days*. One has one's pride.'

'Oh, stop it, Oliver,' said Georgiana, busily pulling out handfuls of antique garments, the very colours of the mud and silt of the estuary. 'Concentrate, everyone. There's so little time.'

She opened the other wardrobe, to reveal a few of Sock's London clothes, a gap, and then cracking leather motoring-coats (each one the hide of a flayed Minotaur), and a line of khaki jackets. A dark-blue oarsman's scarf (one of those enormous things which could easily double as a shroud) was looped up at the end of the row. As soon as he saw these antique garments, Horsfall began to look truly manic in the authentic Holderness style. Georgiana offered him a Major's coat, but he shook his head, and touched one with a Captain's stars at the cuff, saying not a word as she guided his arms into the sleeves. He took out the oarsman's scarf, wrapped it twice round his neck, and threw the end over his shoulder. Dressed thus, he looked like an emblem of old England, up on its hind legs and roaring for blood.

Colin, meanwhile, had put on a dark Norfolk jacket buttoning up to the neck, and looked rather more like one of the Woodbegoods. Adrian had found a massive and splendid overcoat of herringbone tweed, and (as I remarked at the time) resembled I.A. Richards slipping out to a meeting of the Left Book Club. The wretched godson had slipped out of the room, and returned equally discreetly, now wearing a navy tracksuit with his school crest on the pocket.

'Shouldn't we take this nice green umbrella, in case it rains?' I asked merrily.

'You'll get wet and like it,' Horsfall snapped back, without a trace of humour.

'Edward, don't be brutal,' Georgiana (that connoisseur of brutes) said at once, in a tone which gave him every encouragement.

'Alarms,' said Horsfall briskly. 'What's the betting?'

Fair chance,' Adrian said unexpectedly. 'But there's a good possibility that if they've got people staying, they'll have got them turned off. After all, Claudia's a cut above their usual sort. They might want to show off a picture signed on the back.'

'We'll just have to risk it,' Horsfall said, 'and run like the clappers if we're wrong. We'll have to have our retreat in order, just in case.'

'Windows?' Colin asked.

'Again, can't say. There's no operation without risks. A simple lock can be busted, we'll have to take it as it comes.'

Georgiana rummaged in Sock's desk, and came out with a formidable weapon: a clasp knife with a blue steel blade, a good five inches long and quite obviously as sharp as a razor.

'You might as well take this,' she said. 'I think you could open a door with it.'

Horsfall handled the beastly thing with the respect it deserved, and then slipped it into his hip pocket.

They all gathered once more round the table in the study. I noticed that the remains of the bottle of Grouse had gone to join its ancestors. Quietly I removed it, and replaced it with the bottle of Jamieson's.

'Need I remind you,' barked Horsfall, 'that we have ten minutes before we set off? Gather round. I'll tell you what we're going to do.' He took Sock's chair, and the others scraped up plain wooden seats from the corners of the room. Georgiana switched off the top light and came to stand behind him, taking no part in the conversation, but resting her hand on his shoulder like the Muse of Battle. The child was kneeling beside him.

For a moment, the only sound was that of the moths battering at the window. Horsfall had the relevant sheet of the Ordnance map and Adrian's sketch in front of him on the table. Adrian (his second thoughts thoroughly conquered) had a pencil in his hand, which moved over a blank sheet of paper without making a mark. Colin, reverting to the practices of his athletic youth, was pressing the palms of his hands together, counting ten, and letting go. An unholy delight took hold of me as I looked round the room: three men bent over a map, the lad kneeling like the server at a mystery, and Georgiana looking perversely more beautiful, in her own chilly way, than ever. It could have been the doomed toughs of any Thirties novel of travelling and bloodshed. I was reluctant to spoil such a fine effect for a ha'pennyworth of tar, so I opened a packet of Sock's Navy Cut and sent curls of smoke to turn in the chimney of lamplight. Adrian, who smokes other people's cigarettes on his birthday and at the funerals of town planners, reached for the packet and added his smoke to mine. It all looked perfectly splendid.

'Right,' said Horsfall. 'Straight job, silent. We land, we go in, and we retreat in good order. Josh, the boat's sound?'

'Yes, sir.'

'Yes,' Georgiana supplemented. 'Sock took it out this spring to cut the rushes, and he didn't come back any muddier than usual.'

'Right, that's settled. And the boat's big enough for the four of us?' The brat looked at Horsfall with terror that he was to be left behind. Our Captain quickly set his mind at rest.

'Five of us, I mean. Safer that way.' He looked straight at me. I blew smoke back at him, coolly. 'No ratting.'

'It'll take five all right,' confirmed Georgiana. 'It was built for proper picnics.'

'Well, that's settled,' said Horsfall. 'Now, what about these landing-stages on the map?'

'Ours is still all right,' answered Georgiana, 'but I can't answer for the other side. They're not the type to have a boat.'

'If we lived there,' said my godson longingly, 'Taggart and I could have a big boat, and go down to the sea.'

'You could,' said Horsfall indulgently. 'Now. Can we guess that there might be something on the other side to tie a boat to? Right, we'll risk that too. If there isn't, the barrack-room lawyer can bloody well stand in the mud and hold it.'

'Thank you,' I said. Already, other plans were forming as to what I might do if I were forced to cross the water.

'A scramble up the bank won't kill us,' Horsfall went on, 'but we'll have to be quiet about it.' Murmurs of appreciation, and a brisk circulation of the bottle.

'Any chance of servants, clearing up, making up a fire, or whatever?'

'Simply can't tell,' said Georgiana. 'For all the noise they make, they only keep a man and wife. And I should think they'll be pretty busy at table and in the kitchen, but we've no way of guessing how Isabella organises her household. Sorry.'

'Well,' Adrian put in, 'we'd perhaps . . .'

'Quite so,' Horsfall cut in. 'Talk us through the layout, there's a good chap, but keep it short.'

'You're quite sure where the picture is?' I enquired pleasantly.

'Come *on*, Oliver,' said Georgiana. 'In the saloon.'

'With a spotlight on it,' added Colin.

Adrian began his performance.

'Start with the elevation on the drawing.' The drawing showed a boring neo-classical wedding-cake. Five windows in the middle, three storeys under a pediment, unimportant wings on either side. 'Only the central block matters. The three right-hand windows are french windows on to the terrace, the two on the left are the dining-room. The terrace is symmetrical, with four steps running the length of it, and then the lawn going down to the river. There's thick shrubbery on either side of the house . . .'

'If they haven't ripped it out,' said Georgiana grimly. Style wars, style wars. All very tiring.

'So there's no cover to the front of the house, but the landing is screened?'

'Precisely.'

'Aren't there double doors between the two big rooms, though?' said Georgiana suddenly. She might have thought of that before.

'They're either shut or they're open. We'll get through,' said Horsfall, in a tone which boded no good to anyone who got in his way. Georgiana's grip tightened on his shoulder.

'We'll need two men for the picture,' said Colin. 'How are we deploying?'

'Oliver at the boat,' Josh reminded everyone pointedly.

'Yup. Josh as scout and lookout,' said Horsfall. 'Me to open up, keep guard, and cover the retreat. Experts on deck to move the object. Okay?'

'Fine.'

'Right,' said Horsfall, 'we've got to shift. How is it fixed to the wall?'

'Wire and hooks is the usual,' said Adrian.

'Take a screwdriver just in case. We'll play it as it comes. We'd better be off. If the wind holds, we can talk quite safely until we're half-way over. You all see the map? We pull for the lights at Blackwater till we're half over, then up the channel in the middle, and a sharp pull left for the landing. There shouldn't be any bother if the men at the oars take it steady.'

'Colin rows,' I reminded them, 'and has done since infancy.'

'We'll take the oars then,' Horsfall said to him, 'and there shouldn't be any trouble. I've got a compass.'

'Have something to see it with,' I said, passing him a box of matches, and putting some of Sock's cigarettes into my pocket as I did so.

Horsfall pushed back his chair and went into the dressing room. I heard him fumbling and cursing, and experienced a perfectly genuine cold chill of horror when I saw him returning with Sock's loutish twelve-bore over his arm. The gun was open. I am to this day perfectly prepared to swear before any court in the land that there were two cartridges in the chambers. Even in the lamplight, I saw the glint of metal. As he snapped the gun shut and turned to hand it to Georgiana I heard something metallic shift and clink in the pocket of the khaki tunic. It flashed across my mind that if Horsfall had completely taken leave of his senses and was proposing nothing more nor less than armed robbery, I had better prepare to leg it at the earliest opportunity.

'Steady on,' said Adrian weakly.

'Shut up,' said Horsfall.

He picked up the bottle from the table. The others stood up with a clattering of chairs. He took a good pull at it, the whisky catching the lamplight as it tilted. He handed it to Colin without a word, and without wiping the neck of the bottle. Colin drank hard, and gave it to Adrian, who did the same, and then held it out to me. I shook my head, and he pushed it back across the table. Horsfall took the bottle in his right hand, and cupped his left hand behind my godson's head, lifting the bottle very slowly, so that the spirit touched the child's lips. He crashed the bottle down on the table, and took the shotgun from Georgiana.

'What are we waiting for?'

She went before him, and we all filed down the stairs after them. I lagged behind, to pick up my nice dark overcoat and scarf. At the front door, she held him back. 'No further,' she said. 'Oh, good luck. I'll have all the lights on to guide you home. Fire the gun twice as you come in, if you've got it.'

She put her arms round him and kissed him: I saw their lips part. Through the khaki, I could see the muscles of his arm tighten round her. I had a sudden and very unpleasant wish that Sock would loom up out of the dark, and catch them at it.

She touched Adrian and Colin on the arm as they passed. 'Do as you're told,' she said to Josh, as if she were sending him off to school. Inevitably, she was alone with me for a second.

'Don't let me down,' she said, and moved as if to kiss me. I sidestepped, and said, 'Oh, my dear, I hope you know what you're doing,' with precisely the same emphasis on every syllable.

Then I followed Captain Horsfall out into the dark.

VIII

The wind had died. The air was neither hot nor cold, and smelt of trees and standing water. The lapping of the waves on the mud grew louder as we moved from the noisy gravel to the quieter grass. As we passed down the lawn, I thought of various treacheries, but paused to look hard into the lighted drawing room, and to take a calm farewell of the garlanded harvest cart carved on the fireplace which I would never see again. I then prepared, despite the dark, to enjoy myself. A faint hint of light shone from behind the clouds as we came to the landing-stage. While the others fussed over knots and painters, I wandered down to the edge where the lawn usually stopped and the mud began.

I looked down at the unexpected high water nibbling at the grass, and suddenly nausea took me and my mind went fluttering, hunting for a memory which frightened me. No clear image would come. My panic dulled without vanishing, but I was buggered if I was going to give them the satisfaction of seeing me vomit, so (as usual) I did the right deed for the wrong reason, and fought it down. My eyes were growing used to the dark, though the end of my cigarette still dazzled me. They had loaded themselves, soldier, aesthetes, gun, godson and all, into the boat, and Horsfall was shouting at me to get a bloody move on. It takes courage to step from firm land into darkness and the noise of moving water. I have never pretended to be anything but a coward. Somehow, I grabbed Adrian's hand and stepped down on to something damp which shifted unpleasantly. I caught my balance, and saw the brat kneeling in the prow of the boat, and Colin and Horsfall fumbling with the oars on the bench in front of me. Beyond them, I could see a sort of Whistler stroke of grey on black with a single point of light like a pinprick in the paper.

'Is it intended,' I asked, 'that I should sit on something?'

'There's a perfectly good place beside me,' Adrian said from somewhere below my knees.

'Damp, I should imagine,' I said with feeling, folding my handkerchief, and sitting on that.

The heroes, meanwhile, had played a little game with the rowlocks and a bottle of gun-oil to no great effect. The amount they'd drunk was, inevitably, affecting their operational skill.

However, I thought it unlikely that any landed gent of Londonish tendencies would take a confused racket on the river for a boatload of madmen, hell-bent on pinching his most valuable painting out of motives of the purest and most lunatic chivalry.

I didn't enjoy the rocking of the boat, nor the nasty oily gurgle of the water.

'Going well,' said Horsfall, a catch coming in his voice from his exertions at the oar. It seemed only kind to encourage them.

'"All rowed fast, but none rowed faster than stroke," ' I quoted.

'Now men,' he began.

'Dig it, heave it!' (Let me make it quite clear that I picked up these esoterica merely by walking along the banks of the Wear and overhearing the uncouth shouts of men on bicycles.)

'We've only got minutes to do our talking . . .'

'Olly, olly, row like smoke!'

'Shut your mouth, before someone shuts it for you!'

'Terribly sorry,' I said, all tight-lipped and wounded. I fell to whistling very softly, but insistently, Cherubino's song from Figaro: the one about a soft little page going off to be a brave little soldier. Adrian would understand, if no one else did.

'Now, let's run through again. Land as quietly as possible. Lie low by the landing-stage, while I do a recce. We leave the weak link to guard the boat. Then the three of us and the lad crawl up to the terrace, utilising whatever cover we find, Josh keeps guard, three men go in by the sitting-room window. You two lift the thing down, I guard the communicating door. Get it down, proceed to boat, retire in good order. No talking, whatever happens. If there's any resistance, run for it. Are we quite clear?'

'Yes,' the others replied shortly. Light kindled in the sky as the moon drifted from behind the clouds. We must have been caught, a dark silhouette on the moon-silvered water, like the cover of some appalling tale of boyish adventure.

'It's brightening, damn it,' muttered Horsfall.

'Where have we got to?' hissed Colin, leaning a moment on his oar and squinting into the darkness. Horsfall looked cautiously about him, and struck a match over the map.

'Half-way over. We've got to box a bit clever from now on: there's a wreck on the sandbank, steam-launch. Josh, shine your torch down carefully: see anything?'

'Nothing, sir,' piped the infant hero from the bows.

'Pull left, then.' The boat tilted unpleasantly as it swung round towards the bank.

'Enough light to see over now.'

I looked back, but the lights of Jordans had sunk behind the trees. I could imagine Georgiana going from room to room switching on all the lights, clearing things, making preparations for brandy, cocoa and other heroic comforts. For a minute we were out in the dark, then the lights of Blackwater appeared again, and I could see the shadows of the hanging woods beyond the house. We were nearly there. I thought it might be prudent to have my fun while it lasted, and was just about to launch another offensive, when my eyes settled on the treeless piece of shore which was coming nearer. The feeling of nausea rushed back upon me. I was sure that a well-built man, a long shadow stretching behind him, was standing by the water, absolutely still, waiting.

'Look,' I whispered, hoarse with terror.

'At what?'

'There's a man standing waiting by the edge, with something behind him.' My tone must have carried conviction. Horsfall shipped his oar for a second, and looked at the shore.

'There's nothing there,' he said. 'You've got the jitters. It's just as well you're staying with the boat.'

I did not, no, I did *not* like the thought of being alone on that shore. I did not think, somehow, that I would be alone for long. I sighed, and decided to attack to take my mind off things.

'I suppose it makes perfectly good sense. You need me in reserve. I'll smoke on the bank for ten minutes, and then stroll up to the house and explain to my wife and her friends that it was all an undergraduate lark.'

'For the last time, put a sock in it,' said Horsfall, who in the circumstances, could have chosen his words better. Silence. Softly, I began to croon,

'Sunset and evening star . . .'

'Shut up!'

'Can somebody tell me please,' I said softly, with just a hint in my voice that if not answered, I would ask my question again, louder, 'exactly why we are doing this?'

'To get the Stubbs back,' said Adrian, for once, not in the mood for subtexts.

'To show them, and you, and everyone like you,' began Colin, with a somewhat greater grasp on the hidden dynamics of the situation. Horsfall cut across his speech.

'If I had you alone for five minutes, I'd knock the nonsense . . . There's nothing else left to do.' Good. He was very cross indeed, and incoherent with it.

'I see. Well, it's very clear why *you're* doing it. Ane fayre damoyselle has offeryt you ane geste of knightly valour' (and if by now, in some subterranean layer of his mind, Horsfall was not planning on collecting the traditional reward, I was the proverbial monkey's uncle), 'and you're out here proving that the age of chivalry is not dead.'

'That is quite enough, Oliver,' hissed Adrian into my right ear. Horsfall, who cannot have understood the half of what I was saying, took refuge in the secret terms of the soldier's art.

'You Port Mahon soldier, you unspeakably bloody little man!' This outburst was followed by the unexpected bleat of a sheep at bay: Colin had finally had enough.

'Bastard through and through. Oh yes, Oliver *darling*, it's easy enough for you to sneer at anything half decent, isn't it?'

'Now, now.'

'Don't think we don't know about you. You've been seen in the

Salisbury and the Golden Lion a bit too bloody often to get away with it. I'm surprised you're not rotten with disease. No wonder Claudia left you.'

'And you? What's the annual turnover of flyblown trulls these days? I've never met the same slut twice.'

'Sod you, literally and metaphorically!'

'Shut up, the pair of you, before I fucking kill you!' snarled Horsfall, *sotto voce*.

At this point, the clouds had the grace to part, so we rowed the last hundred yards (as it says in the *Aeneid*) through the friendly silence of the peaceful moonlight. There was something of a landing-stage left, enough to tie the boat to. Mercifully, I managed to reach a clearing in the shrubbery without getting wet or dirty.

'Stay here if you know what's good for you,' snapped Horsfall, and led his troops off down the path. Another Navy Cut did nothing to settle my stomach. I directed the rising bile into a consideration of my revenge on the lot of them for a load of drunken, public-school yobbos.

There would have been no use simply making a noise, and I had not the slightest desire to get back into the boat and row it away. What was needed was a course of action which would put a spanner in their works, but give them nothing to pin on me if I decided to go back with them after all. On the other hand, I needed to be somewhere where I could see what was going on, and desert if things looked bad. Inspiration would come to me. There's never any good whatsoever in standing where one has been told to stand, so I folded the lapels of my coat up to my chin and set off for a bit of free-enterprise espionage. I picked my way cautiously down the path after them, and heard noises suggesting that the raiding-party had set up a base-camp in a clearing in the rhododendrons. There was a professionally quiet scuffle, and then the sound of Horsfall's whisper. He had evidently crept up on the terrace for his promised recce, in best Sandhurst style.

'Amazing luck. They're in the dining-room, three of them, two women.' (Oh, come on, Horsfall. You know who they are.) 'The doors between the rooms are open, but only a crack: we can manage, but we'll have to be bloody quiet. There's only one light on in the big room. The curtains on the dining-room windows are open: we'll have to go up from the right. It shouldn't matter if we do our stuff properly. There's a scrap of cover at both ends of the terrace: big stone seats with roofs.'

'Are the french windows open?'

'No, blast them. I'll have to do something about that. You'll have to stay under cover behind the right-hand seat till you see me go in. Right, as soon as the moon's covered, we go for it. Adrian and Colin after me, Josh covers the retreat. Give me the gun.'

Once the tiny feet had pattered off into the night, I slid round the corner, and was confronted by a pale figure raising a threatening arm. I don't like statues, especially ones by my ancestor. This one had done my nerves no good whatsoever. I edged past it, and took up a position in the shadows at the edge of the lawn. In the last light of the disappearing moon, I saw the trio hugging the edge of the shrubbery, and Horsfall dropping to his knees preparing to crawl over the lawn. As darkness descended, the lights of the house sprang into greater prominence: a dull glow burning in three of the long windows on to the terrace, and bright light shining from the other two, sending long ladders of light down the lawn towards the water. Lights flicked on and off on the second floor as someone went from room to room.

My plan of action came clear in my mind. Every minute wasted on this side would enhance the likelihood of grounding in the mud as they tried to make it back to Jordans. I decided to skulk on the terrace and watch Claudia through the dining-room window for a generous ten minutes, and then wander back to the boat. I could always pitch a yarn about a domestic needing to be distracted. By then, they should have had a very pleasant five minutes, stewing like so many aubergines in their own acid juices. And if there was great silliness, I decided to desert there and then, since even a reunion with dear Claudia is marginally better than being shoved in the slammer.

Horsfall was moving: the game had begun.

IX

I don't know what they teach them at Sandhurst, but I have picked up some simple techniques at College garden-parties which enable me to negotiate a shrubbery without getting twigs in my hair or calling attention to myself. Thus, I gained the welcome recess at the left-hand end of the terrace without any particular difficulty, and settled down to watch the dinner party in progress.

There is always something rather haunting about watching people in a well-lit room from the darkness, and somehow my own invisibility, and the fact that I was well placed to watch the whole show as it unfolded, put me in a rather odd mood of dreamy excitement, as if I were seeing a film. I was halfway into a *crise* – the nasty feelings about water and figures by water were still with me – but at the same time, there was a distinct pleasure in being the only person able to apprehend the whole of this bizarre comedy.

In the dining-room, I saw three people grouped about a small round table which had obviously been placed near the windows for them to watch the last of the evening. A vast, formal dining-table shone like a black pool behind them, unused. There were candles on the tables, in Jensen silver holders, and I regret to say that, as Colin had warned us, there were little lights on the wall directed at a number of surprisingly distinguished modern abstract paintings. There was an enormous Rothko in pride of place on what must once have been a neoclassical overmantel: it was the wrong shape for the space, even leaving questions of style out of it, but it suggested, at the very least, a certain vulgar confidence.

Stephen was facing the window, and wearing a sharkskin jacket. The unfortunate phrase 'impotent porpoise' rose spontaneously into my mind: he was sleek, pink, pompous, and stuffed into his evening clothes like a high-quality sausage. Isabella looked decidedly Transatlantic: her hair and her face were equally lacquered, and she was wearing a sharp white jacket, apparently over nothing at all, with the cuffs turned back to disclose a goodly number of heavy gold chains. Claudia had her back to me, silhouetted against the light, so all I could see of her was a penumbra of Venetian red hair glowing against the candle. As I stole up, she must just have said something malicious: the other two were sniggering helplessly into their tiny, jade-green coffee-cups. Isabella recovered herself first, patted at her patent-leather hair, and remarked in the shrill, nasal tones of New York's leaders of style and fashion,

'Well, sweetie, what the hell are we meant to do about them? Seriously, I mean, it's like being related to the Munsters. The last time they were here, the guy lurched in with blood on his jacket, no kidding. I don't imagine he'd killed anyone, he'll just have been murdering some poor little bunny or something. Anyway, he stood in the corner like a Goddamned psychopath, drinking all Steve's whisky and growling. And who's he to look down at us, anyway? He's nothing but some kind of hit-man with a fancy accent. And Georgie – well, she is Steve's cousin, and a lovely little thing, and I don't want to speak ill of the girl, but the last time she was here, she drove me absolutely wild – she drifted in like Little Orphan Annie with walked-over shoes and a string of pearls . . .'

'That was to show she was really trying,' interjected Claudia,

'. . . and she kind of winced and shut her eyes when anyone tried to be civil. He must have her absolutely brainwashed. It's all gone on quite long enough. There's no way we can get through to the guy Holderness: I don't know if he's rude or crazy, and I don't want to, but if we try and make contact with Georgie while he's away, maybe she'll get off her high horse a bit and talk some sense into him. It's just plain ridiculous to be living five miles away, and not to visit. You'll just have to be a good girl, sweetie, and come along like a little lady.'

The significance of all this dawned on me delightedly: Jordans had obviously been being dissected and anatomised for a good hour. 'I really want to see the house, though,' Isabella continued. 'They tell me he hangs dead pheasants in the lounge.'

What followed happened very quickly. The moonlight returned, and I saw Horsfall, knife in hand, wrestling with the lock of the french windows into the drawing-room. Colin, Adrian and the child were flat on their bellies at the bottom of the steps to the terrace. There was a faint click, and Horsfall disappeared into the house. In the dining room, Stephen swirled brandy round his glass, and raised it to his wife. Horsfall's troops, doubled up, sprinted silently for the open window. Adrian hovered, half-visible, at the entrance, glancing up at the moon, which was thinking of breaking cover again. Isabella stretched out one jingling hand to stroke her husband's arm. Adrian vanished. Claudia suddenly turned her head, and seemed to be looking at the doors through to the drawing-room. She passed her hand over her forehead. The faintest of bumping noises came from the drawing-room: they must have just got the thing off the wall. Stephen and Isabella seemed to have heard nothing: they appeared genuinely engrossed in one another, in a faintly disgusting fashion. Claudia's hearing, like mine, is excellent. She pushed her chair back, murmuring 'air': Isabella spared her a glance, saying,

'Sorry, honey. We sort of shut you out for a minute.'

'I'll just go out on the terrace for a bit,' said Claudia. 'My head's gone a bit stuffy.'

'Poor baby,' said Isabella agreeably. Claudia opened the french windows, and came out. Her green dress shimmered, back-lit, and her hair was rich with shadow.

Whatever deity protects clever and elegant young men prompted me to whisper, 'Darling.' Claudia shut the french windows unhurriedly behind her, and came further out into the shadows by the stone seat.

'Oliver,' she whispered, 'what the bloody hell are you doing here?'

'I was brought here by a boatload of mad Englishmen, who are at this very moment stealing your hosts' Stubbs.'

'Are they dangerous?'

'Quite possibly.'

'Okay. In that case, I'll keep quiet, if you stay and explain. Yes or no?'

'Yes.'

'There's a phone-box near the end of the drive. Ring us up in ten minutes – 770846. I'll fix things.'

She turned, and we saw, in the intermittent light, the child racing across the lawn, followed by Adrian and Colin bearing the painting between them: the back of it was towards us: a stretcher, a gilt frame, nothing more. Claudia backed further into the shadows beside me, as we half heard a click from the french windows. Horsfall, having closed them, took a last keen glance all round, and strolled after his troops. The gun was held close to his right side, his finger on the trigger (a posture familiar from newspaper photographs of soldiers on patrol in Belfast), and the faint light played about the gunmetal of the barrels. He was half-way across the lawn before we heard the sound of the safety-catch being re-engaged. Once the lot of them had vanished into the shrubbery, Claudia left me, and returned to the dining-room.

'How're you feeling, Claudia?' enquired Stephen.

'It was nothing at all. I thought I had a migraine coming, but it's gone away. Dearest Isabella, excuse a poor widow-woman. If only my Oliver would come back from Italy: he gets so involved, and forgets to write. Sorry I'm being bad value.'

'Don't worry, sweetie,' said Isabella, with the usual American mania for spelling things out. 'It's a bad time for you, we know that. I'm really sorry if we embarrassed you or made you feel bad: you know it's not meant like that.'

'Let's say no more about it,' suggested Stephen, exhibiting the first flash of civilised feeling this merry gathering had shown. Claudia stretched, extending her thin arms luxuriously, and, it may be assumed, prepared to open another topic of conversation. I meanwhile had turned away, and was beating a swift and silent retreat. So: Claudia had been busily keeping up appearances all summer, all well and good. Five more minutes of jolly British fun, and then I would trot off and phone my wife.

I made my way back to the ancestral statue, and lurked in its shade, where I was fortunate enough to overhear a whispered council of war.

'We got it!' squeaked my godson, who had doubtless not been so happy since his house won the cricket cup.

'Good show,' yipped Horsfall, 'good men all. Should be in the army.'

'Where,' whispered Colin, 'is that shit Oliver?'

Where indeed?

'Told you he was the weak link,' said Horsfall. 'If you ask me, I reckon we should push off while the going's good, and leave the miserable little sod to find his own way back. He's probably gone off to chuck up in the woods or something. He can't rat now, after all, he's in with us up to the bloody neck. Just leave him.'

'Let him rot,' confirmed Adrian. 'He's not going to be doing much harm, he was sweating like a toad in the boat.'

Amid muted cries of mutual congratulation, they slithered back to the boat, hoisted the picture aboard, and rowed for home.

I, meanwhile, dived for the shrubbery, and worked my way round the house. Finally, I made it to the drive, and set off along it, keeping to the shadows. 'White in the moon the long road lies, that leads me from my love . . .' Seldom can those who quote that maudlin lyric have done so with more mixed feelings. In the phone-box, the three pages or so which were left of the directory mercifully included the 'g's and 'h's, since I had completely forgotten the number Claudia had given me. The manservant brought Claudia to the phone quite quickly. Did that luxurious household have a phone in the dining-room? It opened up ghastly vistas of power breakfasting, but in present circs, it obviously had its uses: I did not wish the return of the prodigal and the discovery of the absent 'Horse-Tamer' to happen simultaneously.

'Hello? Hello? Oliver!' she began, her voice pitched to carry. 'So you're back!' She paused. 'Oh, I'm sorry. I should have left some kind of address, I'm such a rat. But I never got the letter . . .' Pause. There was obviously nothing for me to contribute, so I said,

'Rhubarb, rhubarb, rhubarb.' She was off again, acting it up a storm: it had often struck me, in happier days, that the stage had lost a considerable asset to the Bar when she took her final examinations.

'Oh, God, the Italian post. I'm really sorry, darling . . .'

'Rhubarb, rhubarb.'

'Oh, you poor thing, how beastly. Thank God someone told you where I was . . . Oh, you mean the concert at *Snape*! . . . no, cars are the living end, honestly . . . oh, how could they be so stupid? *No*! Death on a bicycle . . . he can't have towed it to Aldeburgh with everything in it . . . how clever of you to ring Micky . . .'

'Clever old you, all round.' I said, with feeling.

'No, I haven't told Steve and Isabella a *thing* . . . They'll be thrilled . . . Oh, God! you took that horrid boat from Harwich, you must be exhausted! . . . no, don't try and tell me, you must be running out of money . . .'

'Rhubarb?' I put in.

'Oh, that's no distance at all. No: I won't hear of it . . . no, you can't bloody walk, it's miles! I'll come down in the car . . . no, stay exactly where you are, I know where to find it. I'm sure Stephen and Isabella won't mind . . .'

Noises off: cries of No! No!, and Isabella's penetrating squawk: 'It's okay, Claudie, we've got the picture. Of course you can bring him!'

'No, they really don't mind. Ten minutes? Stay put, darling: see you soon.'

I had only a couple of minutes in which to reflect on Claudia's virtually supernatural talent for telling lies (a professional qualification, doubtless, for a successful barrister) which had thus provided me with excellent reasons for appearing in Suffolk in the middle of the night with no luggage, before her grey Audi drew up outside the phone box. She opened the passenger door, and I got in. It was only decent (and blast the consequences) to lean over and kiss her.

'Claudia, my love,' I said, 'you're being very sweet about this.'

'I don't think "sweet" is quite the word you're looking for, Oliver. If I were you, I'd try and think in terms of "damage limitation". I take it that you've been involved in some kind of nostalgic jape with the dear old chums?'

'Got it in one.'

'Someone got all romantic?'

'Yes.'

'Well, Stephen and Isabella, who I'm fond of, are going to be very upset. I'm glad I trusted you, though. You didn't tell me they were actually carrying guns. I didn't like the look of that bozo on the lawn – who the hell was he?'

'Some kind of career soldier. He was visiting, and the whole thing went to his head.'

She shrugged. 'Well, we'll try and sort all that out in the next few days. I take it they've kidnapped the bloody thing, and not burnt it in the garden or something?'

'Oh, yes. It's just crossing the river and going to Jordans, like something out of a Negro spiritual. I doubt very much they'll manage to do anything worse than knock a bit of gilt off the corners of the frame, seeing as the party consists of one soldier and two salivating art-historians and not the other way round.'

'Good-oh. Now. I'd better drive us to Snape and back to get our timing right. You might like to know the following things – *try* to remember.' (Claudia's virtually photographic memory for the factual forms, for her, a standard, from which she is intolerant of deviation.)

'You have just listened to Brendel playing three piano concertos by Mozart one after the other, so you can adjust your expression accordingly. You're lucky that there was a concert tonight. Micky told you I was here, and you thought you'd go to a concert and drop in once dinner was safely over. Your car, which is a Renault 4, in which you have been driving round Italy, has something dreadful wrong with its sparking-plugs, as far as you know, and has been towed away to Aldeburgh to be cured. I haven't been able to snatch a moment alone with the Yellow Pages, so I haven't a clue what the garage is called. You'd better be shattered and exhausted tonight . . .'

'My dear, I can assure you that that is no less than the truth . . .'

'And we'll look up the book and pick a name before breakfast.'

The steep roof of the Crown Inn at Snape loomed up in the moonlight. Claudia turned the car expertly in the forecourt.

'Right, home we go. You'd better back me up.'

'Claudia, I'll do my best.'

Her lips tightened. 'You may have to do better than that. Let me remind you of a key point in this grotesque fiction. You scurried up from London in the hopes of seeing me as soon as possible. Really, Oliver, you must believe I haven't engineered this on purpose, but what the bloody hell could I say?'

'Oh, Claudia. I do appreciate that.' It was true. I could not, given such unpromising material, and a mere two minutes' start, have come up with so breathtakingly plausible a yarn. 'I quite take your point. If I am not yearningly uxorious, like your charming host, the whole thing goes out of the window.'

'Right. And Oliver, I know you've sometimes found it hard to believe that I too' (the 'too' hurt) 'have friends that I love and value. I'm fond of Isabella. She's been very good to me, and you may just remember her parents were friends of my father's.' (I had seldom, if ever, listened to tales about Daddy the Diplomat.) 'If you screw up this one, so help me God, I'm going to make bloody sure you end up behind bars with your loutish chums.'

'Yes, darling. It's nice to know where we stand. The dewy, tentative romance of the second honeymoon it is. I promise you, I'll do my best, and if I vomit, we can put it down to over-excitement. Would you believe I tried to stop them?'

'Yes, Oliver. I would.'

We drove along in silence for a while, Claudia negotiating the country lanes with absent-minded efficiency.

'What happened?' she asked, after a while.

'Well. They got terribly tanked, and decided that they'd liberate Stephen's Stubbs to teach Isabella and all dago upstarts that Old England had teeth and claws and could look after itself . . .'

'Is the assassin on the premises?'

'Thankfully not. The military presence on the Blackwater lawns was merely some kind of brainless lieutenant. I was glad enough to see the chap vanish into the shrubbery without a shot being fired, but if it had been Sock who was leading the party, I've a terrible, reluctant feeling that he'd have slit throats all round, just to be sure.'

'Urgh.' It was not, I had to concede, an attractive image, or an implausible one. I had a sudden, momentary vision of Isabella slumped in her modish chair, her white jacket sodden with scarlet. 'As it was,' continued Claudia more cheerfully, 'it was public-school pups on the rampage?'

'Oh, sister. Eton, Harrow, Rugby, the lot. Being a mere woman, and NLCS to boot, you can't guess the half of it . . . Anyhow, they decided to take ship and do the deed. And there we all are.'

'And here we are,' Claudia confirmed, delivering me to the front door of Blackwater with a new and convincing provenance.

X

There was one thing in my favour: I could hardly have looked less like a burglar. Despite this, I felt an increasing sense of crisis and despair as Claudia pushed open the door of Blackwater and propelled me inside. Whatever happened, the rest of the night was going to be unpleasant. If they discovered the thing was missing, there would be scenes, and I was feeling far too tired to invent an art-historical jaunt round the Continent. There had hardly been time to get Claudia to invent one, and in any case, one has one's pride. I began to wish that I had just kept quiet, been a good little soldier, and legged it back to London on the milk-train at five-thirty next morning.

Isabella scurried down the stairs, arms outstretched. Her very high heels clicked busily on the marble.

'Olly! What a surprise! We were just bowled over! You should have seen the expression on Claudie's face! She told us your letters hadn't got through? Come on, sweetie, give me a kiss, and tell us all what you've been doing.'

I took her in my arms, and bent to kiss her cheek. 'Isabella. It's lovely to be here. And so kind of you to put up with me.'

'Oh God, no! You're so welcome.' I began to get a ghastly sense that, if someone was fool enough to put a drink into my hand, I would say that if she would just come into the saloon with me, I would have a surprise for her. Stephen, fortunately, came woofing down the stairs, displaying a vast expanse of blue cummerbund under his tasteless jacket.

'Olly, delighted to see you. You're looking very good.' I bloody well am not, I said to myself, as he pumped away at my hand. In truth, I had seldom felt more dreadful. 'Not much of a tan, eh?' I managed some kind of a smile.

'I've been scurrying from archive to archive,' I said. 'Whatever lies Claudia may have told you, I've really been trying to get on with things as quickly as possible.' I got the bent eye from the partner of my soul for that one, and remembered, with a sudden qualm of vertigo, that the tattier palazzi of Central Italy are crammed with Isabella's European relations. Had Claudia a second layer of bluff? I was going to have to be very careful. Oh, God. Isabella was going to ask me who I'd seen in Italy . . .

As they ushered me up the stairs, Isabella talking all the time, I interjected the odd word about their kindness, and how delightful and unexpected it all was, attempting, meanwhile, to try and work out whether I could make a surreptitious phone-call to some beastly emigré in Florence to sort out the beginnings of an alibi. For the second time that evening, I found myself making frantic use of my remaining scraps of art-historical arcana, trying to come up with one painter who might give me good reason for having spent three months in Italy in some remote place without seeing anyone. Nothing came to mind, and I began (listening to myself talking smoothly) to panic as I had rarely panicked before.

We stood on the first-floor landing, within ten feet of the door of the robbed saloon. There was surely no chance that the french windows had been locked without the loss of the picture being noticed. At any moment, I felt, I was going to be taken in there; at any moment, Isabella was going to say that I ought to be shown the pictures. All this time (I don't know how), my automatic pilot was continuing to talk fluently. I seem to remember that I flirted with Isabella, laughed at Stephen's jokes, and called Claudia 'darling'; all the while almost crying with exhaustion, dying for strong drink, and sinking within myself into overwhelming chasms of despair. It is a very futile luxury to keep a conscience if you live as I do, but during that ghastly five minutes in the hall, I was all set to repent. I had no reason to expect that Claudia would be kind to me. I could only hope that she was enjoying the spectacle of her former husband well and truly landed in it, up to the armpits.

'Well now,' said Isabella, 'you must be dying for a drink.' Never a truer word, madam. 'Let's go on up to my little parlour, it's snug at this time of night. All the fancy stuff can wait till the morning. You're family, Olly, you don't have to get the grand tour.' I could have kissed her.

So we all went upstairs, and found ourselves in the little square room in which eighteenth-century Stradling ladies had done their embroidery. They would hardly have recognised it, though they might have liked the cream damask walls, piped in green cord. It had modern Italian tub-chairs upholstered in a vibrant and astonishing pink tweed. The elegant oval bookcase niches on either side of the fireplace had been glassed in, and held the prize exhibits from Isabella's collection of antique fans, carefully back-lit. The pretty ladies on the mantelpiece were Dresden, not Royal Doulton, and the green carpet was as deep, thick and soft as genuine moss. I was deeply relieved to note that the black lacquer console table held a reasonably comprehensive selection of things to drink – and more than suspected that the odd proportions of the pseudo-eighteenth-century cupboards under the window-seat implied the presence of a small, built-in refrigerator. Adrian, doubtless, would have accepted their hospitality so as not to call attention to himself, and written a savage article for the *Spectator* through his tears. There was one two-seater sofa to match the curious chairs. Plausibility demanded that I take it.

'Whisky, Olly?' asked Stephen.

'Lovely,' I replied.

'Ice?'

'Just one, thanks.' I was right about the fridge. Claudia took her seat beside me, her thigh pressing against mine, while Stephen handed me a more than generous tumbler.

'Anything for you, Claudie?'

'A drop of wine, if there's some open.'

'There's a box. Can you drink Kookaburra Creek?'

'Lovely.'

'I can open a bottle?'

'No, that'll do fine.'

Isabella, true to type, was drinking green chartreuse. She fixed me with a bright, and surprisingly shrewd, eye.

'I don't expect you want to talk about yourself, Olly. You look exhausted.' I took a sizeable swig of my whisky, and looked down into it, swirling it in the glass. Then I looked up. Few older women, in my experience, can resist the melting gaze of a personable blond.

'You're very sweet, Isabella. I don't really want to talk about myself, actually. Not that I mind telling you my adventures, but I might be better value at breakfast.'

'Oh God, I quite understand. I'm sure you're longing to get to bed.' She looked momentarily confused, and an unbecoming flush rose on her neck. She laughed in embarrassment, and Claudia came to the rescue.

'Oh, darling. Well, yes, in both senses. It's awful being this tired – you get a sort of second wind, but it's not like being really awake. Poor Olly's been up for about eighteen hours, I think, and if I'd known I was going out again, I wouldn't have enjoyed your lovely dinner the way I did.'

'You were okay, weren't you?' asked Isabella anxiously.

'Oh, it was fine. But you know, driving when you're a tiny bit over the limit is that much more of a strain.'

'Well,' boomed Stephen, 'we won't keep you. I'll just nip down and lock up, and then we can all get to bed.'

'Claudie, Ollie, I'll just find you some more towels, and a razor, and such,' said Isabella, putting down her minute glass and steaming out in the wake of her husband. I sat rigid, frozen in horror, waiting for a discovery which would find me without strength or resources.

'Put your face straight!' hissed Claudia.

'Claudia, I am going to die. I cannot, I absolutely cannot, handle the next few minutes. What the fuck am I going to do?'

Stephen's heavy tread was heard on the stairs, no faster than usual. He came in, beaming like Mine Host, and I looked at him in stark disbelief. Claudia took my hand, and her nails sank into my palm. I knew what she was saying: 'Accept the miracle. Shut up. Try not to look like a dying duck in a thunderstorm.'

'Claudie, you know the house. If you're moving about, tell Olly what he can and can't do without telling the world.'

'Thanks, Stephen. We'd better go up now, I think.'

We scrambled ourselves up to our bedroom on the third floor, where room-service had already left a prodigal heap of fluffy pink towels, some shaving-foam, a razor, a silk dressing-gown, some too-large underwear and a couple of shirts, and I threw myself on the bed. In the far distance, I heard the report of Sock's shotgun: Horsfall's uncouth announcement of triumph. Claudia, who had of course not registered the sound of a shot, since it held no meaning for her, marched round the room, removing garments, creaming her face, and tying herself into a dressing gown.

'Are you planning some kind of all-night vigil in the armchair?' I enquired.

'Absolutely not. I'm ravenous.' Georgiana's tale of some thundering daughter of the shires dining *chez* Gibb faintly returned to me as Claudia condescended to a little exegesis.

'It's part of Isabella being a New York Princess with a mania for doing everything right. What she assumes is that no one of reasonable income goes out to dinner for the calories. Cuisine minceur is still in, in her circles, so cuisine minceur is what you get. If you're a house-guest, it's understood that you might see fit to raid the kitchen around midnight. Romance or no romance, that's where I'm headed. Coming?'

It occurred to me that I had barely touched Georgiana's school dins, and had not, as was my usual practice, made up the difference with strong drink. The Great Stubbs Crisis seemed to have been postponed till the morning. I was hungry.

'Why are we not, even now, preparing statements for the local constabulary?' I enquired.

'I think Stephen must have gone through both rooms in the dark. He often does. He's quite proud of being able to zip round without falling over anything.'

'Pass me a dressing-gown,' I said, removing my trousers. 'I'm coming with you.'

We padded downstairs, and entered the service quarters of the house. I was not wholly surprised to observe a line of light beneath the kitchen door.

'Hello, chaps,' said Stephen cheerfully, clutching a bagel heavily laden with cold-cuts, mayonnaise, and gherkins. 'Stoking up, eh?' He gave the distinct impression of a man who had learned to take modish cookery in good part.

'Have you left anything in the fridge?' enquired Claudia.

'There's still some chicken, and there's half a Brie on that marble thing over there.' Claudia foraged efficiently, and put rolls, butter, cold chicken and Brie before us.

'I don't think Olly's had a square meal since the day before yesterday,' she said, seriously.

'You poor chap. Can you make do, or shall I open a tin?' I felt hysteria bubbling to the surface, and bit the inside of my cheek.

'No,' I said, 'I'll be fine with this.'

Stephen pottered off and investigated the pantry, bringing me a jar of Branston Pickle just to be on the safe side. I concentrated on stoking bread and chicken. The door swung open.

'Claudie! Hi, kids.' Isabella stood in the doorway. She was wearing a quilted housecoat buttoned up to her chin, and her sleek black hair was in two plaits. Without her makeup, she looked about twelve: her smooth olive complexion and pointed chin were virtually impervious to time. Claudia pushed the wreckage of the carcase towards her companionably.

'No, honey. I just want a couple of crackers and some peanut butter. Have you got all you want, Olly?'

'It's wonderful, Isabella. I've got everything I need.'

Isabella hitched up a stool next to her husband, and began to spread crackers with peanut butter and apple jelly. Claudia, at my side, absorbed Brie with quiet concentration. The whole scene was oddly peaceful: the atmosphere of dormitory feast almost sustaining, almost, momentarily, un-knotting the knots in my gut. Claudia's profile was smooth, creamy, and unreadable. I thought, at last, I had better make a move before I ran screaming out of the room.

'Darling. Shall we go up?'

She pushed away her plate.

'Well, my dears. See you in the morning.'

I took her hand, waist-high, as if we were dancing a minuet, and we left the room. We paced up the stairs in sober silence, side by side. Once into our quarters, Claudia vanished through the further doors to the bathroom. I prowled to and fro, picking at my cuticles. She emerged again, her face soft and young, ambiguous. I could not ask. She removed her dressing-gown, climbed into bed, and lay watching me. I went in my turn to the bathroom, where I brushed my teeth and removed my clothes. I put the light out as I returned to the bedroom, felt my way round the bed, and slipped in at her side. We lay like herrings in a box, silent and cold. My hand, at my side, blundered into the fingers of her hand, at her side, with an electric thrill. Like blind fish meeting in the dark, nothing which happened could possibly be blamed on either one of us.

XI

Having, considerably to my own surprise, performed the deed of kind with grim, ravenous concentration, I found myself lying awake afterwards staring into the dark. Claudia, at my side, was whiffling gently through her small, but perfectly formed, nose. I should have been asleep, I was tired to the point of tears. But I could not help obsessively visualising what was happening at Jordans. Georgiana must, surely, have changed: she owned a long, white, New Romantic dress, with a negligent fall of point-lace round its deep décolleté. It was devastatingly becoming, and absurdly answerable to the Hero's Return: it was impossible to believe that she would not have put it on. With the house lit like the *Queen Mary*, she must have emerged from the french windows, and paced down to the water to meet the men. Her dark hair was piled carelessly, held with a high tortoiseshell comb, exposing her slender, vulnerable nape: she would not have re-dressed it. For the traditional man, there is nothing quite like the moment when one takes the comb out of the hair, and the silky heap slithers, in loose, romantic profusion, down over the white shoulders. What on earth was she going to do with Colin, Adrian and the brat? Infected by the wild licence of the night, the surging adrenaline of the lust to own, what could she do but offer herself to Horsfall? I could not see the others at all: all I could see was Georgiana, with that lout Horsfall crushing handfuls of her white dress in his muddy paws.

I slept at last, in patches, with nasty dreams, and woke again at dawn. I lay watching the light on the ceiling, waiting every moment for the raising of the alarm. It came, at about half-past eight. Despite the well-fitting doors, the thick carpets, and the sheer distance from point to point, I became faintly aware of scuttering: a sense of alarm, unease, and rapid movement oozed under the door and rose gradually to fill the room. Claudia sighed, and stirred.

'It's started,' I said. My wife squiggled herself round, and groped for her glasses (which she needs to find her contact lenses).

'I think we ought to lie doggo for a bit,' she said. 'Let them get over the worst of it.'

I poured myself some mineral water from the bottle so thoughtfully left on the night-table, and propped myself up against the pillows. 'Can we just leave?' I suggested hopefully. 'A mad, romantic dash?'

Claudia gave me a long, bleak look over the top of her glasses.

'They're going to want me,' she pointed out evenly. Yes, my darling. I have heard the five things you have forborne from saying, loud and clear.

'Noblesse oblige,' I said. 'We mustn't let the side down.' Unlike my dear old chums, Claudia did not squirm and bridle to hear me uttering such sentiments. She read my words, accurately, as a statement of capitulation from a man who has finally realised that his scrotum is held in a tiny, vice-like grip.

'There are compensations,' she said dryly. 'You'll find Isabella makes the best coffee in England.' Ah, yes. Well, there she rather had me. I had come, over many years, to form a fixed opinion that Georgiana was in the habit of dumping the water out of the flowers in the hall, and boiling it up of a morning. The Jordans household, generally, tended to favour navvies' tea, made with four teabags to the pot, and for two pins, would have drunk it with condensed milk.

'Oh, God,' I said wearily. 'I'd better go and have a bath.'

'Don't touch the lever in the middle,' warned Claudia. 'It squirts the water into a sort of whirlpool, and it's a bit bracing for this hour of the morning.'

'Don't worry,' I said, wandering through and turning on taps. 'Dear God,' I continued, surveying the glass shelves over the bath. As a connoisseur, would you recommend the Floris, the Crabtree and Evelyn, or the Guerlain?'

'I think you might go for the Floris, on the whole. It contains vetiver and ylang-ylang, which are popularly supposed to promote calm, well-being and clear thinking.'

'Would anyone mind if I finished the bottle?'

'Me,' said Claudia, with feeling.

The morning was unseasonably calm: the sun began to break up the river-mist as soon as it rose. Diffused blue light played up from the water, and shone in our many mirrors.

I had a perfectly lovely bath, and began to feel a little better. Claudia bathed while I shaved, and we began to prepare for the day. I got into Stephen's faintly repulsive socks, shorts and shirt, and reached with the deepest reluctance for my grey flannels. Claudia, meanwhile, was pottering about, donning tights and a cream silk shirt. My wife's physique was made, essentially, for scrawny, wistful, alley-cat charm: in terms of personality and general approach to life, however, she exhibits all the tentative vulnerability of a barracuda. The effect is unsettling. While I was musing, she inserted herself briskly into a mustard-yellow wool suit with a boxy jacket and a short, tight skirt, from which her meagre legs protruded to unattractive effect. She sprayed herself liberally with Chamade, and put a pair of pearl studs in her ears.

I came up behind her, and we stood surveying ourselves in the wardrobe mirror. I am almost exactly a foot taller than she.

'If I don't say anything about your jacket,' said Claudia, getting her blow in first, 'then don't you say anything about my suit.'

'It's a little, um, secretarial, don't you think?'

'Don't you believe it,' said Claudia coolly. 'It's what they call "power dressing". It's going to be absolutely everywhere in the next year or two. And as for the colour, you would really not believe how tired I get of black.' I loathed Claudia reminding me of her life as a barrister, and how different it was from mine, and well she knew it.

'Come on,' she said, 'we'd better go down.'

So we went out to face the music, only to find Isabella hovering on the landing, her face pathetic with worry.

'Oh kids! Thank God you're up!'

'Isabella! What is it?' Claudia strode across to the older woman, and took her hands.

'Someone's stolen our Stubbs!'

'What Stubbs?' I asked.

'It's a very good painting,' said Claudia over her shoulder, 'and it was hanging in the saloon.' She turned her attention back to our hostess.

'When d'you think it went?'

'Oh, Claudie,' said Isabella tearfully, 'we've been racking our brains. We all think it must have gone some time between nine or so, and Steve locking up round midnight.'

'You mean while you were actually eating in the next room?' I asked. The effect was a little stilted, but Isabella, fortunately, was in no state to notice.

'That's the worst bit,' she said. 'It makes me feel really awful, thinking that someone came into my house, and we were just sitting there. We don't want to lock ourselves up like Fort Knox; I mean, a girl's got to be able to walk on to her own terrace, for Pete's sake, but suddenly I don't feel safe here any more.'

'You don't have anyone else here at night, do you?'

'No. No one wants to live in these days. Bill and Clara must have gone round eleven, since it was a party: they'll have loaded the dishwasher and tidied up a bit, and come back about eight. We should maybe get a dog, but we're away so much, it wouldn't be much of a life for him.'

'Have you rung the police?'

'No, honey. That's why I'm so glad you're up. I don't really want to break that lunch date, not when Georgie was being so civil, for once. If we get the police in, will they keep us all day, answering questions?'

'They might,' said Claudia. 'It's not really my area. It's a bit specialist for them: they've got some kind of Fine Art squad, and they've certainly got domestic security experts. I think you and Stephen might end up hanging about for quite a bit while they find the specific people they want you to talk to.'

I took Claudia's hand unobtrusively, and dug my nails in, hard. She knew what I meant: 'Claudia, you double-barrelled cow, you are setting us all up to go and play Georgiana's demented game. For God's sake let's go to the police, and let this all fizzle out.' She returned the squeeze with interest, and I knew what that meant too: the short arm of the law had decided to jump in with both dainty feet and sort everyone out. My only chance of survival was to go along with her.

'That's what I thought,' continued Isabella, unaware of this by-play. 'Do you think it would be too awful if we rang them around three? We could pretend we'd only just found out, since we don't use the saloon in the mornings. Do you think it would make any difference?'

'Probably not,' said Claudia. 'Whatever happened, it must have been highly professional. Was anything else missing?'

'Not a thing. They must have known exactly what they wanted. What I'm wondering now is who even knew it was here: it's not well known, I don't think, and it hadn't been back long. Do you think maybe someone at the restorer's said something?'

'It's a possibility,' said Claudia judiciously. This farce was beginning to get on my nerves, and I found myself starting to fidget.

'Oh, Olly,' said Isabella apologetically, touching my arm. 'You must be dying for your breakfast, and here I am, keeping you talking on the landing. Let's all go down and get some coffee.'

We found Stephen in the kitchen, his normal air of pink and plumpy bonhomie severely deflated. A red-eyed woman in a flowered pinny flitted about in the background, putting things away. The coffee, as Claudia had promised, was all that was excellent: fragrant Arabica, black as tar, which emerged hissing from a Gaggia machine of formidable capacity. Two cups had me as high as a kite, but feeling a good deal better. There were croissants and so forth on the table, which we dutifully worried into crumbs.

I looked at my watch covertly. It was about half-past ten. There were about two hours to get through before we would have to load ourselves into Stephen's big white car and head ineluctably for Jordans. I could not read the situation at all: whatever happened, it promised to be the most unpleasant morning since my wedding day. Had it occurred to Claudia that Adrian and Colin might betray me to Isabella? With a tiny thrill of something like gladness, I realised that it had not: Claudia, burdened as she is with pedantic, schoolgirl notions of honour, had not realised that my dear old chums would shop me as soon as look at me. If she had had any sense, she would have kept the lot of us well apart. Accustomed as she is to the cut and thrust of the courtroom, Claudia seldom puts a foot wrong. Even though I was virtually certain to find myself a victim of the resultant fall-out in one way or another, I found myself almost looking forward to a scene which, no doubt, would come back to haunt the dear girl in the stilly watches of many a subsequent night. Perhaps, as she struggled to deal with the fatal results of her own actions, she might gain some tiny inkling of the unmitigated hell wherein I had dwelt for many a long year. Claudia is sensitive to atmosphere.

She realised that I had inexplicably cheered up, and knew me well enough to shoot me a very dubious glance. I pushed back my chair.

'Stephen,' I said, 'I've never really seen myself as even an armchair detective, but if you fancy playing Sexton Blake, I don't mind being Kipper, or Haddock, or whatever he was called. Seriously though, do you think it would be a good idea if some of us went and had a look round?'

'Good idea,' he said heartily. 'I think Bill's out the back already, but another pair of eyes never does any harm.' We went out together in an unexpected atmosphere of masculine camaraderie.

The male half of the domestic staff was found pottering about on the terrace. Fortunately, it had rained very little for some weeks, or I would never have suggested this useful timewaster. The ground-surface in the shrubbery, as I could remember only too well, was dry leafmould, ill adapted to show symptoms of disturbance, and the dew had long since dried off the lawn. The rhododendrons, with their tenacious leaves and springy branches, had, to the untrained eye, sprung back into shape without leaving any tell-tale signs of broken branches, fallen leaves, and so forth. My lunatic chums had by some miracle stopped short of adorning themselves with false beards, blue spectacles, and other potentially deciduous objects, so no traces of their passage were to be seen. The exercise of ordinary reason suggested, eventually, approach by water; and the area by the landing-stage proved, indeed, to be churned by the passage of a number of feet. We congratulated one another heartily on our use of practical intelligence. I went so far as to spot a genuine clue: a well-preserved footprint on a bit of mud by itself. I wondered, idly, whose it was. It may even have been mine. Butler Bill was sent off to find a tarpaulin and cover the thing up lovingly for the delectation of the police, while Stephen and I went back to the house, and prepared ourselves for luncheon with the enemy.

XII

It is not far from Blackwater to Jordans, as the crow flies. By land, however, it is five miles or more, since the road goes via Snape and round the top of the estuary. I sat passively in the back of Stephen's top-of-the range vehicle, and said nothing at all. My timewasting with Stephen had allowed Claudia only a few moments alone with me, which she had for once had the common humanity not to use: what was there, after all, to say? The reiteration of threats on one side, and promises on the other? The mutual assurance that we would play it by ear? Claudia is a good deal subtler than the appalling Horsfall: she is content to leave the obvious unstated.

It was, I think, precisely as I crossed Sick Heart River for the second time in twenty-four hours that I went mad. The stress of my obscenely peculiar position in this country-house farce was so intolerable that I ceased even to despair. I was helpless in the waters of my recurrent nightmare, the black and slimy current sucking me down. Sock's heavy oxblood shoe pressed down on the top of my head, pushing my face under water with the dispassionate power of an avenging god. My head exploded, I gulped the river into my lungs, and then at last I was dead, and everything was so much easier. Stephen swung the car into the drive, and I found that I was surveying the house of Jordans through a shifting veil of water with the glazed amiability of a corpse.

The Rover drew up, and we all got out. It was obvious even from that point that we were walking into trouble. We were met with complete silence: no welcome committee, not even the dog Taggart, scuttled out to do the decent. As we approached nearer the front door, it became obvious that electric lights were still pallidly burning in all rooms. Claudia began to look anxious.

'Oh my Lord,' said Isabella. 'It doesn't look like they had any better morning than we did. What do you think we should do, guys?'

Claudia tried the handle of the front door, which opened.

'I think we should go in and at least leave a message,' she said firmly. 'Do you know your way in this house, Olly?'

'Sort of,' I said.

She opened the door, and we went into the hall. As we entered, someone hurled himself recklessly down the stairs from, apparently, the attics.

'Colin? Have you found him – Oh, dear Christ.' He skidded to a halt, and regarded us helplessly. His face was disfigured by a night's growth of beard – Adrian is one of these dark, jowly men who starts looking like a carpet-salesman in no time, and in all but the direst of circumstances, he is obsessive about scraping himself smooth. Dirty, distraught and unshaven as he was, he looked shifty, unreliable and, so deceptive are appearances, considerably madder than I did. Isabella regarded him with disfavour.

'Hi,' she said firmly. 'What the hell is going on? I'm Isabella Gibb. Mrs Holderness is expecting us?'

'It's the child,' said Adrian hoarsely. 'Josh. He's gone missing. They're all out looking for him.'

'Oh, my God,' said Isabella. 'Poor Georgie. I think we'll maybe wait here awhile and see if there's anything we can do – if we can help, at all, you know we'll do anything we can.'

She led us decisively across the hall, while Adrian stood gaping at her from the bottom landing, opened the drawing-room door, and stopped dead. The three of us piled up behind her in a singularly foolish fashion. Over her shoulder, I saw the length of Georgiana's familiar drawing-room, desolate and sordid with empty glasses and full ashtrays, and 'The Horse-Tamer' propped against the wall. Isabella walked slowly across the room, came to a halt in front of the picture, and surveyed it for signs of damage. All four of us trooped after her, mesmerised by her eerie silence. Having completed her inspection, she turned suddenly. Her face held a quality of concentrated rage which had even her husband taking an involuntary step backwards. It is the only time in my life when the expression 'blazing eyes' has seemed to me genuinely expressive. She ignored us, and addressed herself only to Adrian.

'Tell Georgiana she's got just one hour. If that picture's not back at Blackwater by' – she consulted a minute watch – half-past one, I'm ringing the police.' She turned on her heel and stalked out, trailed by Stephen.

'Don't forget,' said Claudia pleasantly, 'I have a lot of friends here and there in the law. I can make life very difficult for you.'

Adrian turned away from us and slumped against the wall with a very English gesture of despair.

'Just what's been going on here?' she asked, with calm, forensic curiosity. Adrian looked at me, and being dead, I met his gaze with indifferent calm.

'I hope you're feeling pleased with yourself, Olly. You've succeeded beyond your wildest dreams.' What could have happened? I doubted, since I heard the jubilant report of Horsfall's shotgun on the midnight air, that they had mislaid my beastly godson in a patch of quick-mud on the way home. A first inkling began to dawn on me.

'Did Horsfall end up in bed with Georgiana?' I enquired.

'Of course he fucking did,' said Adrian exhaustedly. 'What I don't think even you had reckoned on is that Josh had a pain in the tummy' (I was hardly surprised, since the evening's excitements, from the child's point of view, had included first steps in heroic boozing) 'and walked in on them.'

'Oh, dear Lord,' said Claudia, in her turn. He turned to her, since she was manifestly a better audience.

'It was all about as bad as it could be,' he told her. 'Josh ran out of the house, we think, and Georgiana rooted us out of bed to go and look for him. She's like a bloody Fury, I've never seen anything like it. Horsfall's already pissed off into the night.' He glared at me. 'If anything's happened to Josh, it will all be your fault.'

'All?' I asked gently.

'Oh, shut up. It makes me ill just looking at you.'

'Adrian,' said Claudia, 'we've got to go. Isabella and Stephen will be waiting for us in the car. Don't let Georgiana forget about the picture, will you?'

The picture. It was the first moment I had had actually to see the thing. I turned to look at the canvas. Somewhere, roaring through the water in my ears, I heard the crunch of car-wheels pulling up on the gravel, and this is what I saw, though Claudia has told me a hundred times since that it probably was not. I stared at the figure who held the great horse by the edge of the water, and found that I was looking at Sock Holderness's handsome and indifferent face.

The front door slammed, shaking the house. I heard a slow, heavy step on the boards: the footfall of Ulysses sounding in the halls of Ithaca while Penelope ran mad in the woods, her honour gone. Only one more door. I stood petrified, waiting in black, surging panic for the moment when it would open behind me and I would see the face of Holderness reflected in the mirror. Claudia seized my wrist in an iron grip, and propelled me bodily towards the french windows. Legging it round the house to the land side, we ran like maniacs towards Isabella, life, London, home.